Jer

His Lives and His Times

The Michael Moorcock Collection

The Michael Moorcock Collection is the definitive library of acclaimed author Michael Moorcock's SF & fantasy, including the entirety of his Eternal Champion work. It is prepared and edited by John Davey, the author's long-time bibliographer and editor, and will be published, over the course of two years, in the following print omnibus editions by Gollancz, and as individual eBooks by the SF Gateway (see http://www.sfgateway.com/authors/m/moorcock-michael/ for a complete list of available eBooks).

ELRIC

Elric of Melniboné and Other Stories

Elric: The Fortress of the Pearl

Elric: The Sailor on the Seas of Fate

Elric: The Sleeping Sorceress

Elric: The Revenge of the Rose

Elric: Stormbringer!

Elric: The Moonbeam Roads
comprising –
Daughter of Dreams
Destiny's Brother
Son of the Wolf

CORUM

Corum: The Prince in the Scarlet Robe
comprising –
The Knight of the Swords
The Queen of the Swords
The King of the Swords

Corum: The Prince with the Silver Hand
comprising –
The Bull and the Spear
The Oak and the Ram
The Sword and the Stallion

HAWKMOON

Hawkmoon: The History of the Runestaff
comprising –
The Jewel in the Skull
The Mad God's Amulet
The Sword of the Dawn
The Runestaff

Hawkmoon: Count Brass
comprising –
Count Brass
The Champion of Garathorm
The Quest for Tanelorn

JERRY CORNELIUS

The Cornelius Quartet
comprising –
The Final Programme
A Cure for Cancer
The English Assassin
The Condition of Muzak

Jerry Cornelius: His Lives and His Times (short-fiction collection)

A Cornelius Calendar
 comprising –
  The Adventures of Una Persson
   and Catherine Cornelius in
   the Twentieth Century
  The Entropy Tango
  The Great Rock 'n' Roll Swindle
  The Alchemist's Question
  Firing the Cathedral/Modem
   Times 2.0

Von Bek
 comprising –
  The War Hound and the World's
   Pain
  The City in the Autumn Stars

The Eternal Champion
 comprising –
  The Eternal Champion
  Phoenix in Obsidian
  The Dragon in the Sword

The Dancers at the
End of Time
 comprising –
  An Alien Heat
  The Hollow Lands
  The End of all Songs

Kane of Old Mars
 comprising –
  Warriors of Mars
  Blades of Mars
  Barbarians of Mars

Moorcock's Multiverse
 comprising –
  The Sundered Worlds
  The Winds of Limbo
  The Shores of Death

The Nomad of Time
 comprising –
  The Warlord of the Air
  The Land Leviathan
  The Steel Tsar

Travelling to Utopia
 comprising –
  The Wrecks of Time
  The Ice Schooner
  The Black Corridor

The War Amongst the Angels
 comprising –
  Blood: A Southern Fantasy
  Fabulous Harbours
  The War Amongst the Angels

Tales From the End of Time
 comprising –
  Legends from the End of Time
  Constant Fire
  Elric at the End of Time

Behold the Man

Gloriana; or, The Unfulfill'd Queen

SHORT FICTION
My Experiences in the Third World
War and Other Stories: The Best
Short Fiction of Michael Moorcock
Volume 1

The Brothel in Rosenstrasse and
Other Stories: The Best Short Fiction
of Michael Moorcock Volume 2

Breakfast in the Ruins and Other
Stories: The Best Short Fiction of
Michael Moorcock Volume 3

Jerry Cornelius:
His Lives and His Times

MICHAEL MOORCOCK

Edited by John Davey

Copyright © Michael and Linda Moorcock 1968 – 1974,
1976, 1980, 1981, 1987, 1990, 1991, 1993, 1998, 2006, 2011
Revised versions Copyright © Michael and Linda Moorcock 2014
Interior Artwork Copyright © Harry Douthwaite 1965, 1968;
Mal Dean 1968, 1969; David Britton 1972, 1979
All characters, the distinctive likenesses thereof, and all related
indicia are™ and © 2014 Michael & Linda Moorcock.

This edition published in Great Britain in 2014 by
Gollancz
An imprint of the Orion Publishing Group
Orion House, 5 Upper St Martin's Lane,
London WC2H 9EA

An Hachette UK Company

3 5 7 9 10 8 6 4

A CIP catalogue record for this book is
available from the British Library

ISBN 978 1 473 20072 2

Typeset by Jouve (UK), Milton Keynes

Printed and bound in Great Britain by Clays Ltd, Elcograf S.p.A.

The Orion Publishing Group's policy is to use papers
that are natural, renewable and recyclable products and
made from wood grown in sustainable forests. The logging
and manufacturing processes are expected to conform to
the environmental regulations of the country of origin.

www.multiverse.org
www.sfgateway.com
www.gollancz.co.uk
www.orionbooks.co.uk

Introduction to
The Michael Moorcock Collection

John Clute

H E IS NOW over 70, enough time for most careers to start and
end in, enough time to fit in an occasional half-decade or so
of silence to mark off the big years. Silence happens. I don't think
I know an author who doesn't fear silence like the plague; most of
us, if we live long enough, can remember a bad blank year or so,
or more. Not Michael Moorcock. Except for some worrying
surgery on his toes in recent years, he seems not to have taken
time off to breathe the air of peace and panic. There has been no
time to spare. The nearly 60 years of his active career seems to
have been too short to fit everything in: the teenage comics; the
editing jobs; the pulp fiction; the reinvented heroic fantasies;
the Eternal Champion; the deep Jerry Cornelius riffs; NEW WORLDS;
the 1970s/1980s flow of stories and novels, dozens upon dozens
of them in every category of modern fantastika; the tales of the
dying Earth and the possessing of Jesus; the exercises in postmodernism that turned the world inside out before most of us had
begun to guess we were living on the wrong side of things; the
invention (more or less) of steampunk; the alternate histories; the
Mitteleuropean tales of sexual terror; the deep-city London riffs:
the turns and changes and returns and reconfigurations to which
he has subjected his oeuvre over the years (he expects this new
Collected Edition will fix these transformations in place for good);
the late tales where he has been remodelling the intersecting
worlds he created in the 1960s in terms of twenty-first-century
physics: for starters. If you can't take the heat, I guess, stay out of
the multiverse.

His life has been full and complicated, a life he has exposed and hidden (like many other prolific authors) throughout his work. In *Mother London* (1988), though, a nonfantastic novel published at what is now something like the midpoint of his career, it may be possible to find the key to all the other selves who made the 100 books. There are three protagonists in the tale, which is set from about 1940 to about 1988 in the suburbs and inner runnels of the vast metropolis of Charles Dickens and Robert Louis Stevenson. The oldest of these protagonists is Joseph Kiss, a flamboyant self-advertising fin-de-siècle figure of substantial girth and a fantasticating relationship to the world: he is Michael Moorcock, seen with genial bite as a kind of G.K. Chesterton without the wearying punch-line paradoxes. The youngest of the three is David Mummery, a haunted introspective half-insane denizen of a secret London of trials and runes and codes and magic: he too is Michael Moorcock, seen through a glass, darkly. And there is Mary Gasalee, a kind of holy-innocent and survivor, blessed with a luminous clarity of insight, so that in all her apparent ignorance of the onrushing secular world she is more deeply wise than other folk: she is also Michael Moorcock, Moorcock when young as viewed from the wry middle years of 1988. When we read the book, we are reading a book of instructions for the assembly of a London writer. The Moorcock we put together from this choice of portraits is amused and bemused at the vision of himself; he is a phenomenon of flamboyance and introspection, a poseur and a solitary, a dreamer and a doer, a multitude and a singleton. But only the three Moorcocks in this book, working together, could have written all the other books.

It all began – as it does for David Mummery in *Mother London* – in South London, in a subtopian stretch of villas called Mitcham, in 1939. In early childhood, he experienced the Blitz, and never forgot the extraordinariness of being a participant – however minute – in the great drama; all around him, as though the world were being dismantled nightly, darkness and blackout would descend, bombs fall, buildings and streets disappear; and in the morning, as though a new universe had taken over from the old one and the world had become portals, the sun would rise on glinting rubble, abandoned tricycles, men and women going about their daily tasks as though nothing had happened, strange shards of ruin poking into altered air. From a very early age, Michael Moorcock's security reposed in a sense that everything might change, in the blinking of an eye, and be *rejourneyed* the next day (or the next book). Though as a writer he has certainly elucidated the fears and alarums of life in Aftermath Britain, it does seem that his very early years were marked by the epiphanies of war, rather than the inflictions of despair and beclouding amnesia most adults necessarily experienced. After the war ended, his parents separated, and the young Moorcock began to attend a pretty wide variety of schools, several of which he seems to have been expelled from, and as soon as he could legally do so he began to work full time, up north in London's heart, which he only left when he moved to Texas (with intervals in Paris) in the early 1990s, from where (to jump briefly up the decades) he continues to cast a Martian eye: as with most exiles, Moorcock's intensest anatomies of his homeland date from after his cunning departure.

But back again to the beginning (just as though we were rimming a multiverse). Starting in the 1950s there was the comics and pulp work for Fleetway Publications; there was the first book (*Caribbean Crisis*, 1962) as by Desmond Reid, co-written with his early friend the artist James Cawthorn (1929–2008); there was marriage, with the writer Hilary Bailey (they divorced in 1978), three children, a heated existence in the Ladbroke Grove/Notting Hill Gate region of London he was later to populate with Jerry Cornelius and his vast family; there was the editing of NEW WORLDS, which began in 1964 and became the heartbeat of the British New Wave two years later as writers like Brian W. Aldiss and J.G. Ballard, reaching their early prime, made it into a tympanum, as young American writers like Thomas M. Disch, John T. Sladek, Norman Spinrad and Pamela Zoline found a home in London for material they could not publish in America, and new British writers like M. John Harrison and Charles Platt began their careers in its pages; but before that there was Elric. With *The Stealer of Souls* (1963) and

Stormbringer (1965), the multiverse began to flicker into view, and the Eternal Champion (whom Elric parodied and embodied) began properly to ransack the worlds in his fight against a greater Chaos than the great dance could sustain. There was also the first SF novel, *The Sundered Worlds* (1965), but in the 1960s SF was a difficult nut to demolish for Moorcock: he would bide his time.

We come to the heart of the matter. Jerry Cornelius, who first appears in *The Final Programme* (1968) – which assembles and co-ordinates material first published a few years earlier in NEW WORLDS – is a deliberate solarisation of the albino Elric, who was himself a mocking solarisation of Robert E. Howard's Conan, or rather of the mighty-thew-headed Conan created for profit by Howard epigones: Moorcock rarely mocks the true quill. Cornelius, who reaches his first and most telling apotheosis in the four novels comprising *The Cornelius Quartet*, remains his most distinctive and perhaps most original single creation: a wide boy, an agent, a *flaneur*, a bad musician, a shopper, a shapechanger, a trans, a spy in the house of London: a toxic palimpsest on whom and through whom the *zeitgeist* inscribes surreal conjugations of 'message'. Jerry Cornelius gives head to Elric.

The life continued apace. By 1970, with NEW WORLDS on its last legs, multiverse fantasies and experimental novels poured forth; Moorcock and Hilary Bailey began to live separately, though he moved, in fact, only around the corner, where he set up house with Jill Riches, who would become his second wife; there was a second home in Yorkshire, but London remained his central base. *The Condition of Muzak* (1977), which is the fourth Cornelius novel, and *Gloriana; or, The Unfulfill'd Queen* (1978), which transfigures the first Elizabeth into a kinked Astraea, marked perhaps the high point of his career as a writer of fiction whose font lay in genre or its mutations – marked perhaps the furthest bournes he could transgress while remaining within the perimeters of fantasy (though *within* those bournes vast stretches of territory remained and would, continually, be explored). During these years he sometimes wore a leather jacket constructed out of numerous patches of varicoloured material, and it sometimes seemed perfectly fitting that he bore the semblance, as his jacket flickered and fuzzed from across a room or road, of an illustrated man, a map, a thing of shreds and patches, a student fleshed from dreams. Like the stories he told, he seemed to be more than one thing. To use a term frequently applied (by me at least) to twenty-first-century fiction, he seemed equipoisal: which is to say that, through all his genre-hopping and genre-mixing and genre-transcending and genre-loyal returnings to old pitches, *he was never still*, because 'equipoise' is all about *making stories move*. As with his stories, he cannot be pinned down, because he is not in one place. In person and in his work, it has always been sink or swim: like a shark, or a dancer, or an equilibrist...

The marriage with Jill Riches came to an end. He married Linda Steele in 1983; they remain married. The Colonel Pyat books, *Byzantium Endures* (1981), *The Laughter of Carthage* (1984), *Jerusalem Commands* (1992) and *The Vengeance of Rome* (2006), dominated these years, along with *Mother London*. As these books, which are non-fantastic, are not included in the current *Michael Moorcock Collection*, it might be worth noting here that, in their insistence on the irreducible difficulty of gaining anything like true sight, they represent Moorcock's mature modernist take on what one might call the rag-and-bone shop of the world itself; and that the huge ornate postmodern edifice of his multiverse *loosens* us from that world, gives us room to breathe, to juggle our strategies for living – allows us ultimately to escape from prison (to use a phrase from a writer he does not respect, J.R.R. Tolkien, for whom the twentieth century was a prison train bound for hell). What Moorcock may best be remembered for in the end is the (perhaps unique) interplay between modernism and postmodernism in his work. (But a plethora of discordant understandings makes these terms hard to use; so enough of them.) In the end, one might just say that Moorcock's work as a whole represents an extraordinarily multifarious execution of the fantasist's main task: which is to *get us out of here*.

Recent decades saw a continuation of the multifarious, but with a more intensely applied methodology. The late volumes of the long Elric saga, and the Second Ether sequence of meta-fantasies – *Blood: A Southern Fantasy* (1995), *Fabulous Harbours* (1995) and *The War Amongst the Angels: An Autobiographical Story* (1996) – brood on the real world and the multiverse through the lens of Chaos Theory: the closer you get to the world, the less you describe it. *The Metatemporal Detective* (2007) – a narrative in the Steampunk mode Moorcock had previewed as long ago as *The Warlord of the Air* (1971) and *The Land Leviathan* (1974) – continues the process, sometimes dizzyingly: as though the reader inhabited the eye of a camera increasing its focus on a closely observed reality while its bogey simultaneously wheels it backwards from the desired rapport: an old Kurasawa trick here amplified into a tool of conspectus, fantasy eyed and (once again) rejourneyed, this time through the lens of SF.

We reach the second decade of the twenty-first century, time still to make things new, but also time to sort. There are dozens of titles in *The Michael Moorcock Collection* that have not been listed in this short space, much less trawled for tidbits. The various avatars of the Eternal Champion – Elric, Kane of Old Mars, Hawkmoon, Count Brass, Corum, Von Bek – differ vastly from one another. Hawkmoon is a bit of a berk; Corum is a steely solitary at the End of Time: the joys and doleurs of the interplays amongst them can only be experienced through immersion. And the Dancers at the End of Time books, and the Nomad of the Time Stream books, and the Karl Glogauer books, and all the others. They are here now, a 100 books that make up one book. They have been fixed for reading. It is time to enter the multiverse and see the world.

September 2012

Introduction to
The Michael Moorcock Collection

Michael Moorcock

B Y 1964, AFTER I had been editing NEW WORLDS for some
months and had published several science fiction and fantasy
novels, including *Stormbringer*, I realised that my run as a writer
was over. About the only new ideas I'd come up with were mini-
ature computers, the multiverse and black holes, all very crudely
realised, in *The Sundered Worlds*. No doubt I would have to return
to journalism, writing features and editing. 'My career,' I told my
friend J.G. Ballard, 'is finished.' He sympathised and told me he
only had a few SF stories left in him, then he, too, wasn't sure
what he'd do.

In January 1965, living in Colville Terrace, Notting Hill, then an
infamous slum, best known for its race riots, I sat down at the
typewriter in our kitchen-cum-bathroom and began a locally
based book, designed to be accompanied by music and graphics.
The Final Programme featured a character based on a young man
I'd seen around the area and whom I named after a local green-
grocer, Jerry Cornelius, 'Messiah to the Age of Science'. Jerry was
as much a technique as a character. Not the 'spy' some critics
described him as but an urban adventurer as interested in his
psychic environment as the contemporary physical world. My
influences were English and French absurdists, American noir
novels. My inspiration was William Burroughs with whom I'd
recently begun a correspondence. I also borrowed a few SF ideas,
though I was adamant that I was not writing in any established
genre. I felt I had at last found my own authentic voice.

I had already written a short novel, *The Golden Barge*, set in a
nowhere, no-time world very much influenced by Peake and the

surrealists, which I had not attempted to publish. An earlier auto-biographical novel, *The Hungry Dreamers*, set in Soho, was eaten by rats in a Ladbroke Grove basement. I remained unsatisfied with my style and my technique. *The Final Programme* took nine days to complete (by 20 January, 1965) with my baby daughters sometimes cradled with their bottles while I typed on. This, I should say, is my memory of events; my then wife scoffed at this story when I recounted it. Whatever the truth, the fact is I only believed I might be a serious writer after I had finished that novel, with all its flaws. But Jerry Cornelius, probably my most successful sustained attempt at unconventional fiction, was born then and ever since has remained a useful means of telling complex stories. Associated with the 60s and 70s, he has been equally at home in all the following decades. Through novels and novellas I developed a means of carrying several narratives and viewpoints on what appeared to be a very light (but tight) structure which dispensed with some of the earlier methods of fiction. In the sense that it took for granted the understanding that the novel is among other things an internal dialogue and I did not feel the need to repeat by now commonly understood modernist conventions, this fiction was post-modern.

Not all my fiction looked for new forms for the new century. Like many 'revolutionaries' I looked back as well as forward. As George Meredith looked to the eighteenth century for inspiration for his experiments with narrative, I looked to Meredith, popular Edwardian realists like Pett Ridge and Zangwill and the writers of the *fin de siècle* for methods and inspiration. An almost obsessive interest in the Fabians, several of whom believed in the possibility of benign imperialism, ultimately led to my Bastable books which examined our enduring British notion that an empire could be essentially a force for good. The first was *The Warlord of the Air*.

I also wrote my *Dancers at the End of Time* stories and novels under the influence of Edwardian humourists and absurdists like Jerome or Firbank. Together with more conventional generic books like *The Ice Schooner* or *The Black Corridor*, most of that work was done in the 1960s and 70s when I wrote the Eternal Champion supernatural adventure novels which helped support my own and others' experiments via NEW WORLDS, allowing me also to keep a family while writing books in which action and fantastic invention were paramount. Though I did them quickly, I didn't write them cynically. I have always believed, somewhat puritanically, in giving the audience good value for money. I enjoyed writing them, tried to avoid repetition, and through each new one was able to develop a few more ideas. They also continued to teach me how to express myself through image and metaphor. My Everyman became the Eternal Champion, his dreams and ambitions represented by the multiverse. He could be an ordinary person struggling with familiar problems in a contemporary setting or he could be a swordsman fighting monsters on a far-away world.

Long before I wrote *Gloriana* (in four parts reflecting the seasons) I had learned to think in images and symbols through reading John Bunyan's *Pilgrim's Progress*, Milton and others, understanding early on that the visual could be the most important part of a book and was often in itself a story as, for instance, a famous personality could also, through everything associated with their name, function as narrative. I wanted to find ways of carrying as many stories as possible in one. From the cinema I also learned how to use images as connecting themes. Images, colours, music, and even popular magazine headlines can all add coherence to an apparently random story, underpinning it and giving the reader a sense of internal logic and a satisfactory resolution, dispensing with certain familiar literary conventions.

When the story required it, I also began writing neo-realist fiction exploring the interface of character and environment, especially the city, especially London. In some books I condensed, manipulated and randomised time to achieve what I wanted, but in others the sense of 'real time' as we all generally perceive it was more suitable and could best be achieved by traditional nineteenth-century means. For the Pyat books I first looked back to the great German classic, Grimmelshausen's *Simplicissimus* and other early picaresques. I then examined the roots of a certain kind of moral fiction from Defoe through Thackeray and Meredith then to modern times where the picaresque (or rogue tale) can take the form of a road movie, for instance. While it's probably fair to say that Pyat and *Byzantium Endures* precipitated the end of my second marriage (echoed to a degree in *The Brothel in Rosenstrasse*), the late 70s and the 80s were exhilarating times for me, with *Mother London* being perhaps my own favourite novel of that period. I wanted to write something celebratory.

By the 90s I was again attempting to unite several kinds of fiction in one novel with my Second Ether trilogy. With Mandelbrot, Chaos Theory and String Theory I felt, as I said at the time, as if I were being offered a chart of my own brain. That chart made it easier for me to develop the notion of the multiverse as representing both the internal and the external, as a metaphor and as a means of structuring and rationalising an outrageously inventive and quasi-realistic narrative. The worlds of the multiverse move up and down scales or 'planes' explained in terms of mass, allowing entire universes to exist in the 'same' space. The result of developing this idea was the *War Amongst the Angels* sequence which added absurdist elements also functioning as a kind of mythology and folklore for a world beginning to understand itself in terms of new metaphysics and theoretical physics. As the cosmos becomes denser and almost infinite before our eyes, with black holes and dark matter affecting our own reality, we can explore them and observe them as our ancestors explored our planet and observed the heavens.

At the end of the 90s I'd returned to realism, sometimes with a dash of fantasy, with *King of the City* and the stories collected in *London Bone*. I also wrote a new Elric/Eternal Champion sequence, beginning with *Daughter of Dreams*, which brought the fantasy worlds of Hawkmoon, Bastable and Co. in line with my realistic and autobiographical stories, another attempt to unify all my fiction, and also offer a way in which disparate genres could be reunited, through notions developed from the multiverse and the Eternal Champion, as one giant novel. At the time I was finishing the Pyat sequence which attempted to look at the roots of the Nazi Holocaust in our European, Middle Eastern and American cultures and to ground my strange survival guilt while at the same time examining my own cultural roots in the light of an enduring anti-Semitism.

By the 2000s I was exploring various conventional ways of story-telling in the last parts of *The Metatemporal Detective* and through other homages, comics, parodies and games. I also looked back at my earliest influences. I had reached retirement age and felt like a rest. I wrote a 'prequel' to the Elric series as a graphic novel with Walter Simonson, *The Making of a Sorcerer*, and did a little online editing with FANTASTIC METROPOLIS.

By 2010 I had written a novel featuring Doctor Who, *The Coming of the Terraphiles*, with a nod to P.G. Wodehouse (a boyhood favourite), continued to write short stories and novellas and to work on the beginning of a new sequence combining pure fantasy and straight autobiography called *The Whispering Swarm* while still writing more Cornelius stories trying to unite all the various genres and sub-genres into which contemporary fiction has fallen.

Throughout my career critics have announced that I'm 'abandoning' fantasy and concentrating on literary fiction. The truth is, however, that all my life, since I became a professional writer and editor at the age of 16, I've written in whatever mode suits a story best and where necessary created a new form if an old one didn't work for me. Certain ideas are best carried on a Jerry Cornelius story, others work better as realism and others as fantasy or science fiction. Some work best as a combination. I'm sure I'll write whatever I like and will continue to experiment with all the ways there are of telling stories and carrying as many themes as possible. Whether I write about a widow coping with loneliness in her cottage or a massive, universe-size sentient spaceship searching for her children, I'll no doubt die trying to tell them all. I hope you'll find at least some of them to your taste.

One thing a reader can be sure of about these new editions is that they would not have been possible without the tremendous and indispensable help of my old friend and bibliographer John Davey. John has ensured that these Gollancz editions are definitive. I am indebted to John for many things, including his work at

Moorcock's Miscellany, my website, but his work on this edition has been outstanding. As well as being an accomplished novelist in his own right John is an astonishingly good editor who has worked with Gollancz and myself to point out every error and flaw in all previous editions, some of them not corrected since their first publication, and has enabled me to correct or revise them. I couldn't have completed this project without him. Together, I think, Gollancz, John Davey and myself have produced what will be the best editions possible and I am very grateful to him, to Malcolm Edwards, Darren Nash and Marcus Gipps for all the considerable hard work they have done to make this edition what it is.

Michael Moorcock

Contents

Illustrated by Harry Douthwaite, Mal Dean
and David Britton

To the memory of Mal Dean — painter, illustrator and musician
— who died of cancer on Sunday, 24 February, 1974, aged 32

Freedom of thought and action is this century's most terrible gift to Western civilisation, our most fearful burden. I for one would gladly relinquish that burden.

– Lobkowitz, 1965

THE CONFLICTING TIME STREAMS OF THE 20TH CENTURY WERE MIRRORED IN JERRY CORNELIUS

The Peking Junction

I

Out of the rich and rolling lands of the West came Jerry Cornelius, with a vibragun holstered at his hip and a generous message in his heart, to China.

Six feet two inches tall, rather fat, dressed in the beard and uniform of a Cuban guerrilla, only his eyes denied his appearance or, when he moved, his movements. Then the uniform was seen for what it was and those who at first had admired him loathed him and those who had at first despised him loved him. He loved them all, for his part, he kissed them all.

On the shores of a wide lake that reflected the full moon stood a tall, ruined pagoda, its walls inlaid with faded mosaic of red, pale blue and yellow. In the dusty room on the first floor Jerry poured Wakayama Sherry for three disconcerted generals whose decision to meet him in this remote province had been entirely a matter of instinct.

'Substantial,' murmured one general, studying the glass.

Jerry watched the pink tongue travel between the lips and disappear in the left-hand corner of the mouth.

'The tension,' began a second general carefully. 'The tension.'

Jerry shrugged and moved about the room very swiftly. He came to rest on the mat in front of them, sat down, folded his legs under him.

A winged shadow crossed the moon. The third general glanced at the disintegrating mosaic of the wall. 'Only twice in...'

Jerry nodded tolerantly.

For Jerry's sake they were all speaking good Mandarin with a certain amount of apprehensive self-contempt, like collaborators who fear reprisals from their countrymen.

'How is it now, over there?' asked one of the generals, waving towards the West.

'Wild and easy,' said Jerry, 'as always.'

'But the American bombing...'

'A distraction, true.' Jerry scratched his palm.

The first general's eyes widened. 'Paris razed, London gutted, Berlin in ruins...'

'You take a lot from your friends before you condemn them.'

Now the shadow had vanished. The third general's right hand spread its long fingers wide. 'But the destruction... Dresden and Coventry were nothing. Thirty days – skies thick with Yankee pirate jets, constant rain of napalm, millions dead.' He sipped his sherry. 'It must have seemed like the end of the world...'

Jerry frowned. 'I suppose so.' Then he grinned. 'There's no point in making a fuss about it, is there? Isn't it all for the best in the long run?'

The general looked exasperated. 'You people...'

2

Tension, resulting in equilibrium: the gestures of conflict keep the peace. A question of interpretation.

3

Having been Elric, Asquiol, Minos Aquilinas, Clovis Marca, now and for ever he was Jerry Cornelius of the noble price, proud prince of ruins, boss of the circuits. Faustaff, Muldoon, the eternal champion...

Nothing much was happening in the Time Centre that day; phantom horsemen rode on skeletal steeds across worlds as fantastic as those of Bosch or Breughel, and at dawn when clouds of giant scarlet flamingoes rose from their nests of reeds and wheeled through the sky in bizarre ritual dances, a tired, noble figure would go down to the edge of the marsh and stare over the water at the strange configurations of dark lagoons and tawny islands that seemed to him like hieroglyphs in some primeval language. (The marsh had once been his home, but now he feared it his tears filled it.)

Cornelius feared only fear and had turned his albino beast from the scene, riding sadly away, his long mane flowing behind him so that from a distance he resembled some golden-haired madonna of the lagoons.

4

Imposition of order upon landscape; the romantic vision of the age of reason, the age of fear. And yet the undeniable rhythm of the spheres, the presence of God. The comforts of tidiness; the almost unbearable agony of uncompromising order. Law and Chaos. The face of God, the core of self:

> For the mind of man alone is free to explore the lofty vastness of the cosmic infinite, to transcend ordinary consciousness, or roam the secret corridors of the brain where past and future melt into one... And universe and individual are linked, the one mirrored in the other, and each contains the other.

> – *The Chronicle of the Black Sword*

5

It was extremely subtle, he thought, staring out of the window at the waters of the lake. In another room, the generals slept. The appearance of one thing was often almost exactly that of its diametric opposite. The lake resembled a spread of smoothed silver; even the reeds were like wires of pale gold and the sleeping herons could have been carved from white jade. Was this the ultimate mystery? He checked his watches. Time for sleep.

6

In the morning the generals took Cornelius to the site of the crashed F111A. It was in fair condition, with one wing buckled and the tailplane shot away, its ragged pilot still at his controls, a dead hand on the ejector lever. The plane stood in the shadow of the cliff, half-hidden from the air by an overhang. Jerry was reluctant to approach it.

'We shall expect a straight answer,' said a general.

'Straight,' said Jerry, frowning. It was not his day.

'What was the exact nature of the catastrophe?' enquired one general of another.

Jerry forced himself to climb up onto the plane's fuselage and strike a pose he knew would impress the generals. It was becoming important to speed things up as much as he could.

'What do you mean by that?' The general raised his eyes to him, but Jerry was not sure that he had been addressed. 'What does it mean to you, Mr Cornelius?'

Jerry felt cornered. 'Mean?' He ran his hand over the pitted metal, touching the USAF insignia, the star, the disc, the bar.

'It will go in the museum eventually,' said the first general, 'with the '58 Thunderbird, of course, and the rest, But what of the land?' A gesture towards the blue-green plain which spread away beyond their parked jeeps. 'I do not understand.'

Jerry pretended to study the cliff. He didn't want the generals to see him weeping.

Later they all piled into the jeep and began to roar away across the dusty plain, protecting their mouths and eyes with their scarves.

Returning to the pagoda by the lake, one of the generals stared thoughtfully back across the flat landscape. 'Soon we shall have all this in shape.'

The general touched a square object in one uniform pocket. The sound of a raucous Chinese brass band began to squall out. Herons flapped from the reeds and rose into the sky.

'You think we should leave the plane where it is, don't you?' said General Way Hahng.

Cornelius shrugged. But he had made contact, he thought complacently.

7

The heavy and old-fashioned steam locomotive shunted to a stop. Behind it the rickety carriages jostled together for a moment before coming to rest. Steam rose beneath the locomotive and the Chinese engineer stared pointedly over their heads at the plain as they clambered from the jeep and approached the train.

A few peasants occupied the carriages. Only one stared briefly through the window before turning his head away. The peasants, men and women, wore red overalls.

Walking knee-deep through the clammy steam they got into the carriage immediately behind the tender. The locomotive began to move.

Jerry sprawled across the hard bamboo seat and picked a splinter from his sleeve. In the distance he could see hazy mountains. He glanced at General Way Hahng but the general was concentrating on loosening a belt-buckle. Jerry craned his head back and spotted the jeep, abandoned beside the rails.

He switched on his visitaper, focusing it on the window. Shadowy figures began to move on the glass, dancing to the music which had filled the carriage. The generals were surprised but said nothing. The tune was 'Hello Goodbye' by The Beatles.

It was not appropriate. Jerry turned it off. There again, he thought, perhaps it was appropriate. Every plugged nickel had two sides.

He burst into laughter.

General Way Hahng offered him a swift, disapproving glance, but no more.

'I hear you are called the Raven in the West,' said another general.

'Only in Texas,' said Jerry, still shaking.

'Aha, in *Texas*.'

General Way Hahng got up to go to the lavatory. Jacket removed, the general's tight pants could be seen to stretch over beautifully rounded buttocks. Jerry looked at them feeling ecstatic. He had never seen anything like them. The slightly rumpled material added to their attraction.

'And in Los Angeles?' said another general. 'What are you called in Elay?'

'Fats,' said Jerry.

8

Even though he was a physicist, he knew that important biological objects come in pairs.

– Watson,
The Double Helix

With sinology, as with Chinese food, there are two *kinds*…

– Enright,
Encounter, July 1968

9

General Lee met them at the station. It was little more than a wooden platform raised between the railroad line and the Yellow River.

He shook hands with Jerry. 'My apologies,' he said. 'But under the circumstances I thought it would be better to meet here than in Weifang.'

'How much time have you got?' Jerry asked.

General Lee smiled and spread his hands. 'You know better than that, Mr Cornelius.' They walked to where the big Phantom IV staff car was parked.

General Way Hahng called from the window as the train moved off. 'We will go on to Tientsin and journey back from there. We will wait for you, Mr Cornelius.'

Jerry waved reassuringly.

General Lee was dressed in a neat Ivy League suit that was a little shiny, a little frayed on one sleeve. He was almost as tall as Jerry, with a round face, moody eyes and black chin whiskers. He returned his driver's salute as he personally opened the door of the limousine for Jerry. Jerry got in.

They sat in the stationary car and watched the river. General Lee put a hand on Jerry's shoulder. Jerry smiled back at his friend.

'Well,' said the general eventually, 'what do you think?'

'I think I might be able to do it. I think I'm building something up there. With Way Hahng.'

Lee rubbed at the corner of his mouth with his index finger. 'Yes. I thought it would be Way Hahng.'

'I can't promise anything,' Jerry said.

'I know.'

'I'll do my best.'

'Of course. And it will work. For good or ill, it will work.'

'For good and ill, general. I hope so.'

IO

'Too much,' said Jerry back in the pagoda, drinking tea from cracked Manchu bowls, eating shortbread from elegant polystyrene-ware that had been smuggled from the factories at Shimabara or Kure.

The generals frowned. 'Too much?'

'But the logic,' said General Way Hahng, the most beautiful of the three.

'True,' said Jerry, who was now in love with the generals and very much in love with General Way Hahng, For that general in particular he was prepared (temporarily or metatemporally, depending how it grabbed him) to compromise his principles, or at least not speak his mind fully. In a moment of self-exasperation he frowned. 'False.'

General Way Hahng's expression was disappointed. 'But you said...'

'I meant "true",' said Jerry. It was no good. But the sooner he was out of this one the better. Something had to give shortly. Or, at very least, someone. He suddenly remembered the great upsurge of enthusiasm among American painters immediately after the war and a Pollock came to mind. 'Damn.'

'It is a question of mathematics, of history,' said the second general.

Jerry's breathing had become rapid.

II

'I do not read French,' said General Way Hahng disdainfully handing the piece of paper back to Jerry. This was the first time they had been alone together.

Jerry sighed.

12

A SHOUT.

13

As always it was a question of gestures. He remembered the way in which the wing of the F111A had drooped, hiding the ruin of the undercarriage. Whatever fallacy might exist – and perhaps one did – he was prepared to go along with it. After all, his admiration and enthusiasm had once been generous and it was the sort of thing you couldn't forget; there was always the sense of loss, no matter what you did to cover it up. Could he not continue to be generous, even though it was much more difficult? He shrugged. He had tried more than once and been rejected too often. A clean break was best.

But the impulse to make yet another gesture – of sympathy, of understanding, of love – was there. He knew no way in which such a gesture would not be safely free of misinterpretation, and he was, after all, the master forger. There was enormous substance there, perhaps more than ever before, but its expression was strangled. Why was he always ultimately considered the aggressor? Was it true? Even General Lee had seen him in that rôle. Chiefly, he supposed, it was as much as anything a question of equilibrium. Perhaps he simply had to reconcile himself to a long wait.

In the meantime, duty called, a worthy enough substitute for the big search. He stood on the top floor of the pagoda, forcing himself to confront the lake, which seemed to him as vast as the sea and very much deeper.

14

Memory made the martyr hurry; duality. Past was future. Memory was precognition. It was by no means a matter of matter. Karl Glogauer pinioned on a wooden cross by iron spikes through hands and feet.

> But if you would believe the unholy truth – then Time is an agony of Now, and so it will always be.

> – 'The Dreaming City'

Do Not Analyse.

15

Devious notions ashamed the memory of his father's fake Le Corbusier château. But all that was over. It was a great relief.

'It is cool in here now,' said General Way Hahng.

'You'd better come out,' he said cautiously. 'Quick. The eye. While it is open.'

They stood together in the room and Jerry's love filled it.

'It is beautiful,' said the general.

Weeping with pity, Jerry stroked the general's black hair, bent and kissed the lips. 'Soon.' The vibragun and the rest of the equipment was handy.

16

A SWEET SHOUT.

17

The voice of the flatworm. Many-named, many-sided, metatemporal operative extraordinary, man of the multiverse, metaphysician metahealed metaselfed. The acid voice.

'God,' said Renark and he lived that moment for ever.

– The Sundered Worlds

18

The flow of the Mandarin, the quality of the Sanskrit that the general spoke in love. It all made sense. Soon. But let the victim call once more, move once more.

19

Jerry went to the window, looked out at the lake, at the black and shining water.

Behind him in the room General Way Hahng lay naked, smoking a powerful dose. The general's eyes were hooded and the general's lips curved in a beatific, almost stupid, smile. The little visitaper by the side of the mattress cast abstract images on the mosaic of the wall, played 'What You're Doing', but even that made Jerry impatient. At this moment he rarely wanted complete silence, but now he must have it. He strolled across the room and waved the visitaper into silence. He had the right. The general did not dispute it.

Jerry glanced at his discarded outfit and touched his clean chin. Had he gone too far?

His own heavy intake was making his heart thump as if in passion. There had been his recent meeting with the poet he admired but who denied himself too much. 'Irony is often a substitute for real imagination,' the poet had said, speaking about a recent interplanetary extravaganza.

But all that was a distraction now. It was time.

Jerry bowed his head before the lake. Sentiment, not the water, had overcome him momentarily. Did it matter?

20

Jerry pointed the vibragun at the general and watched the body shake for several minutes. Then he took the extractor and applied it. Soon the infinitely precious nucleotides were stored and he prepared to leave. He kissed the corpse swiftly, put the box that was now the general under his arm. In Washington there was a chef who would know what to do.

He climbed down through the floors to where the remaining generals were waiting for him.

'Tell General Lee the operation was conducted,' he said.

'How will you leave?'

'I have transportation,' said Jerry.

21

The Lovebeast left China the next morning carrying Jerry Cornelius with it, either as a rider or against his will: those who saw them pass found it impossible to decide. Perhaps even Jerry or the Beast itself no longer knew, they had moved about the world together for so long.

Like a dragon it rose into the wind, heading for the ruined, the rich and rolling lands of the West.

The Delhi Division

I

A smoky Indian rain fell through the hills and woods outside Simla and the high roads were slippery. Jerry Cornelius drove his Phantom V down twisting lanes flanked by white fences. The car's violet body was splashed with mud and it was difficult to see through the haze that softened the landscape. In rain, the world became timeless.

Jerry switched on his music, singing along with Jimi Hendrix as he swung around the corners.

Were they finding the stuff? He laughed involuntarily.

Turning into the drive outside his big wooden bungalow, he brought the limousine to a stop. A Sikh servant gave him an umbrella before taking over the car.

Jerry walked through the rain to the verandah; folding the umbrella he listened to the sound of the water on the leaves of the trees, like the ticking of a thousand watches.

He had come home to Simla and he was moved.

2

In the hut was a small neatly made bed and on the bed an old toy bear. Above it a blown-up picture of Alan Powys had faded in the sun. A word had been scratched into the wall below and to the left of the picture:

ASTRAPHOBIA

By the side of the bed was a copy of *Vogue* for 1952, a *Captain Marvel* comic book, a clock in a square case. The veneer of the clock case had been badly burned. Propping up the clock at one corner was an empty Pall Mall pack which had faded to a pinkish colour and was barely recognisable. Roaches crawled across the grey woollen blankets on the bed.

Rain rattled on the corrugated asbestos roof. Jerry shut and locked the door behind him. For the moment he could not concern himself with the hut. Perhaps it was just as well.

He looked through the waving trees at the ruined mansion. What was the exact difference between synthesis and sensationalism?

3

Jerry stayed in for the rest of the afternoon, oiling his needle rifle. Aggression sustained life, he thought. It had to be so; there were many simpler ways of procreating.

Was this why his son had died before he was born?

A servant brought in a silver tray containing a bottle of Pernod, some ice, a glass. Jerry smiled at it nostalgically, then broke the rifle in order to oil the barrel.

4

The ghost of his unborn son haunted him; though here, in the cool bungalow with its shadowed passages, it was much easier to bear. Of course, it had never been particularly hard to ignore; really a different process altogether. The division between imagination and spirit had not begun to manifest itself until quite late, at about the age of six or seven. Imagination – usually displayed at that age in quite ordinary childish games – had twice led him close to a lethal accident. In escaping, as always, he had almost run over a cliff.

Soon after that first manifestation the nightmares had begun, and then, coupled with the nightmares, the waking visions of twisted, malevolent faces, almost certainly given substance by *Fantasia*, his father's final treat before he had gone away.

Then the horrors increased as puberty came and he at last found a substitute for them in sexual fantasies of a grandiose and sado-masochistic nature. Dreams of jewelled elephants, cowed slaves and lavishly dressed rajahs parading through baroque streets while crowds of people in turbans and loincloths cheered them, jeered at them.

With some distaste Jerry stirred the fire in which burned the collection of religious books for children.

He was distracted by a sound from outside. On the verandah servants were shouting. He went to the window and opened it.

'What is it?'

'Nothing, sahib. A mongoose killing a cobra. See.'

The man held up the limp body of the snake.

5

From the wardrobe Jerry took a coat of silk brocade. It was blue, with circles of a slightly lighter blue stitched into it with silver threads. The buttons were diamonds and the cloth was lined with buckram. The high, stiff collar was fixed at the throat by two hidden brass buckles. Jerry put the coat on over his white silk shirt and trousers. Carefully he did up the buttons and then the collar. His long black hair fell over the shoulders of the coat and his rather dark features, with the imperial beard and moustache, fitted the outfit perfectly.

Crossing the bedroom, he picked up the rifle from the divan. He slotted on the telescopic sight, checked the magazine, cradled the gun in his left arm. A small drop of oil stained the silk.

Pausing by a chest of drawers he took an old-fashioned leather helmet and goggles from the top drawer.

He went outside and watched the ground steam in the sun. The ruined mansion was a bright, sharp white in the distance. Beyond it he could see his servants wheeling the light Tiger Moth biplane onto the small airfield.

6

A journey of return through the clear sky; a dream of flying; wheeling over blue-grey hills and fields of green rice, over villages and towns and winding yellow roads, over herds of cattle; over ancient, faded places, over rivers and hydro-electric plants; a dream of freedom.

In the distance, Delhi looked as graceful as New York.

7

Jerry made his way through the crowd of peons who had come to look at his plane. The late Victorian architecture of this suburb of Delhi blended in perfectly with the new buildings, including a Protestant church, which had been erected in the last ten years.

He pulled the flying goggles onto his forehead, shifted the gun from his left arm to his right and pushed open the doors of the church.

It was quite fancifully decorated, with murals in orange, blue and gold by local artists, showing incidents from the life of Jesus and the Apostles. The windows were narrow and unstained; the only other decoration was the altar and its furnishings. The pulpit was plain, of polished wood.

When Jerry was halfway down the aisle a young Indian priest appeared. He wore a buff-coloured linen suit and a dark blue shirt with a white dog-collar and he addressed Jerry in Hindi.

'We do not allow guns in the church, sir.'

Jerry ignored him. 'Where is Sabiha?'

The priest folded his hands on his stomach. 'Sabiha is in Gandhi-nagar, I heard this morning. She left Ahmadabad yesterday...'

'Is the Pakistani with her?'

'I should imagine so.' The priest broke into English. 'They have a tip-top car – a Rolls-Royce. It will get them there in no time.'

Jerry smiled. 'Good.'

'You know Sabiha, then?' said the priest conversationally, beginning to walk towards Jerry.

Jerry levelled the needle rifle at his hip. 'Of course. You don't recognise me?'

'Oh, my god!'

Jerry sighed and tilted the rifle a little. He pulled the trigger and sent a needle up through the priest's open mouth and into his brain.

In the long run, he supposed, it was all a problem of equilibrium. But even considering his attitude towards the priest, the job was an unpleasant one. Naturally it would have been far worse if the priest had had an identity of his own. No great harm had been done, however, and on that score everybody would be more or less satisfied.

8

THERE are times in the history of a nation when random news events trickling from an unfriendly neighbour should be viewed not as stray birds but as symbols of a brood, the fingerposts of a frame of mind invested with sinister significance.

WHAT is precisely happening in Pakistan? Is there a gradual preparation, insidiously designed to establish dangerous tensions between the two neighbours?

WHY are the so-called Majahids being enrolled in large numbers and given guerilla training? Why have military measures like the setting up of pill-boxes and similar offensive-defensive steps on the border been escalated up to an alarming degree?

Blitz news weekly,
Bombay, 27 July, 1968

9

Through the half-constructed buildings of Gandhinagar Jerry wandered, his flying helmet and goggles in one hand, his rifle in the other. His silk coat was grubby now and open at the collar. His white trousers were stained with oil and mud and his suède boots were filthy. The Tiger Moth lay where he had crash-landed it, one wheel completely broken off its axle. He wouldn't be able to use it to leave.

It was close to sunset and the muddy streets were full of shadows cast by the skeletons of modern skyscrapers on which little work had been done for months. Jerry reached the tallest building, one that had been planned as the government's chief administration block, and began to climb the ladders which had been placed between the levels of scaffolding. He left his helmet behind, but held the rifle by its trigger guard as he climbed.

When he reached the top and lay flat on the roofless concrete wall he saw that the city seemed to have been planned as a spiral, with this building as its axis. From somewhere on the outskirts of the city a bell began to toll. Jerry pushed off the safety catch.

Out of a side street moved a huge bull elephant with curling tusks embellished with bracelets of gold, silver and bronze. On its head and back were cloths of beautifully embroidered silk, weighted with tassels of red, yellow and green; its howdah was also ornate, the wood inlaid with strips of enamelled brass and silver, with onyx, emeralds and sapphires. In the howdah lay Sabiha and the Pakistani, their clothes disarrayed, making nervous love.

Jerry sighted down the gun's telescope until the back of the Pakistani's head was in the cross hairs, but then the man moved as Sabiha bit his shoulder and a strand of her blue nylon sari was caught by the evening wind, floating up to obscure them both. When the nylon drifted down again Jerry saw that they were both close to orgasm. He put his rifle on the wall and watched. It was over very quickly.

With a wistful smile he picked up his gun by the barrel and dropped it over the wall so that it fell through the interior of the building, striking girders and making them ring like a glockenspiel.

The couple looked up but didn't see Jerry. Shortly afterwards the elephant moved out of sight.

Jerry began to climb slowly back down the scaffolding.

10

As he walked away from the city he saw the Majahid commandos closing in on the street where he supposed the elephant was. They wore crossed ammunition belts over their chests and carried big Lee-Enfield .303s. The Pakistani would be captured, doubtless, and Sabiha would have to find her own way back to Delhi. He took his spare keys from his trouser pocket and opening the door of the violet Rolls-Royce, climbed in and started the engine. He would have to stop for petrol in Ahmadabad, or perhaps Udaipur if he went that way.

He switched on the headlights and drove carefully until he came to the main highway.

11

In the bath he examined the scar on his inner thigh; he had slipped while getting over a corrugated iron fence cut to jagged spikes at the top so that people wouldn't climb it. He had been seven years old: fascinated at what the gash in his flesh revealed. For hours he had alternately bent and straightened his leg in order to watch the exposed muscles move through the seeping blood.

He got out of the bath and wrapped a robe around his body, walking slowly through the bungalow's passages until he reached his bedroom.

Sabiha had arrived. She gave him a wry smile. 'Where's your gun?'

'I left it in Gandhinagar. I was just too late.'

'I'm sorry.'

He shrugged. 'We'll be working together again, I hope.'

'This scene's finished now, isn't it?'

'Our bit of it, anyway, I should think.' He took a brass box from the dressing table and opened the lid, offering it to her. She looked into his eyes.

When she had taken all she needed, she closed the lid of the box with her long index finger. The sharp nails were painted a deep red.

Exhausted, Jerry fell back on the bed and stared at her vaguely as she changed out of her nylon sari into khaki drill trousers, shirt and sandals. She bunched up her long black hair and pinned it on top of her head.

'Your son...' she began, but Jerry closed his eyes, cutting her short.

He watched her turn and leave the room, then he switched out the light and very quickly went to sleep.

12

THE unbridled support given to the Naga rebels by China shows that India has to face alarums and excursions on both sides of her frontier. It is not likely that China would repeat her NEFA adventure of 1962, as she might then have to contend with the united opposition of the USSR and the USA.

THAT is precisely why the stellar role of a cat's paw appears to have been assigned to Pakistan...

OUR Intelligence service should be kept alert so that we get authentic information well in advance of the enemy's intended moves.

AND once we receive Intelligence of any offensive being mounted, we should take the lesson from Israel to strike first and strike hard on several fronts before the enemy gets away with the initial advantages of his blitzkrieg.

Blitz, ibid.

13

'Waterfall' by Jimi Hendrix was playing on the tape as Jerry ate his breakfast on the verandah. He watched a mongoose dart out from under the nearby hut and dash across the lawn towards the trees and the ruined mansion. It was a fine, cool morning.

As soon as the mongoose was safe, Jerry reached down from the table and touched a stud on the floor. The hut disappeared. Jerry took a deep breath and felt much better. He hadn't accomplished everything, but his personal objectives had been tied up very satisfactorily. All that remained was for a woman to die. This had not, after all, been a particularly light-hearted episode.

14

KRISHNAN MOHAN JUNEJA (Ahmadabad): How you have chosen the name BLITZ and what does it mean?
It was started in 1941 at the height of Nazi blitzkrieg against Britain.

Blitz, ibid., correspondence column.

15

At least there would be a little less promiscuous violence which was such a waste of everybody's life and time and which depressed him so much. If the tension had to be sustained, it could be sustained on as abstract a level as possible. And yet, did it finally matter at all? It was so hard to find that particular balance between law and chaos.
It was a dangerous game, a difficult decision, perhaps an irreconcilable dichotomy.

16

As he walked through the trees towards the ruined mansion he decided that in this part of the world things were narrowing down too much. He wished that he had not missed his timing where the Pakistani was concerned. If he had killed him, it might have set in motion a whole new series of cross-currents. He had slipped up and he knew why.

The mansion's roof had fallen in and part of the front wall bulged outwards. All the windows were smashed in the lower storeys and the double doors had been broken backwards on their hinges. Had he the courage to enter? The presence of his son was very strong.

If only it had not been here, he thought. Anywhere else and the Pakistani would be dead by now.

Until this moment he had never considered himself to be a coward, but he stopped before he got to the doorway and could not move forward. He wheeled round and began to run, his face moving in terror.

The Phantom V was ready. He got into it and drove it rapidly down the drive and out into the road. He went away from Simla and he was screaming, his eyes wide with self-hatred. His scream grew louder as he passed Delhi and it only died completely when he reached Bombay and the coast.

He was weeping uncontrollably even when the SS *Kao An* was well out into the Arabian Sea.

The Tank Trapeze

01.00 hours

Prague Radio announced the move and said the Praesidium of the Czechoslovak Communist Party regarded it as a violation of international law, and that Czechoslovak forces had been ordered not to resist.

*   *   *

Perfection had always been his goal, but a sense of justice had usually hampered him. Jerry Cornelius wouldn't be seeing the burning city again. His only luggage an expensive cricket bag, he rode a scheduled corpse-boat to the Dubrovnik depot and boarded the SS *Kao An* bound for Burma, arriving just in time.

After the ship had jostled through the junks to find a berth, Jerry disembarked, making his way to the Rangoon public baths where, in a three-kyat cubicle, he took off his brown serge suit and turban, changing into an elaborately embroidered Russian blouse loose enough to hide his shoulder holster. From his bag he took a pair of white flannels, soft Arabian boots and an old-fashioned astrakhan shako. Disguised to his satisfaction he left the baths and went by pedicab to the checkpoint where the Buddhist monk waited for him.

The monk's moody face was fringed by a black 'Bergman' beard making him look like an unfrocked BBC producer. Signing the safe-conduct order with a Pentel pen that had been recharged in some local ink, he blinked at Jerry. 'He's here today.'

'Too bad.' Jerry adjusted his shako with the tips of his fingers then gave the monk his heater. The monk shrugged, looked at him curiously and handed it back. 'Okay. Come on. There's a car.'

'*Every gun makes its own tune*,' murmured Jerry.

As they headed for the old Bentley tourer parked beyond the guard hut, the monk's woolly saffron cardigan billowed in the breeze.

*   *   *

02.15

All telephone lines between Vienna and Czechoslovakia were cut.

* * *

They drove between the green paddy fields and in the distance saw the walls of Mandalay. Jerry rubbed his face. 'I hadn't expected it to be so hot.'

'Hell, isn't it? It'll be cooler in the temple.' The monk's eyes were on the twisting white road.

Jerry wound down the window. Dust spotted his blouse but he didn't bother to brush it off. 'Lai's waiting in the temple, is he?'

The monk nodded. 'Is that what you call him? Could you kill a child, Mr Cornelius?'

'I could try.'

* * *

03.30

Prague Radio and some of its transmitters were off the air.

* * *

All the roofs of Mandalay were of gold or burnished brass. Jerry put on his dark glasses as they drove through the glazed gates. The architecture was almost primitive and somewhat fierce. Hindu rather than Buddhist in inspiration, it featured as decoration a variety of boldly painted devils, fabulous beasts and minor deities.

'You keep it up nicely.'

'We do our best. Most of the buildings, of course, are in the later Pala-Sena style.'

'The spires in particular.'

'Wait till you see the temple.'

The temple was rather like an Anuradhapuran ziggurat, rising in twelve ornate tiers of enamelled metal inlaid with silver,

bronze, gold, onyx, ebony and semi-precious stones. Its entrance
was overhung by three arches, each like an inverted 'V', one upon
the other. The building seemed overburdened, like a tree weighted
with too much ripe fruit. They went inside, making their way

between pillars of carved ivory and teak. Of the gods in the carvings, Ganesh was the one most frequently featured.

'The expense, of course, is enormous,' whispered the monk. 'Here's where we turn off.'

A little light entered the area occupied chiefly by a reclining Buddha of pure gold, resting on a green marble plinth. The Buddha was twenty feet long and about ten feet high, a decadent copy in the manner of the Siamese school of U Thong. The statue's thick lips were supposed to be curved in a smile but instead seemed fatuously pursed.

From the shadow of the Buddha a man moved into the light. He was fat, the colour of oil, with a crimson fez perched on his bald head. His hands were buried in the pockets of his beige jacket. 'You're Jeremiah Cornelius? You're pale. Haven't been out East long...'

'This is Captain Maxwell,' said the monk eagerly.

'I was to meet a Mr Lai.'

'This is Mr Lai.'

'How do you do.' Jerry put down his cricket bag.

'How do you do, Mr Cornelius.'

'It depends what you mean.'

Captain Maxwell pressed his lips in a red smile. 'I find your manner instructive.' He waved the monk away and returned to the shadows. 'Will it matter, I wonder, if we are not simpatico?'

*   *   *

03.30

Russian troops took up positions outside the Prague Radio buildings.

*   *   *

In the bamboo bar of the Mandalay Statler-Hilton Jerry looked through the net curtains at the rickshaws passing rapidly on both sides of the wide street. The bar was faded and poorly stocked and its only other occupants, two German railway technicians on their way through to Laos, crossed the room to the far corner and began a game of bar billiards.

Jerry took the stool next to Captain Maxwell who had registered at the same time, giving his religion as Protestant and his occupation as engineer. Jerry asked the Malayan barman for a Jack Daniel's that cost him fourteen kyats and tasted like clock oil.

'This place doesn't change,' Maxwell said. His bloated face was morose as he sipped his sherbet. 'I don't know why I come back. Nowhere else, I suppose. Came here first...' He rubbed his toothbrush moustache with his finger and used the same finger to push a ridge of sweat from his forehead. Fidgeting for a moment on his stool he dismounted to tug at the material that had stuck to the sweat of his backside. 'Don't touch the curries here. They're murder. The other grub's okay though. A bit dull.' He picked up his glass and was surprised to find it empty. 'You flew in, did you?'

'Boat in. Flying out.'

Maxwell rolled his sleeves up over his heavy arms and slapped at a mosquito that had settled among the black hairs and the pink, torn bites. 'God almighty. Looking for women?'

Jerry shrugged.

'They're down the street. You can't miss the place.'

'See you.' Jerry left the bar. He got into a taxi and gave an address in the suburbs beyond the wall.

As they moved slowly through the teeming streets the taxi driver leaned back and studied Jerry's thin face and long blond hair. 'Boring now, sir. Worse than the Japs now, sir.'

*   *   *

03.45

Soviet tanks and armoured cars surrounded the party Central Committee's building in Prague.

*   *   *

From the other side of the apartment's oak door Jerry heard the radio, badly tuned to some foreign station, playing the younger Dvořák's lugubrious piano piece, *The Railway Station at Čierna nad Tisou.* He rang the bell. Somebody changed the channel and the radio began to play 'Alexander's Ragtime Band', obviously performed by one of the many Russian traditional jazz bands that had become so popular in recent years. A small woman in a blue cheong sam, her black hair piled on her head, opened the door and stepped demurely back to let him in. He winked at her.

'You're Anna Ne Win?'

She bowed her head and smiled.

'You're something.'

'And so are you.'

On the heavy chest in the hallway stood a large Ming vase of crimson roses.

The rest of the apartment was full of the heavy scent of carnations. It was a little overpowering.

*   *   *

03.47

Prague Radio went off the air completely.

*   *   *

The child's body was covered from throat to ankles by a gown onto which intricately cut jewels had been stitched so that none of the material showed through. On his shaven head was a similarly worked cap. His skin was a light, soft brown and he seemed a sturdy little boy, grave and good-looking. When Jerry entered the gloomy, scented room, the child let out a huge sigh, as if he had been holding his breath for several minutes. His hands emerged from his long sleeves and he placed one on each arm of the ornate wooden chair over which his legs dangled. 'Please sit down.'

Jerry took off his shako and looked carefully into the boy's large almond eyes before lowering himself to the cushion near the base of the chair.

'You've seen Lai?'

Jerry grinned. 'You could be twins.'

The boy smiled and relaxed in the chair. 'Do you like children, Mr Cornelius?'

'I try to like whatever's going.'

'Children like me. I am different, you see.' The boy unbuttoned his coat, exposing his downy brown chest. 'Reach up, Mr Cornelius, and put your hand on my heart.'

Jerry leaned forward and stretched out his hand. He placed his palm against the child's smooth chest. The beat was rapid and irregular. Again he looked into the child's eyes and was interested by the ambiguities he saw in them. For a moment he was afraid.

'Can I see your gun, Mr Cornelius?'

Jerry took his hand away and reached under his blouse, tugging his heater from his holster. He gave it to the child who drew it up close to his face to inspect it. 'I have never seen a gun like this before.'

'It's a side-product,' Jerry said, retrieving the weapon, 'of the communications industry.'

'Ah, of course. What do you think will happen?'

'Who knows? We live in hope.'

Anna Ne Win, dressed in beautiful brocade, with her hair hanging free, returned with a tray, picking her way among the cushions that were scattered everywhere on the floor of the gloomy room. 'Here is some tea. I hope you'll dally with us.'

'I'd love to.'

* * *

04.20

The Soviet Tass Agency said that Soviet troops had been called into Czechoslovakia by Czechoslovak leaders.

*   *   *

In the hotel room Maxwell picked his nails with a splintered chopstick while Jerry checked his kit.

'You'll be playing for the visitors, of course. Hope the weather won't get you down.'

'It's got to get hotter before it gets cooler.'

'What do you mean by that?' Maxwell lit a Corona from the butt of a native cheroot he had just dropped in the ashtray, watching Jerry undo the straps of his bag.

Jerry upended the cricket bag. All the equipment tumbled noisily onto the bamboo table and hit the floor. A red cricket ball rolled under the bed. Maxwell was momentarily disconcerted, then leaned down and recovered it. His chair creaked as he tossed the ball to Jerry.

Jerry put the ball in his bag and picked up a protector and a pair of bails. 'The smell of brand-new cricket gear. Lovely, isn't it?'

'I've never played cricket.'

Jerry laughed. 'Neither have I. Not since I had my teeth knocked out when I was five.'

'You're considering violence, then?'

'I don't get you.'

'What is it you dislike about me?'

'I hadn't noticed. Maybe I'm jealous.'

'That's quite likely.'

'I've been aboard your yacht, you see. The *Teddy Bear*. In the Pool of London. Registered in Hamburg, isn't she?'

'The *Teddy Bear* isn't my yacht, Mr Cornelius. If only she were. Is that all...?'

'Then it must be Tsarapkin's, eh?'

'You came to Mandalay to do a job for me, Mr Cornelius, not to discuss the price of flying fish.'

Jerry shrugged. 'You raised the matter.'

'That's rich.'

* * *

04.45

Prague radio came back on the air and urged the people of Prague to heed only the legal voice of Czechoslovakia. It repeated the request not to resist. 'We are incapable of defending these frontiers,' it said.

* * *

Caught at the wicket for sixteen off U Shi Jheon, Jerry now sat in his deckchair watching the game. Things looked sticky for the visitors.

It was the first few months of 1948 that had been crucial. A detailed almanac for that period would reveal a lot. That was when the psychosis had really started to manifest itself. It had been intensifying ever since. There was only a certain amount one could do, after all.

* * *

06.25

Russian troops began shooting at Czechoslovak demonstrators outside the Prague Radio building.

* * *

While Jerry was changing, Captain Maxwell entered the dressing room and stood leaning against a metal locker, rubbing his right foot against his fat left leg while Jerry combed his hair.

'How did the match go?'

'A draw. What did you expect?'

'No less.'

'You didn't do too badly out there, old boy. Tough luck, being caught like that.'

Jerry blew him a kiss and left the pavilion, carrying his cricket bag across the empty field towards the waiting car that could just be seen through the trees.

* * *

06.30

Machine-gun fire broke out near the Hotel Esplanade.

* * *

Jerry strolled among the pagodas as the sun rose and struck their bright roofs. Shaven-headed monks in saffron moved slowly here and there. Jerry's boots made no sound on the mosaic paths. Looking back, he saw that Anna Ne Win was watching him from the corner of a pagoda. At that moment the child appeared and took her hand, leading her out of sight. Jerry walked on.

* * *

06.30

Prague television was occupied.

* * *

Maxwell stared down through the window, trying to smooth the wrinkles in his suit. 'Rangoon contacted me last night.'

'Ah.'

'They said: "It is better to go out in the street".' Maxwell removed his fez. 'It's all a matter of profits in the long run, I suppose.' He chuckled.

'You seem better this morning. The news must have been good.'

'Positive. You could call it positive. I must admit I was beginning to get a little nervy. I'm a man of action, you see, like yourself.'

*   *   *

06.37
Czech National Anthem played.

*   *   *

Anna Ne Win moved her soft body against his in the narrow bed, pushing his legs apart with her knee. Raising himself on one elbow he reached out and brushed her black hair from her face. It was almost afternoon. Her delicate eyes opened and she smiled.

He turned away.

'Are you crying, Jerry?'

Peering through the slit in the blind he saw a squadron of L-29 Delfins fly shrieking over the golden rooftops. Were they part of an occupation force? He couldn't make out the markings. For a moment he felt depressed, then he cheered up, anticipating a pleasant event.

*   *   *

06.36

Prague Radio announced: 'When you hear the Czech National Anthem you will know it's all over.'

*   *   *

Jerry hung around the post office the whole day. No reply came to his telegram but that was probably a good sign. He went to a bar in the older part of the city where a Swedish folk-singer drove him out. He took a rickshaw ride around the wall. He bought a necklace and a comb. In Ba Swe Street he was almost hit by a racing tram and while he leaned against a telephone pole two *Kalan cacsa* security policemen made him show them his safe conduct. It impressed them. He watched them saunter through the crowd on the pavement and arrest a shoeshine boy, pushing him aboard the truck which had been crawling behind them. A cathartic act, if not a kindly one.

Jerry found himself in a deserted street. He picked up the brushes and rags and the polish. He fitted them into the box and placed it neatly in a doorway. A few people began to reappear. A tram came down the street. On the opposite pavement, Jerry saw Captain Maxwell. The engineer stared at him suspiciously until he realised Jerry had seen him, then he waved cheerfully. Jerry pretended he hadn't noticed and withdrew into the shade of a tattered awning. The shop itself, like so many in the street, had been closed for some time and its door and shutters were fastened by heavy iron padlocks. A proclamation had been pasted on one door panel. Jerry made out the words *Pyee-Daung-Su Myanma-Nainggan-Daw*. It was an official notice, then. Jerry watched the rickshaws and cars, the trams and the occasional truck pass in the street.

After a while the shoeshine boy returned. Jerry pointed out his equipment. The boy picked it up and walked with it under his arm towards the square where the Statler-Hilton could be seen. Jerry decided he might as well follow him, but the boy began to run and turned hastily into a side street.

Jerry spat into the gutter.

*　　*　　*

07.00

President Svoboda made a personal appeal over the radio for calm. He said he could offer no explanation for the invasion.

*　　*　　*

As Jerry checked the heater's transistors, Maxwell lay on the unmade bed watching him. 'Have you any other occupation, Mr Cornelius?'

'I do this and that.'

'And what about political persuasions?'

'There you have me, Captain Maxwell.'

'Our monk told me you said it was as primitive to hold political convictions as it was to maintain belief in God.' Maxwell loosened his cummerbund.

'Is that a fact?'

'Or was he putting words into your mouth?'

Jerry clipped the heater back together. 'It's a possibility.'

*　　*　　*

08.20

Pilsen Radio described itself as 'the last free radio station in Czechoslovakia'.

*　　*　　*

A Kamov Ka-15 helicopter was waiting for them on the cricket field near the pavilion. Maxwell offered the pilot seat to Jerry. They clambered in and adjusted their flying helmets.

'You've flown these before,' said Maxwell.

'That's right.' Jerry lit a cheroot.

'*The gestures of conflict keep the peace*,' murmured Maxwell nostalgically.

*   *   *

10.00

The Czechoslovak agency Četeka said that at least ten ambulances had arrived outside Prague Radio station, where a Soviet tank was on fire.

*   *   *

When they had crossed the Irrawaddy, Jerry entered the forest and headed for the shrine. He had a map in one hand and a compass in the other.

The atmosphere of the forest was moist and cool. It would begin to rain soon; already the sky was becoming overcast. The air was full of little clusters of flies and mosquitoes, like star systems encircling an invisible sun, and in avoiding them Jerry knocked off his shako several times. His boots were now muddy and his blouse and trousers stained by the bark and foliage. He stumbled on.

About an hour later the birches began to thin out and he knew he was close to the clearing. He breathed heavily, moving more cautiously.

He saw the chipped green tiles of the roof first, then the dirty ivory columns that supported it, then the shrine itself. Under the roof, on a base of rusting steel sheeting, stood a fat Buddha carved from local stone and painted in dark reds, yellows and blues. The statue smiled. Jerry crawled through the damp undergrowth until he could get a good view of the boy.

A few drops of rain fell loudly on the roof. Already the ground surrounding the shrine was churned to mud by a previous rainfall. The boy lay in the mud, face down, arms flung out towards

the shrine, legs stiffly together, his jewelled gown covering his body. One ankle was just visible; the brown flesh showing in the gap between the slipper and the hem. Jerry touched his lips with the tip of his finger.

Above his head monkeys flung themselves through the green branches as they looked for cover from the rain. The noise they made helped Jerry creep into the clearing unobserved. He frowned.

The boy lifted his head and smiled up at Jerry. 'Do you feel like a woman?'

'You stick to your prayers, I'll stick to mine.'

The boy obeyed. Jerry stood looking down at the little figure as it murmured the prayers. He took out his heater and cleared his throat, then he adjusted the beam width and burned a thin hole through the child's anus. He screamed.

Later Maxwell emerged from the undergrowth and began removing the various quarters from the jewelled material. There was hardly any blood, just the stench. He shook out the bits of flesh and folded the parts of the gown across his arm. He put one slipper in his right pocket and the other in his left. Lastly he plucked the cap from the severed head and offered it to Jerry.

'You'd better hurry. The rain's getting worse. We'll be drowned at this rate. That should cover your expenses. You'll be able to convert it fairly easily in Singapore.'

'I don't often get expenses,' said Jerry.

* * *

10.25

Četeka said shooting in the centre of Prague had intensified and that the 'Rude Pravo' offices had been seized by 'occupation units'.

*   *   *

Waiting near the Irrawaddy for the Ka-15 to come back, Jerry watched the rain splash into the river. He was already soaked.

The flying field had only recently been cleared from the jungle and it went right down to the banks of the river. Jerry picked his teeth with his thumbnail and looked at the broad brown water and the forest on the other side. A wooden landing stage had been built out into the river and a family of fishermen were tying up their sampan. Why should crossing this particular river seem so important?

Jerry shook his umbrella and looked up at the sound of the helicopter's engines. He was completely drenched; he felt cold and he felt sorry for himself. The sooner he could reach the Galapagos the better.

*   *   *

11.50

Pilsen Radio said: 'The occupation has already cost 25 lives.'

*   *   *

He just got to the post office before it closed. Anna Ne Win was standing inside reading a copy of *Dandy*. She looked up. 'You're British, aren't you? Want to hear the Test results?'

Jerry shook his head. It was pointless asking for his telegram now.

He no longer had any use for assurances. What he needed most at this stage was a good, solid, undeniable fact; something to get his teeth into.

'A Captain Maxwell was in earlier for some money that was being cabled to him,' she said. 'Apparently he was disappointed. Have you found it yet – the belt?'

'I'm sorry, no.'

'You should have watched where you threw it.'

'Yes.'

'That Captain Maxwell. He's staying at your hotel, isn't he?'

'Yes. I've got to leave now. Going to Singapore. I'll buy you two new ones there. Send them along.' He ran from the post office.

'Cheerio,' she called. 'Keep smiling.'

*   *   *

12.28

Četeka said Mr Dubček was under restriction in the Central Committee building.

*   *   *

Naked, Jerry sat down on his bed and smoked a cheroot. He was fed up with the East. It wasn't doing his identity any good.

The door opened and Maxwell came in with a revolver in his hand and a look of disgust on his fat face. 'You're not wearing any damned clothes!'

'I wasn't expecting you.'

Maxwell cocked the revolver. 'Who do you think you are, anyway?'

'Who do you think?'

Maxwell sneered. 'You'd welcome suggestions, eh? I want to puke when I look at you.'

'Couldn't I help you get a transfer?'

'I don't need one.'

Jerry looked at the disordered bed, at the laddered stockings Anna Ne Win had left behind, at the trousers hanging on the string over the washbasin, at the woollen mat on the floor by the bed, at

the cricket bat on top of the wardrobe. 'It would make me feel better, though.' He drew on his cheroot. 'Do you want the hat back?'

'Don't be revolting, Cornelius.'

'What do you want, then, Captain Maxwell?'

'Justice.'

'I'm with you.' Jerry stood up and reached for his flannels. Maxwell raised the Webley & Scott .45 and fired the first bullet. Jerry was thrust against the washbasin and he blinked rapidly as his vision dimmed. There was a bruise five inches in diameter on his right breast and its centre was a hole with red, puckered sides; around the edges of the bruise a little blood was beginning to force its way out. 'There certainly are some shits in the world,' he said.

A couple of shots later, when Jerry was lying on the floor, he had the impression that Maxwell's trousers had fallen down. He grinned. Maxwell's voice was faint but insulting. 'Bloody gangster! Murderer! Fucking killer!'

Jerry turned on his side and noticed that Anna Ne Win's cerise suspender belt was hanging on a spring under the bed. He reached out and touched it and a tremor of pleasure ran through his body. The last shot he felt hit the base of his spine.

He shuddered and was vaguely aware of the weight of Maxwell's lumpen body on his, of the insect-bitten wrists, of the warm Webley & Scott still in one hand and the cordite smell on the captain's breath. Then Maxwell whispered something in his ear and reaching around his face carefully folded down his eyelids.

(All quotes from the *Guardian*, 22 August, 1968)

The Nature of the Catastrophe

Introduction

The One Part Actress

Miss Brunner was firm about it. With her lips pursed she stood in the school's dark doorway. She knew she had him over a barrel.

Pretending to ignore her, Jerry Cornelius leafed through the tattered copy of *Business Week*. 'The future that rides on Apollo 12 ... Hunt for cancer vaccine closes in ... What delayed the jumbo jets? ... New sales pitch for disposables...'

Miss Brunner moved fast. She snatched the magazine from his hands.

'Look at me,' she said. 'Look at me.'

He looked at her. 'I'll be too many people by 1980. By 1980 I'll be dead,' he said.

Her nostrils flared. 'You've got to go.'

His legs trembled. 'It'll be murder.'

She smiled. 'It'll be murder,' she said, 'if you don't. Won't it?'

Jerry frowned. 'It had to come. Sooner or later.'

'It'll clear the air.'

'What fucking air?' He gave her a hurt look. 'Then?'

'Get busy, eh. You've got fifty years to play about in, after all.'

'Fuck you!'

'And we'll have no more of that.'

In the gym a wind-up gramophone played 'Bye, Bye, Blackbird'.

Le Fratricide de la rue Clary

Genes began to pop.
    Scenes fractured.
    Jerry screamed.

They took his bicycle away. It was a gent's black roadster: 'The Royal Albert'. He had kept it up nicely.

'Hang on tight, Mr Cornelius.'

'I'll bloody go where I...'

'This is it!'

The seedy street in Marseilles disappeared.

He didn't mind that.

In the Net

There was a drum beating somewhere and he could bet he knew who was beating it. Of all the superstitious notions he had encountered, the notion of 'the future' was the most ludicrous. He was really lumbered now.

Development

The nerve gas plant at Portreath, Cornwall, is a pilot establishment for the Ministry of Defence, which has been manufacturing small quantities of gas for some time. Mrs Compton said the widow of one victim has not been allowed to see the pathologist's report or any other medical papers on her husband.

Guardian, 21 November, 1969

Fantasy Review

After the gas attack Jerry Cornelius finished the washing-up and went out into the street. A rainbow had formed over Ladbroke Grove. Everything was very still. He bent to put on his bicycle clips.

'Jerry!'

'Yes, Mum?'

'You come back and dry up properly, you little bugger!'

The Impatient Dreamers

5 June, 1928: Fifty-two years since Owen Nares and Jeanne de Casalis opened in Karen Bramson's *The Man They Buried* at the Ambassadors Theatre, London. The *Daily News* had said: '... at the end of all the tumult of life is "Time and the unresolved hypothesis".'

People Like You

Jerry groped his way from the car and turned his sightless eyes upward. Sunlight would not register. He was completely blind.

So it hadn't paid off.

Tears began to cruise down his cheeks.

'Mum?'

Somewhere in the distance the chatter of the Graf Zeppelin's engines died away.

He was abandoned.

Am I blue? You'd be too. If each plan with your man done fell through. Watcha gonna do? Watcha gonna do?

World to Conquer

We regret to say that Prince Jewan Bukht, son of the late Shah Bahudur Sha, the last titular King of Delhi, is dangerously ill ... He is the last of his race that was born in the purple. He leaves a son, also in bad health, who was born in Rangoon while his father was in confinement. With Prince Jewan Bukht passes away the last direct descendant of the once famous house of Timour.

Rangoon Times, 28 July, 1884

He struggled out of that.

Number 7

Jerry stumbled and fell, gashing his knee. He felt about him with his stone-cold hands. He touched something as smooth as steel. He stroked the surfaces. A discarded suit of armour? And yet everywhere now were sounds. Engines. Screams.

Didn't he know there was a war on? Was he making it back?

He heard a bus draw up nearby, its motor turning over.

He shouted.

There was silence again. A V1 silence.

Coming in on a wing and a prayer...

The Ill Wind

The rush of water.

He was grasping at anything now.

He should never have tried it. A certain amount of diffusion could have been anticipated, but nothing as terrifying as this. He'd been conned.

Distantly: *One o'clock, two o'clock, three o'clock rock...*

The Adapters

There were strong sexual overtones which only became apparent as he concentrated, speaking aloud into the thinning air:

'Miss Jeanne de Casalis, who is the subject this week for our "Is the Child Mother to the Woman?" series...'

'My father, who came from le pays Basque, had gone to Basutoland for the purpose of scientific investigations in connection with cancer and probable cures for this terrible disease, when a baby was announced...'

'Once the best and most popular fellow at Greyfriars – now the worst boy in the school! Such is the unhappy pass to which Harry Wharton's feud with his form-master leads him! You cannot...'

'Issued 15 July, 1931, to be used to prepay postage on mail carried aboard the Graf Zeppelin on its prospective flight to the North Pole. It was on this voyage that the *Nautilus*, a submarine commanded by Sir Hubert Wilkins, was to meet the Graf Zeppelin and transfer mail from one ship to the other at the North Pole. The *Nautilus* did not keep the rendezvous.'

'Long Service Certificate. Presented by the Board of Directors to Ernest Frederick Cornelius of the W.D. & H.O. Wills Branch of the Imperial Tobacco Company (of Great Britain and Ireland), Limited, in Recognition of Faithful Service Rendered During the Past 25 Years and as a mark of Appreciation and Goodwill. Signed on behalf of the Board, Date 28 March, 1929. Gilbert A.H. Wills, Chairman.'

'Georges Duhamel, who has discovered a serum for cancer, is suddenly stricken with pain. He lives for the rest of the play in dread expectation of death. His whole nature changes ... [He] will not face an operation because that will proclaim to the world that his serum is a failure.'

Jerry closed the scrapbook and opened the stamp album. It contained hundreds of Zeppelin issues from Paraguay, Liechtenstein, Latvia, Italy, Iceland, Greece, Germany, Cyrenaica, Cuba, Canada, Brazil, the Argentine, the Aegean Islands, the United States of America, San Marino, Russia. There were also a couple of Spanish autogiro issues and an Italian issue showing Leonardo da Vinci's flying machine.

From the little linen envelope beside the album, Jerry took with his tweezers his latest discovery, a set of Salvador airmail stamps issued on 15 September, 1930. The stamps had become so brittle that they would split unless handled with great care. They were deep red (15c), emerald green (20c), brown violet (25c), ultramarine (40c) and all showed a biplane flying over San Salvador. This issue had just preceded the Simón Bolivar airmail issue of 17 December, 1930.

'Jerry! You get down outa there an' 'elp yer mum!'

Jerry was oscillating badly.

The Merit Award

Jerry wandered over the bomb site, kicking at bits of broken brick. The catharsis had come at last, then. But wasn't it a trifle disappointing?

Now he could go for miles and nothing would interrupt him.

Taking an apple from his pocket, he bit it, then spat, flinging the thing away. It had tasted of detergent.

He looked down at his hands. They were red and grey and they shook. He sat on a slab of broken concrete. Nothing moved. Nothing sang.

Shapers of Men

Changes in jewellery design styles tend to take place over a period of many years. In the past one could think in terms of millennia, centuries or generations, at the very least. Not so today.

– Brian Marshall,
Illustrated London News, 22 November, 1969

Coming Next Issue

Jerry wondered why the scene had got so hazy. A few buildings stood out sharply, but everything else was drowned in mist. He put the Phantom X into reverse.

He wished they'd let him keep his bike.

How little time you were allowed for yourself. Twenty-five years at most. The rest belonged to and was manipulated by the ghosts of the past, the ghosts of the future. A generation was a hundred and fifty years. There was no escape.

A rocket roared by.

When the red, red robin comes bob, bob, bobbin'...

Prisoner in the Ice

By 1979, industrial technology will make the sixties seem like the dark ages. Automatic highways – computerized kitchens – person-to-person television – food from under the sea. They are ideas today, but industrial technology will make them a part of your life tomorrow ... Our measuring devices are so accurate they're used by the US Bureau of Standards to measure other measuring devices. Our fasteners were selected for the space suits on the men who walked the moon. Our plastic parts are in almost every automobile made in the USA.

In these ways, and more, we help make today's ideas tomorrow's realities.

US Industries Inc., ad,
New York Times, 16 October, 1969

'The waterline length is 1,004 ft, and when completed her tonnage will probably exceed 73,000. The *Queen Mary's* maiden voyage (from Southampton to New York) begins on 27 May, 1936...'

'Britain's toy soldiers have been...'

'By 1980 there will be...'

His voice was hoarse now. Fifty years was too long. He had no-one, and no-one to blame but himself.

Little man you're crying; I know why you're blue...

Lucifer!

A hundred and fifty years itched in his skull and yet he could not get back to the only year in which he could survive.

From time to time his sight would return, allowing him horrifying visions – fragments of newspapers, buildings, roadways, cars, planes, skulls, ruins, ruins, ruins.

'MUM!'

'DAD!'

(CRASHED CONCORDE HAD RECEIVED FULL OVERHAUL)

'CATHY!'

'FRANK!'

(MARS MEN BACK IN DOCK)

'GRANDMA!'

'GRANDPA!'

(CHINESE MAKE FRESH GAINS)

'JERRY!'

(METS DO IT AGAIN – TEN IN A ROW!)

'Je...'

His voice whispered into near vacuum.

If only he had been allowed to bring his 'Royal Albert' bike. It would have seen him through. It would have been an anchor.

But he was alone.

'M...'

Rootless, he was dying.

The cold was absolute. His body fell away from him.

The resurrection, if it came, would be painful.

Conclusion

A Man of Qualities

'That's a boy!'

'That's what you say.' Jerry had had enough of it all. He shivered.

They unstrapped him from the chair. 'Don't you feel better now?'

Jerry glanced around the Time Centre. All the chronographs were going like clockwork. 'I told you it didn't exist,' he said, 'because I don't exist. Not there.'

'It was worth a try, though, wasn't it?'

Jerry bunched himself up and tried to stop shaking.

A Kind and Thoughtful Friend

'It boils down to a question of character, doesn't it?' Miss Brunner said. 'Character. Character.'

She always knew how to get to him. She always chose a moment when his energy was at a low ebb.

He looked miserably up from the desk, hoping to touch her heart.

She knew he was confused. 'And if I told your mother...'

He lowered his head again. Maybe it would all blow over.

It's a Beautiful, Glamorous Age

It had all gone now, of course. He'd used up the last of it. No more past to draw on. He felt at his skin.

'Smooth,' he said.

'You see.' She held her thin body in an attitude of triumph. 'It was all for the best.'

Other texts used:
The Sketch, 13 January, 1926
The Bystander, 5 October, 1927
T.P.'s Weekly, 26 November, 1927
Daily Mail, 15 December, 1927
Le Petit Marseillais, 22 October, 1930
The Story of Navigation, Card No. 50,
published by The Imperial Tobacco Co., 1935
Standard Catalogue of Air Post Stamps, Sanabria,
New York, 1937
Modern Boy, 9 July, 1938
The Illustrated Weekly of India, 6 July, 1969
Vision of Tomorrow, November 1969

The Swastika Set-Up

Introduction

Often Dr Cornelius has said he should not interfere with the calendar, for he almost invariably removes two sheets at the same time and so produces even more confusion. The young Xaver, however, apparently delights in this pastime and refuses to be denied his pleasure.

– Thomas Mann,
Disorder and Early Sorrow

The Fix

His early memories were probably no longer reliable: his mother lying on the bed with her well-muscled legs wide apart, her skirt up to her stomach, her cunt smiling.

'You'll have to be quick today. Your father's coming home early.'

The school satchel, hastily dumped on the dressing table, contained his homework: the unified field theory that he had eventually destroyed, save for the single copy on a shelf somewhere in the Vatican Library.

Jerry took out his cigar case and selected an Upmann. Time moved swiftly and erratically these days. With the little silver syringe he cut the cigar and lit it, staring through the rain-dappled window at the soft summer landscaping surrounding his isolated Tudor Mansion. It had been some while since he had last visited the West Country.

He adjusted the stiff white shirt cuffs projecting an inch beyond the sleeves of his black car coat, placed his hand near his heart and shifted the shoulder holster slightly to make it lie more comfortably. Even the assassination business was getting complicated.

On the Job

The conflicting time streams of the 20th century were mirrored in Jerry Cornelius.

– Early reference

At the Time Centre

Alvarez, a man of substance, sniggered at Jerry as they climbed into their orange overalls. Jerry pursed his lips good-humouredly. The brightly coloured lab was humming with activity and all the screens gleamed. Alvarez winked.

'Will you want the use of the mirror tonight, Mr Cornelius?'

'No thanks, Alvarez. Enough's enough, right?'

'Whatever you say, though there's not much time left.'

'Whichever – we'll get by.'

They strolled towards the machine, a shimmering web of crimson and gold, so sophisticated.

With some poise Alvarez adjusted a dial, darting a glance at Jerry who seated himself, placed the tips of his fingers on his forehead, and stared into the shimmering web.

'How would you like it, Mr Cornelius?'

'Medium,' Jerry said.

As Alvarez busied himself with the little controls he murmured incidentally. 'Do you think mouth-to-mouth fertilisation will make much difference, sir? What's your bet? How do you fancy their chances?'

Jerry didn't bother to reply. The web was beginning to bulge near N¾E.

'Look to your helm, Mr Alvarez.'

'Aye, eye, sir.'

The Dessert

Jerry hated needling a dead man, but it was necessary. He looked down at the twice-killed corpse of Borman, the first Nazi astronaut. The riding britches had been pulled below his thighs. Perhaps it had been a last-minute attempt to gain sympathy, Jerry thought, when Borman had unbuttoned the britches to expose the thin white scars on his pelvis and genitals.

The seedy Sherman Oaks apartment was still in semi-darkness. Borman had been watching a cartoon show when Jerry had called. An arsenical Bugs Bunny leapt along a mildew-coloured cliff.

Jerry turned off the cheap TV and left.

Tense

Curling his hair with his fingers, Jerry looked quizzically at the mirror. Then he looked hard. But it didn't work.

The mirror.

He pinched the tip of his nose.

Reflecting on the enigma, he got into his purple brocade bell-bottoms, his deep crimson shirt, and delicately strapped on his heater, setting the holster comfortably on his hip.

The room was cool, with white walls, a gold carpet, a low glass table in the middle of the floor.

From the floor, Catty Ley reached smoothly up to stroke his trousers. 'You got...?'

She wore the bra that showed her nipples, the black stockings, the mauve garters and boots. 'You object...'

'Oh, yes.'

'Darling.'

He smiled, began to comb his hair, taking the long strands down so that they framed his face. 'There's been a bulge,' he said, 'and it's still bulging. We're trying to do something about it. Fuck it.'

'A rapture?'

'Who's to say?'

'An eruption?'

'Perhaps.'

'Will you be needing me for anything?'

'It depends how everything goes.'

'Jerry!'

'Catty...'

It was time to get back to the Time Centre.

Facts

There were two sexes, he thought, *plus permutations. There is death, there is fear, there is time. There is birth, serenity, and time. There is identity, maybe. There is conflict. Robbed of their ambiguities, things cease to exist. Time, as always, was the filter.*

Double Lightning

A whole school of ships lay at anchor in the bay and the tall cranes on the dockside formed a long wedding arch for Jerry as he walked lightly towards the pier where the *Teddy Bear* was berthed. The sun shone on the rainbow oil, on the crisp, white shrouds of the ship, on the schooner's bright brass. She was a beautiful vessel, built in 1920 for Shang Chien, the playboy warlord, who had sailed her regularly from the opium-rich ports of the China Seas to Monte Carlo until Mao had paid him off to settle in France where he had recently died.

What was the ship doing in Frisco?

Jerry went aboard.

A tatty jack tar greeted him, rolling along the deck whistling 'So Sad'.

'Master in the cabin?' Jerry asked. Something was shaping.

The sailor sighed. 'Won't be.' He went to the rail and ran his fingers along the brasswork. He gave Jerry a secret, sardonic look. 'Larger things have come up.'

The sailor didn't stop him as he sauntered to the main companionway and descended.

The schooner's fittings were really Edwardian; all gilt and red plush. Jerry's feet sank into the soft carpet. He withdrew them, moving with difficulty. Finding the cabin he walked in, sniffing the musty air. Korean tapestries in the manner of Chong Son covered the walls; ceramics – mainly Yi dynasty – were fixed on all the shelves. He knew at once that, for the moment at least, the action was elsewhere. But where?

As he made his way back he saw that the holes his feet had made were filling with masses of white maggots. He grinned. There was no doubt in his mind: sooner or later the schooner would be scuppered by someone. A woman? He paused, trying to get the feel of it. Yes, possibly a woman. He lit an Upmann. The maggots began to squirm over his shoes. He moved on.

As he reached the gangplank, the sailor reappeared.

'You know what's wrong with you...' the sailor began.

'Save it, sailor.'

Jerry swung down to the pier, making it fast to where his Phantom III was parked.

He got the big car going. His spirits had risen considerably.

'It's all essential,' he laughed.

Facts

It was so elusive. There were events that frightened him; relationships that he could not cope with directly. Were his own actions creating some particular kind of alchemy?

There was birth.

Beckett had written a letter to a friend. 'What can I do? Everything I touch turns to art in my hands.'

After thirty or forty years, even Duchamp's readymades had come to be objects of interest for him.

Tolerance. Tension. Integrity. Why was he running away?

I am tired, he thought; exhausted. But he had to finish the job in hand.

There was murder.

The Map

Jerry studied the map. His father would have known what to do, and he would have done the right or the wrong thing.

The map was a little faded in places, but it offered a clue. Now he had to wait for a phone call.

'The next great American hero will be a Communist'

Jerry grinned as he drove along. The recent discovery of sex and drugs had taken their minds off the essential problems. Time was silting up. Sooner or later there would be the Flood and then, with a spot of luck, everything would be cooler. It was his job to get the muck shifted as fast as possible. It was a dirty but essentially satisfying job.

His car hit an old man with an extraordinary resemblance to Walt Disney's Pinocchio. No, there was an even closer likeness. He got it. Richard Nixon. He roared with laughter.

It had all started to work out nice with the folding, at long last, of the *Saturday Evening Post*.

Development I

Really, one only had to wait for death to kiss the bastards. Those who wouldn't die had to be killed. Kinetically, of course, it was very simple.

He switched on the car radio and got 'Your Mother Should Know' by The Beatles.

Fact

There was death.

Supposition

You had to keep your eye on the facts.

Falsehood

There was no such thing as falsehood.

Uncomfortable Visions

Toronto was grey, square and solid. The sun wasn't shining and the traffic wasn't moving. There was a crowd in the street.

Andrew Wells was due to speak at and inspire the big Civil Rights Convention in Toronto where all the American exiles (or 'yellow bellies' as they were known) had gathered.

True to the spirit of convention, Andrew, dressed in a neat grey business suit, addressed the exiles and their friends from a balcony on the second floor of Rochdale College, the squarest block in the city. From the roof of the building opposite Jerry had an excellent view of the balcony, the crowd below, and the speaker. Jerry was dressed in the full ceremonial uniform of a Royal Canadian Mounted Policeman. The only difference was that the gun in the neat leather holster on his belt was his trusty heater.

As Andrew began his conventional address concerning universal brotherhood, freedom and the New Apocalypse, Jerry drew the heater, levelled it on his crooked left arm, sighted down it and burned Andrew right in the middle of his black mouth, moving the beam about to cauterise the face. Naturally, there wasn't much blood.

He got into the Kamov Ka-15 helicopter and ascended to the clouds where he made a quick getaway, wondering which poor bastard would claim the credit this time.

Muscle Trouble

In mutable times like these, thought Jerry as he walked back into Lionel Himmler's Blue Spot Bar, everything was possible and nothing was likely. His friend Albert the émigré nodded to him from the shadowy corner by the bar, lifting his glass of schnapps in the strobe light, saluting both Jerry and the stripper on the stage.

Jerry flickered to a table, sat down and ordered scotch and milk. Once history ceased to be seen in linear terms, it ceased to be made in linear terms. He glanced at his new watch. It consisted of eight yellow arrows radiating from a purple central hub. There were no figures marked on it, but the arrows went rapidly round and round. He could check the time only in relation to the speed at which the arrows moved. The arrows were moving very rapidly now.

Albert finished his schnapps, wiped his hands over his shaggy, grey beard and staggered towards the Wardour Street exit of the bar, on his way back to his sad little bedsitter decorated from floor to ceiling with dusty old charts, sheets of equations and eccentric geometric figures.

In these days of temporal and social breakdown the human psyche suffered enormously. Jerry felt sorry for the little Jew. History had destroyed him.

The drums stopped beating. The strobe gave way to conventional lighting. Suddenly it seemed he was the only customer. The waiter arrived, put his drink down, tucking the bill under the glass.

'How about that – Symphony Sal,' said the MC, coming on clapping. 'Give her a big hand,' he said quietly, looking around the deserted bar. 'Give her a big hand,' he told Jerry.

Jerry started to clap.

The MC went away. The bar was silent.

Only in dreams did karma continue to have any meaning, thought Jerry. Or, at least, so it sometimes seemed.

He turned.

She was standing there in the doorway, smiling at him, her wide-brimmed hat like a halo. A Tory woman in garden-party good taste.

She came to his table and picked up the tag with her gloved fingers.

'I'll take that, sonny.'

The gloves were of blue lace, up to the elbow. She wore a dark blue cotton suit that matched her hat. Her hair was black and her oval face was beautiful. She parted her lips.

'So?' said Jerry.

'Soon,' she purred. 'I've got some answers for you. Are you interested?'

'What do you think?'

She glanced demurely at her blue shoes. 'To stop now would severely complicate things. You and your friends had better call it a day. You could always come in with me.'

'In there?' Jerry shook his head.

'It's not so different.' She gave him a hard little smile.

'About as different as yin from yang. Sure.' Jerry reached out and placed his right palm hard against her stomach. She shrugged.

'It's too late, I think,' she said. 'We should have got together earlier.' With a movement of her hips she took a small step away from him.

'You could always get some new sex stars, couldn't you?' Jerry sipped his scotch and milk.

'Certainly.'

'Are the current ones essential?'

She smiled more openly and gave him a candid look. 'I see. You know a lot, Mr Cornelius.'

'My job.'

'And you want a new one?'

'Maybe.'

'I'm Lady Susan Sunday,' she said.

'Lady Sue.'

She shrugged. 'You're out of luck, I think. We're really moving. Frightfully nice to have met you, Mr Cornelius.'

Jerry watched her pay the waiter. He knew her from the file. A close associate of his old enemy Captain Maxwell, from the Burma and China days. The opposition was organising a freeze, if he wasn't mistaken. She had told him everything. A stasis situation. He sniffed.

When she had gone, he went up to the bar. 'Have you a mirror?'
'Lovely for you,' said the barman.

The Pieces

When he got back, Catty was still in her uniform. He took her soft
shoulders and kissed her on the mouth. He put his hands in her
pants.

'Look,' she said, waving at the centre of the room where an
ornate crystal chess set was laid out on a low table. 'Want a game?'

'I can't play chess,' he said.

'Oh, fuck,' she said.

He regarded her with compassionate anticipation. 'You'd
better fetch me those levitation reports,' he said.

The Music of Time

The road was straight and white between avenues of cedars and
poplars. Jerry idled along doing forty.

The Inkspots were singing 'Beautiful Dreamer' on the Duesenberg's tapes. It amused Jerry to match his tapes to his cars. They
finished that one and began 'How Deep is the Ocean?'.

On the seat beside him Jerry had a Grimshaw guitar with the
shaped resonator. They had appeared just too late and had been
quickly superseded by the electric guitar. Now George Formby's
ukelele thrummed.

> *In a young lady's bedroom I went by mistake*
> *My intentions were honest you see*
> *But she shouted with laughter,*
> *I know what you're after:*
> *It's me Auntie Maggie's remedy.'*

1957 had marked the end of the world Jerry had been born into.
Adapting was difficult. He had to admit that he had special advan-
tages. Already people were beginning to talk about him as 'The
Messiah of the Age of Science' and a lot of apocryphal stores

were circulating. He laughed. He wasn't the archetype. He was a stereotype.

Still, he did what he could.

Science, after all, was a much more sophisticated form of superstition than religion.

After this little episode was completed (if 'completed' was the word) he would go and relax among that particularly degenerate tribe of head-hunters who had adopted him on his last visit to New Guinea.

He smiled as large drops of rain hit the windscreen and were vapourised. On that trip he had been responsible for starting at least eight new cargo cults.

Don't Let Me Down

That great big woman had almost been the death of him. There had been so much of her. A hungry woman who had fed his own greed. He sucked breath through clenched teeth at the memory, expelled a shivering sigh.

He had probably been the last of the really innocent mother-fuckers. It had been her slaughter, not society, that had put a stop to it. His funny old father, Dr Cornelius (a lovable eccentric, a visionary in his own way), had killed her when she got cancer of the cervix, running a white-hot poker into her cunt without so much as a by your leave.

His eyes softened nostalgically. He remembered her wit.

Once, when his sister Catherine had come out with a particularly sour remark, his mother had rounded on her from the table where she had been cutting up onions.

'Say that again, love, and I'll carve me fucking name on your womb.'

As it turned out, she'd made something of a prophetic retort.

His childhood had been, until his voluntary entry into the Jesuit seminary, an unspoiled and relatively uncomplicated one. But he couldn't complain. It had been much more interesting than many.

He turned the Duesenberg into a side lane. Through the
twilight he could see the silhouette of the Tudor Mansion. He
needed a fresh car coat. The brown leather one, in the
circumstances.

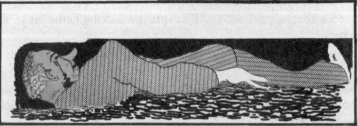

Get Back

An expectancy of change grew out of the dynamic of a search
for the 'new politics', a kind of quest-epic which had to end on
schedule on 5 November. Disappointment followed when the
search produced nothing new. All the found objects were cast
in old forms. Humphrey's coalition was virtually indistinguish-
able from Roosevelts's, Truman's or Johnson's – except that
crucial sections had fallen away. McCarthy and Nixon were
both relying on a Fifties phenomenon – the ascendancy of the
suburban elite. John Kennedy had used that class already in
1960. In their separate ways, Nixon and McCarthy both sought
its allegiance, and if they had contested each other directly,
1968 would have been a delayed-replay of 1960. McCarthy
would probably have won: precisely because he could recap-
ture the old spirit, not because he could fashion the new.

– Andrew Kopkind,
America: The Mixed Curse

Pour les originaux

Jerry looked through the mail that had accumulated since he had
been away.

Outside the French windows the sky was overcast and rain still
swished among the oaks. Softly from the stereo came The Beatles'
'Only a Northern Song'.

There was a request to open a local fête. It was from the vicar
of the village church and began 'I know you have a very full schedule but...' He was a month behind on his Telstar rental and there
was a final demand from the firm who had supplied the aircraft
carrier which he had lost on the abortive Antarctic expedition
where they had failed to find the opening to Pellucidar. A pot
scheme if ever there had been one.

A folded sheet marked *Plattegrond van Amsterdam*. Several post-
cards without messages.

At last he found what he'd been expecting. The envelope had been resealed and forwarded from his Ladbroke Grove convent. He opened it and shook out the contents.

A torn envelope. Small brown manila with the address ripped off and a stamp that said 'Join the sun set in Eastbourne this year'. A fivepenny stamp, postmarked Eastbourne, Sussex, the date indecipherable. On the back, three words: Assassin – Assassin – Assassin.

An Imperial Reply Coupon stamped Juliasdale, Rhodesia, 23 Jan. '69: 'Valid only for exchange within the British Empire. Southern Rhodesia. Selling 3d price. This coupon may be exchanged in any part of the BRITISH EMPIRE for a postage stamp or stamps representing the postage on a single rate letter to a destination within the Empire. Exceptionally the exchange value in India and Burma is 2½ annas.' The engraving, blue on oatmeal, was of a standing Britannia looking out over the sea at a square-rigged sailing ship.

An empty book match folder marked UCS.

A postcard with a fourpenny Concorde stamp postmarked Weston-S-Mare, Somerset, 15 Apr. 1969. It showed a big wave breaking on a rock and the caption read: 'The Cornish Seas. A study of the waves breaking on the rocks. There is nothing but the open Atlantic between the Cornish coast and America: A Natural Colour Photograph.'

The last item was a rather dog-eared sheet of paper, folded several times and secured with a paper clip. Jerry removed the paper clip and unfolded the paper.

There was a message. A single handwritten line in separated upper and lower case letters. 'The ship is yours. B.'

Jerry frowned and put the various bits and pieces back into the envelope. He sipped his mug of black coffee as The Beatles sang 'Altogether Now' and he studied the envelope to see if it gave him any further clues. It had four stamps on it. A fivepenny showing the *Queen Elizabeth* II; a shilling showing the RMS *Mauretania*; another shilling showing the SS *Great Britain*. It bore his Ladbroke Grove address and the forwarding number circled in blue ballpoint – 93. In the top left-hand corner was written in black felt pen: Urgent Special Delivery. The fourth stamp was in the bottom right-hand corner. Another fourpenny Concorde.

What was he to make of it?

There was nothing else but to go down to the harbour in the morning and look at the ships.

For the rest of the evening, before he went to bed, he read the comic strip serial in his back issues of *International Times*. The strip was called 'The Adventures of Jerry Cornelius. The English Assassin'.

Maybe it would add up to something, after all.

The Golden Apples of the Sun

Dylan and the rest, unable to face the implications of their own subject matter, had beaten a quick retreat. Those few whom they had urged on were left stranded, staring around them in bewilderment.

Now the times had, indeed, changed. But the prophets had not. They had only been able to predict – not adapt.

Multivalue logic.

Was it logic, in any real sense, at all?

Or was he really only imposing his own vision on reality; a vision so strong that, for a short time, it would seem to be confirmed by the events around him?

Be that as it may, it was time for some action. He stripped and cleaned his needle gun, drew on his black car coat, his black bell-bottoms, his white shirt with the Bastille-style collar, put the gun in its case, put the case in his pocket, left the Tudor Mansion, locked the doors behind him, looked up at the morning sun slanting through the clouds, and walked on his cuban-heeled feet towards the blue and sparkling sea.

In his dress and his methods of operation he, too, was an anachronism. But he knew no other way. Perhaps there would, in human terms, never be another way. Equilibrium had to be maintained somehow and as far as Jerry was concerned, only the ontologists had any kind of satisfactory answer.

The New Man

Pope Paul turned saint-slayer in the interests of historical accuracy. Out go the saints whose existence is now doubted. St Barbara, whose name has been given to millions of girls and an American city, is struck off. So are Susanna, Boniface of Tarsus, Ursula and her fellow martyrs. An English saint whose existence cannot be doubted moves into the Calendar...

The Sun, 10 May, 1969

Capacity

At Harbour Street Jerry paused to rest. His boots weren't suitable for cobbled lanes.

There was hardly anyone about in the little Cornish village. A smell of fish, a few inshore trawlermen mending their nets, white stone walls of the cottages, grey slate roofs, the masts of the boats that had not yet put out to sea.

Looking down the narrow street at the harbour and beyond it, Jerry saw the yacht anchored at the far end of the stone mole that had been built during the village's better days.

It was the *Teddy Bear*. The yacht had been given a lick of fresh white paint. A corpse of a boat. Is that where the meeting was to take place?

He began to trudge along the mole. The mole was also cobbled. His feet were killing him.

Development II

The War is Over

The kind of chromosomes a person has is called his genotype, and the appearance of a person is called his phenotype. Thus, males have the genotype XY and the phenotype male. Women have the genotype XX and the phenotype female ... In every war in history there must have been a considerable flow of genes one way or another. Whether the genes of the victors or of the vanquished have increased most is a debatable point.

– Papazian,
Modern Genetics

Miss Brunner

The boat smelled as if she had been fouled by a score of cats. Jerry stood on the rotting deck and waited.

Eventually Miss Brunner emerged from the wheelhouse. She was dressed as severely as ever in a Cardin trouser suit as dated as Jerry's own clothes. She held a baby in her crooked right arm, a Smith and Wesson .44 revolver in her left hand.

She gave him a bent smile. 'Good morning, Mr Cornelius. So our paths come together again.'

'I got your note. What's up, Miss Brunner?'

She shook her short red hair in the wind and turned her feline face down to regard the baby.

'Do you like children, Mr Cornelius?'

'It depends.' Jerry moved to look at the baby and was shocked.

'It's got your eyes and mouth, hasn't it?' said Miss Brunner. She offered it to him. 'Would you like to hold it?'

He took a wary step backward. She shrugged and tossed the little creature far out over the rail. He heard it hit the water, whine, gurgle.

'I only hung on to it in case you'd want to have it,' she said apologetically. 'Okay, Mr Cornelius. Let's get down to business.'

'I might have kept it,' Jerry said feelingly. 'You didn't give me much of a chance to consider.'

'Oh, really, Mr Cornelius. You should be able to make up your mind more quickly than that. Are you going soft?'

'Just crumbling a little, at the moment.'

'Ah, well, it's all written in the quasars, I suppose. Come along.'

He followed her down the companionway, along the passage and into the cabin decorated with the Korean tapestries.

'Could we have a porthole open?' Jerry asked.

Pettishly Miss Brunner flung open a porthole. 'I didn't know you cared that much for fresh air.'

'It's to do with my upbringing.' Jerry saw that there were charts unfolded on the ornate mother-of-pearl chart table. He gave them the once-over. A cockroach crawled across a big detailed plan of Hyde Park.

'I suppose you know it's Maxwell and his gang,' Miss Brunner said. 'Trying the old diversion game again. I don't know who that woman thinks she is...' She glared at Jerry and turned her head to stare out of the porthole. 'They're building up a sex scene that could set us back by I don't know how long. Essentially a red herring – but we'll have to nip it in the bud, if we can. Fight fire with fire. I'm not unsympathetic, Mr Cornelius...'

'Any clues?' Jerry lit an Upmann in the hope that it would overlay some of the stink.

Miss Brunner made an agitated gesture.

He gave her a cool, slightly contemptuous look. She couldn't work that one on him. There was no background.

She crossed rapidly to a locker set high in the bulkhead near the door. Taking something from the locker she tossed it to him. 'Recognise that?'

Jerry turned the dildo in his hands. It had a crude, unaesthetic feel to it. 'Don't know. It looks slightly familiar, but...'

'Have a look at the stem.'

Jerry stared closely at the stem. A brand name. *Maxwell's Deviant Devices, London, W.8.*

'Overloaded. He's not happy in his work. That links it with the captain, all right,' Jerry agreed.

She brought something else out of the locker and put it on the chart table. It was a vial of processed DNA.

'Makes sense,' said Jerry. 'They're attempting to slow down the transmogrification by fucking about with identity – concentrating on the heaviest sex angles they can find. It's the easiest way, of course. But crude. I can't believe that anyone these days... Such an old trick...'

'But it could be an effective one. You know how unstable things have been getting since 1965. These people are pre-1950!'

They laughed together.

'I'm serious, though,' added Miss Brunner, sitting down. 'They won't even use chrono-barometers.'

'Bugger me. How do they tell the Time?'

'They don't admit it's here. It's our main advantage, of course.'

Fact

There were a great many instincts in common between *Homo sapiens* and the other animals.

As Barrington Bayley had pointed out in his book *Structural Dynamism*, man was not an intelligent animal. He was an animal with intelligence that he could apply to some, not all, of his activities.

Supposition

$E = mc^2$

Falsehood

Truth is absolute.

Cutting the Mustard

Miss Brunner handed him a beef sandwich. He bit it and grimaced. 'It tastes of grass.'

'It's all a question of how you process it, I suppose,' she said.

She began to strap on her underclothes. 'Well, that's our pact sealed. Where do you intend to go from here?'

'Back to London first. Then I'll start sniffing around.'

She darted him an admiring look.

'You're coarse, darling – but you know how to get down to the nitty-gritty.'

'I don't suppose you'll be around when the shit hits the fan.'

'You never know. But we'd better say goodbye, just in case.'

She handed him a cardboard carton full of old Beatles singles and a photograph. 'Don't lose it. It's our only contact.'

'You anticipate a wax situation?'

'Maybe something a little more sophisticated than that. Is your equipment okay?'

'Ready to go.'

'Oh, sweetie...'

She fell on his erection.

Electric Ladyland

Jerry took the Kamov Ka-15 to London. From there he would call Oxford.

The sound of the copter's rotors drummed in his ears. The fields fled by below. He didn't care for this sort of backtracking operation.

He would need Catty. And he would need one of them. A particular one.

He'd better check his circuits and get in any chemicals he was short on. He sighed, knowing that he would soon be immersed, but not relishing the prospect.

Reaching to the far side of the cockpit, he adjusted the Ellison meter.

Ladbroke Grove lay ahead. He began to drop her down.

If his mother hadn't taken it into her head that he should have a hobby, he wouldn't be in this situation now. He supposed he was grateful, really.

Consequences

When he had made the phone call, Jerry looked through his mother's recipe books to refresh his memory.

Then he made a list of ingredients.

Captain Maxwell

Captain Maxwell left the Austin Princess and crossed the grass verge at the agreed point. They were meeting on the banks of the Cam, just to the north-east of Cambridge. The towpath was lined with fishermen. The river was full of punts. It was a lovely day.

'I thought this would constitute neutral territory, old boy.' Maxwell smiled as he came briskly up to where Jerry was standing watching an angler.

'Neutral territory?' Jerry looked up absently.

Maxwell had lost weight since Jerry had last seen him. He wore a Harris Tweed jacket with leather patches on the sleeves and leather bands round the cuffs, cream cricket flannels, an old Etonian tie. His lips were as red as ever, his round face as bland. 'How are you, old chap? I thought you were dead!' He insinuated a smile onto his features. 'What can I do for you? Say the word.'

'I felt like a chat,' said Jerry. Although the day was warm, he wore his double-breasted black coat buttoned up and his hands were in his pockets. 'You seem to have done well for yourself since Burma.'

'I can't complain, old sport.'

'You've expanded your business interests, I hear. Getting the export market.'

'You could put it like that. The American tie-up with Hunt seems to be working all right.'

Maxwell put his hand on Jerry's elbow and they began to trudge along the towpath, side by side. The air was full of sweet summer smells. Crickets chirped and bees buzzed.

'I was talking to the bishop about you only the other day,'

continued Maxwell. 'He doesn't approve of you at all, old son.' He gave a short, plummy laugh. 'I told him it was nothing more than high spirits. "Spawn of the Antichrist", indeed!'

Jerry grinned.

Maxwell glanced at him, looked disconcerted, cleared his throat. 'You know the bishop. A bit of a romantic. A bit High Church, too, for my taste. Since I became PM, I've had to think about things like that.'

'How is the government?'

'Oh, well – it's *small*, y'know, but generally pretty effective in what it tries to do, I think.'

'I haven't seen much about it recently.'

'We don't often get into the media these days, of course. But we remain realistic. In the meantime we're thinking of building a smaller House of Commons. The one we're using now can accommodate over a hundred members. It's far too big for us to manage.' Maxwell stopped by the river and kicked at a stone. 'But we'll see, we'll see…'

'You're hoping people will get interested in politics again?'

'I *am* rather hoping that, old boy, yes.' Maxwell tried to cover up a sudden secretive expression.

'But for politics, they need surrogates…'

Maxwell looked up sharply. 'If you mean *issues* – I think we can find *issues* for them all right.'

Jerry nodded. 'On the other hand, captain, you can't turn back the clock, can you?'

'Don't intend to, old boy. I'm thinking of the future. The swing of the pendulum, you know.'

Jerry began to giggle uncontrollably.

He stepped into a passing punt. 'Well, so long, captain.'

'TTFN, old chap. Hope I could assist…'

Jerry developed hiccups. He fell backwards into the water. 'Oh, shit!' he laughed. He signalled for his helicopter to come down and pick him up.

The only depressing thing about the encounter was that briefly, at any rate, he had to take the captain's plan seriously.

Popcorn

Jerry tuned his guitar to modal G and played 'Old Macdonald Had a Farm' with a Far Eastern feeling.

He looked through the leaded and barred window of the

converted convent that was his Ladbroke Grove HQ. Maxwell's opium business was booming. The captain disguised his consignments as penicillin and antitetanus serum and shipped them mainly to underdeveloped nations. They were, in fact, developing rapidly with the captain's help.

The sun went in. It began to rain.

Jerry got up and put on his coat. Then he went down the long, dark staircase to the front door and out into the courtyard where he climbed into his Phantom VI.

As he drove down Ladbroke Grove, he pulled out the dusty drawer in the dashboard containing the 45 player and stacked the old Beatles singles onto it. 'The Inner Light' began to play. Jerry smiled, taking a hand-rolled from the nearby tray and sticking the liquorice paper between his lips. It was all such a long time ago. But he had to go through with it.

He remembered the Burma days.

Every gun makes its own tune...

It wasn't the first time Maxwell had succeeded in buggering the equilibrium. But in those days he hadn't liked working with women.

Jerry cheered up at the prospect of his next action.

Cause and Effect

The three men who took the Apollo 8 spaceship on its Christmas journey round the moon were awarded a trophy in London yesterday – for providing 'the most memorable colour TV moment of the past year or any other year' ... Others who were honoured for the year's best achievements in colour TV were comedian Marty Feldman and actress Suzanne Neeve. Derek Nimmo, famous for his parts in 'Oh Brother' and 'All Gas and Gaiters' won the Royal Television Society's silver medal for 'outstanding artistic achievement in front of the camera.'

The Sun, 10 May, 1969

Sweet Child

Jerry got what he needed. It was the last thing on his list.

In Holland Park he wandered hand in hand with Helen who was happy. Her long blonde hair was thick and delicate and her little mini-dress had a gold chain around the waist. Her breasts were sixteen years old and full and she was just plump enough all over. She had a great big red mouth and delicious teeth and huge dark eyes that were full of surprises.

It was a silent summer day and all the trees were green and still and Jerry sang and sprang along the leafy paths.

Helen, behind him, gave a slightly condescending smile.

Jerry shrugged and folded his arms across his chest, turning. He narrowed his eyes and said softly, 'Do you love me, Helen?'

'More or less.'

'More or less?'

'Oh, Jerry!' She laughed.

He looked about him, through the trees. The park was deserted.

He drew his needle gun.

Helen looked at it curiously. 'You are silly, Jerry.'

He gestured with his weapon.

'Come here, Helen.'

She stepped lightly towards him. With his left hand he reached out and felt below her pelvis. He shook his head.

'Is that yours?'

'Of course it's mine.'

'I mean real or false?'

'Who can say?'

'Take it off.'

She pulled up her skirt and undid the little pin that released it into her hand. She gave it to him. 'I feel funny now,' she said. 'More or less.'

'You'd better go ahead of me,' said Jerry, replacing his needle gun.

Resolution

Because man is an animal, movement is most important for him ... Long distance running is particularly good training in perseverance.

– Mao Tse-tung,
Hsin ch'ing-nien, April 1917

Customs

His mouth was full of blood. He popped the last of the liver down his throat and sucked his lower lip, appraising Helen, who stood shivering in the centre of the pentagram. Then he took the speakers and placed one on each of the star's five points, turned to the console on the wall and switched on.

Sparks leapt from point to point and settled into a blue-green flow. Helen hugged her naked breasts.

'Keep your arms at your sides, please,' said Miss Brunner from the darkness on the other side of the lab.

'It's only a temporal circuit. There's nothing to worry about yet.'

Jerry turned a dial. Softly, at first, the music issued from the speakers. Jimi Hendrix's 'Still Raining, Still Dreaming'. Helen began to sway to the sound.

Jerry switched tracks, studying the girl carefully. He got the Deep Fix and 'Laughing Gods'. She jerked, her eyes glazing.

Jerry gave Miss Brunner the thumbs-up sign, turned off the power for a moment to let her into the pentagram, switched on and increased the volume.

His eyes stopped blinking. His face was bathed in the blue-green glow as he watched Miss Brunner move in on the girl.

Grand Guignol

It was telekinesis of a sort, Jerry supposed. You had to act it all out. That was the drag, sometimes. Still – desperate days, desperate measures.

When the drums started to beat, you had to dance.

Na Chia

Delicately Jerry removed Catty's lights and threw them steaming into the kidney dish. Miss Brunner picked up the dish and left the room. 'I'll be getting on with these.'

'Okay,' said Jerry. His job involved much more precise surgery, for he was attempting nothing less than necromancy.

And there wasn't much time.

T'si i

He pumped Catty's corpse full of methane wishing that Miss Brunner had not used up Helen so completely. This was the dark period. The low point. Even if they were successful in cleaning up the Maxwell problem, there was still much to do.

A *kalpa*, after all, was a *kalpa*. It sometimes seemed it would last for ever. Nonetheless, he would be glad when this particular job was wound up.

The drums were beating faster now. His pulse-rate rose, his temperature increased. In the strobe light his face was flushed, his eyes burning, and there was a rim of blood around his lips. The lab was in chaos where he had ransacked it in his haste, searching out the equipment and chemicals he needed.

Squatting by the gas cylinder, he howled along with the Deep Fix.

Scream

'BELPHEGOR!' shrieked Maxwell as Jerry appeared in the window, his car coat unbuttoned and flapping in the sudden wind, his heater in his hand.

Jerry was incapable of speech now. His glowing eyes scanned the opulent room and he remained stock-still, framed against the full moon.

He would never know if Maxwell had identified him as Belphegor or whether that was who the captain had called for. He crouched.

He sprang.

The Prime Minister ran across the room. From somewhere The Beatles began to sing 'Sexy Sadie'. Maxwell touched the door handle and whimpered.

Jerry burned him.

Then, while Maxwell was still hot, he bit off everything he could find.

This was politics with a vengeance.

Baby's in Black

Jerry flattened the accelerator. The world swam with blood. Walpurgis Eve. Trees and houses flashed past.

The breath hissed in through his tight fangs.

Gradually the drums slowed their tempo and Jerry cooled, dropped down to sixty and began to pick his teeth.

A nervous tick. He couldn't help laughing.

Anarchists in Love

He stopped off at the tenement in Robert Street on the borders of Soho. The house was empty now. It had been condemned for years. He pushed open the broken door and entered the damp darkness, treading the worm-eaten boards. His mother had claimed that this was where he had been born, with thick hair down to his shoulders and a full set of teeth, dragged feet first into the world. But towards the end his memory had been better than hers, though by no means reliable.

He struck a match, frowning, trod the groaning stairs to the first floor and found two tall black candles in bronze holders screwed on either side of the entrance to the room he had come to see. He lit the candles.

The place was being used. Neat symbols had been carved in the walls and there were signs of recent occupation. Rats had been crucified near the candles. Some of them were still alive, moving feebly. An early portrait of himself, framed between two sheets of dark glass, hung on the door.

So the place had already become a shrine of some kind.

Below the portrait was a row of equations, quoted from one of his books. Jerry felt sick. Standing by the room he might have been born in, he bent and vomited out the blood that had bloated his stomach.

Weakly, he stumbled down the stairs and into the festering street.

They had taken the hubcaps off his car. He glanced around, conscious of eyes peering at him. He buttoned his coat about his body, got into the driving seat and started the engine.

Perhaps the future would forget him. It had better, for its own sake. He was, after all, only standing in until something better turned up.

Mrs Cornelius

After his mother's death they had moved, finally, to his father's fake Le Corbusier château. Somehow Jerry had always identified the house with his misfortune, though there was no particular evidence to support the idea.

The brain and the womb. Which had created him?

Perhaps neither.

She had begun to claim, as the cancer became more painful, that he had not been conceived by his father. His father had denied this.

'Who else would want to fuck you?' he used to say.

This of course had amused Jerry.

There had been a lot of laughter in the family in those days. Catherine, his brother Frank, his mother and father. Each had a particular kind of humour which had complemented that of the others.

But enough of the past.

He saw Miss Brunner bathed in his headlights and stopped the car.

'Perhaps you could drop me off at the coast,' she said as she climbed in beside him. 'The rest is up to you.'

He smiled sweetly.

'Maxwell's out of it for the time being, I take it,' said Miss Brunner. 'There's only the residual bits and pieces to tidy up. Then the job's over.'

'I suppose so.'

The drums had started up again.

His and Hers

Then is there no such thing as justice? ... His scientific mind is irradiated by this idea. Yet surely the question is, in itself, scientific, psychological, moral, and can therefore be accepted without bias, however disturbing? Lost in these deliberations Dr Cornelius discovers he has arrived back at his own door.

– Thomas Mann,
Disorder and Early Sorrow

The Sex Complex

Holland House was a sixteenth-century manor reconstructed as a façade in 1966. On the white battlements stood guards in yellow leather.

'Helen?' called one.

'Okay, Herschel.'

They went through the iron doors and the floor began to sink under their feet, taking them down and down through crawling light.

At the bottom Jerry drew his heater and pushed what was left of the fake Helen through the opening into the huge hall where the freaks turned to glance at them before looking back at Lady Sue Sunday, still in her Tory set, who stood in an ornate pulpit at the far end.

'Helen!' Lady Sue looked prim.

'It was inconclusive,' said what was left of the fake Helen defensively. 'Really.'

'So...'

Jerry glimmed Lady Sue's freaks. 'Jesus,' he said. There were little boys dressed as little girls. There were men dressed as women and women decked out like men in almost every detail. There were androgynes and hermaphrodites. There were little girls dressed as little boys. There were hugely muscled women and tiny, soft men. 'Irony, Lady Sue, is no substitute for imagination.'

He shook his head and unbuttoned his car coat with his free hand.

Lady Sue put a glove to her lips.

'You're a naughty boy, Jerry. Naughty, naughty, naughty boy...'

Jerry laughed. 'Evidently you never knew my mother.'

Lady Sue scowled.

'Maxwell's had it,' Jerry said. 'I only dropped in to let you know. You can go home. It's all over.'

'Naughty...'

'Oh, shut up.' He raised his gun.

She licked her lips.

Jerry watched the urine as it began to drip from the floor of the pulpit. Lady Sue looked uncomfortable. She spread her arms to indicate her creatures.

Jerry sighed. 'If you hadn't been so damned literal-minded...'

'You can accuse...' With an impatient gesture she touched a button on the pulpit's console. Little Richard music began to roar about the hall.

Jerry relaxed. No good getting excited.

'This is a one-way ticket,' he called, waving his heater at the scene. 'A line. Just a line.'

'Who needs angles, you little horror?' She picked up her wide-brimmed blue hat and adjusted it on her head.

'At best a spiral,' Jerry murmured wearily.

'A chain!' she cried. 'A chain! Vitality! Don't you get it?'

'Off you go, Lady Sue.'

Little Richard changed to James Brown. It was too much for Jerry. He began to race through the freaks towards the pulpit. The freaks kept touching him.

Lady Sue picked up a small vanity bag. 'Well...' She was defeated. 'Back to Hampstead, I suppose. Or...'

'You get a passage on a boat,' he said. 'The *Teddy Bear*. She's in the Pool of London now. Hurry up...'

'Why...?'

'Off you go. I might see you later.'

She stepped out of the pulpit and walked towards the elevator immediately behind her – a golden cage. She got into the cage. It began to rise. Through the glass bottom Jerry could see right up her skirt, saw the damp pants.

When she had disappeared, he took his heater and burned down the pulpit. The lights began to fade, one by one.

The flaming pulpit gave him enough light to work. He cleaned up Lady Sue's mess, much more in sorrow than in anger. The mess recoiled then rushed at him. It was shouting. He backed away. Normally he would have used his heater, but he was now too full of melancholy. He had been very busy, after all.

They were never grateful.

The freaks pursued him to the lift; he got there first and went up fast.

He left Holland House and the guards shot at him as he raced through the door and out into the park. He ducked behind a statue and burned his initials into the chest of each of them.

That did it.

It was one for mother.

A Cure for Cancer

Jerry watched the *Teddy Bear* sail out into the calm oil of the Pool and start to sink.

Lady Sue leaned moodily on the rail, staring at him as the ship went down. Soon only her hat and the topmast were visible.

Jerry looked at his watches. They had almost stopped.

As he made his way back through the decrepit warehouses on the quayside he became aware of groups of figures standing in the shadows staring at him. Each of the figures was dressed in a moth-eaten black car coat he recognised as one of his cast-offs.

He shuddered and climbed into the Phantom VI.

His tongue was sweating. His heart was cold.

It had been a much tougher job than he expected.

Time Off Time

'Adjustment okay,' said Alvarez, coughing cheerfully. 'Well, well, well...'

Jerry sat tired in his chair and inspected the shimmering web of crimson and gold. Apart from tiny and perfectly logical fluctuations in the outer strands, it was sweet and perfect.

'Aquilinas on tomorrow, isn't he?' Alvarez said as he tidied up.

Jerry nodded. He took a deep breath. 'I'll have that mirror now. I'm looking forward to the change.'

'That's a fact,' said Alvarez.

The Sunset Perspective

A Moral Tale

I

MOGADISCIO, Somalia, Oct. 15 – President Abirashid Ali Shermarke of Somalia was assassinated today by a member of the police force, an official announcement said here. The announcement said that a man had been arrested and accused of the murder at Las Anod in northern Somalia, where the President was touring an area stricken by drought. No reason for the assassination was suggested.

New York Times, 16 October, 1969

Energy Quotient

Jerry Cornelius lay on his back in the sweet warm grass and looked across the sunny fields, down the hill towards the bright, smart sea. Overhead a flight of friendly Westland Whirlwinds chattered past, full of news. Soon it was silent again.

Jerry stretched and smiled.

A small fox terrier wriggled through the stile at the bottom of the hill and paused, wagging its tail at him.

A cloud moved in front of the sun and the day chilled. Jerry first watched the cloud and then watched the dog. He listened to the grasshoppers. They were scraping their legs together in the long grass by the hedge. He sniffed the wind.

It was all a matter of how you looked at it, thought Jerry, getting tired of waiting for the cloud to pass. He took a deep breath and sprang to his feet, dusting off his brown velvet bell-bottoms. The dog started to bark at him. On the other side of the hedge a cow's heavy body shook the leaves. In the distance a woman's voice called the dog. Things were moving in on him.

Time to be off.

Jerry buttoned up his black car coat and adjusted the collar to frame his pale face. He tramped along the footpath towards the village.

Seagulls screamed on the cliffs.

The church bell began to clank.

Jerry sighed. He reached the field where his Gates Twinjet was parked. He climbed in, revved the chopper's engine, and buzzed up into the relative peace of the skies over Cornwall, heading for London.

One was allowed such short periods of rest.

2

> There was something in that blind, scarred face that was terrifying ... He did not seem quite human.

> – W. Somerset Maugham,
> Preface, *Ashenden*

Time Quotient

When Jerry got to the Time Centre only Alvarez was on duty. He was boredly watching the chronographs, his bearded face a pale green in the light from the machines. He heard the footsteps and turned large, liquid brown eyes to regard Jerry.

'Looks salty,' Jerry quipped, indicating the web model in the centre of the operations room. The web bulged badly along one of its straights.

'Miss Brunner said she'd see to the adjustments,' Alvarez told him pettishly. Morale seemed to have declined since Jerry had been away. 'But between you and me, Mr C., I think the whole bloody structure's going out of phase.'

'Oh, come now...' Jerry made a few minor adjustments to Number Six 'graph, studied the results for a moment and then shrugged. 'You haven't located the central cause of the bulge?'

'Miss Brunner's gone a bit funny, if you ask me.'

Alvarez began to pick his teeth. '*On* the quiet,' he added, 'I'm pissed off with that bird.'

'We all have our ups and downs, Mr Alvarez.'

He went into the computing room. Miss Brunner's handbag was on her desk. There were some sheets of calculations near it, but they hadn't gone very far. The face of each wall was a section of the huge computer she had built. But the machine was dormant.

Miss Brunner had turned off the power.

That meant something. She was probably having another identity crisis.

But what had caused it?

3

Life proceeds amid an incessant network of signals...

– George Steiner

Rise of the Total Energy Concept

Jerry finally managed to track Miss Brunner down. She was burying a goat in the Hyde Park crater and didn't see him come up and stand looking over the rim at her.

He watched as she mumbled to herself, hitching her Biba maxiskirt up to her thighs and urinating on the new mound of earth.

'Well, you're really in a bad way, aren't you, Miss B?'

She raised her head. The red hair fell over her foxy face; the eyes were glassy. She hissed and smoothed down her muddy clothes. 'It's a difficult situation, Mr Cornelius. We've got to try everything.'

'Isn't this a bit dodgy?'

She picked up a stick and began to draw her usual mandala in the steaming earth. 'If I can't be allowed to do my own job in my own way...'

'You've been working too hard.'

'I've got eight toads and four newts buried around here!' She glared at him. 'If you think I'm going to go round digging them up for you or anybody else...'

'Not necessary. Anyway, Alvarez obviously thinks we'll have to rephase.'

'Bugger off.'

'Look at yourself. You always revert to type in a crisis.'

She paused, pushing back her hair and offering him a pitying smile. 'Electricity's all you ever think about, isn't it? There are other methods, you know, which...'

Jerry dug inside his black car coat and took the needler from the shoulder holster. He waved it at her.

'Come up out of there. You'll ruin your clothes.'

She sniffed and began to climb, the loose earth falling away behind her.

He nudged her in the ribs with the needler and marched her to the Lear Steamer. Alvarez was in the driving seat. He had already got up enough pressure to start moving. Jerry sat beside Miss Brunner in the back seats of the car as it drove towards Bayswater Road.

'You reckoned the emanations vectored back to New York, didn't you?' he asked her. She had calmed down a bit now. 'I read your initial calculations.'

'New York was just involved in the first phase. I could have told you much more if you'd've let me finish with the goat...'

'I don't think goats are very efficient, Miss B.'

'Well, what can we do about New York, anyway? We can't sort one AA Factor out from that lot there!'

'But the factor might sort us out.'

4

WASHINGTON, Oct. 15 – Congress voted today to coin a new dollar that would honor former President, Dwight D. Eisenhower, but the Senate and the House of Representatives differed on whether it should be a silver dollar. Flourishing a letter from Mrs Eisenhower, a group of Western legislators got the Senate to override the Administration's proposal to produce a copper and nickel coin. A similar effort, backed by the same letter, failed in the House, which opted for the administration's non-silver dollar. Mrs Eisenhower's letter disclosed that the former President had loved to collect and distribute silver dollars as mementos.

New York Times, 16 October, 1969

Horror Rape of the Kidnapped Teenage Beauty

Jerry pared the black mixture of oil and blood from the nail of the little finger of his right hand and carefully licked his upper lip. Then he put both hands back on the steering wheel of the wavering Cadillac limousine. The car was as hard to control as a hovercraft. The sooner it was used up the better. He saw the toll barrier ahead on the multilane highway and brought the car down to seventy.

Cars pulled into the sides of the road as his siren sounded. Jerry's six outriders, in red and orange leather, moved into position at front and back of the Cadillac, their arms stretched on the crucifixes of their apehanger bars.

Jerry pressed a switch.

The Who began to sing 'Christmas'. The sign hanging over the highway said DRIVERS WITH CORRECT CHANGE – THIS LANE.

Jerry paid his twenty-five cents at the turnpike and drove into New Jersey.

This was a noisy situation. There were either too many facts, or no facts at all – he couldn't be sure at this stage. But he had the feel of it. There was no doubt about one thing – it was a morality syndrome of the worst sort.

He checked his watches. The arrows whirled rapidly round the dials. Not much longer now.

The car lolloped along between the overgrown subsidy fields and the ramshackle internment centres.

Jerry lit a brown Sherman's Queen-Size Cigarettello.

Why Homosexuals Seek Jobs in Mental Hospitals

On George Washington Bridge Jerry decided to change the Cadillac for one of his outriders' BMW 750s. He stopped. The riders got off their bikes and parked them neatly in a line along the rail. Drivers behind them on the highway hooted, their horns dying as they approached, pulled up, looked elsewhere.

He slid from the car, was passed the leather helmet and mirror goggles by the blonde who took his place in the driving seat.

Jerry tucked his black flare pants into the tops of his ornate Cherokee boots, buckled up and mounted the vacated bike. He kicked the starter and had reached eighty by the time he hit Manhattan and entered the island's thick haze of incense.

The Holy City

The babble of the charm-sellers, the fortune-tellers, the fakirs, the diviners, the oracles, the astrologers, the astromancers and necromancers mingled with the squeal of the tyres, the wail of the sirens, the caterwauling of the horns.

Corpses swayed on steel gibbets spanning the streets. Broadsheets pasted on the sides of buildings advertised spectacular entertainments, while on the roofs little parties of marauders crept among the chimneys and the collapsing neon signs.

The popping of distant gunfire occasionally signified a clash.

Shacked up for Slaughter!

Jerry and his riders got all the way down 7th Avenue to West 9th Street before they were blocked by a twelve-foot-high pile-up and had to abandon their bikes.

From what Jerry could see, the pile-up went down as far as

Sheridan Square and West 4th Street. The faggots had probably closed off the area again and were defending their territory. They had had a lot of bad luck up to now. Maybe this time they would be successful.

Jerry took out his glasses and scanned the fire escapes – sure enough, the faggots, sporting the stolen uniforms of the Tactical Riot Police, were lobbing B-H5 gas grenades into the tangled heaps of automobiles.

Sheltering under a sign saying DOLLARS BOUGHT AT COMPETITIVE PRICES, Jerry watched for a few seconds.

It looked like a mince-over for the faggots.

My God, Wild Dogs are Attacking the Kids!

Eventually Jerry reached his headquarters at the Hotel Merle on St Mark's Place – the other side of the battle area. He had bought the hotel cheap when the Mafia had moved out to Salt Lake City.

Leaving his riders to go to the aid of their comrades on West 4th, he entered the seedy gloom of the lobby.

Shakey Mo Collier was on the desk. His black face was caked with white clay and his expression was unusually surly. He cheered up when he saw Jerry.

'Mornin', guv. Vere's a bloke waitin' fer yer in 506.'

'What's his name?'

Mo screwed up his eyes in the poor light and his lips moved as he tried to read something he had scribbled on a checking-in card. 'Robin – nar – Reuben – nar – Robert – de – Fate? Nar! Rob...'

'Robert D. Feet.' Jerry felt relieved. His trip hadn't been wasted. He recognised the 'whimsical' pseudonym. 'Foreign Office.'

Mo sniffed and picked at the clay on his face. 'I'll buy it, won' I?'

Jerry chucked him under his chin. 'We bought it.'

He took the groaning elevator to the fifth floor. The warren of narrow corridors was everywhere painted the same chocolate brown. Jerry found 506.

Cautiously, he opened the door.

The darkened room contained a bed without sheets and

blankets. It had a striped, stained mattress. On the floor was a worn green carpet. A bedside table, lamp and secretaire were all coated with several layers of the same brown paint. The blind had been pulled down. On the secretaire stood a half-full bottle of Booth's Gin and a plastic cup.

Jerry opened the door into the bathroom. The pipes gurgled and shook, but the room was empty. He checked the shower stall just the same.

He went back into the bedroom and looked at the bottle of gin. Obviously, his visitor had left it as a message.

It made sense.

The trip had paid off.

5

The New York Mets moved to within one victory of the pot of gold yesterday when they defeated the Baltimore Orioles 2–1, in 10 innings and took a lead of three games to one in the World Series. The victory was the third straight for the underdog Mets over the champions of the American League and it was laced with potent doses of the 'magic' that has marked their fantastic surge to the top in 1969.

New York Times, 16 October, 1969

Upset or Equilibrium in the Balance of Terror?

Miss Brunner appeared to have cooled down the reversion process somewhat when Jerry returned to the Centre. She was still mumbling, half the doodles on her pads were astrological equations she was either feeding into or receiving from her computer, but the worst part of her work was over now Jerry had isolated the key mark's identity type.

She licked her lips when he handed her the paper with the name on it.

'So it's a morality syndrome?'

'Yes, the poor sod.' Jerry rubbed the back of his neck. 'I'll have to take him out as soon as possible. No time for a transmogrification. This'll have to be a termination. Unless...' He narrowed his eyes as he looked at her. 'Are you sure you're all right?'

'Yes, of course. It's this bloody pattern. You know what it does to me.'

'Okay. Well, can you pin him down in a hurry? We had a break in that he's evidently going "guilty" on us, like a lot of them. They do half our work for us. Very few are even one hundred per cent sure of themselves. That's why they say they are.'

She started to sort through her notes, stopped and picked up a bottle of cologne. She unscrewed the cap, upended the bottle and dabbed some of the cologne on her forehead.

Jerry rocked on the balls of his feet.

'At least it's a familiar pattern,' she said. 'A standard British resurrection plan of the old type. With "conscience" overtones. What does Alvarez say?'

Jerry went into the next room. 'How's it shaping, Mr Alvarez?'

Alvarez shrugged and spread his hands helplessly. 'Most of the Middle East's breaking up. Complete temporal entropy in many areas. It'll be South-East Asia next, and you know what that means.'

Jerry frowned.

Almost shyly, Alvarez glanced at Jerry. 'It's never been this bad, has it, Mr Cornelius?'

Jerry scratched his left hand with his right hand. 'How about other sectors?'

Alvarez made a radio call. He listened to the headphones for a while and then swivelled to face Jerry who was now leaning against a console smoking an Upmann Exquisitos.

'Moscow's completely out. New York more or less the same. Half of Peking's down – its southern and western districts. Singapore's completely untouched. No trouble in Shanghai. None in Sydney or Toronto. No trouble in Calcutta, but New Delhi's had it...'

Jerry dropped his cigar on the floor and stood on it.

The factor was overplaying his hand.

He went back into Miss Brunner's room and told her the news.

She spoke distantly. 'I've got it down to eight localities.' She started to tap out a fresh programme and then stopped.

She went to her handbag, picked it up, squatted on the floor of the computing room. She was breathing heavily.

Jerry watched her as she took something from her bag and threw it on the ground. It was a handful of chicken bones. Miss Brunner was casting the runes.

'For God's sake, Miss Brunner!' Jerry took a step towards her. 'The whole balance is gone and you're fucking about with bones...'

She raised her head and cackled. 'You've got to have faith, Mr C.'

'Oh, Christ!'

'Exactly,' she mumbled. 'It's a sort of progress report on the Second Coming, isn't it? You ought to know, after all!'

'Mother of God!'

He pressed the button marked POWER OFF and the computer went dead.

Sometimes he would admit that one form of superstition was as good as another, but he still preferred to rely on the forms he knew. He flung himself on top of Miss Brunner and began to molest her.

They were all operating on instinct at the moment.

Systems Theory and Central Government

Jerry was running.

The backlash was bound to hit London soon and the whole equilibrium would be thrown. Alvarez's dark suggestions about rephasing might have to be implemented. That meant a great deal of work – a long job involving a lots of risks. He wasn't sure he was up to it at the moment.

He would have to play his hunch, picking one locality from the list of eight Miss Brunner had shown him before she reverted.

He ran through a deserted Holland Park. The autumn leaves slapped his face. He headed for the Commonwealth Institute.

Whither ESRO?

The sun had set by the time Jerry arrived outside the Institute where a few lights were burning.

He turned up the collar of his black car coat, walked under the flags, past the pool and into the main hall. It was deserted. He crossed the hall and opened a door at the back. It led into a small corridor. At the end of the corridor was another door. Jerry approached it and read the name on it:

COLONEL MOON

The name seemed right.

Jerry turned the handle of the door. It was unlocked. He walked into absolute blackness.

An electric light went on.

He was in a steel office. There were steel filing cabinets, steel shelves and a steel desk. At the desk sat Colonel Moon, a stiff-backed man, no longer young. A cigarette in a black plastic holder was clamped between his teeth. He had a square, healthy face, a little touched by drink. His eyes were blue and slightly watery. He wore the tweed jacket of a minor Civil Service 'poet'.

As Jerry entered, Colonel Moon closed a boxfile with one hand. His other hand was still by the light switch on the wall near the desk.

'Miss Brunner is dead, eh? It was just as well, Mr Cornelius. We couldn't have her running wild.'

'So you're the Great Terror.' Jerry rubbed his left eyelid with his left index finger. He looked casually about. 'They don't give you much room.'

Moon presented Jerry with a patronising smile. 'It serves my simple needs. Won't you sit down?'

Jerry crossed to the far wall and seated himself in the wicker rocker. 'Where did you pick this up?'

'Calcutta. Where else?'

Jerry nodded. 'I got your message in New York.'

'Jolly good.'

'I'm not really up to this, but what was it – "guilt" or something?'

'Sense of fair play, old boy.'

Jerry burst out laughing.

'I'll be seeing *you*, colonel.'

6

While the strategic importance of large air-launched weapons declines in the age of ICBMs and submarine-launched ballistic missiles, airborne guided weapons for tactical use grow in importance. Vietnam has become a 'testing ground' for a wide range of weapons from the Walleye TV-guided bomb to Bullpup and the radar-homing Shrike. The lessons learned from actual operations are rapidly being applied to new weapons systems such as the AGM-80A Viper and the AGM-79A Blue Eye, both conceived as Bullpup replacements.

Flying Review International, November 1969

Emotion and the Psychologist

In mutable times like these, thought Jerry as he walked into Lionel Himmler's Blue Spot Bar, everything was possible and nothing was likely. His friend Albert the émigré nodded to him from the shadowy corner by the bar, lifting his glass of schnapps in the strobe light, saluting both Jerry and the stripper on the stage.

Jerry flickered to a table, sat down and ordered scotch and milk. Once history ceased to be seen in linear terms, it ceased to be made in linear terms. He glanced at his new watch.

Moon's machinery could be useful if used in conjunction with their own. He was sorry that he'd have to blow up Bhubaneswar, though.

The problems, of course, would be 'psychological' rather than 'moral' – if 'moral' meant what he thought it did. That was, he admitted, one of his blind spots. It was a pity Miss Brunner wasn't herself (or, rather, was too much herself). She had a much better grasp of that sort of thing.

From behind the curtain a record of Mozart's 41st Symphony began to play.

Jerry settled back in his chair and watched the act.

7

Peace rallies drew throngs to the city's streets, parks, campuses and churches yesterday in an outpouring of protest against the Vietnam war. The Times Square area was hit by a colossal traffic jam during rush hour as tens of thousands of demonstrators marched to the culminating event of the day – a rally in Bryant Park, west of the New York Public Library. The park was saturated with people, many of them unable to see the speakers' stand or hear the denunciations of war ... Mayor Lindsay had decreed a day of mourning. His involvement was bitterly assailed by his political opponents and by many who felt that the nationwide demonstrations were not only embarrassing President Nixon's efforts to negotiate an honorable peace but were giving aid and comfort to the enemy as well.

New York Times, 16 October, 1969

Technology Review

Miss Brunner would be a complete write-off soon, if she wasn't saved.

She was up to her old tricks. She had constructed a pentagram circuit on the floor of the computer room and she had dug up her goat. It lay in the centre of the pentagram, its liver missing.

Jerry watched for a moment and then closed the door with

a sigh. He'd have to deal with Moon himself – and what's more it wouldn't now be a simple take-out.

Moon had known what he was doing when he had arranged events so that Miss Brunner's logic patterns would be scattered. He had doubtless hoped that with Miss Brunner's reversion, the whole Time Centre would be immobilised. It had been a clever move – introducing massive chaos factors into twelve major cities, like that. Moon must have been working on the job a long time.

Now Miss Brunner was doing the only thing she could, under the circumstances.

He turned to Alvarez who was sipping a cup of hot Ribena. 'They keep turning up, don't they?'

Alvarez's tone was sardonic. 'Will it ever end?'

Westminster Scene

Jerry needed sleep. Miss Brunner could get by on a drop or two of blood at the moment, but it wouldn't do for him. Moon would make a good substitute, of course, if he wasn't now needed as an antidote, but that would anyway mean rushing things, probably buggering them up altogether. It was something of a vicious circle.

He went back to his Ladbroke Grove HQ and took the lift up to the tower where he had his private apartments. He switched on the stereo and soothed himself down with a rather mannered version of Beethoven's 9th, conducted by von Karajan. He typed his notes on the IBM 2000 and made a hundred copies on his Xerox 3600. It wasn't like the old days, when the Centre had only needed one chronograph and the entire works could be run by a single operator. Perhaps the whole thing should be folded. It was becoming a large randomising feature in its own right.

He followed the Beethoven with a Del Reeves album, after considering a Stones LP. There were some perversions left in the world, but he didn't feel up to that one at present. It would have been like drinking Wild Turkey bourbon in an Austin Princess.

He lay down on the leather ottoman by the window.

He dozed until Alvarez called.

'Absolute Crisis Situation just about to break,' Alvarez told him. 'I'd say you have three hours. After that, there won't even be a chance of rephasing, if I'm any judge.'

'Check,' said Jerry and winked at his reflection in the mirror.

Tantalizer

It had to be this way. Jerry couldn't have managed it alone, otherwise. He had been forced to wait for the moment when the feedback would start to hit Moon.

He found him in his office, completely naked, sitting in the middle of a huge and tattered Union Jack, the empty cigarette holder between his teeth. It was the flag that had been missing from the pole Jerry had passed on his way in.

Moon's well-preserved body was pale and knotted with muscle. He was remarkably hairy. He saw Jerry and got up.

'Nice to see you, dear boy. As a matter of interest, how did you find me, originally?'

'Originally? The only person sentimental enough to look after those old outposts was you. I knew you would have left NY. I had a hunch you'd be here.'

Moon pursed his lips.

'Coffee?' he said at length. He crossed to a gas-ring set up on one of the steel filing cabinets. He put the kettle on and measured spoonfuls of Camp Coffee into orange plastic cups.

'No, thanks,' said Jerry.

Moon began to pour the coffee back into the bottle. It flooded over the neck and ran down the sides, staining the label.

'It's a shame you refused to fall back on the old methods,' he said. 'I thought you would when Miss Brunner went.'

'They aren't suitable, in this case,' Jerry told him. 'Anyway, I've been in a funny mood for some time.'

'You've got jolly moralistic all of a sudden, haven't you?' Colonel Moon raised his eyebrows in his 'quizzical' expression.

'You shouldn't have done that, colonel.' Jerry began to tremble. 'I've never understood the death-wish you people have.'

'Ah, well, you see – you're younger than me.'

'We'll have to wipe out most of your bloody logic sequence. That's not a "moralistic" reaction. I'm just annoyed.'

Again the 'quizzical' expression. 'So you say.'

Jerry smacked his lips.

'I would have thought,' Moon added, 'that in your terms my sequence was a fairly simple one.'

Jerry couldn't answer. He knew Moon was right.

'Everything's so boringly complicated these days, isn't it?' Moon put his hand on the handle of the kettle and winced. He stiffened his lips and began to pour the water into the cup.

Jerry stopped trembling. He felt quite sympathetic towards Moon now. 'It's a question of attitude, I suppose.'

Moon looked surprised. There were tears in his eyes; just a few. 'Yes, I suppose so.'

'Shall we be off?' Jerry removed his black gloves and put one in each pocket of his car coat. He reached inside the coat, pulling his needler free of its holster.

'Mind if I finish my coffee?'

'I'd appreciate it if you'd hurry up, though.' Jerry glanced at his watches. 'After all, there's Miss Brunner to think of.'

8

Today as an extensive auto trip has confirmed, the only danger along Route 4 is the traffic, which is dreadful, and the potholes, which can shatter an axle. The improved security along the road is one of the more visible examples of the progress achieved over the last year by the allied pacification program.

New York Times, 16 October, 1969

People

Jerry took Colonel Moon to the basement of the Ladbroke Grove HQ.

The colonel smoothed his iron-grey hair and looked around the bare room. 'I thought – well – Miss Brunner?'

'That's next. We're going to have to soften you up a bit first. Jimi Hendrix, I'm afraid.'

Jerry went to the hidden panel and opened it. He flipped a toggle switch to turn on the power.

Colonel Moon said: 'Couldn't you make it George Formby?'

Jerry thought for a moment and then shook his head. 'I'll tell you what. I'll make it early Hendrix.'

'Very well. I suppose there isn't much time left. You can't blame me for trying, eh?'

Jerry's eyes were glazed as he waltzed over to Colonel Moon and positioned him. 'Time? Trying?'

Colonel Moon put his head in his hands and began to sob.

Jerry took aim with the needler, pulled the trigger. The needles passed through the hands and through the eyes and into the brain. Jerry pulled his little transmogrifier from his pocket and stuck the electrodes on Moon's skull.

Then he switched on the music.

Books

It was 'And the Gods Made Love' that did it.

His hands rigid over his eyes, Colonel Moon fell down. He murmured one word: Loyalty. And then was supine.

Jerry reduced the volume and picked up a wrist. It was completely limp.

Thoroughly into it now, Jerry licked his lips, heaved the body onto his back, and left for the Time Centre.

9

ROME, Oct. 15 – Cardinal Cooke, Archbishop of New York, urged the Roman Catholic Synod of Bishops today to consider the present period of 'stress and strain' in the church 'frankly and positively, with great charity.'

New York Times, 16 October, 1969

He Smashed the 'Death Valley' Terror Trap

Jerry stumbled through the door with the body over his shoulder. 'All ready. Where's Miss B?'

Alvarez was chewing a beef sandwich. 'Still in there. She locked the door a while ago.'

'Use the emergency lock to open it, will you?'

'You haven't given yourself much margin.' Alvarez spoke accusingly as he operated the lock. The computing room door sank into the floor.

Jerry stepped through. 'Close it up again, Mr A.'

'Aye, aye, Mr C.'

Alvarez was getting very edgy about the whole thing. Jerry wondered if he would have to go.

Blue lights flickered on five points. Red lights, close together, shifted on the far side of the room. The red lights were Miss Brunner's beautiful eyes.

'I've come to help you.' Jerry grinned and his teeth felt very sharp.

She screamed.

'Oh, do shut up, Miss B. We're going to break the spell together.'

'*BELPHEGOR!*'

'Anything you say.'

We Survived the Cave of the 10,000 Crazed Bats

Jerry sucked his lower lip.

Colonel Moon now stood shivering in the centre of the pentagram, an inane grin on his face.

Jerry took the speakers and placed one on each of the five

points, then turned the computer to FULL INPUT and switched on the rest of the equipment.

Sparks leapt from point to point and settled into a blue-green flow. It was all very familiar. Colonel Moon's mouth went slack.

'Cheer up, colonel. You never saw an act like this at the Empire!'

From the darkness, Miss Brunner cackled stupidly.

Jerry turned a dial. The music came out softly at first, but it got to the colonel in no time. It was the Mothers of Invention and 'Let's Make the Water Turn Black'.

He heard Miss Brunner through it all. 'Tasty,' she was saying. At least she was responding a bit.

'In you go, Miss B.'

He watched her scrawny, naked body in silhouette as it moved through the blue-green glow into the pentagram.

Colonel Moon hissed as Miss Brunner took her first nip.

Jerry's part of it was over. He slipped from the room.

The antidote had been administered, but there was still a lot of tidying up to do.

Sex Habits of Bonnie Parker and the Women Who Kill

Alvarez was smiling now. He looked up from his headphones. 'The situation's static. We've got a silly season on our hands by the smell of it.'

Jerry was worn out. 'Reset all the chronographs, will you? It's not over yet.'

Miss Brunner could be a great asset, but her habits sometimes put him off her.

He yawned. 'Poor old Moon.'

'Hoist by his own petard, eh?' grinned Alvarez.

'Silly bugger. He didn't really believe in what he was doing.'

'But Miss Brunner did.'

'Well, Moon felt he ought to have a "sense of purpose", you see. It lets them all down in the end.'

10

It would be foolish to speculate further.

– George Steiner

Facts by Request

Miss Brunner and Jerry Cornelius walked hand in hand through Hyde Park and paused where the crater had been.

'It's very hazy,' she said. 'So I did it again.'

'Moon set you up. You knocked him down.'

'*C'est la vie!*'

'You could put it like that.'

She stopped and removed her hand from his. 'Really, Mr Cornelius, you do seem *down*.'

'Well, it's all over now. Here's your transport.'

He pointed through the trees at the Sikorsky SH-3D which began to rev up, blowing the last of the leaves from the branches, blowing the other leaves up into the air. The day was cold and sunny.

She paused, looking in her handbag for something and not finding it. 'You sympathise with them, yet you'll never understand their morality. It was such a long while ago. You're a kind little chap, aren't you?'

Jerry folded his arms and closed his face.

He watched her walk towards the helicopter, her red hair ruffled by the wind. She was full of bounce. Moon had agreed with her.

He thought she called something out, but he couldn't hear her above the whine of the rotors.

The helicopter shuddered and lumbered into the sky.

Soon it was gone.

Jerry looked at his watches. The arrows were revolving at a moderate speed. It was all he could hope for.

The gestures of conflict keep the peace.

It was a motto that even Moon had understood, but he had chosen to ignore it. Those old men of action. They were the ones you had to watch.

Jerry lay down on the grass and closed his eyes. He listened to the lazy sound of the distant traffic, he sniffed the scents of autumn.

It had been a rotten little caper, all in all.

Other texts consulted include:
Real Detective Yearbook, No. 101, 1969
Confidential Detective Cases, March 1969
Women in Crime, May 1969
Male, June 1969
Encounter, August 1969
New Scientist, 13 November, 1969

Sea Wolves

It occurs to us that while we've been saying 'you need your computer' we'd also like to emphasize something equally important.

'Your computer needs you.'

You see, without you your computer is nothing.

In fact, it's people like yourself that have made the computer what it is today.

It's people like you that have made their computer do some pretty exciting things.

Like help them keep on top of sales trends.

Or design a bridge.

Or keep track of all the parts that go into a giant whirlybird.

To do things like that, your computer needs some help.

It needs you to get more involved with it. So you can use it to help you do more than just the payroll and the billing.

And it needs some terminals.

Terminals let you get information in and out of your computer fast.

They let you get up close to your computer.

Even though you might be miles away...

But terminals are nothing unless something happens between you and your computer.

Unless you get involved with your computer.

You need your computer.

Your computer needs you.

KNOW YOUR BUSINESS.

KNOW YOUR COMPUTER.

IBM

I

Running, grinning, apeing the movements of the mammals milling about him, Jerry Cornelius made tracks from the menagerie that was My Lai, the monster tourist attraction of the season, and threw his Kamov Ka-15 into the sky, flew over the tops of the tall hotels and novelty factories, away from there; away to the high privacy of Bangkok's Hotel Maxwell where, panting, he froze his limbs in the angles of sleep.

A posture, after all, was a posture.

2

Jerry's uniform was that of the infamous Brigade of St Basil. These Osaka-based White Cossack Mercenaries had recently changed from the Chinese to the American side; a half-hearted move; a compromise. But the uniform – cream, gold and fawn – overrode most other considerations.

Meanwhile revolutionary troops continued to march on the great automated factories of Angkor Wat and Anuradhapura. It would all be over by the Festival of Drakupolo.

A week passed. Jerry continued to sleep, his well-cut jacket and jodhpurs uncrumpled, for he did not stir and his breathing was minimal, neither did he perspire. There was a complete absence of REMs.

3

The war ended with a complete victory for the factories. The defected revolutionaries made their way back to Simla and Ulan

Bator. Jerry woke up and listened to the news on Radio Thai. He frowned.

A fine balance had to be maintained between man and machine, just as between man and man, man and woman, man and environment.

It was as good as it was bad.

Regretfully he stripped off his uniform. He was not sure he looked forward to civvy street.

4

The gestures of conflict keep the peace. The descendants of Tompion and Babbage toyed with inaccurate engines while their enemies entertained impossible debates concerning the notion that an electronic calculating device could not possess a 'soul'. The old arguments perpetuated themselves: resolved in the ancient formulae of warfare.

5

When Jerry arrived in Phnôm Penh the streets were full of bunting. Rickshaws, bicycles, cars and trams were hung with paper banners, streamers and posters. The Central Information Building shuddered with bright flame. The factories had won, but others were suffering for them. It was as it should be, thought Jerry.

Cheerfully he mounted an abandoned British-made Royal Albert gent's black roadster and pedalled along with the procession, avoiding the wreckage of cash registers and adding machines that had been hurled from shops and offices that morning, heading for the suburbs where his bungalow housed a Leo VII cryogenic storage computer which he had, before the war, been programming on behalf of the monks at the new temple on Kas

Rong. But the anti-religious riots had not only been directed at the machines. The monastery had been hastily disbanded by the authorities in the hope that this measure would save the new research wing of the Hospital of the Secret Heart at Chanthaburi. It had not.

6

Jerry entered the bungalow and shivered. The temperature was almost at zero. He pushed back the steel sliding doors of the inner room. The computer glistened under a thick coating of ice.

Was entropy setting in again?

Turning up the collar of his black car coat he inspected the power inputs. Something had overloaded Leo VII.

Jerry sniffed the sharp air. A problem of cardinal importance. He twitched his lips. Time to be moving.

He paused, studying the computer. It trembled under its sheathing of ice. He went to the wall and took his kid gloves from his pocket. He pulled them on, pressed the DESTRUCT button, but it would not move. It was frozen solid.

Jerry reached inside his coat and brought out his needle gun. With the butt he hammered the button home.

He left the computer room. In the living room ice had formed traceries on the walls and windows, whorls and lines spelling out equations of dubious importance. A little bile came into his throat.

All the signs pointed West.

He went to the garage at the side of the bungalow, wheeled his big BMW 750cc hog onto the path, put it between his legs, kicked the starter and whisked wild and easy off down the concrete road towards the jungle.

Yellow sun.

Blue sky.

Green trees.

Monkeys screaming.

7

Zut alors!
Maxim's in Paris
buys its fish
from a machine.

Part of the reason that fish at Maxim's is so fabulous is because it's so fresh. Fresh from General Electric data-processing equipment. When a French fisherman unloads his catch at the port of Séte, a unique data-gathering and display system takes over...

Progress is our most important product
GENERAL ELECTRIC

8

A LOUD SHRIEK.

9

The Dnieper flowed slowly, its muddy waters churned by the wind. In the brown land some snow remained. The great sky was low and grey over the steppe. A small wooden landing stage had moored to it a carved fishing boat, its sail reefed.

On the landing stood three Cossacks. They had long moustaches, smoked large pipes, wore big fur caps on the sides of their shaven heads. Heavy burkas swathed their burly bodies and they wore baggy trousers of blue or green silk, boots of red or yellow morocco leather. There were sabres at their sides, rifles on their backs. They watched the horseman as he galloped nearer on his shaggy, unshod pony.

The rider had bandoliers of cartridges crossing his chest, an

M60 on his back. He wore the Red Army uniform of the 'Razin' 11th Don Cossack Cavalry and he carried the horsehair standard of an ataman. He was young, with long pale hair and sharp blue eyes. He drew his horse to a skidding halt and saluted the three men whose expressions remained set.

'Cossacks of the Zaporozhian Sech, greetings from your brothers of the Don, the Yaik and the Kukan.' He spoke with a strong Ukrainian accent, driving the standard into the hard ground.

The nearest Zaporozhian reached down and picked up a sack that lay at his feet. 'The Sech is no more,' he said. 'We and this are all that remains. The great horde came four days ago from the East.' He upended the sack and emptied it.

Jerry dismounted and went to stare at the collection of small metal cogs, transistors and tapes.

'The krug is dead.' Tears came to the leading Zaporozhian's hard, grey eyes. 'The Khan rules. This is the end of our ancient freedom.'

Jerry got back onto his horse and rode away. He left the horsehair standard waving in the wind. He left the Cossacks weeping. He left the bank of the muddy Dnieper and headed out across the steppe, riding south again, towards the Black Sea.

IO

The Anthropomorphic View:

The Bug Slayer

No computer stamps out program bugs like RCA's Octoputer. It boosts programming efficiency up to 40%.

Programming is already one-third of computer costs, and going up faster than any other cost in the industry. A lot of that money is eaten up by bugs...

11

He wandered along the grassy paths between the ancient ruins. Everywhere was litter. Broken tape spools crunched beneath his boots, printouts snagged his feet; he was forced to make detours around buckled integrator cabinets. A few white-coated technicians tried to clean up the mess, haul the torn bodies away. They ignored Jerry, who went past them and hit the jungle once more. In his hand he held an ice pick.

One of the technicians jerked his thumb as Jerry disappeared.

'Asesino...' he said.

Jerry was glad to be out of Villahermosa.

12

He was cleaning his heat in his hut when the pale young man came in, shut the flimsy door and shuddered. Outside, the jungle stirred.

Jerry replaced rod, rag and oil in their case and carefully closed the lid.

The young man was dressed in a brown tropical suit with sweat stains under arms and crutch. He had noticed the three weapons in the case: the needler, the heater, the vibragun. He crossed himself.

Jerry nodded and drew on his black leather Norfolk jacket. From the tops of his dark Fry boots he untucked his pink bell-bottomed Levis and smoothed them down with the tips of his fingers, watching the pale young man with amused, moody eyes.

An Aeroflot VC 10 began its approach to the nearby Mowming drome. The windows vibrated shrilly and then subsided.

'The sense of oneness known to the Ancients.' The young man waved his hands vaguely in all directions. 'At last it is within our grasp.'

Jerry rubbed his nose with his case.

133

'I'm sorry, Mr Cornelius. I am, of course, Cyril Tome.' A smile of apologetic patronage. 'What a nightmare this world is. But the tide is turning…'

Jerry began vigorously to brush his fine blond hair, settling it on his shoulders. 'I wasn't expecting you, Mr Tome.'

'I left a message. In Kiev.'

'I didn't get it.'

'You mean you didn't receive it?'

'If you like.'

'Mr Cornelius, I gathered from a mutual acquaintance that we were of a similar mind. "Science is only a more sophisticated form of superstition" – didn't you say that?'

'I'm told so. Who was the acquaintance?'

'Dennis.' He raised his eyebrows. 'Beesley? But don't you agree that in place of the old certainties, rooted in the supreme reality of existence, we have transferred our faith to science, the explanation for everything which explains nothing, the ever more fragmented picture of reality which becomes ever more unreal…'

'How is Bishop Beesley?'

'Carrying on the fight as best he can. He is very tired.'

'He is indeed.'

'Then you don't agree…'

'It's a question of attitude, Mr Tome.' Jerry walked to the washstand and picking up a carton of Swedish milk poured out half a saucer for the half-grown black-and-white cat which now rubbed itself against his leathered leg. 'Still, we don't need emotional rapport, you know, to do business.'

'I'm not sure…'

'Who is, Mr Tome?'

'I am sure…'

'Naturally.'

Tome began to pace about the floor of the hut. 'These machines. They're inhuman. But so far only the fringes have been touched.'

Jerry sat down on the bed again, opening his gun case. He

began to fit the vibragun together, snapping the power unit into place.

Tome looked distastefully on. 'I suppose one must fight fire with fire.'

Jerry picked his teeth with his thumbnail, his brows furrowed. He did not look at Tome.

'What's the pattern?' he murmured, stroking the cat.

'Is there a pattern to anarchy?'

'The clearest of all, I'd have thought.' Jerry slipped the vibragun into his shoulder holster. 'In Leo VII all things are possible, after all.'

'A machine is –'

'– a machine is a machine.' Jerry smiled involuntarily.

'I don't understand you.'

'That's what I was afraid of.'

'Afraid?'

'Fear, Mr Tome. I think we might have to book you.'

'But I thought you were on my side.'

'Christ! Of course I am. And their side. And all the other sides. Of course I am!'

'But didn't you start the machine riots in Yokohama? When I was there?'

Tome burst into tears.

Jerry rubbed at his face in puzzlement.

'There's been a lot of that.'

Tome made for the door. He had started to scream.

Some beastly instinct in Jerry responded to the movement and the sound. His vibragun was slipped from its holster and aimed at Tome as the pale young man fumbled with the catch.

Tome's teeth began to chatter.

He broke up.

All but insensate, Jerry fell back on the bed, his mad eyes staring at the ceiling.

Eventually they cooled.

Jerry left the hut and struck off through the jungle again. He had an overwhelming sense of déjà vu.

13

The Mechanistic View:

Horace is Hornblower's remarkable new computer system. And what he does with confirmations is a Hornblower exclusive...

Only Horace prints complete confirmations in Seconds

14

Jerry was lost and depressed. Thanks to Tome, Beesley and their fellow spirits, a monstrous diffusion process was taking place.

He stumbled on through the jungle, followed at a safe distance by a cloud of red and blue macaws. They were calling out phrases he could not quite recognise. They seemed malevolent, triumphant.

A man dressed in the tropical kit of an Indian Army NCO emerged from behind a tree. His small eyes were almost as confused as Jerry's.

'Come along, sir. This way. I'll help.'

For a moment Jerry prepared to follow the man, then he shook his head. 'No, thank you, Corporal Powell, I'll find my own way.'

'It's too late for that, Mr Cornelius.'

'Nonetheless...'

'This jungle's full of natives.'

Jerry aimed a shot at the NCO, but the little man scurried into the forest and disappeared.

Several small furry mammals skittered out into the open, blinking red eyes in the direct sunlight. Their tiny thumbs were opposable. Jerry smiled down indulgently.

Around him the Mesozoic foliage whispered in the new, warm wind.

15

He had reached the sea.

He stood on the yellow shore and looked out over the flat, blue water. Irresolutely he stopped as his boots sank into the sand. The sea frightened him. He reached inside his coat and fingered the butt of his gun.

A white yacht was anchoring about a quarter of a mile away. Soon he heard the sound of a motor boat as it swept towards him through the surf.

He recognised the yacht as the *Teddy Bear*. It had had several owners, none of them particularly friendly. He turned to run, but he was too weak. He fell down. Seamen jumped from the boat and pulled him aboard.

'Don't worry, son,' one of them said. 'You'll soon be back in Blighty.'

'Poor bastard.'

Jerry whimpered.

They'd be playing brag for his gear soon.

> *Because of the sins which ye have committed before God, ye shall be led away captives into Babylon by Nabuchodonosor king of the Babylonians.*

(Baruch 6: 2)

He was feeling sorry for himself. He'd really blown this little scene.

16

Need to improve customer service? Salesman productivity? Here's your answer – Computone's portable computer terminal, the world's smartest briefcase. It weighs only 8¾ pounds, and it costs as little as $20 per month. Through a telephone in the prospect's home or office, your salesman can communicate directly with a computer, enter orders and receive answers to inquiries within seconds. The terminal converts your salesman into a team of experts who bring to the point of sale the vast memory of a computer and its ability to solve problems immediately and accurately.

COMPUTONE SYSTEMS INC.
the company that put the computer in a briefcase

17

Jerry was dumped outside the Time Centre's Ladbroke Grove HQ. He got up, found his front door, tried to open it. The door was frozen solid. The Leo VII had spread its cryogenic bounty throughout the citadel.

Jerry sighed and leaned against the brick wall. Above his head someone had painted a new slogan in bright orange paint:

NO POPERY

There were only two people who could help him now and neither was particularly sympathetic to him.

Was he being set up for something?

18

Hans Smith of Hampstead, Last of the Left-Wing Intellectuals, was having a party to which Jerry had not been invited.

Because of his interest in the statistics of interracial marriage in Vietnam in the period 1969/70, Hans Smith had not heard about the war. There had been few signs of it on Parliament Hill. Late one night he had seen a fat, long-haired man in a tweed suit urinating against a tree. The man had turned, exposing himself to Smith, grinning and leering. There had also been some trouble with his Smith-Corona. But the incidents seemed unrelated.

Balding, bearded, pot-bellied, and very careful, Hans Smith had codified and systemised his sex-life (marital, extramarital and intermarital) to the point where most discomfort and enjoyment was excluded. His wife filed his love letters and typed his replies for him and she kept his bedroom library of pornography and sex-manuals in strict alphabetical order. Instead of pleasure, Smith received what he called 'a healthy release'. The sexual act itself had been promoted into the same category as a successful operation for severe constipation. Disturbed by the Unpleasant, Smith belonged to a large number of institutions devoted to its extinction. He lived a smooth existence.

Jerry opened the front door with one of the keys from his kit and walked up the stairs. Somewhere The Chants were singing 'Progress'.

He was late for the party. Most of the remaining guests had joined their liberal hosts in the bedroom, but Smith, dressed in a red-and-gold kimono that did much to emphasise the pale obscenity of his body, came to the door at his knock, a vibro-massager clutched in one thin hand. He recognised Jerry and made a Church Army smile through his frown.

'I'm sorry, bah, but...'

But Jerry's business was urgent and it was with another guest.

'Could I have a word with Bishop Beesley, do you think?'

'I'm not sure he's...'

Jerry drew out his heater.

'There's no need to be boorish.' Smith backed into the bedroom. Unseen middle-aged flesh made strange, dry sounds. 'Bishop. Someone to see you...' He fingered his goatee.

Mrs Hans Smith's wail: 'Oh, no, Hans. Tell them to fiddle off.'

Smith made another of his practised smiles. 'It's Cornelius, kitten.'

'You said you'd never invite –'

'I didn't, lovey...'

Jerry didn't want to look inside, but he moved a step nearer. 'Hurry up, bishop.'

Naked but for his gaiters and mitre, the gross white form of Bishop Beesley appeared behind Hans Smith. 'What is it?'

'A religious matter, bishop.'

'Ah, in that case.' The bishop bundled up his clothes and stepped out. 'Well, Mr Cornelius?'

'It's the Leo VII cryogenics. They seem to be trying to convert. I can't make it out. They're freezing up.'

'Good God! I'll come at once. A clearing needed, eh? An exorcism?'

Jerry's hunch had been a good one. The bishop had been expecting him. 'You'd know better than I, bishop.'

'Yes, yes,' Beesley gave Jerry's shoulder a friendly pat.

'Well, the shit's certainly hit the fan,' said Jerry. He winked at Smith as he left.

'I'm very glad you called me in, dear boy.' Bishop Beesley hopped into his trousers, licking his lips. 'Better late than never, eh?'

Jerry shivered.

'It's your baby now, bishop.'

He had another old friend to look up.

19

'One down, eight letters, *To Lucasta, faithful unto death...*' Jerry shrugged and put the newspaper aside. They had arrived. He tapped the pilot on the shoulder. 'Let's descend, Byron.'

As the cumbersome Sikorsky shuddered towards the ground, Jerry had an excellent view of the ruins on the headland. All that remained of the castle was grass-grown walls a foot or two high, resembling, from this perspective, a simplified circuit marked out in stones – a message to an extraterran astronomer. The archaeologists had been at work again in Tintagel.

Beyond the headland the jade sea boomed, washing the ebony beach. The Sikorsky hovered over the ocean for a moment before sweeping backwards and coming to rest near Site B, the monastery.

Dressed in his wire-rimmed Diane Logan black corduroy hat, a heavy brown Dannimac cord coat, dark orange trousers from Portugal, and near-black Fry boots, Jerry jumped from the Sikorsky and walked across the lawn to sit on a wall and watch the helicopter take off again. He unbuttoned his coat to reveal his yellow Sachs cord shirt and the Lynn Stuart yellow-and-black sash he wore in place of a tie. He was feeling light in his gear but he was still bothered.

In the hot winter sunshine, he pranced along the footpath that led to the Computer Research Institute – a series of geodesic domes stained in bright colours.

'A meaning is a meaning,' he sang, 'is a meaning is a meaning.'

He was not altogether himself, these days.

Outside the gates he grinned inanely at the guard and displayed his pass. He was waved through.

The Institute was a private establishment. The red moving pavement took him to the main admin building and the chrome doors opened to admit him. He stood in the white-tiled lobby.

'Mr Cornelius!'

From a blue door marked DIRECTOR came Miss Brunner, her auburn hair drawn back in a bun, her stiff body clothed in a St Laurent tweed suit. She stretched her long fingers at him. He grasped them.

'And what's your interest in our little establishment, Mr C?' Now she led him into her cool office. 'Thinking of giving us a hand?' She studied a tank of small carp.

'I'm not sure I know the exact nature of your research.' Jerry glanced around at all the overfilled ashtrays.

She shrugged. 'The usual thing. This and that. We're checking analogies at present – mainly forebrain functions. Amazing how similar the human brain is to our more complex machines. They can teach us a lot about people. The little buggers.'

He looked at the graphs and charts on her walls. 'I see what you mean.' He rubbed a weary eye and winced. He had a sty there.

'It's all very precise,' she said.

'Get away.'

Jerry sighed. Didn't they know there was a war on?

20

'Sweet young stuff,' said Miss Brunner. 'Tender. Only the best goes into our machines.'

Jerry looked at the conveyor, at the aluminium dishes on the belt, at the brains in the dishes.

'They feel nothing,' she said, 'it's all done by electronics these days.'

Jerry watched the battery brains slipping like oysters into the gullets of the storage registers.

'You will try it, won't you?'

'It works both ways,' she said defensively.

'I bet it does.'

Miss Brunner smiled affectionately. 'It's beautifully integrated. Everything automatic. Even the pentagrams are powered.'

'This isn't religion,' said Jerry, 'it's bloody sorcery!'

'I never claimed to be perfect, Mr Cornelius. Besides, compared with my methods the narrow processes of the orthodox...'

'You've been driving the whole bloody system crazy, you silly bitch! You and that bastard Beesley. I thought there were only two polarities. And all the while...'

'You've been having a bad time, have you? You bloody puritans...'

Jerry pursed his lips. She knew how to reach him.

21

When he got back to Ladbroke Grove he found the door open. It was freezing inside.

'Bishop Beesley?' His voice echoed through the dark passages. The cold reached his bones.

'Bishop?'

Time was speeding. Perhaps his counter-attack had failed.

He found Beesley in the library. The bishop had never got to the computer. His round, flabby face peered sadly out of the block of ice encasing him. Jerry drew his heater and thawed him out.

Beesley grunted and sat down. 'I suppose it was a joke. Doubtful taste...'

'Sorry you were bothered, bishop...'

'Is that all...?'

'Yes, I must admit I was desperate, but that's over now, for what it was worth.'

'You treacherous little oik. I thought you had made a genuine repentance.'

Jerry had been triggered off again. His eyes were glowing a deep red now and his lips were curled back over his sharp teeth. His body radiated such heat that the air steamed around it. He waved his gun.

'Shall we press on into the computer room?'

Beesley grumbled but stumbled ahead until they stood before the iced-up Leo VII.

'What point is there in my presence here,' Beesley chattered, 'when your claims – or its – were plainly insincere?'

'The logic's changed.' Jerry's nostrils widened. 'We're having a sacrifice instead.'

Jerry thought he smelled damp autumn leaves in the air.

He snarled and chuckled and forced the bishop towards the appropriate input.

'Sacrilege!' howled Beesley.

'Sacrosanct!' sniggered Jerry.

Then, with his Fry boot, he kicked Beesley's bottom.

The clergyman yelled, gurgled and disappeared into the machine.

There was a sucking sound, a purr, and almost immediately the ice began to melt.

'It's the price we pay for progress,' said Jerry. 'Your attitudes, bishop, not mine, created the situation, after all.'

The computer rumbled and began a short printout. Jerry tore it off.

A single word:

TASTY.

22

Like it or not, the Brunner programme had set the tone to the situation, but at least it meant things would calm down for a bit... Time to work on a fresh equation.

These alchemical notions were, he would admit, very commonplace. The pattern had been begun years before by describing machines in terms of human desires and activities, by describing human behaviour in terms of machines. Now the price of that particular logic escalation was being paid. Beesley had paid it. The sweet young stuff was paying it. The mystical view of science had declined from vague superstition into positive necromancy. The sole purpose of the machines was confined to the raising of dead spirits. The polarities had been the Anthropomorphic View and the Mechanistic View. Now they had merged, producing something even more sinister: the Pathological View.

A machine is a machine is a machine... But that was no longer the case. A machine was anything the neurotic imagination desired it to be.

At last the computer had superseded the automobile as the focus for mankind's hopes and fears. It was the death of ancient freedoms.

23

It was raining as Jerry picked his way over the Belgrade bomb sites followed by crowds of crippled children and the soft, pleading voices of the eleven- and twelve-year-old prostitutes of both sexes.

His clothes were stained and faded. Behind him were the remains of the crashed Sikorsky which had run out of fuel.

On foot he made for Dubrovnik, through a world ruled by bad

poets who spoke the rhetoric of tabloid apocrypha and schemed for the fruition of a dozen seedy apocalypses.

At Dubrovnik the corpse-boats were being loaded up. Fuel for the automated factories of Anuradhapura and Angkor Wat. On one of them, if he was lucky, he might obtain a passage East.

Meanwhile machines grew skeletons and were fed with blood and men adopted metal limbs and plastic organs. A synthesis he found unwelcome.

24

Out of the West fled Jerry Cornelius, away from Miss Brunner's morbid Eden, away from warm steel and cool flesh, on a tanker crammed with the dead, to Bombay and from there to the interior, to rest, to wait, to draw breath, to pray for new strength and the resurrection of the Antichrist.

A posture, after all, was a posture.

> You won't make an important decision
> in the 70s without it
> Your own personal desk-top computer
> terminal

Remember the 1970s are just around the corner. A call to Mr A.A. Barnett, Vice President – Marketing, Bunker-Ramo, could be your most important decision for the new decade.

(All ad quotes from *Business Week*, 6 December, 1969)

Voortrekker

A Tale of Empire

My Country 'Tis of Thee

Mr Smith said that the new Constitution would take Rhodesia further along the road of racial separate development – although he preferred to call it 'community development and provincialisation.' He agreed that, initially, this policy would not improve Rhodesia's chances of international recognition, but added: 'I believe and I sincerely hope that the world is coming to its senses and that this position will change, that the free world will wake up to what international communism is doing.'

Guardian, 14 April, 1970

Think It Over

The group was working and Jerry Cornelius, feeling nostalgic, drew on a stick of tea. He stood in the shadows at the back of the stage, plucking out a basic pattern on his Futurama bass.

> 'She's the girl in the red blue jeans,
> She's the queen of all the teens...'

Although the Deep Fix hadn't been together for some time Shakey Mo Collier was in good form. He turned to the console, shifting the mike from his right hand to his left, and gave himself a touch more echo for the refrain. Be-bop-a-lula. Jerry admired the way Mo had his foot twisted just right.

But it was getting cold.

Savouring the old discomfort, Jerry peered into the darkness at the floor where the shapes moved. Outside the first Banning cannon of the evening were beginning to go off. The basement shook.

Jerry's numb fingers muffed a chord. A whiff of entropy.

The sound began to decay. The players blinked at each other. With a graceful, rocking pace Jerry took to his heels.

None too soon. As he climbed into his Silver Cloud he saw the first figure descend the steps to the club. A woman. A flatfoot.

It was happening all over again.

All over again.

He put the car into gear and rippled away. Really, there was hardly any peace. Or was he looking in the wrong places?

London faded.

He was having a thin time and no mistake. He shivered. And turned up the collar of his black car coat.

HOPES FOR U.S. VANISH, he thought. If he wasn't getting older then he wasn't getting any younger, either. He pressed the button and the stereo started playing *Sgt Pepper*. How soon harmony collapsed. She never stumbles. There was no time left for irony. A Paolozzi screenprint. She likes it like that. Rain fingered his windscreen.

Was it just bad memory?

Apple crumble. Fleeting scene. Streaming screen. Despair.

At the head of that infinitely long black corridor the faceless man was beckoning to him.

Not yet.

But why not?

Would the time ever be right?

He depressed the accelerator.

Diffusion rediffused.

Breaking up baby.

Jump back...

He was crying, his hands limp on the wheel as the car went over the ton.

All the old men and children were dying at once.

HANG

ON

'No!'

Screaming, he pressed his quaking foot right down and flung

his hands away from the wheel, stretching his arms along the back of the seat.

It wouldn't take long.

I Love You Because

What the Soviet Union wants in Eastern Europe is peace and quiet...

Hungarian editor quoted,
Guardian, 13 April, 1970

Clearwater

'How's the head, Mr Cornelius?'

Miss Brunner's sharp face grinned over him. She snapped her teeth, stroked his cheek with her hard fingers.

He hugged at his body, closed his eyes.

'Just a case of the shakes,' she said. 'Nothing serious. You've got a long way to go yet.'

There was a stale smell in his nostrils. The smell of a dirty needle. Her hands had left his face. His eyes sprang open. He glared suspiciously as she passed the chipped enamel kidney dish to Shakey Mo who winked sympathetically at him and shrugged. Mo had a grubby white coat over his gear.

Miss Brunner straightened her severe tweed jacket on her hips. 'Nothing serious...'

It was still cold.

'Brrr...' He shut his mouth.

'What?' She whirled suddenly, green eyes alert.

'Breaking up.'

'We've been through too much together.'

'Breaking up.'

'Nonsense. It all fits.' From her large black patent leather satchel she took a paper wallet. She straightened her... 'Here are your tickets. You'll sail tomorrow on the *Robert D. Feet.*'

Shakey Mo put his head back round the tatty door. The surgery belonged to the last backstreet abortionist in England, a creature of habits. 'Any further conclusions, Miss Brunner?'

She tossed her red locks. 'Oh, a million. But they can wait.'

Heartbreak Hotel

Refugees fleeing from Svey Rieng province speak of increasing violence in Cambodia against the Vietnamese population. Some who have arrived here in the past 24 hours tell stories of eviction and even massacre at the hands of Cambodian soldiers sent from Phnôm Penh.

Guardian, 13 April, 1970

Midnight Special

The *Robert D. Feet* was wallowing down the Mediterranean coast. She was a clapped-out old merchantman and this would be her last voyage. Jerry stood by the greasy rail looking out at a sea of jade and jet.

So he was going back. Not that it made any difference. You always got to the same place in the end.

He remembered the faces of Auchinek and Newman. Their faces were calm now.

Africa lay ahead. His first stop.

That's When Your Heartaches Begin

Four rockets were fired into the centre of Saigon this evening and, according to first reports, killed at least four people and injured 37.

... When used as they are here, in built-up areas, rockets are a psychological rather than a tactical weapon.

Guardian, 14 April, 1970

Don't Be Cruel

Could the gestures of conflict continue to keep the peace? Was the fire dying in Europe? 'Ravaged, at last, by the formless terror called Time, Melniboné fell and newer nations succeeded her: llmiora, Sheegoth, Maidahk, S'aaleem. All these came after Melniboné. But none lasted ten thousand years.' ('The Dreaming City'.) In the flames he watched the shape of a teenage girl as she ran about dying. He turned away. Why did the old territorial impulses maintain themselves ('sphere of influence') so far past their time of usefulness? There was no question about it in his mind. The entropy factor was increasing, no matter what he did. The waste didn't matter, but the misery, surprisingly, moved him. Een Schmidt, so Wolenski had said, now had more personal power than Hitler or Mussolini. Was it take-out time again? No need to report back to the Time Centre. The answer, as usual, was written in the hieroglyphs of the landscape. He smiled a rotten smile.

The Facts of Death

'Name your poison, Mr Cornelius.'

Jerry raised distant eyes to look into the mad, Boer face of Olmeijer, proprietor of the Bloemfontein *Drankie-a-Snel-Snel*. Olmeijer had the red, pear-shaped lumps under the eyes, the slow rate of blinking, the flushed neck common to all Afrikanders.

Things were hardening up already. At least for the moment he knew where he was.

'Black velvet,' he said. 'Easy on the black.'

Olmeijer grinned and wagged a finger, returning to the bar. '*Skaam jou!*' He took a bottle of Guinness from beneath the counter and half-filled a pint glass. In another glass he added soda water to three fingers of gin. He mixed the two up.

It was eleven o'clock in the morning and the bar was otherwise deserted. Its red flock fleur-de-lis wallpaper was studded with the dusty heads of gnu, hippo, aardvark and warthog. A large fan in the centre of the ceiling rattled rapidly round and round.

Olmeijer brought the drink and Jerry paid him, took a sip and crossed to the jukebox to select the new version of 'Recessional' sung by the boys of the Reformed Dutch Church School at Heidelberg. Only last week it had toppled the Jo'burg Jazz Flutes' 'Cocoa Beans' from number one spot.

> The tjumelt end the shouwting days;
> The ceptens end the kengs dep'haht:
> Stell stends Thine incient secrefize,
> En umble end e contriteart.
> Loard Goed ev Osts, be with us yit,
> List we fergit – list we fergit!

Jerry sighed and checked his watches. He could still make it across Basutoland and reach Bethlehem before nightfall. Originally he had only meant to tank-up here, but it seemed the Republik was running out of the more refined kinds of fuel.

If things went slow then he knew a kopje where he could stay until morning.

Olmeijer waved at him as he made for the door.

'Christ, man – I almost forgot.'

He rang No Sale on the till and removed something from beneath the cash tray. A grey envelope. Jerry took it, placed it inside his white car coat.

The Silver Cloud was parked opposite the *Drankie-a-Snel-Snel*. Jerry got into the car, closed the door and raised the top. He fingered the envelope, frowning.

On it was written: *Mr Cornelius. The Items.*

He opened it slowly, as a man might defuse a bomb.

A sheet of cheap Russian notepaper with the phrase *Hand in hand with horror: side by side with death* written in green with a felt pen. A place mat from an American restaurant decorated with a map of Vietnam and a short article describing the flora and fauna. Not much of either left, thought Jerry with a smile. A page torn from an English bondage magazine of the mid-fifties period. Scrawled on this in black ballpoint: *Love me tender, love me sweet!!!* Although the face of the girl in the picture was half-obscured by her complicated harness, he was almost sure that it was Miss Brunner. A somewhat untypical pose.

The handwriting on envelope, notepaper and picture were all completely different.

Jerry put the items back into the envelope.

They added up to a change of direction. And a warning, too? He wasn't sure.

He opened the glove compartment and removed his box of chessmen – ivory and ebony, made by Tanzanian lepers, and the most beautiful pieces in the world. He took out the slender white king and a delicate black pawn, held them tightly together in his hand.

Which way to switch?

Not Fade Away

SIR: I noticed on page three of the *Post* last week an alleged Monday Club member quoted as follows: 'I have listened with increasing boredom to your streams of so-called facts, and I would like to know what you hope to achieve by stirring up people against coloured immigrants.'

In order that there should be no doubt whatsoever in the minds of your readers as to the position of the Monday Club in this matter, I would quote from *The New Battle of Britain* on immigration: 'Immigration must be drastically reduced and a scheme launched for large-scale voluntary repatriation. The Race Relations Acts are blows against the traditional British right to freedom of expression. They exacerbate rather than lessen racial disharmony. They must be repealed.'

In a letter from the Chairman of the Monday Club to Mr Anthony Barber, Chairman of the Conservative Party, it is stated: 'Our fourth finding, and it would be foolish to brush this under the carpet, was that references to immigration were thought to be inadequate. In view of the very deep concern felt about this matter throughout the country, failure to come out courageously in the interests of the indigenous population could threaten the very existence of the party ... However, it was thought there was no good reason to restrict the entry of those people whose forefathers had originally come from these islands...'

It would be quite wrong to leave anybody with the impression that the Monday Club was not wholly in support of the interests of the indigenous ... population ... of these islands.

– D.R. Bramwell,
letter to *Kensington Post*, 27 March, 1970

That'll Be the Day

Sebastian Auchinek was a miserable sod, thought Jerry absently as he laid the last brick he would lay for the duration.

Removing his coolie hat he stood back from the half-built wall and looked beyond at the expanse of craters which stretched to the horizon.

All the craters were full of muddy water mixed with defoliants. Not far from his wall a crippled kid in a blue cotton smock was playing in one of the holes.

She gave him a beautiful smile, leaning on her crutch and splashing water at him. Her leg-stump, pink and smooth, moved in a kicking motion.

Smiling back at her Jerry reflected that racialism and imperialism were interdependent but that one could sometimes flourish without the other.

The town had been called Ho Thoung. American destroyers had shelled it all down.

But now, as Jerry walked back towards the camp, it was quiet.

'If the world is to be consumed by horror,' Auchinek had told him that morning, 'if evil is to sweep the globe and death engulf it, I wish to *be* that horror, that evil, that death. I'll be on the winning side, won't I? Which side are you on?'

Auchinek was a terrible old bit of medieval Europe, really. Doubtless that was why he'd joined the USAF. And yet he was the only prisoner in Ho Thoung Jerry could talk to. Besides, as an ex-dentist, Auchinek had fixed Jerry's teeth better than even the Australian who used to have a surgery in Notting Hill.

Several large tents had been erected amongst the ruins of the town which had had 16,000 citizens and now had about 200. Jerry saw Auchinek emerge from one of these tents, his long body clothed in stained olive drab and his thin, pasty Jewish face as morose as ever. He nodded to Jerry. He was being led to the latrine area by his guard, a boy of fourteen holding a big M60.

Jerry joined Auchinek at the pit and they pissed in it together.

'And how is it out there?' Auchinek asked again. 'Any news?'

'Much the same.'

Jerry had taken the Trans-Siberian Express from Leningrad to Vladivostok and made the rest of his journey on an old Yugoslavian freighter now owned by the Chinese. It had been the only way to approach the zone.

'Israel?' Auchinek buttoned his faded fly.

'Doing okay. Moving.'

'Out or in?'

'A little of both. You know how it goes.'

'Natural boundaries.' Auchinek accepted a cigarette from his guard as they walked back to the compound. 'Vietnam and Korea. The old Manchu Empire. It's the same everywhere.'

'Much the same.'

'Pathetic. Childlike. Did you get what you came for?'

'I think so.'

'Still killing your own thing, I see. Well, well. Keep it up.'

'Take it easy.' Jerry heard the sound of the Kamov Ka-15's rotors in the cloudy sky. 'Here's my transport.'

'Thank you,' said Auchinek's guard softly. 'Each brick brings victory a little closer.'

'Sez you.'

Crying

'That's quite a knockout, Dr Talbot,' agreed Alar. 'But how do you draw a parallel between Assyria and America Imperial?'

'There are certain infallible guides. In Toynbeean parlance they're called "failure of self-determination", "schism in the body social" and "schism in the soul". These phases of course all follow the "time of troubles", "universal state" and the "universal peace". These latter two, paradoxically, mark every civilisation for death when it is apparently at its strongest.'

... Donnan remained unconvinced. 'You long-haired boys are always getting lost in what happened in ancient times. This is here and now – America Imperial, June Sixth, Two Thousand One Hundred Seventy-seven. We got the Indian sign on the world.'

Dr Talbot sighed. 'I hope to God you're right, Senator.'

Juana-Maria said, 'If I may interrupt...'

The group bowed.

– Charles L. Harness,
The Paradox Men, 1953

Rave On

In Prague he watched while the clocks rang out.

In Havana he studied the foreign liberals fighting each other in the park.

In Calcutta he had a bath.

In Seoul he found his old portable taper and played his late, great Buddy Holly cassettes, but nothing happened.

In Pyongyang he found that his metabolism had slowed so much that he had to take the third fix of the operation a good two months early. Where those two months would come from when he needed them next he had no idea.

When he recovered he saw that his watches were moving at a reasonable rate, but his lips were cold and needed massaging.

In El Paso he began to realise that the alternatives were narrowing down as the situation hardened. He bought himself a second-hand Browning M35 and a new suède-lined belt holster. With ammunition he had to pay $81.50 plus tax. It worked out, as far as he could judge at that moment, to about £1 per person at the current exchange rate. Not particularly cheap, but he didn't have time to shop around.

It Doesn't Matter Anymore

It was raining on the grey, deserted dockyard. The warehouses were all boarded up and there were no ships moored any more beneath the rusting cranes. Oily water received the rain. Sodden Heinz and Campbell cartons lurked just above the surface. Broken crates clung to the edge. Save for the sound of the rain there was silence.

Empires came and empires went, thought Jerry.

He sucked a peardrop, raised his wretched face to the sky so that the cold water fell into his eyes. His blue crushed-velvet toreador hipsters were soaked and soiled. His black car coat had a tear in the right vent, a torn pocket, worn elbows. Buttoned tight, it pressed the Browning hard against his hip.

It was natural. It was inevitable. And the children went on burning – sometimes a few, sometimes a lot. He could almost smell them burning.

A figure emerged from an alley between Number Eight and Number Nine sheds and began to walk towards him with a peculiar, rolling, flatfooted gait. He wore a cream trench coat and a light brown fedora, light check wide-bottomed trousers with turn-ups, tan shoes. The trench coat was tied at the waist with a yellow Paisley scarf. The man had four or five days' beard. It was the man Jerry was waiting for – Sebastian Newman, the dead astronaut.

A week earlier Jerry had watched the last ship steam out of the Port of London. There would be none coming back.

Newman smiled when he saw Jerry. Rotten teeth appeared and were covered up again.

'So you found me at last,' Newman said. He felt in the pocket of his coat and came out with a pack of German-made Players. He lit the cigarette with a Zippo. 'As they say.'

Jerry wasn't elated. It would be a long while before he re-engaged with his old obsessions. Perhaps the time had passed or was still to come. He'd lost even the basic Greenwich bearings. Simple notions of Time, like simple notions of politics, had destroyed many a better man.

'What d'you want out of me?' Newman asked. He sat down on the base of the nearest crane. Jerry leaned against the corrugated door of the shed. There was twenty feet separating them and, although both men spoke quietly, they could easily hear each other.

'I'm not sure,' Jerry crunched the last of his peardrop and swallowed it. 'I've had a hard trip, Colonel Newman. Maybe I'm prepared to give in...'

'Cop out?'

'Go for a certainty.'

'I thought you only went for outsiders.'

'I didn't say that. I've never said that. Do you think this is the Phoney War?'

'Could be.'

'I've killed twenty-nine people since El Paso and nothing's happened. That's unusual.'

'Is it? These days?'

'What are "these days"?'

'Since I came back I've never known that. Sorry. That wasn't "cool", eh?' A little spark came and went in the astronaut's pale eyes.

Jerry tightened his face. 'It never stops.'

Newman nodded. 'You can almost smell them burning, can't you?'

'If this is entropy, I'll try the other.'

'Law and Order?'

'Why not?'

Newman removed his fedora and scratched his balding head. 'Maybe the scientists will come up with something...'

He began to laugh when he saw the gun in Jerry's hands. The last 9mm slug left the gun and cordite stank. Newman rose from his seat and bent double, as if convulsed with laughter. He fell smoothly into the filthy water. When Jerry went to look there were no ripples in the oil, but half an orange box was gently rocking.

Bang.

Listen to Me

Europe undertook the leadership of the world with ardour, cynicism and violence. Look at how the shadow of her palaces stretches out ever farther! Every one of her movements has burst the bounds of space and thought. Europe has declined all humility and all modesty; but she has also set her face against all solicitude and all tenderness.

She has only shown herself parsimonious and niggardly where men are concerned; it is only men that she has killed and devoured.

So, my brothers, how is it that we do not understand that we have better things to do than to follow that same Europe?

Come, then, comrades, the European game has finally ended; we must find something different. We today can do everything, so long as we do not imitate Europe, so long as we are not obsessed by the desire to catch up with Europe...

Two centuries ago, a former European colony decided to catch up with Europe. It succeeded so well that the United States of America became a monster, in which the taints, the sickness and the inhumanity of Europe have grown to appalling dimensions.

Comrades, have we not other work to do than to create a third Europe? The West saw itself as a spiritual adventure. It is in the name of the spirit, in the name of the spirit of Europe, that Europe has made her encroachments, that she has justified her crimes and legitimised the slavery in which she holds four-fifths of humanity...

The Third World today faces Europe like a colossal mass whose aim should be to try to resolve the problems to which Europe has not been able to find the answers...

– Frantz Fanon,
The Wretched of the Earth, 1961

I Forgot to Remember to Forget

The references were all tangled up. But wasn't his job really over? Or had Newman been taken out too soon? Maybe too late. He rode his black Royal Albert gent's roadster bicycle down the hill into Portobello Road. He needed to make better speed than this. He pedalled faster.

The Portobello Road became impassable. It was cluttered by huge piles of garbage, overturned stalls, the corpses of West Indians, Malays, Chinese, Indians, Irish, Hungarians, Cape Coloureds, Poles, Ghanaians, mounds of antiques.

The bike's brakes failed. Jerry left the saddle and flew towards the garbage.

DNA (do not analyse).

As he swam through the stinking air he thought that really he deserved a more up-to-date time machine than that bloody bike. Who was he anyway?

Back to Africa.

Everyday

At the rear of the company of Peuhl knights Jerry Cornelius crossed the border from Chad to Nigeria. The horsemen were retreating over the yellow landscape after their raid on the Foreign Legion garrison at Fort Lamy where they had picked up a good number of grenades. Though they would not normally ride with the Chad National Liberation Front, this time the sense of nostalgia had been too attractive to resist.

Along with their lances, scimitars, fancifully decorated helmets and horse-armour the Peuhl had .303s and belts of ammo crossed over the chainmail which glinted beneath their flowing white surcoats. Dressed like them, and wearing a bird-crested iron helmet painted in blues, reds, yellows and greens, Jerry revealed by his white hands that he was not a Peuhl.

The big Arab horses were coated by the dust of the wilderness and were as tired as their masters. Rocks and scrub stretched on all sides and it would be sunset before they reached the hills and the cavern where they would join their brother knights of the Rey Bouba in Cameroon.

Seigneur Samory, who led the company, turned in his saddle and shouted back. 'Better than your old John Ford movies, eh, Monsieur Cornelius?'

'Yes and no.' Jerry removed his helmet and wiped his face on his sleeve. 'What time is it?'

They both spoke French. They had met in Paris. Samory had had a different name then and had studied Law, doing the odd review for the French edition of Box Office – Cahiers du Cinéma.

'Exactly? I don't know.'

Samory dropped back to ride beside Jerry. His dark eyes glittered in his helmet. 'You're always so anxious about the time. It doesn't bother me.' He waved his arm to indicate the barren landscape. 'My Garamante ancestors protected their huge Saharan empire from the empire of Rome two and a half millennia ago. Then the Sahara became a desert and buried our chariots and our cities, but we fought the Vandals, Byzantium, Arabia, Germany and France.'

'And now you're on your way to fight the Federals. A bit of a come down, isn't it?'

'It's something to do.'

They were nearing the hills and their shadows stretched away over the crumbling earth.

'You can take our Land-Rover to Port Harcourt if you like,' Samory told him. The tall Peuhl blew him a kiss through his helmet and went back to the head of the company.

I Love You Because

SIRS: I'm so disgusted with the so-called 'American' citizen who knows little or nothing about the Vietnam war yet is so ready to condemn our gov't and soldiers for its actions. Did any of these people that are condemning us ever see their closest friend blown apart by a homemade grenade made by a woman that looks like an 'ordinary villager'? Or did they ever see their buddy get shot by a woman or 10-year old boy carrying a Communist rifle? These people were known VC and Mylai was an NVA and VC village. If I had been there I probably would of killed every one of those goddamned Communists myself.

– SP4 Kurt Jacoboni,
Life, 2 March, 1970

I'll Never Let You Go

Sometimes it was quite possible to think that the solution lay in black Africa. Lots of space. Lots of time.

But when he reached Onitsha he was beginning to change his mind. It was night and they were saving on street lighting. He had seen the huts burning all the way from Awka.

A couple of soldiers stopped him at the outskirts of the town but, seeing he was white, waved him on.

They stood on the road listening to the sound of his engine and his laughter as they faded away.

Jerry remembered a line from Camus's *Caligula*, but then he forgot it again.

Moving slowly against the streams of refugees, he arrived in Port Harcourt and found Miss Brunner at the Civil Administration Building. She was taking tiffin with Colonel Ohachi, the local governor, and she was evidently embarrassed by Jerry's dishevelled appearance.

'Really, Mr Cornelius!'

He dusted his white car coat. 'So it seems, Miss B. Afternoon, colonel.'

Ohachi glared at him, then told his Ibo houseboy to fetch another cup.

'It's happening all over again, I see.' Jerry indicated the street outside.

'That's a matter of opinion, Captain Cornelius.'

The colonel clapped his hands.

Can't Believe You Wanna Leave

Calcutta has had a pretty rough ride in the past twelve months and at the moment everyone is wondering just where the hell it goes from here. There aren't many foreigners who would allow the possibility of movement in any other direction. And, in truth, the problems of Calcutta, compounded by its recent vicious politics, are still of such a towering order as to defeat imagination; you have to sit for a little while in the middle of them to grasp what it is to have a great city and its seven million people tottering on the brink of disaster. But that is the vital point about Calcutta. It has been tottering for the best part of a generation now, but it hasn't yet fallen.

Guardian, 14 April, 1970

True Love Ways

'I thought you were in Romania,' she said. 'Are you off schedule or what?'

She came right into the room and locked the door behind her. She watched him through the mosquito netting.

He smoked the last of his Nat Sherman's Queen-Size brown Cigarettellos. There was nothing like them. There would be nothing like them again.

She wrinkled her nose. 'What's that bloody smell?'

He put the cigarette in the ashtray and sighed, moving over to his own half of the bed and watching her undress. She was all silk and rubber and trick underwear. He reached under the pillow and drew out what he had found there. It was a necklace of dried human ears.

'Where did you get this?'

'Jealous?' She turned, saw it, shrugged. 'Not mine. It belonged to a GI.'

'Where is he now?'

Her smile was juicy. 'He just passed through.'

I Want You, I Need You, I Love You

Relying on US imperialism as its prop and working hand in glove with it, Japanese militarism is vainly trying to realise its old dream of a 'Greater East Asia Co-Prosperity Sphere' and has openly embarked on the road of aggression against the people of Asia.

Communiqué issued jointly from Chou-en-Lai and
Kim-il-Sung (President of North Korea)
quoted in *Newsweek*, 20 April, 1970

Maybe Baby

Jerry's colour vision was shot. Everything was in black and white when he arrived in Wenzslaslas Square and studied the fading wreaths which lay by the monument. Well-dressed Czechs moved about with briefcases under their arms. Some got into cars. Others boarded trams. It was like watching a film.

He was disturbed by the fact that he could feel and smell the objects he saw. He blinked rapidly but it didn't help.

He wasn't quite sure why he had come back to Prague. Maybe he was looking for peace. Prague was peaceful.

He turned in the direction of the Hotel Esplanade.

He realised that Law and Order were not particularly compatible.

But where did he go from here?

And why was he crying?

It's So Easy

Weeping parents gathered in the hospital and mortuary of the Nile Delta farming towns of Huseiniya last night as Egypt denounced Israel for an air attack in which 30 children died. The bombs were reported to have fallen on a primary school at Bahr el Bakar, nearby, shortly after lessons had begun for the day. A teacher also died, and 40 children were injured.

In Tel-Aviv, however, the Israeli Defence Minister, General Dayan, accused Egypt of causing the children's deaths by putting them inside an Egyptian army base. The installations hit, he said, were definitely military. 'If the Egyptians installed classrooms inside a military installation, this, in my opinion, is highly irresponsible.'

Guardian, 9 April, 1970.

All Shook Up

Back to Dubrovnik, where the corpse-boats left from. As he waited in his hotel room he looked out of the window at the festering night. At least some things were consistent. Down by the docks they were loading the bodies of the White South Afrikan cricket team. Victims of history? Or was history their victim? His nostalgia for the fifties was as artificial as his boyish nostalgia, in the fifties, for the twenties.

What was going on?

Time was the enemy of identity.

Peggy Sue Got Married

Jerry was in Guatemala City when Auchinek came in at the head of his People's Liberation Army, his tanned face sticking out of the top of a Scammell light-armoured car. The sun hurt Jerry's eyes as he stared.

Auchinek left the car like toothpaste from a tube. He slid down the side and stood with his Thompson in his hand while the photographers took his picture. He was grinning.

He saw Jerry and danced towards him.

'We did it!'

'You changed sides?'

'You must be joking.'

The troops spread out along the avenues and into the plazas, clearing up the last of the government troops and their American Advisors. Machine guns sniggered.

'Where can I get a drink?' Auchinek slung his Thompson behind him.

Jerry nodded his head back in the direction of the pension he had been staying in. 'They've got a cantina.'

Auchinek walked into the gloom, reached over the bar and took two bottles of Ballantine from the cold shelf. He offered one to Jerry who shook his head.

'Free beer for all the workers.' The thin Jew broke the top off the bottles and poured their contents into a large schooner. 'Where's the service around here?'

'Dead,' said Jerry. 'It was fucking peaceful...' Warily, Jerry touched his lower lip.

Auchinek drew his dark brows together, opened his own lips and grinned. 'You can't stay in the middle for ever. Join up with me. Maxwell's boys are with us now.' He looked at the bar mirror and adjusted his Che-style beret, stroked his thin beard. 'Oh, that's nice.'

Jerry couldn't help sharing his laughter. 'It's time I got back to Ladbroke Grove, though,' he said.

'You used to be a fun lover.'

Jerry glanced at the broken beer bottles. 'I know.'

Auchinek saluted him with the schooner. 'Death to Life, eh? Remember?'

'I didn't know this would happen. The whole shitty fabric in tatters. Still, at least you've cheered up...'

'For crying out loud!' Auchinek drank down his beer and wiped the foam from his moustache. 'Whatever else you do, don't get dull, Jerry!'

Jerry heard the retreating forces' booby traps begin to go off. Dust drifted through the door and swirled in the cone of sunlight. Miss Brunner followed it in. She was wearing her stylish battledress.

'Revolution, Mr Cornelius! "Get with it, kiddo!" What do you think?' She stretched her arms and twirled. 'It's all the rage.'

'Oh, Jesus!'

Helpless with mirth, Jerry accepted the glass Auchinek put in his hand and, spluttering, tried to swallow the aquavit.

'Give him your gun, Herr Auchinek.' Miss Brunner patted him on the back and slid her hands down his thighs. Jerry fired a burst into the ceiling.

They were all laughing now.

Any Way You Want Me

Thirty heads with thirty holes and God knew how many hours or minutes or seconds. The groaning old hovercraft dropped him off at Folkestone and he made his way back to London in an abandoned Ford Popular. Nothing had changed.

Black smoke hung over London, drifting across a red sun.

Time was petering out.

When you thought about it, things weren't too bad.

Oh, Boy

He walked down the steps into the club. A couple of cleaners were mopping the floor and the group was tuning up on the stage.

Shakey Mo grinned at him, hefted the Futurama. 'Good to see you back in one piece, Mr C.'

Jerry took up the bass. He put his head through the strap.

'Cheer up, Mr C. It's not the end of the world. Maybe nothing's real.'

'I'm not sure it's as simple as that.' He screwed the volume control to maximum. He could still smell the kids. He plucked a simple progression. Everything was drowned. He saw that Mo had begun to sing.

The 1,500-watt amp roared and rocked. The drummer leaned over his kit and offered Jerry the roll of charge. Jerry accepted it, took a deep drag.

He began to build up the feedback.

That was life.

Other references:
Buddy Holly's Greatest Hits (Coral)
This is James Brown (Polydor)
Elvis' Golden Records (RCA)
Little Richard All-time Hits (Specialty)
Roy Orbison's Greatest Hits (Monument)

Dead Singers

'It's the old-fashioned Time Machine method again, I'm afraid.'
Bishop Beesley snorted a little sugar, gasped, grinned, put the
spoon back in the jade box and tucked the box into the rich folds
of his surplice. 'Shoot.'

'Shot,' said Jerry reminiscently. He was really in the shit this
time. He plucked the used needle from his left forearm and looked
intently at the marks. He rolled down his white sleeve. He pulled
on the old black car coat.

Rubbing his monstrous belly, Beesley pursed his little lips. 'I've
never appreciated your humour, Mr Cornelius. Like it or not,
you're tripping into the future. Where, I might add, you richly
belong.'

Jerry rolled his eyes. 'What?'

'That's all in the past now.' Beesley waddled to the other side of
the tiled room and wheeled the black Royal Albert gent's roadster
across the clean floor. He paused to flip a switch on the wall.
'Belly Button Window' flooded through the sound system. They
were turning his own rituals against him. Now the devil had all
the songs.

'All aboard, Mr C.'

Reluctantly, Jerry mounted the bike. He was getting a bit too
old for this sort of thing.

To the people living in it, no matter how 'bad' it might seem by
different standards, thought Jerry as he pedalled casually along the
Brighton seafront, the future will have its ups and downs. Not too
good, not too bad. Society isn't destroyed; it merely alters. Different superstitions; different rituals. We get by. And (he avoided the
dead old lady with the missing liver who lay in the middle of the
road) we make the rules to fit the situation. He turned up Station
Road, pedalling hard. Mind you, you couldn't escape the fucking
smell. Oh, Jesus! Nowadays all the fish were frozen.

*

Faithful to the bishop's briefing, Jerry was doing his best to hate the future, but he'd lived with it too long. A series of useful small events always prepared you for the main one. Soldiers in Bogside prepared the way for soldiers in Clydeside and martial law. Shooting prisoners at Attica made it easier to shoot strikers in Detroit. So you got used to it. And when you were used to it, it wasn't so bad. He cycled past the burnt-out remains of the Unicorn Bookshop, an early casualty of the Brighton Revival. Who was invoking what, for Christ's sake? One man's future was another man's present.

The dangers were becoming evident. It was cold and still. Entropy had set in with a vengeance. He carefully stowed the bike on the back seats of the Mercedes G4/W31. The bike was his only real transport. He started the convertible's 5,401cc engine and rolled away past the Pavilion making it into the South Downs where the seeds of the disaster had been sown all those years ago. Rural thinking; rural living. His only consolation was that the Rats had got the cottage-dwellers first.

When the Screamers had finally turned on Lord Longford and cast him forth after he'd dared voice the mildest suggestion that perhaps things were going just a trifle too far in some directions, a sweet-faced, mad-eyed girl had a vision which proved Longford had been the Antichrist all along. The circumstances surrounding his death, two weeks later, remained mysterious, but the event itself improved morale tremendously amongst his ex-followers. At the following Saturday's book-burning in Hyde Park observers had noted a surge of fresh enthusiasm.

A death or two would do it every time.

Jerry had decided not to resign from the Committee, after all. But now the job was done; the ball had rolled. It was peaceful at last. A wind hissed through the wasted hills. Jerry wondered what had happened to his own family. But there wasn't time for that. He kept going. It was getting colder.

*

The turning point must have been in the Spring of 1970. Given a slightly different set of circumstances, it should have been nothing more than the last death-kick of the Old Guard and everything would have been okay. But somehow the thing had gathered impetus. By Spring 1972 he realised the Phoney War had become a shooting war. Maybe Lobkowitz had been right when they'd last met in Prague. 'The war, Jerry, is endless. All we can ever reasonably hope for are a few periods of relative peace. A lull in the battle, as it were.' Just as the middle-class 'liberals' and 'radicals' had got the Attica rebels ready for the massacre, so they had set up British workers for the chop. The final joke of the dying middle class. Lawyers, managers, TV producers and left-wing journalists: they had been the real enemy. Still, it was too late in 1967 to start worrying about that and it was certainly too late now. If, of course, it *was* now. He was feeling a bit vague. Images flickered on the windscreen. A fat, middle-aged woman in a cheap pink suit ran a few yards in front of him and vanished. She reappeared where she had started and did it all over again. She kept doing it. He was losing any cool he'd thought he had.

'Shit.'

From the sky he heard Jefferson Airplane. It was all distorted, but it seemed to be 'War Movie'. Someone was trying to reach him, and halfway down Croydon High Road at that. Some misguided friend who didn't realise that that sort of thing couldn't possibly work here. The buildings on either side of him were tall, burnt-out and crazy, but it was still Saturday afternoon. The ragged people traipsed up and down the pavements with their empty shopping bags in their hands, looking for something to buy. A few Rats in a jeep cruised past them, the Rats were too interested in Jerry's Mercedes to do anything about the shoppers. Jerry reached into the back and grasped the crossbar of the Royal Albert. The scene was slicing up somewhat. He heard a shout from a roof. A woman in a black leather trench coat was shouting to him from the top of Kennard's Department Store. She was waving an M16 in each hand.

'Jerry!' There was some nasty echo there. 'Jerry!'

It could have been anyone. He put his foot down on the accelerator and got moving. Speed could do nothing but worsen this frozen situation. There again, he'd no other choice.

In London he slowed down, but by that time he'd blown it completely. Still, he'd got what Beesley wanted. Nothing stayed the same. Tiny snatches of music came from all sides, trying to take hold. Marie Lloyd, Harry Champion, George Formby, Noël Coward, Cole Porter, Billie Holliday, MJQ, Buddy Holly, The Beatles, Jimi Hendrix and Hawkwind. He hung on to Hawkwind, turning the car back and forth to try to home in, but then it was Gertrude Lawrence and then it was Tom Jones and then it was Cliff Richard and he knew he was absolutely lost. Buildings rose and fell like waves. Horses, trams and buses faded through each other. People grew and decayed. There were too many ghosts in the future. In Piccadilly Circus he brought the Mercedes to a bumping stop at the base of the Eros statue and, grabbing the Royal Albert, threw himself clear. He was screaming for help. They'd been fools to fuck about with Time again. Yet they'd known what they were getting him into.

Bishop Beesley stood looking down at him. The bishop had one foot in Green Park, one foot resting on the roof of the Athenaeum. His voice was huge and distant. 'Well, Mr Cornelius, what did you find?'

Jerry whimpered.

'If you want to come back, you'll have to have some information with you.'

Jerry pulled himself together long enough to say: 'I've got some.'

He stood in the clean, tiled room. The Royal Albert was scratched and rusty. Its tyres were flat. It had taken as bad a beating as he had. Munching a Mars, Bishop Beesley leaned against the steel door which opened onto the street.

'Well?'

Jerry dropped the bike to the floor and stumbled up to him,

trying to push past, but the bishop was too heavy. He was immovable. 'Well?'

'It's what you wanted to know.' Jerry looked miserably at the shit on his boots. 'The clean-up succeeded. All the singers are dead.'

Bishop Beesley smiled and opened the door to let him into Ladbroke Grove. He went out of a house he had once thought was his own. 'Bye, bye, now, Mr C. Don't do anything I couldn't do.'

The cold got to Jerry's chest. He began to cough. As he trudged along the silent street in the grey autumn evening, the birds stood on their branches and window ledges, shifting from foot to foot so that their little chains chinked in the staples. They didn't take their unblinking eyes off him. As Jerry turned up the collar of his threadbare coat he had to smile.

The Longford Cup

The following narrative appears to be incomplete. It was discovered in the fireplace of a ruined convent in London's so-called Forbidden Sector. It is largely a record of conversations held by the notorious criminal Cornelius and some of his associates during the period shortly before and immediately during the Re-affirmation of Human Dignity. It is published for the Committee alone. It is imperative that it be in no manner whatsoever made public. The notes were probably compiled by one of our special workers (several of whom came to be on terms of intimacy with Cornelius and, as the Committee already knows from the Report PTE5, are still missing). We regret that much of the narrative is likely to distress members of the Committee but present it unedited so that they may exactly understand the depths of depravity to which persons such as Cornelius had sunk before the Re-affirmation. We have retained the original title – though we recognise that it is obscure. We have numbered the items. Cornelius is believed to be still at large and it is likely that extra efforts will he needed before he can be apprehended.

– MEW

I

Nothing in my work points to any impulse to develop hostility to the sexual deviant, homosexual, or 'gay' individual – whatever one may call them. But it is obvious from the way in which one's work on these problems is received (and often suppressed), that there is a kind of freemasonry in the background, by which those with bizarre sexual tastes are trying to censor debate. This is dangerous...

– David Holbrook,
letter to the *Guardian*, 28 September, 1972

2

'Well, the rich are getting richer and the poor are getting poorer, Mr C.' Shakey Mo Collier held the door of the Phantom VII while Jerry stepped, blinking, out. Mo's long greasy hair emerged from under an off-white chauffeur's cap and spread over the shoulders of his grubby white uniform jacket. Mo was looking decidedly seedy, as if the brown rice and mandrax diet Jerry had recommended wasn't doing him all the good it should.

Jerry smoothed the pleats of his blue midi-skirt and ran the tips of his fingers under the bottom of his fawn Jaeger sweater. He looked every inch the efficient PA. There were auburn highlights in his well-groomed shoulder-length coiffure and the long chiffon scarf tied at his throat, coupled with the neatly overdone make-up, gave him the slight whorish look that every girl finds useful in business. Opening a tooled leather shoulder bag he looked himself over in the flap mirror. He winked a subtly mascara'd eye and offered Mo a jolly grin.

'Cor!' said Mo admiringly. 'You little yummy.'

Jerry stepped through the glass doors and into the foyer, his pleats swinging to just the right tempo.

In the lift he met Mr Drake from Publicity.

'It must be a heavy responsibility,' said Mr Drake. His pallor was at odds with his thick, red lips. He fingered his green silk tie and left a tiny sweat stain near the knot. 'Working for such a busy and influential man. Doesn't it ever get on top of you? How does he fit it all in?'

'It's a question of technique really,' said Jerry. He giggled.

The doors opened.

'See you,' said Mr Drake. 'Be good.'

Jerry stepped along the corridor.

This particular job was beginning to get dull. He'd never been fond of undercover work. Besides, he had the information now. The crucial decision had come at the last full meeting of the Committee (Jerry had been taking the minutes) when it had been agreed, in the words of Jerry's boss, to 'use the devil's own troops against him'. Files on the sexual preferences of people in high places had been compiled. In return for the original copies of their files they had to give their active help in the campaign. It was surprising how smoothly the method worked already. The police in particular, who had once been able to control and profit from the distribution of erotica, had been only too pleased to see a return to the old status quo. Everything and everyone was settling back nicely, by and large. Even the taste for the stuff was a pre-seventies habit.

At the end of this week, Jerry decided, he would give his notice.

He walked through the oak door and into the untidy office. His employer, who almost always got in early, beamed at him. 'There you are, my dear.' He rose from behind the desk, putting his ugly fingers to the top of his bald head and with his other hand gesturing towards his visitor.

The visitor – in clerical frock-coat and gaiters – took up a lot of space. Flipping through a piece of research material, he had his huge back to Jerry, but he was immediately identifiable.

'This is Bishop Beesley. He is to take poor Mr Tome's place on the Committee.'

The bishop slowly presented his front, like an airship man-oeuvring to dock, his jowls shaking with the effort of his smile. It was impossible for Jerry to tell from the expression in the tiny twinkling eyes if he had, in turn, been recognised by his old enemy.

'My dear.' Beesley's voice was as warm and thick as butter-scotch sauce.

'Bishop.' Jerry let his lips part a fraction. 'Welcome aboard.

Well...' He continued towards his own office on the far side of the desk.

'Allow me,' Bishop Beesley lumbered to the door and opened it for Jerry.

That was what the power struggle was all about really, thought Jerry as, with a graceful smile, he swept past. He could almost feel the bishop's hand on his bottom.

3

A revival of the fifties sexual aesthetic had never been that far away. How swiftly people recoiled from even a hint of freedom. Lying amidst the tangled sheets Jerry watched as Miss Brunner togged herself up in her stockings, her suspenders, her chains. She had an awful lot in common with Bishop Beesley. Jerry frowned, considering a new idea. Using the last of his Nepalese, he rolled himself a fat joint. He began to drift. Even he could understand the sense of relief she must have. His own girdle hung on the chair to his right.

Her voice was controlled and malicious as she tugged the zip of the black silk sheath dress, a Balenciaga copy. 'That's much better, isn't it?' Gazing savagely into the mirror, she began to brush her dark red hair.

'Comfortable?' Jerry offered her the joint.

She shook her head and picked up an atomiser. The room became filled with Mon Plaisir. Jerry reeled.

'Maybe I should get myself one of those Ted suits?' he said. 'What else? A fancy waistcoat. A yellow Paisley cravat?' His memory was poor on the details. 'Crêpes?'

Miss Bruner was disapproving. She bent to powder her nose. 'I don't think you really understand, Mr Cornelius.'

He reached for another pillow. Propping it behind him he sat up. 'I think I do. The cards had already been punched. What's happening was inevitable. Is there a safer bolt-hole than the plastic fifties?'

'Some people take these things seriously.' Her face was now a mask of moral outrage. 'You talk of fashion while I speak of morality.'

It was true that Jerry had never been able to see much of a difference between the two.

'But the clothes...?' he began. 'All this tight gear.'

'They make me feel dignified.'

Jerry's laughter was amazed and coarse. 'Well,' he said. 'Fuck that.'

'A typical masculine reaction.' She put the lipstick to her mouth. 'You should know.'

It was obviously time to go home and look up the family.

4

Mrs Cornelius waddled to the door at Jerry's knock. He saw her coming through the cracked and dirty glass. He had had a haircut and a shave and was wearing a nice blue suit. She unbolted the door.

'Hello, Mum.'

'Blimey! Look who it isn't!' Her red face was almost the exact match to her dirty dress. Blowsy as ever, she was disconcerted, pushing her stiff peroxide locks back from her forehead. Then she guffawed. 'Cor! 'Ullo, stranger.' She called back into the dank darkness of her home. 'Caff! Wot a turn up! It's yer bruvver!'

As she closed and locked the door behind Jerry she added: 'This we got ter celebrate!'

In the kitchen Jerry saw his sister Catherine. She was looking pale but beautiful, her blonde hair in a score of tiny braids. She was wearing a blue-and-white Moroccan dress from under which her beaded sandals poked. The room itself was in its usual state, disordered and decrepit, with piles of old newspapers and magazines on every surface.

'I didn't know you were living here, Cathy,' he said.

'I'm not. I just dropped in to see Mum. How are things with you, then?'

'Up and down.' He selected a relatively safe chair, removed about thirty copies of *Woman* and *Woman's Own* and seated himself opposite her at the table while their mother rummaged in the warped sideboard for a quarter-bottle of gin.

'Yore lookin' nice.' Mrs Cornelius found the gin and unscrewed the cap, pouring half the bottle into a cup, offering the rest vaguely, knowing they would refuse. 'More than I can say for 'er – all dressed up like a bleedin' wog. I bin tellin' 'er – she thought she was pregnant – 'ow can she be bloody pregnant, 'angin' rahnd with a lot of long-'aired nanas? One thing she *don't* 'ave ter worry abart – gettin' pregnant off of one of them bloody 'ippies. I said – wait till yer find yerself a *real* man – then yer'll be up the stick fast enough.'

'Mum!' Catherine's protest was mild and automatic. She hadn't really been listening.

Mrs Cornelius sniffed. 'I'm not sayin' anyfink was different in my day – we all 'ave ter 'ave our fun – but in my day we didn't bloody go on abart it all the time. Kept ourselves to ourselves.'

'It was the middle classes finding out.' Jerry winked at his sister. 'They had to shout it all over the street, eh, Mum?'

'Dunno wot yer talkin' abart.' She smiled as the gin improved her spirits.

'What did they all do before they discovered sex?' Jerry wondered.

'Pictures and dancing,' said Catherine, 'to Ambrose and his Orchestra. It was the war buggered that. That's how they found out. But it took them till 1965 before it really hit them. Now they've gone and spoiled it for the rest of us. Trust the bloody BBC.'

Mrs Cornelius glared stupidly at her children, feeling she was being deliberately excluded.

'Well,' she said brutally, 'it's love what makes the world go rahnd.' With an air of studied reminiscence she reached out and began to finger a tarnished gilt model of the Eiffel Tower. 'Paris in the spring,' she said. She was referring to her favourite and most familiar love affair. Presumably it had been with Jerry's father, but she had always been unclear on that particular detail of the story, though her children knew everything else by heart.

'There *was* more romance then.' Catherine seemed genuinely regretful. Jerry found himself loving them both. He tried to think of something comforting to say.

'We're trying to find our moral and sexual balance at present, maybe,' he said. 'Things will sort themselves out in time. Meanwhile the old apes drape themselves in wigs and gowns and mortar-boards and play at judges and scholars, gnashing their yellow fangs, wagging their paws, scampering agitatedly about. Wasted Longford, lost Muggeridge and melancholy Mrs W. Somewhere you can hear them whimpering, as if the evidence of their own mortality were emphasised by the knowledge of other people's happiness.'

They stared at him in astonishment.

He blushed.

5

'Bugger me!' said Shakey Mo. He leaned against the Phantom VII, his jacket open to reveal the purple Crumb T-shirt covering his underprivileged chest. Jerry sat on the far side of the garage, working at the bench, checking his heat. He wore heavy shades, a long-skirted jacket of black kid, black flared trousers and black high-heeled cowboy boots with yellow decorative stitching. The buckle of his wide plaited-leather belt must have measured at least six inches across; it was solid brass. 'Well, bugger me. What are we up to now, Mr C?'

Jerry smeared grease on his needle gun. He checked the action and was happy.

'Nice one,' said Mo.

Jerry grinned. His sharp teeth gleamed. His movements were fast and neat as he tucked the gun into his shoulder holster.

'Things are speeding up again, Mo.'

Jerry got into the back of the car and stretched out with a

satisfied sigh. Mo leapt happily into the driving seat and started the engine.

'It's always a relief when tenderness transmutes into violence,' said Jerry.

'Not that violence is without its responsibilities, too. But it's so much easier.'

Mo, on the other side of the glass partition, didn't hear a word.

Jerry got a flash then. The dope was making him silly. He shrugged. 'We can't all be perfect.'

6

Miss Brunner looked him over admiringly. 'That's more like it. That's what I call a man.'

Jerry sneered.

At this an expression of adoration swiftly came and went in her eyes. She moved greedily towards him, touching his belt-buckle, stroking his jacket, fingering the pearl buttons of his shirt.

'Oh, what slaves we are to fashion, after all!'

'Glad to be back in the game.' Jerry's hand was on her neck, touching filmy fabric, soft skin, delicate hair. 'When's Beesley due?'

'Any minute. But I could stall him.' Her lips trembled.

Jerry removed his hand. 'We'll save that up for the celebration.'

Her flat was luxurious, with white fluffy carpets, deep armchairs, lots of multicoloured cushions, pleasant prints on the pale walls; the sort of hideout any tired businessman would have welcomed.

There was a knock on the door of this nest. Jerry crossed the carpet and entered the bedroom. He heard Bishop Beesley's muffled voice, a parody of courtliness.

'Your adoring servant, dear lady, I have only an hour. The Committee calls. But how better to spend an hour than in the company of the most beautiful, the *sweetest* woman in London?'

'What a flatterer you are, bishop!' Her voice was a mixture of vanity and contempt. Jerry, who was having trouble sustaining his rôle, felt deeply sorry for her. As usual when his tenderness and his love were aroused, his head became filled with a variety of pompous and speciously philosophical observations. He controlled himself, promising that he would indulge all that later. Standing with his back to her fitted wardrobe he could see himself in the mirror of her kidney-shaped dressing table, his hair hanging long and straight and black, his shades glinting. The mirror helped him resume his proper attitude of mind. He snarled at himself.

Miss Brunner entered the bedroom, calling back: 'With you in a second, bishop.'

She had known that he would follow. He heaved his huge body after her, beaming affectionately, his fat little hands outstretched to touch her.

'A kiss, dear lady. A token...' He shivered. His red lips blubbered. His hot eyes were damp with anticipation. 'After last night I would – you could – oh, I am yours, dear lady. Yours!'

Miss Brunner's laughter was perhaps not as harsh as she would have liked. Indeed, there was something of a quaver in it.

'Pig,' she said.

It did not have quite the expected effect. He fell to his fat knees. 'And sinner, too,' he agreed. He buried his head in her thighs, his saliva gleamed on the black silk, he threatened her balance; she almost fell. She clutched at the tufts of hair on both sides of his head and steadied herself.

'Yes!' he groaned. 'Yes!'

Jerry had begun to enjoy the scene so much (including Miss Brunner's discomfort) that he was reluctant to act; but he pulled himself together, gave his reflection a parting snarl, and moved round the bed.

'Bishop.'

Beesley paused, drew back a fraction and stared enquiringly up into Miss Brunner's unhappy face.

She cleared her throat. 'I'm afraid we are discovered, bishop.'

Beesley considered this. Then, with a certain amount of studied dignity, he got to his feet, his back still towards Jerry. He turned.

'Afternoon, bishop,' said Jerry. 'So much for the sanctity of the home, eh?'

Beesley looked hopefully at Miss Brunner.

'My husband,' she explained.

'Cornelius?' Beesley was indignant. 'You hate him. You can't stand him. You told me so. Not your type at all.'

'He does have his off days,' she agreed.

'The fact remains,' said Jerry. 'You ought to know what marriage means, bishop. After all, you're a married man yourself.'

'You intend to blackmail me?' Now that he felt he understood their motives Bishop Beesley relaxed a trifle.

'Of course not.' Jerry slipped his needle gun from its holster. 'It's time you got undressed. Isn't that what you came for?'

7

Afterwards, while Bishop Beesley lay grunting in uncomfortable slumber on the edge of the rug, Jerry stretched himself fully clothed beside Miss Brunner's wet, warm and naked body. He put an arm round her triumphant shoulders and felt her melt.

'I'm still not clear about your motives,' she said. 'And I'm not sure I support them, either.'

'I'm certain you don't,' Jerry stared idly at the bishop's flesh as little ripples ran from the back of his pink neck, over his grey bottom and down his legs. 'You've tired him out.'

She kissed his shoulder and wriggled against his coat. 'It wasn't hard.'

'I could see that.' Still, thought Jerry, it was a shame to see the great predator brought low.

'What's it got to do with the Committee?' she asked.

'Well, I can't beat it. Not at present. And I don't want to join it. I've seen enough of it. It gets so boring. Besides, it won't last that long. But while it does it will reintroduce so much in the way of guilt that the next era's bound to get off to a slower start than I'd have liked. I still indulge these visions of Utopia, you see.' He waved a hand at the bishop. 'A lesson in tolerance.'

'I didn't know you were interested in politics.'

'I'm not. This is an artistic impulse. Like Bukaninism.' He sniffed. 'I've a horror of the Law of Precedent. It's bad logic. Could you put the new Hawkwind album on?'

While she went into the next room he swallowed a couple of tabs of speed.

The music began to fill the room. She came back and she was looking lovely. He smiled at her.

'We've got to struggle on somehow,' he said. 'Everything fades. Only love can conquer disintegration. Only love denies the second law of thermodynamics. Love love, it's the best thing we have.' Jerry groaned as she fell upon him, biting and caressing. 'Oh, my love! Oh, my love!'

It took her five long minutes to unbuckle his belt. While she did it he reflected that if he'd achieved nothing else he had almost certainly re-programmed Beesley. It was bound to make a difference. A small victory was all he had a right to expect at this stage.

8

Jerry's mum was furious. 'Wot they wanna call it a bloody "Forbidden Sector" for, then?' She put down her bag on a pile of newspapers. 'I was aht shoppin' when I saw 'em puttin' up the fuckin' barbed wire. I asked the bloke – "It's 'cause of all them prossies," 'e sez. "Fuck that!" I sez – "Wot abart the decent people?" – "Yer can always move aht," 'e sez. Well, fuck that! Anyway, Jer – they're lookin' for *you*. Wotcher bin up to? Don' tell me.' She lowered herself into her armchair and kicked her shoes off. Jerry poured her a cup of tea.

'I just made it,' he said.

She became nervous. 'Thinkin' of stayin' 'ere?'

He shook his head. 'Just want to change my appearance a bit, then I'll be off.'

'Be as well,' she said. 'Yore not lookin' too chipper.'

'I've had a busy time.'

'Boys!' she said. 'Give me girls any day of the week. They're a lot less trouble.'

'Well, I suppose it's all a question of circumstances.'

'Too right!' She offered him a look that was a mixture of affection and introspection. 'It's a man's world, innit?'

Jerry had discarded his gear and was now dressed in the dark blue suit he usually wore to his mum's.

'You got a good place to go to?' she asked.

'It'll do.'

'Not to worry. Everythin' blows over.'

'Let's hope so.'

'Your trouble is, Jerry, yore too fuckin' confident and then you get too fuckin' low. Yore dad was the same. I've 'ardly known a man that wasn't. All puff and strut one minute and like a little kid the next. Men. Want yore own way all the time. Then when you don't get it...'

'I know, Mum.'

'It's women that suffers, Jerry.' She gave a satisfied sniff.

Jerry sighed and reached down to pick up his suitcase. 'I know. Well, I'll just go and change. Then I'll be off.'

When he reappeared in the kitchen he was wearing his miniskirt, his Jaeger sweater, his court shoes, his auburn wig, his pearls. Mrs Cornelius screeched. Her body shook and tears of laughter filled her eyes. Sweat brightened her forehead. 'Cor!' She gasped and paused. 'Yore full o' surprises, Jerry. You shoulda bin in show-biz. That's a disguise and an 'alf all right!'

'It always was,' said Jerry. He blew her a kiss and left.

Outside, Mo was waiting in the Mercedes. The armour plates were in position at most of the windows. Mo had a Banning Mark Four on the floor beside the passenger seat. He patted the big gun as he got the car moving. Jerry settled himself in the back. It was dusk and the first searchlight beams of the evening were already swinging over the grey streets.

'Time for some business, Mr C?'

'Get you,' said Jerry. He noticed that his left stocking had started to run. He wetted his finger and dabbed at the ladder. 'You can't win them all.'

The Mercedes jumped forward. Jerry cradled his own Banning, stroking its cool metal barrel, working its action back and forth. There was an explosion to the west, near Ladbroke Grove, a short burst of machine-gun fire. Jerry saw a tank cross the street at the intersection just ahead of them.

'At least it's simpler than sex.' He began to load the Banning.

'And a bloody sight more fun!' Mo grinned, wound down the window and lobbed a grenade at a sub-post-office. There was a flash, a bang and a lot of glass flew about.

'Here we go again, Mr C.'

The Entropy Circuit

I

Cosmology

'It is impossible to guess what the human race will do in the next ten years...'

Everything was getting sluggish.

Jerry Cornelius: stumbling upon the boards of his bare bedsitter; trying to find water for his consumptive girl-wife who coughed, heated and naked, under the thin grey sheet; who trembled. He would have been glad of a drink, something to smoke, a tab of limbitrol, perhaps.

The water in the jug was low and warm. He found a cup, unable to see in the gloom if it was clean, and poured. He stopped, jug in hand, staring through the cracks and the grime of the window at the unlit, deserted street, reviewing suddenly the future, contemplating the past, unwilling to consider a present which at that moment appeared to have betrayed him. A wind moved the palms flanking the avenue; the sea, unseen, the Mediterranean, gasped against the shingle below the promenade onto which the pension fronted. It was winter and Jerry had been waiting in Menton since the previous summer.

Jerry returned to the bed, offering the cup, but she was asleep again; her light snores were uneven, sickly. He drank and turned to the table; it was covered in papers, abandoned forms. Nearly a year ago he had set off for the Vatican with a plan owing more to drug euphoria than to logic, knowing nothing of the new regulations limiting border traffic into Italy from France. Here, in Menton, he had planned to stay a couple of nights at most, but first he had had to wait for a new benzine permit (it had not been granted and his postal request to London had been unacknowledged). Later, trying to cross into San Remo on foot he had been informed that passage was granted on certain days only, each case being considered individually, and he would need a visa. It had taken a month for the visa to arrive and during that time there had come further restrictions; the border had been opened with only a day's warning in advance five times in the past six months, and the rule was simply first come, first served. If you stood in line, there was a chance that you would be allowed to cross (barring official disapproval) before the barrier came down again. Twice Jerry had got as close as ten or fifteen people before the line and been turned away; three times he had failed to hear the news that the border was to be opened. In attempting to conserve his various resources, he had not followed the example of other travellers and tried, fruitlessly, to find a less heavily trafficked crossing point, but now he was running out of cash, and he had little left to sell.

He touched the stud of his Pulsar watch; the numerals seemed to glow more faintly and soon the power cell would give out altogether, for all that he had made every effort to preserve it as long as possible. The red numerals said 5.46; he released the stud before the seconds had time to register. He wondered if Mo Collier would be able to get here in time. Mo had promised to smuggle some money through to him, if he could. He knew that he was luckier than many; he had seen the pathetic tents and shanties in the hills above the town; he had seen the corpses on the coast road near the entrance to the tunnel; he had seen the children who had been left behind.

He shuffled the papers and found Mo's postcard again. It had taken over three weeks to arrive and read: 'Wish you were here, Mr C. Should be taking a holiday myself in a month or so.' Checking the London postmark, Jerry had worked out that this could put the time of Mo's arrival within the fortnight since he had received it. Turning over one of several spoiled forms, he came across some lines written either by himself or the girl he had married in Menton on Christmas Day (there had been a rumour, then, since discounted, that married couples received preferential treatment at the border):

> The power of love is harder to sustain
> By far than that easy instrument
> The brutal power of pain.

His lips moved as he stared at the sheet; he frowned, plucking at the frayed cuff of his black car coat. Were the words a quotation; had he or the girl been inspired to write them down? He was unable to interpret them. He screwed the paper up and let it fall amongst its fellows.

He folded his arms against an unanticipated chill.

2

Cosmogonies

> 'The first principle of the universe to take form was Chronos, or Time, which came out of Chaos, symbolising the infinite, and Ether, symbolising the finite.'

'It's all falling apart, Jerry,' said Shakey Mo Collier as he handed over the last of the cash (each £1 overstamped to the value of £100). 'Sorry it had to be sterling. How much longer can it go on for? A few million years and nobody will have heard of the South of France, or Brighton, for that matter. I know I'm in a gloomy mood – but who *has* got the energy these days? That's what I'd like to know.'

Jerry held up his heater. The ray of watery sunlight from the window fell on it. 'Here's some, for a start.'

'And what did it cost you?'

'Oh, well...' Jerry looked in the mirror at the bags under his eyes, the lines on his face. 'That's entropy for you.'

'I brought you some petrol, too,' said Mo.

'How did you get it through?'

Mo was pleased with himself. 'It's in spare tanks, in the tanks themselves. It's worth twice the value of the car, for all it looks very flash on the outside. I'm going to get a boat from Marseilles, first chance.'

'Going straight back?'

'Straight? That's a laugh, these days.'

The girl was better today. Coughing only a little, she moved slowly from the lavatory and back to the bed. She tried to smile at Mo, who winked at Jerry. 'Doing all right, still, I see.'

'We pooled our resources.' Jerry felt he should explain.

'I know what you mean.' Another wink.

With a sigh the girl got into the bed and pulled the sheet around her thin body. She pushed back dirty fair hair from her oval face while, with her other hand, she fumbled for cigarettes and matches on the bamboo table beside her. She struck a match. It failed to light. She struck another and the same thing happened. After several tries, she abandoned the box. Mo stepped forward, snapping a gold Dunhill lighter. Nothing happened.

'That's funny,' he said. 'It was working okay this morning.' He peered at it, flicking the wheel. 'Not a spark. But the flint's new.'

Aggrieved, but at the same time reconciled, Mo replaced the lighter in his pocket. He glanced at his watch. 'Oh, shit,' he said, 'that's fucking stopped as well.'

Jerry murmured an apology.

Mo said: 'It's not your fucking fault, Jerry. Not really. Or is it?'

There was a knock on the thin wood of the door. Quickly, Jerry opened the drawer in the table and slipped the tight wad of notes into it. 'Come in.'

It was Miss Brunner. She was precisely clothed, in a dark blue tweed costume. She looked disdainfully at Mo's long, greasy hair, his untidy moustache, his dirty denims, but when she saw Jerry and the condition of his room, she smiled with genuine relish. 'My, you have come down in the world.'

'I think that's true of most of us. What brings you to Menton out of season?'

'You can't afford to be sulky, I'd have thought.' She cast a cool eye at the girl. 'Or choosy, it seems. I heard you were hard up, stuck, in trouble. I came to help.'

202

Mo moved uneasily, making for the door. 'Well, I'll be seeing you, Jerry. You don't want me...?'

'Take it easy, Mo.'

Mo allowed himself a quick, almost cheerful grin. 'What there is left to take, Mr C. I hope things work out. Keep in touch.'

As the door closed, Miss Brunner stopped her speculative eyeing of the girl and turned to Jerry. 'I've a job,' she said, 'which could solve all your problems. Would you like the details? What about your friend?'

'Don't worry about her,' said Jerry. He stood beside the girl, stroking her soft cheek. 'She's dying.'

'You were on your way to the Vatican, I heard.'

'A year ago. I was getting used to it here, though.'

'This would take you to the Vatican. You know it's been closed off for months – hardly anyone allowed in or out. Why were you going? Somebody offer you work?'

'It sounded tasty.'

'I got an offer, too – on the computer. But I wanted complete autonomy. Anyway, I heard what they're up to and it would, I think, be mutually convenient if you were to throw a spanner or two in the works.'

'Mutually convenient? Who else is involved?'

'I'm representing a consortium.'

'Beesley?'

'He has special reasons for being interested in the project,' she admitted.

'Maxwell.'

'Oh, you don't have to name them all, Mr Cornelius.'

'The usual gang, in fact. I'm not sure. Every time I've thrown in my lot with you I've come out of it –'

'Wiser,' she said. 'And that's the main thing. Besides, we haven't always won.'

'It's spending the time that I mind. And the energy.'

'In this case, if you're successful, you get all you need of both.'

She explained what she thought was happening at the Vatican.

3

Fundamentals

'Probably the most extraordinary coincidence discovered by science is the fact that the basic formulae for three separate, and apparently unrelated, energy systems are almost identical.'

It was good to be on the road again, though the forty-five-kilometre speed limit didn't exactly make for a zippy trip. Sitting beside him as they negotiated the winding coast road beyond Genoa, the girl looked almost healthy. She had the window of the Ambassador station wagon all the way down and a light rain fell on her bare arm.

'We can only be kind to one another,' she said, 'there is scarcely any alternative if we are to resist chaos.'

Jerry was saved from replying by the stereo's groan, indicating that the tape was running too slow. It had been getting worse and worse. He tugged the cartridge from the player and turned the radio on long enough to hear a few bars of some song for Europe. He despaired. He switched it off. Behind them, in the drizzle, the grey, square towers of Genoa were overshadowed by huge neon signs showing stylised pictures of rats and warning them to be vigilant for new plagues.

'Love among the predators,' said Jerry reminiscently. 'Is this your first trip to Rome?'

'Oh, no,' she said. 'My last.'

Their surroundings widened out. On their right they could see the remains of a small hillside town which had been burned in an effort to contain a plague.

'The world's filling up with fucking metaphors.' Jerry kept his eyes on the road. 'Too fucking many metaphors.'

4

Universe

> 'To the old ones, the sun was energy or god or both, but the stars were different.'

The car padded through the wet streets of the Roman night as Jerry sought the address Miss Brunner had given him; without any kind of street lighting, it was almost impossible to read the signs, for the moon appeared only intermittently through the heavy cloud. Police cars, impressed by the size of the station wagon, were curious, but left him alone. There were even more police in Rome now. During Jerry's last trip the various kinds of policemen had at last begun to outnumber the male civilians in the city.

Someone had been standing in a doorway and began to approach when they saw the car, flagging it down. Jerry pulled into the side, touching the control panel on his door to lower the left front window (the girl had fallen asleep).

'Still managing to keep up appearances, then,' said the man in the trench coat. It was his brother Frank, seedy as ever. He leered in. 'Going to give me a lift, Jerry? I've been waiting for you.'

Jerry leaned across and opened the rear door. Frank climbed in with a sigh and began to unbutton his coat. The faint smell of mould filled the car.

Frank rubbed comfortably at his stubble. 'It's like old times, again.'

'You said it,' said Jerry despondently.

'Make a right,' said Frank. 'Then a left. How long is it since you were welcome at the Vatican?'

'Quite a while.' Jerry followed the instructions. They went over the river.

'Head for St Peter's.'

The girl woke up, sniffing. 'Dope?' she murmured.

'Frank,' said Jerry.

'This'll do,' Frank told him. They stopped by a toyshop; they were about a hundred yards from the Vatican City.

Frank left the car and let himself into the toyshop. Jerry and the girl followed. At last, as they reached the back of the shop, Jerry recognised where he was.

Frank grinned. 'That's right. One of your old hotspots. And the tunnel's been reactivated. We were lucky. Most of the catacombs are filled up with stolen cars, these days. It's conservation, of sorts, I suppose.' He pulled aside a gigantic, soft bear to reveal a hole in the wall. Taking a flashlight from his pocket, he led the way.

Within a few moments they had descended into ancient darkness. Frank's thin beam touched the carved face of Mithras. Jerry glared back at it. He considered it a poor likeness.

5

God

'There is no figure in modern developed societies to compare with that of the shaman.'

Jerry's boots crushed the gross, leprous toadstools which grew between the cracks in the flagstones; their smell reminding him of Frank, their flesh of Bishop Beesley, their toxicity of Miss Brunner, all of whom now stood in the chamber at the end of the tunnel, together with Captain Maxwell, the Protestant engineer, his huge backside turned towards Jerry as he fiddled with a piece of equipment.

'It's got a lot warmer, at any rate.' Jerry noticed that his watch burned brighter; the girl's face had lost its pallor.

'That's because we're under the bloody Vatican,' said Frank. 'Well, is it a complete set, Miss Brunner?'

'It would have been nice to have had Doktor von Krupp, but she's faded away altogether, I'm afraid. A termination, we can safely say.'

Most of the equipment in the chamber was familiar to Jerry.

Captain Maxwell straightened up, wiping sticky sweat from his choleric features. He pursed his lips when he saw Jerry, but made no comment. 'She's still acting up a bit,' he told Miss Brunner. 'Perhaps we could try a modified programme?'

'That would take us back to square one,' she said.

Jerry said: 'It looks like we're there already.'

'It's our last chance.' Unexpectedly, her tone was defensive.

'I'd say His Holiness has already beaten you.' Jerry wondered at his own glow of satisfaction; previously, he had always been inclined to associate their consortium with that of the Papal Palace. 'He's got the brains, the equipment, the power.'

'Not all of it, Mr Cornelius.' Bishop Beesley unwrapped an Italian chocolate bar. 'I think I speak for everyone here when I say we've no time for your brand of cynicism. And I might remind you that *we* have the experience. Besides,' he added with a smirk, indicating a tangle of thick cables disappearing into a hole in the ceiling, 'we're tapping a lot of his resources.'

'Undetected?'

'The energy situation throughout the world is so unstable,' Miss Brunner told him, 'that they're putting the fluctuation down to the increased entropy rate.'

'You know how mystical people can get about energy,' said Frank. 'That's where we have the edge on them. Half their problems are semantic – there's a lot of confusion just because most of their people can't distinguish between the specific meanings of, well, "energy".'

'They're still thrashing about in a lot of metaphors,' said Miss Brunner.

'I know how they feel,' said Jerry.

6

Body

> 'While questions of origin tickle the imagination, they are, on the whole, insoluble.'

Jerry glanced idly at the dials, but he was impressed. 'He's certainly accumulating energy at a pretty fast lick. You know what he's using it for, do you? Specifically?'

'He's just trying to consolidate. It's a human enough ambition in times like these.' Miss Brunner ran a pale hand over a console. 'After all, it's only what we're aiming for.'

'I think it's greedy,' said the girl.

Miss Brunner sighed and turned away.

Frank wasn't upset by the remark. 'It's the logical extension of capitalist philosophy,' he said. He moistened his lips with his tongue. His eyes were already wet, and hot. Jerry could tell he was trying to be agreeable.

'God knows what would happen if this lot blew.' Captain Maxwell could not disguise the note of glee in his voice. 'Boom!'

Jerry was beginning to regret his weakness in throwing in with them.

'It's the Pope's last bid for divinity, I suppose,' said Bishop Beesley enviously. 'That's why we've got to stop him. And that's why we need you, Mr Cornelius, as a – um –?'

'Hit man,' supplied Frank. 'With the Pope knocked over, they'll never get round to sussing us. We know you've got a lot of other talents, Jerry, but, well, we've got Miss Brunner's computer doing your old job, and this was the only other opening.'

Captain Maxwell put an affectionate hand on the machine.

'Standard Hexamerous and Multiple Axis Noumena,' he said.

Jerry stared at him in astonishment. 'What a load of rubbish.'

'You work it out,' said Miss Brunner. 'Anyway, I think we're all too grown up for silly jealousies, don't you? The fact is, you agreed to do a job.'

'I thought you wanted...?'

'Your noumena? You must realise, Mr Cornelius, that you're getting a bit stale.' She became sentimental. 'You've done a lot of interesting work in your time, but you're past thirty now. Face up to it. You ought to be glad of any work.' She reached out a hand, but he avoided it. 'How much longer could you have lasted in Menton? You were fading yourself.'

'I think I'll go back to Menton, just the same.'

'You won't find much of it left,' she said with a self-satisfied smirk. 'I had to pull all sorts of strings to get you out, not to mention the deals I made with the French governments.'

'You'll have everything we can give you, to help,' said Bishop Beesley encouragingly. 'We're diverting a whole section of the grid for your use alone.'

Jerry shrugged. He had avoided the knowledge for too long. Now he didn't care. He was a has-been. 'I'll need some music,' he murmured pathetically.

'Oh, we've got all your old favourites.' Frank presented him with a case of tapes.

7

World

> 'Until Elizabethan days there had been a comparatively low level of national energy consumption.'

Jerry and the girl climbed the cracked steps, side by side. She was dressed as a nun, a Poor Clare; he was in his old Jesuit kit. The steps ended suddenly and Jerry pushed at the panel which blocked their way. They saw that the corridor beyond the panel was deserted and they climbed out, dusting down their habits. Jerry pushed the Rubens back into place. They found themselves surrounded by the tatty opulence, the vulgarity, of the Papal Palace itself. Commenting on it in a murmur, Jerry added: 'It was the main reason I finally copped out. Of course I was much younger then. And idealistic, I suppose.'

'Still,' she said consolingly, 'they offered you the research facilities you needed.'

'Oh, yes,' he agreed, 'I'm not knocking it.' He was pleased by the irony, that his last caper should take place where his first had begun. There would be no chance of resurrection, if this plan worked out.

Two cardinals went by, carrying small pieces of electronic gear. They whispered as they walked. As he and the girl approached a small side door, Jerry took some keys from his pocket. He stopped by the door, selected a key and slid it into the lock. It turned. They went into a cramped, circular room with a high ceiling.

The room was furnished with three chairs in gilt and purple plush, a brass table. On the table was a telephone. Jerry picked up the receiver, pausing until a voice answered in good, but affected, Italian.

'Could you tell him Cornelius is here?' asked Jerry politely, in English. He replaced the receiver and turned to the girl. 'We might as well sit down.'

They waited in silence for nearly half an hour before the Pope arrived through the other door. His thin lips were curved in a smile, his thin hands embraced one of Jerry's. 'So you made it, after all. You're not feeling good, Jerry?' He laughed. 'You look almost as old as me. And that's pretty old, eh? Is this your assistant?'

'Yes,' said Jerry.

'My child.' He acknowledged the girl who was staring at him in some astonishment; he spoke again to Jerry: 'There isn't much time.' He sighed, sitting down in the vacant chair. 'Ah, Jerry, I had such hopes for you, such faith. For a while I thought you were really Him...' He chuckled, dismissing his regrets. 'But you passed your chance, eh?'

'Maybe the next time round.'

'This is the last ride on the circuit for all of us, I fear.'

'That's my guess, too,' Jerry agreed. 'Still, we've had a good run.'

'Better than most.'

Jerry told him what was happening in the catacombs.

8

Earth

'The solar wind also distorts the magnetic field.'

Miss Brunner snarled. 'Judas!' she said. She had a Swiss Guard holding a naked arm each. 'Oh, you revert to type, you Corneliuses.'

'Common as muck,' agreed Captain Maxwell, his accent thickening.

'Do you mind?' asked Frank. He had been allowed to keep his raincoat on after it had been revealed what lay beneath it.

'Is there any chance of getting our clothes back, Your Holiness?' The bishop's tones were plummy and placatory.

'In your case,' said the Pope with a wave of his hand which made his rings sparkle, 'I'm not sure.'

'I hope,' said Captain Maxwell, 'that you don't think we were deliberately...'

'Stealing my power?' The Pope shrugged. 'It's an instinct with you, captain – like a rat stealing grain. I don't blame you, but I might have to pray for you.'

Maxwell shuddered.

'You are altruistic, Your Holiness,' began Bishop Beesley conversationally, 'and I am sure you recognise altruism in others. We are interested in the pursuit of knowledge for its own sake. It never occurred to us that we were so close to the Vatican City. If we had known...'

Only Miss Brunner preserved silence, listening with some

amusement to her colleagues' patently unconvincing lies; she contented herself with the odd glare in Jerry's direction.

The Pope settled himself comfortably in his throne. 'In a case of this kind, I'm afraid that the old-fashioned methods seem to be the best.'

'You'll make a lovely Joan of Arc,' said Jerry, but he was not really happy with the course that events had taken. He was feeling very lively, thanks to the transference jolts they had given him before they sent him on his mission.

'There's nothing in this for you, Mr Cornelius,' said Miss Brunner. 'I hope that's clear. You're all used up.'

'Recriminations aside,' murmured the Pope, rising again, 'I think I've worked out a practical scheme which should secure your repentance and further our own work here. Forgive me if I admit to having a concern for expediencies; my office demands it from me. Few of us can survive the present crisis, and it's my job to ensure the continuance of the Faith, by whatever means are available to me.'

'You people would pervert technology to the most superstitious, the most primitive ends imaginable.' Miss Brunner turned her rage upon the old man. 'At least I had the cause of Science at heart. And that –' directing her attention to Jerry once more – 'is what you've betrayed, Mr Cornelius.'

'Ah,' said the Pope, 'come in, my son.'

A fat Indian teenager waddled in. He had the dazed, self-important air of the partially lobotomised. 'The fog is getting thicker,' he explained. 'My plane was delayed. Hello, Mr Cornelius.'

'Guru.' Jerry took a packet of cigarettes from his cassock. 'Got a light?'

The Indian boy sighed and ignored the request. 'How does our work progress, Your Holiness?'

'I think we can expect it to go much faster now. For that we must thank Mr Cornelius.' The Pope beamed at Jerry. 'You will not be forgotten. This could mean a canonisation for you. Better than nothing, eh?' He signed to the guards. 'Please take the prisoners down to the input room.'

9

Mind

'But when it comes to psychological activity which apparently involves no physical movement whatsoever, we are hard pressed to state a satisfactory cause or energy source.'

An hour later, when he accompanied his new friends to the input room, Jerry found it hard to recognise his own brother, let alone the others. They all had the anonymity of the very old, the very senile. They quivered a little and made the electrode leads shimmy on their way to the central accumulator, but otherwise they were incapable of movement. Bishop Beesley's loose skin hung on his body like an old overcoat. Somewhere in the background came the sounds of the Deep Fix playing 'Funeral March', a big hit in the mid-seventies. This was by no means the first time Jerry had seen them die, but this was certainly the most convincing death he had witnessed.

Miss Brunner's washed-out eyes located him, but it was not certain that she had recognised him. Her shrunken lips moved, her grey skin twitched.

Jerry began to walk towards her, but the Pope held him back and went forward himself, cupping his hand around his ear as he bent to listen to her. He straightened up, an expression of gentle satisfaction upon his carefully cosmeticised features. 'She repents,' he said. The machines clicked and muttered, as if in approval.

Jerry took out his heater and gunned the guards down before they could lift their old-fashioned M16s into position.

'So you don't stand for Religion, either,' said the Pope. He fingered the complicated crucifix at his throat. 'And you don't stand for Science. You stand for nothing, Jerry. You are alone. Are you sure you have the courage for that?' He took a step, reaching a hand towards the gun. 'Consider...'

Jerry shot him through the crucifix. He sat down on the clean floor.

The Indian teenager's face bore the calm of absolute fear, a familiar expression which many, in the past, had mistaken for tranquillity of mind. He spoke mechanically. 'You must love something.'

'I love her,' said Jerry, with a movement of his head in the direction of the girl who stood uncertainly by the door. 'And Art,' he added with some embarrassment, 'the foundation for both your houses.' He grinned. 'This is for Art's sake.'

He shot the boy in his fat little heart. He put his gun away and drew the bomb from his cassock, activating it as he slapped it against the metal of the nearest machine. 'It's beautiful equipment,' he said regretfully, 'but it's useless now.'

He took the girl's hand in his and led her from the room. They did not hurry as they made their way back to the passage behind the Rubens, through the tunnel, through the toyshop and out into the dawn street.

He helped her into the car. 'How are you feeling?'

She dismissed his concern. 'Can you justify so much violence?'

He got into the driving seat and started the car. 'No,' he said, 'but it's become a question of degrees, these days, hasn't it? Besides, I'm an egalitarian at heart.'

'Won't this mean chaos?'

'It depends what you mean by chaos.' He drove steadily, at forty-five kph, towards the outskirts of the city. The rain had stopped and a pale, gold sun was rising in a cloudless sky. 'To the fearful all things are chaotic. That's how you get religion (and its bastard child, politics).'

'And science, too?'

'Their kind.'

She shook her head. 'I'm not convinced.'

He laughed, speeding up as they took the road to Tivoli, passing the ruined façades of a dozen defunct film studios. 'Neither am I.'

Behind them, Rome was burning. Jerry checked the position of the sun, he opened his window and threw the gun into the road. He kissed her. Then he began to head east. With a sigh, she closed her eyes and sank back into sleep.

(All quotes from *An Index of Possibilities*)

The Entropy Tango

(fragment)

Lyrics by Michael Moorcock

Music by Pete Pavli and Michael Moorcock

The Murderer's Song

'... and then, from that dungeon in the West,
There rises up a melody, beguiling and forlorn.
It is the sweet, sad, self-deceiving murderer's song,
And it will not end 'til morn...'

– Wheldrake,
The Prisoners

I

Baby Shot in Womb Survives

A baby girl has been born in a Belfast hospital with a gunman's
bullet lodged in her side, it was revealed last night. The baby
was born prematurely in the Mater Hospital late on Friday a
few hours after her mother was sprayed by shots from a passing car in Crumlin Road.

Sunday Times, 4 July, 1976

Rolling through the twisting twittens of his idea of Camelot, clad
in scarlet velvet stitched with an excess of gold thread, black fur
jumping on his head, flapping gallant's boots upon his feet, the
tune of some uncomplicated galliard slipping from tongue and
teeth, Romain de la Rose raised bottle to lips, revelling in the
effect which the alcohol was having upon his brain. 'Quite unself-
conscious!' He was amazed. The stuff was not at all disappointing.
Unlike so many things discovered from the ancient world, this
booze, this grog, this fruit of the vine was everything its original
inventors claimed. He sought control of his legs, his vision; he
failed. He saw a blank stone wall ahead. He fumbled for a power
ring, forgot his intention, and sat down.

Miss Una Persson, her co-ordinates as conservative as ever, had
landed in Camelot's central plaza. Until now the location had
been a deserted pine mine, an abandoned artefact of the Duke of
Queens. She had left her time machine (merely a gent's Royal
Albert black bicycle) where it was and had been stretching her legs
when she bumped into the inebriated re-creator of Arthur's
ancient seat – in a cul-de-sac he had not meant to invent.

Romain de la Rose was not one of Una's acquaintances at the
End of Time. His round blue eyes regarded her from handsome,

if plump, pink features. His legs moved a little, as if he were trying to regain his feet. He smiled at her. He studied her.

It was unusual for her to feel, these days, embarrassed. She wondered what was remarkable about her dark green military greatcoat with its red facings, the cavalry boots, the beret, which were her standard time-travelling costume.

She had already swallowed her translation pill. 'Excuse me,' she said, 'but until today this spot was always deserted.'

'The old ruin was yours?'

'Not at all. Although there was a sentimental attachment…'

He regained his feet; made a leg. Bottles fell from his pockets as he bent. They smashed on the flagstones (he wasn't sure if the flags were contemporary; he had chosen them primarily for their colours) and scents of whiskey, gin and Cinzano gathered under her nose. She took a backward step.

'My drunkenness is not to your taste?' He could be as sensitive to nuance as his friend Werther de Goethe.

'Ah…' She waved an ambiguous hand.

'I can produce any beverage.' Another bottle materialised. Sake.

She refused. 'This is the End of Time?'

'A chrononaut!' He began to fiddle with one of the power rings of his left index finger.

She reached to stop him. 'I've no desire to join your collection.'

'Forgive me.' He drew pink brows together. 'It was unbionic of me.' He explained. 'The appropriate slang for the period.' He indicated Camelot, its minarets, turrets and skyscrapers.

Una smiled and accepted the bottle. One sip. It was pure alcohol and could kill her. She spat politely and returned the sake. 'Have you any idea where I might discover the Duke of Queens? Or Lord Jagged, perhaps?'

'They're both adrift, I heard. In Time.' He made no further attempt at coherence. He sank down. He grinned, his head on one side. He hiccupped.

'There go my hopes,' said Una.

His lids fell.

She walked back towards her bicycle.

'Sometimes –' she spoke to herself – 'there seems no point at all in trying for a linear mode.'

2

Mystery Boy

A teenager was suffering from loss of memory yesterday after staggering off the beach at Polperro, Cornwall.

Daily Mirror, 6 July, 1976

Jerry Cornelius was peering at his chest, picking at his hairs. He held something up. 'Is that gangrene?' he asked her. 'Or egg?'

'Egg.' She was tired of rowing. She let the current take the boat, now that they were past Oxford's filthy ruins. He sat in the stern, the tiller lines over his thin, silk-clad shoulders. The shirt was dirty, as were his black velvet britches. There was a dash or two of blood on one sleeve.

'A lot of people resent me for that,' he told her, lighting a soiled Sullivans. 'My wounds heal so quickly.'

She yawned and leaned forward to take the cigarette from his lips. She still wore her greatcoat, although the temperature was in the nineties. The river was low. Consequently the rocks were higher. She puffed. 'Where to, now?' They peered together at the bank and the fire-blackened landscape beyond. 'I've never known it so quiet at this time of year.'

'It's the same everywhere,' he told her. He tried to get his cigarette back, but failed. He contemplated the slime at his feet.

As a concession, she put on a pair of government shades which gave her the appearance of a surprised lemur. He seemed to think this gesture significant, for he looked over his shoulder. 'Is anyone following us?'

'Probably not.'

He was disappointed. 'The freedom of pursuit,' he said. 'It's the only one we've got.'

As was normal of late, he had automatically assumed his Pierrot posture, just as she fell into the Harlequin mode. Back at base Columbine was controlling the Time Centre's operations as best she could. Catherine had always preferred to take the important passive rôles when they came up. She said she only thoroughly relaxed if typecast. Besides, she was still mourning her short-lived colleague, the American-Greek, Minos Aquilinas, who had been killed in the line of duty while on a visit to an obscure half-focused zone; some mythical twentieth-century Atlanta where a black emperor ruled over a Utopian Western Hemisphere. Aquilinas, who specialised as a metatemporal investigator, had been asked to look into the only case of suspected corruption in Atlanta in fifty years. Almost certainly he had been able to find confirming evidence and had been put out of the picture before he could pass his information on to the authorities. He had been the only Greek on regular call. Now Catherine would have to find a replacement.

'You'd better take over the oars,' said Una. She rose and rocked the boat.

Jerry was reluctant to move. 'I'm not well,' he complained. 'I was shot.' He frowned. 'Wasn't I?'

'You should be used to it. Row.'

He obeyed, muttering, taking her place and pulling on the oars with deliberate clumsiness. 'It's time I had a more important part. I used to be famous, you know, in some places. I was a living legend. Now I'm just a bloody stale joke.'

'Every dog has his day. And you've had yours.' She enjoyed being ruthless when he was in his moods of self-pity.

He continued to mutter. 'Apoca-bloody-alypse after apoca-bloody-alypse. Arma-fucking-geddon on Arma-fucking-geddon. I was promised a reward.'

'Heaven?'

'Full control.'

'Of heaven?'

'I thought that's what they all meant.'

'Con men like you, Jerry, are always the easiest men to con.'

'Shit!' His oars found mud. 'Oh, shit!' He hesitated on the edge of hysteria, eyeing her, wondering if he'd be able to get away with it. He withdrew the oar and pushed the boat further into the stream that had been the Thames. 'Are you sure this is the way to London?'

'It was.'

'Sod you!' He attempted to blame her for their predicament. His eyes filled with tears. 'Oh, sod you!'

'You were told you could have a spell of R and R, but you had to come and see the damage.'

'I always hated Oxford. Pater and that.'

'It was the hardest bloody gemlike flame I ever saw.'

'It happened so fast,' he said. 'I had my back turned.'

'It's the story of your life.'

Having failed to involve her, he improved his rowing. The landscape became brown and then an indeterminate green. Undamaged houses appeared on the banks. Children and stock-brokers gambolled on smooth lawns; tea-things clattered; women with well-bred voices called to their loved ones, terrifying Jerry so much that his speed doubled. They left the china, the deckchairs, the climbing frames, the garden hoses and sprinklers behind. Again the landscape grew black: stumps of trees, dark roots, and the smell.

'Oh, fuck,' said Jerry trembling. 'All that work. Everything wiped out except the middle classes.'

'They're like ants,' said Una, commiserating. 'They survive anything.' She chewed on some slices of meat.

'I've got to get away,' he said. 'Where did you leave the bikes?'

'You shouldn't rely on bikes.'

'You do.'

'That's habit, not reliance. There's a difference.' She became uncomfortable. 'I left them in Oxford. We'll have to go to London to get some new ones.'

Jerry cheered up at this admission of incompetence. 'We all make mistakes,' he said.

She rejected his attempt. 'Nobody makes as many as you.'

Relationships were, as always, breaking down as a result of the ambiguous nature of the disaster. She could not for the life of her determine the exact nature of the catastrophe. She felt guilty. 'I'm sorry.'

He shrugged, letting his intelligence through for an instant.

'Tropes,' he said. 'That's all. They might have a function, though. And all the time I thought I'd found Romance.'

3

Climbdown after Language Riots

South Africa yesterday gave in to demands to drop Afrikaans as the compulsory language to schools for black children – the cause of last month's bloody race riots in which 176 people died. In future the staff of black schools will be able to teach in English if they want to.

Daily Mirror, 7 July, 1976

'I suppose that my faith is based firmly on the principle that people are stupider than they look and talk,' said Una. She puffed on the cheroot which Catherine lit for her. They were on a verandah, facing the jungle. Various harsh-voiced birds blundered about in the foliage.

'That's not fair.' Catherine wore a sarong. She kissed Una's gauze-clad shoulder. 'Some people are very clever. Quite ordinary people.'

'That's indisputable.' Una lay back in the rattan chair and tried to see if there were any clouds in a sky only barely visible through the leaves. 'But it isn't what I said. That is, you didn't understand me.'

'You're not in a very democratic mood.' Catherine pushed sweaty blonde hair back from her face. 'Did you have a bad trip?' She glanced into the darkened interior of the bungalow. The instruments were operating normally. She was not really listening to Una's arguments. 'Feeling a bit élitist, eh? You're always like this when you come home.'

'Not at all. Experience shows that most people are thick. They are insensitive. They lack imagination. They are boring. I regard such qualities as pernicious.'

'They can't help it...'

'They can help it if they don't possess the decency, the humility, to realise what fools they are.'

'You used to try to encourage people to have self-confidence. You believed in Education and that.'

'I still do. I'm all for improving the tone, if not the quality, of life.'

Catherine signed to her poor brother Frank who mindlessly began to work the punkah with his big toe. She was anxious to cool Una down. Frank, dressed in a ragged pair of tennis shorts, his body covered in large sores of identical size and shape, smiled into the distance as he sat on one side of the bungalow's front door. Una continued:

'Most intellectuals are pretty stupid, which is why the education systems of the world remain so bad. A perfect system would reveal the best of us. Then we could do away with democracy which nobody really wants anyway. I know it's unfashionable, but we could certainly do with an intelligent intellectual élite running the world. Like in H.G. Wells or some of those others.'

'Nobody thinks that any more.' Catherine seated herself beside her friend. She stared with some dismay at the unchanging rainforest. 'Do they?'

'Not in the democracies,' said Una, 'only in the Marxist countries. And what lets them down, of course, is their puritanism, their certainties. Only idiots are certain of anything.'

'I can't disagree with you there.' Catherine took one of the glasses from the tray between them and sipped her julep through a big straw.

'Bugger democracy.' Una took the other drink. 'I'm fed up with it. It forces intelligent people to pretend to be stupid. What good does that do for anybody?'

'You're just disappointed things haven't worked out too well.'

'If you like.'

For an instant a great macaw perched on the verandah railing and regarded them through chilly black eyes before flying off into the jungle. It seemed to be laughing.

'In lieu of sane politics we're forced towards drama.' Una shifted her weight. 'But how many are prepared to admit we spend most of our lives in a fictive mode? We're all characters in a bad novel. The best we can hope for is to have some share in the writing.'

'But once we realise that, surely time travel becomes a possibility?' Catherine continued to stare at the forest. 'There are advantages.'

'Instinct forces us again and again towards catharses that are unnecessary and often destructive. But if one picks one's own ground, says goodbye to that sort of instinct; follows, perhaps, a higher, more human instinct, then one begins to smell freedom. Identity, time, the human condition, no longer enslave one. Then one can choose any slavery one desires, for as long as one desires it.' She removed the cheroot and threw it as far as she could towards a clump of magnolia trees of a particularly vulgar variety.

'You mean it all comes down to nothing more than a choice of slavery?'

'Don't expect too much of yourself,' said Una. 'Most of us seek only that. True freedom is terrifying. It involves a high risk of destruction.'

'And one's immortal soul?' Catherine smiled sardonically. 'You sound like any black magic fascist.' She sighed. 'I can't resist them.'

Una held firmly to her sad philosophy. 'You can see why the Arabs are astonished by the Jews. A race like that will do anything for a catharsis, no matter what the cost. Heaven save us from Zionism.'

As if summoned by an incantation Sebastian Auchinek showed his miserable face on the stoop. 'Am I the only one doing any work around here?'

Una smiled at an unsmiling Catherine. 'Don't worry, Seb. Glogauer will relieve you in an hour or two.' She sank back into the luxury of the cane, the cushions and the Campari-soda. She giggled at the expression of hopeless pain in Auchinek's martyred eyes.

4

The Hi-Joker

A man who hijacked a Libyan airliner on an internal flight was flown to Majorca yesterday. There he meekly gave himself up to police and surrendered his weapons ... two toy guns.

Daily Mirror, 7 July, 1976

'People seem to get angry about the silliest things.' Una put down the half-read paperback copy of Guy Boothby's *The Beautiful White Devil* and looked again at Auchinek's incoherent note to her. 'Can he survive in the jungle? What's the time in the outside world?'

'About 1070,' said Catherine. 'This part of the continent's virtually unpopulated, but there are all kinds of beasts.'

'I'll drink to that.' Una used the note to mark her place.

5

People

Dai Llewelyn, brother to Roddy (you know, Princess Margaret's friend), has been escorting three American girls around town. They're all black and from New York. 'They're my ethnic friends,' says Dai who is shortly going to America, and, I am told, will stay in their empty flat.

'The Inside World',
Daily Mirror, 7 July, 1976

Auchinek was weeping when they found him on the banks of a stagnant lagoon four miles from the Centre. 'You're all fascists.

Fucking fascists!' Leeches covered his neck, shoulders and upper arms. He had been trying to drown himself – lying on the shore and immersing his head – in his usual compromising fashion. Una took some salt from her kit and began to remove the creatures. Shadows moved in the jungle. Captain Bastable, in his khaki tropical kit, his solar topee on his fine crown, fiddled with the heavy dial of his Banning cannon, using all his strength to keep the weapon off the ground. He had forgotten to bring the stand. Una supposed it was unfortunate that Bastable had been the only member of personnel available for the expedition; his remarks about Jews had not gone down at all well with Glogauer or Auchinek in the canteen a few nights before. His attempts to explain that he 'meant no harm' and that his remarks didn't apply to 'an awful lot of Jews who are jolly good sorts' had made matters worse.

Una pulled off the last leech. Auchinek continued to swear at her. 'You're the kind of people who put Hitler in power!'

Bastable, of course, had no idea what Auchinek was talking about, since he didn't come from Auchinek's zone, but Una couldn't help telling the truth. 'As a matter of fact,' she said, 'I did.'

Auchinek fell silent.

'Everybody agreed later that he went too far,' she added.

Auchinek was shocked, disbelieving. 'You played a part in the Russian revolution!'

'That's right. But not the counter-revolution. The Bolsheviks kicked me out. What's that got to do with it? The Slavs have never been fond of Jews either, you know.'

'Oh, my God!' Auchinek shrieked. He loved Una. He still loved her.

'I am only stating facts,' she continued reasonably, helping him towards the trees. 'It's this way.' She supported him as he limped. 'You Jews always bring things down to a personal level.'

'Oh, Una! Una! Una!'

She looked sardonically at a bemused Captain Bastable and shrugged.

After they had returned to the bungalow and sedated Auchinek, putting him to bed, she confided to Catherine.

'It seems I'm getting up everyone's noses here. I'd better move on.

Catherine could only agree.

'There are times, Una, when you're less than tactful.'

6

Public Opinion

The Israelis are magnificent. They must be the only people in the world with the courage to deal with terrorists, hijackers, bombers, hooligans or the like. What a pity that this country cannot act in such a forthright manner. We used to, many years ago.

> – H.J. Smith,
> Banbury, Oxfordshire,
> *Daily Mirror*, 7 July, 1976

Shakey Mo Collier came running out of the blazing building with oil and blood all over his face, an M16 in his fearful hands, a grin on his face. From the upper floors of the building issued wailing of a kind Una hadn't heard since Kiev, 1919, during one of the pogroms which had relieved the tensions and uncertainties of the civil war for so many of the citizens. 'They nearly got me, Miss P. Christ! It's appalling in there...' He stood beside her, looking up, panting. 'I suppose there's nothing we can do for them now?'

'We've got to go.' She glanced at her calendar. The figures fluttered and died on the display panel. 'It's 1943. Only another three years before Einstein's Revenge. You have to hand it to them. They know how to get back at people.'

Mo was disapproving. 'Well, I call it discrimination.'

Una made an attempt to follow his logic. He was suffering from minor shell shock and would continue to do so for the rest of his days, no matter what part of the twentieth century he operated in.

'Reprisals are all very well,' Mo went on, 'but why take it out on the innocent?'

'We're all innocent,' said Una. 'We're all guilty. What does it mean?' She was in worse shape than he was.

7

People

Marlene Dietrich is to make her first appearance since before the Hitler era in Berlin where her stage career began more than half a century ago. But it is not purely a sentimental journey for Miss Dietrich, now 75. She is being paid £4,000 a show – plus expenses and travel.

Daily Mirror, 7 July, 1976

Jerry shuffled towards the gas-ring and took the aluminium pot from it, pouring coffee into two earthenware bowls. He was naked, but on a nail on the door of the room hung his white Pierrot suit, the black skull-cap.

'I haven't worked in two years,' he said. 'The drink.'

He was unshaven. The room smelled of urine and rotting food. Una had heard about it. She now held a handkerchief to her nose. The handkerchief was soaked in Mitsouko, her favourite perfume.

'You don't have to black up for this one,' she told him.

He showed a fraction of interest, explaining: 'It was those bloody Panthers gave the whole coon business a bad name. I blame them for the death of Vaudeville.'

'It wasn't just them,' Una said reasonably. 'It's like the boxing business. Improved educational opportunities lured the talent away.' She was being as conventional as possible. She still regretted opening up to Auchinek. 'Look at England. All those Irish and Pakistani jokes. No wonder they bombed the Palladium.'

'It was my first big break.' He sighed. 'I was going on the next day. Minimum of two weeks. Then the sods take out the venue. You must be able to understand why I'm so bitter.'

'I've had the same experience myself.' Una inspected his costume. It was covered in stains. 'You'll have to get this cleaned. I know what it's like. But it was probably all for the best.'

Jerry poured the last of his brandy into his coffee. 'You're going to pay my fare home, then? Things haven't been easy. Surabaya's a tough town to find work in.'

She chucked him under the chin. 'Mein Gott, and ich liebe dich so.'

He was not to be placated. 'Warum bin ich nicht froh?'

'Because you're not in your natural element. Because you're not doing the work which suits you best.' She ignored his coffee. 'Come on. There's a schooner waiting in the harbour.'

'I seem to remember a time,' he murmured, climbing into the Pierrot suit, 'when racialism was punishable by death. Where was that?'

She was on her knees, drawing his battered wickerwork suitcase from under the bed. 'Oh.' She was vague. 'That must have been before the war.'

8

Four Women Anarchists Escape

Four women anarchists, including Inge Viett, 32, whose release was demanded by pro-Palestinian hijackers in Uganda last week, escaped from a top security women's jail in West Berlin yesterday. Police are concentrating their search on border crossings.

Daily Telegraph, 8 July, 1976

Jerry as Pierrot and Una as Pierrette danced across the tiny stage erected on the beach at St Ives while behind the curtain Shakey

Mo, Catherine and Frank Cornelius played their banjos for all they were worth.

'Hello again! Hello again! We're here to entertain you!' Jerry and Una sang as brightly as possible to the four or five stern-faced children who so far made up their audience. They lifted their legs, they crossed their legs, they tap danced, they grinned.

Soon they were singing the last number of the show, the reprise of 'The Entropy Tango', at something more than twice its normal speed.

> For a while at least it's all right
> We're safe from Chaos and Old Night
> The Cold of Space won't chill our veins
> And Fimbulwinter's fazed again
> We have danced the Entropy Tango.

Now the curtain fell back and there was the entire ensemble to join in. Jerry and Una went to their respective corners and found their ukeleles, came back to the centre of the stage while Catherine, Frank and Mo formed up behind them.

> And it's kiss, kiss, kiss
> Fear and hate we have dismissed
> And it's wish, wish, wish
> For a better world than this...
> So say goodbye to pain and woe
> And we'll stop the Entropy Tango...

For the first time, the children began to clap enthusiastically, whistling, stamping their feet in the worn-out sand, yelling for more.

The company took its bow. It took several more. It gave them an encore.

'Well,' Jerry removed his skull-cap as the curtain fell. 'If we can get the same response from an adult audience this evening, we're on our way to the big time. It could mean a renaissance of the Concert Party.' He was panting. 'A comeback for Variety.'

'It's the variety I miss,' said Frank vaguely. A little saliva inched down his chin.

9

Amin Alert on Air Raid that Never Was

President Amin yesterday mobilised Uganda to face what he
said was imminent attack from the air. At the same time reports
in East African capitals indicated that Col. Gadaffi, the Libyan
leader, had stepped in to restore the strength of the shattered
Ugandan Air Force. The dramatic warning broadcast over
Radio Uganda early yesterday and repeated throughout the
day was made by a military spokesman – generally believed to
be President Amin himself. He said that 30 Israeli and American warplanes were approaching Uganda from Kenya and that
they had been picked up on radar.

Daily Telegraph, 8 July, 1976

Success had given Jerry a bloom which Una found sickening. She
discovered him checking his heat in his hotel room and waited
until he had finished. He slipped the needler into the shoulder holster and grinned at her. 'Tasty,' he said.

'Tasteless, I'd call it. What a vulgar little wanker you are! Now
that the show's over, where are you going?'

'Tel Aviv, I thought. Some unfinished business.'

'Not you too! Auchinek's there.'

'So I understood.' He pulled on his well-tailored black velvet
jacket. 'How do I look?'

'Handsome,' she said disapprovingly. 'When are you coming
back to work?'

'I'll be working over there.' He winked. He was cheeky. He was
loathsome. 'I've got four weeks at the Tel Aviv Apollo and then, if
I'm lucky, another fortnight at the Sydney Steak and Opera House.
Auchinek says that it's almost certain I'll be picked to represent
Israel in next year's Eurovision Song Contest.' He opened his
wardrobe and chose a striped tie. 'Then it's on to South Africa.'

'So you're selling out?' She sank onto his neat bed.

'Not exactly. Buying in, really.' He knotted the tie about his throat. 'I'm grateful to you, Una. You restored my confidence.'

'Heaven forbid!'

'I had to take the jobs offered. You weren't exactly specific.'

'You can't afford to be.'

'That's the difference between us, Una. I believe in positive action. Cutting through the ambiguities.'

'All that attitude produces is further complications.'

'Complications aren't necessarily ambiguities, though. Life is action.' He condescended to kiss her. The kiss was cold on her forehead. 'I'll never forget what you've done.'

But it was evident he had already forgotten. That was what made him a survivor of sorts.

10

Pretoria to be White by Night

Building will start next April of hostels to house 26,000 to 30,000 Black Africans miles outside Pretoria the South African capital so that the city can be 'white by night'. The scheme will cost millions of pounds and is due to be completed by 1983. Each hostel will accommodate about 1,000 men. All Blacks who are not considered officially to be key workers in the White area – such as those in hotels, hospitals, old people's homes, blocks of flats – will be affected.

Daily Telegraph, 8 July, 1976

Una's co-ordinates were evidently out. The whole landscape was seething, semi-liquid. Terrifying shapes formed and disappeared. Armies of half-human figures rode through billowing black smoke and hungry flame. Confronting them, on a rearing stallion, a white-faced warrior in dark baroque armour lifted a shrieking sword to the skies, voicing a challenge in a rich, lilting language only vaguely familiar to her. She remounted her Royal

Albert and began to pedal as fast as she could, studying the instrument strapped to her left wrist. It told her nothing. Chaos controlled everything. She was drifting. She concentrated and reset the speedometer on her bike. Gradually the world turned to ice and became peaceful. Somewhere in the distance a huge clipper ship raced by. She considered trying to reach it, but her tyres would not grip the ice. Again, she reset her instruments and a burning wind seized her. She was in a desert and above her the sun was small, dull red. In this world, the society at the End of Time had almost certainly failed to flourish. She went sideways through the Shifter, desperately. She knew what was happening to her now. She pulled herself together, hitched up her greatcoat and pedalled as fast as she could. The bike crossed the desert and reached a thick, salt sea. Her concentration faltered. She tried again. Her attempts to get back to her original base had been foolish; she had been too long away from it. Linear logic was virtually a mystery to her now. The larger world beckoned. She accepted it. It was what she had always wanted. She gave up her soul.

Auchinek, in tweeds, came running towards her across a lawn. 'Una! We thought we'd lost you.'

'Fat chance,' she said. 'Hello, Seb. Nice to see you.' Behind him was a large country mansion, probably Georgian, with the usual offensive Adam flourishes. There were ornamental hedges, yews, cypresses, poplars, creating a pleasant Romantic landscape. 'Is this your new house?'

'Do you like it?' He flung an arm around her shoulders, wheeling the bike for her with his free hand.

'It suits you.'

'Thanks.' He took a deep breath of his air.

'I thought most of these places were owned by Arabs, these days.'

'Oh!' He was expansive, relaxed. 'There's still a few of the original old Jews left, you know.'

Frank Cornelius came shuffling through the gravel of the wide drive. He had a scythe in one hand and a bucket in the other. He touched his cap as they passed. 'Evening, squire.'

Sebastian Auchinek took Una through the French windows and into the library, showing her his Buchan first editions, his collection of Chesterton manuscripts, his illustrated Tolkiens and Lewises. 'And for politics –' He knew her tastes. He drew back a velvet cloth to reveal a case. 'Beaconsfield manuscripts!'

She was disappointed. 'No Marx.'

'For what?' He became agitated and replaced the velvet. 'What do you mean?'

'Nothing. Honestly.'

'Catherine's here. And Jerry, of course. It's going to be quite a weekend. Maxwell's coming down from London. Feet, and Tome, and Markham will represent the arts. The Nyes live quite near and they've promised to call over on Sunday. There's not much shooting, but there's plenty of fishing.' They entered a cool hall. 'And I know you like riding. You must ask the groom to pick you out a horse. I'd recommend the chestnut filly.' They walked into a sunny room full of soft furniture covered in some sort of tapestry work. A dark-skinned servant was already pouring tea into thin cups. Bishop Beesley, in purple and black, rose from his chair, a large slice of yellow seed cake in his chubby hand. 'Miss Persson. Such a long time.'

'It doesn't seem it, bishop.'

From the security of her sofa, his daughter Mitzi regarded Una with naughty eyes. 'So you've turned up,' she said. She licked a crumb or two from her thin, experienced lips.

'It's a good old reunion,' said Auchinek with considerable innocence.

II

The Ambassador of Israel, Mr Gideon Rafael

unable to reply individually to the stream of messages, wishes to thank the great many well-wishers who expressed, by telephone, telegram, or by letter, their congratulations and rejoicing at the rescue of the hijacked hostages held captive by terrorists in Entebbe.

Ad, *Daily Telegraph*, 8 July, 1976

Catherine, Jerry and Una lay cuddled together in the huge four-poster. Candlelight filled the room with shadows. It was about three in the morning and outside, on the lawn, peacocks were hooting. It was this noise which had awakened them all from their semi-slumber.

'I'm thirsty.' Jerry, after his Oxford experience, had become rather more attractive again. 'Do you think there's any sort of room service, Una?'

'I doubt it. But one of us could go down and get some drinks from the cabinet. Or the kitchen, perhaps.'

'I'm not going downstairs on my own!' Jerry was adamant. 'Christ. I've seen too many thrillers on telly. You know what happens to the first one.'

'We could all go,' suggested Catherine.

'I'm not thirsty.' Una was too tired to move. Her recent experiences had taken a great deal out of her. She stared stupidly at Jerry's clothes, piled on the floor near her. She saw that he still had his weapons. 'Take a gun.'

'And get blamed when I find the corpse in the library? Not likely!' Jerry was openly contemptuous. 'I'm too fly for that.'

'Oh, sod. I'll go.' Catherine began to climb out of the tangle of sheets. 'Blimey, you don't half sweat a lot these days, Jerry.'

'That wasn't me,' he said. 'It was Una.'

'I never sweat.' She sat up, offended. 'Not that much, anyway. It must have been you, Jerry.'

'I don't sweat. Not at the moment. Really.'

'Well, it must have been me,' said Catherine, to keep the peace as usual.

'It was him,' said Una.

'It bloody wasn't.' Jerry was on his knees facing her. 'Smell it! That's your Mitsouko. It reeks of it.' He held up part of a sheet.

'Just because it smells of my perfume doesn't mean it was my sweat,' said Una evenly. 'You little shit. What are you trying to put over?'

'It was me!' cried Catherine, falling between them. 'Me! Me! Ahhh!'

The door had opened. Sebastian Auchinek, in dressing gown and slippers, stood there. He looked horrified. 'Oh, Una!'

'I'm sorry, Sebby. We got carried away.'

'Oh, Christ.' Una reached towards him as Jerry and his sister slowly got off the bed and rose to their feet.

Auchinek raised his arm. There was something in his hand. Una pulled the sticky sheet over her head. 'Go away, the lot of you! Vampires!'

There came a movement, a sound, then a strong smell of burning meat. She sat up. In the doorway was Auchinek's quartered corpse. There was no blood, just blackened edges to the wounds. Jerry had used his heater. A box lay near Auchinek's hand. From the box spilled some sort of jewellery. A gift.

Jerry began to apologise. Una rounded on him. 'You knew it wasn't a weapon!'

Jerry began to sulk. 'What if I did? It could have been.'

'He hardly ever used one.'

'Just the fucking eyes. Just the fucking guilt.' Jerry holstered the heater. 'I couldn't stand it. He wasn't going to pull that one on me again. I remember when he could handle a machine gun with the best of them. In Macedonia. In Chile. In Kenya. But he couldn't keep it up. He fell back on old tricks. And they didn't work for him. Not this time.'

'This always happens,' said Una, 'when you're around.' The smell was sickening her. 'Poor Sebby.'

'He'll pop up again. You'll see.'

'It's sordid.'

'He set the rules.' Jerry was unrepentant. 'Everything else led from there.'

'How can you say that? You sound like some bloody Palestinian. You fought beside him in the Irgum Tsva'i Leumi. Remember your pledge – to kill every British man, woman or child in Palestine if they wouldn't leave? Does 1947 mean nothing to you?'

Jerry couldn't remember. It was only Una who seemed to worry about keeping track of events. He blinked. 'When?'

Catherine was puzzled. 'But you were on the other side, weren't you, Una?'

'Somebody has to be. The status quo...'

'Ah, of course,' said Jerry. 'But that's what I'm into, too, Una.' He bent to pick up the box. 'Are these real diamonds?' He held them to the light. 'Look at the facets. Look how they sparkle, Una.'

He had won her over. She joined him to stare into the gems.

'He was a self-righteous little bugger, after all.'

12

Widow Disappears from Amin Hospital

A 75-year-old grandmother, Mrs Dora Bloch, has disappeared in Uganda after being caught up in the Entebbe skyjack affair. Her potentially ominous disappearance has led to a diplomatic row between Britain and Uganda. Mr Ted Rowlands, Minister of State, said in the Commons yesterday that it was causing 'grave concern'. Mr James Hennessy, the British High Commissioner to Kampala who was on leave in Britain, has been ordered to fly to Uganda immediately to seek the release of Mrs Bloch who has dual British-Israeli nationality.

Daily Telegraph, 8 July, 1976

'My dear Miss Persson!' Lord Jagged of Canaria, tall and grave in his yellow finery, looking somewhat gaunt, brought the huge swan that was his air car down over the bluff where she stood supporting her Royal Albert by its saddle and handlebars. 'I received your message and came as soon as I could. Time, you know, presses at present. How beautiful you are!' He stepped down beside her and dismissed the swan. He bowed. He kissed her hand. He was irresistible, bearing, as he did, the nobler characteristics of his large family. 'You came earlier?'

'Briefly.' She smiled. 'You are weary?'

'Less so, now that we meet.' A movement of a power ring and he provided their picnic. There were salads, meats, champagnes.

She lowered her bicycle and sat down beside the cloth. He joined her. Another kiss. This time to the cheek. Another, gently, to the lips. 'Una.'

'My darling Jagged.' It was impossible for them to keep a liaison for more than an hour or two at a time. The chronic megaflow denied them anything but that.

'I've little gossip for you today,' he said. He reached for an avocado. 'My own affairs take me away from society. But I heard that the Duke of Queens fought a duel, recently.'

'A duel? Here?'

'A droll episode.'

'Someone was killed?'

'In a sense.' He began to speak of the affair, but it was evident that he made an effort. When he had finished she did not press him for details. 'And you?' he enquired. 'Are you active, still? And fulfilled?'

For his sake she was bright. 'In general, yes.'

'Generalities,' he said, almost to himself, 'are all we have, of course, at the End of Time. I envy you your specifics.'

'They blur. Everything blurs.'

'Perhaps that is Time's most attractive function, eh?' He seized a tiny melon, then a nectarine. The shadow of his circling swan fell across the meal.

'Soon,' he murmured, 'I must leave.'

'Your experiments? Are they successful?'

'They are interesting. I dare not say more.'

'I'll wish you luck, though, I think.'

He inclined his head.

'So the Duke of Queens continues to encourage Romance at the End of Time.'

'This is a world of Romance.' He laughed. 'Of generalities, as I said. Sometimes I envy you your realities.'

'They are no less romantic, I suppose.'

'Everything is a matter of attitudes, in the long run. Of interpretation.'

The shadow returned. He stood up. 'You have eaten enough?'

She nodded.

He dissipated the picnic. He sighed. The swan descended. Fingers touched, lips were joined. 'I will get a message to you,' he told her, 'if I am successful.'

'To the Time Centre,' she said. 'You can always reach me here, I hope.'

'Very well.' He had boarded the swan. It swung upwards into dark blue air.

Una was smiling as he departed. She stooped to recover her bicycle, bouncing it on its tyres to rid it of the dust. She glanced at her wrist. Her instruments were giving stable readings for the moment. She did not mount her machine immediately, but strolled with it along the edge of the bluff, looking out over the brilliant gold, scarlet and blue of the plain below. The patterns were mysterious and it was impossible to guess what the creator of the design had planned.

She swung her leg and seated herself on her saddle. She began to pedal, making adjustments to the dials on the handlebars. Soon she was on her way through Time again, pursuing her lonely, optimistic explorations; searching for one world where tolerance and intelligence were paramount and where they existed by design rather than by accident.

The End of Time fell away behind her, closed, and all the

Earth's history opened up before her as she rode, singing, along the megaflow:

> 'Oh, it's up the trope I go, up I go
> It's up the trope I go, up I go
> It's up the trope I go –
> And the crowd all down below
> Sez – girl, we told you so!
> God damn their eyes!
> God blast their souls!
> To bloody hell!'

The Gangrene Collection

I

The Real Sickness

When he said that people at risk from AIDS were 'swirling around in a human cesspit of their own making', James Anderton, Chief Constable of Manchester, used strong language but uttered the broad truth.

AIDS is, as he said, 'a self-inflicted scourge' ... Free needles will not stop the rot, nor will free contraceptives. The rot is the permissive society itself.

Daily Mirror, 17 December, 1986

Jerry Cornelius crossed the last vision of the future from his list and settled back to watch the end of civilisation as they knew it. It was good to be relaxing again. All in all, it had been a nasty little century.

Una Persson, trying to revive Jerry's mother where she lay on the concrete, still heaving, between a waterlogged sofa and the wall, offered him a look of weary resentment. 'Mrs C! Mrs C! Don't swallow it!' But the old Cockney merely grinned to herself then uttered a confident burp before slipping back into comfy oblivion.

'I wish to God you'd never thought of London.' Una tried to lug the antique Lee-Enfield from under Mrs Cornelius's bottom. 'I can't believe that even you think this is Paradise.'

Jerry rubbed an uncertain lip.

2

Health risk as Pollution levels rise

A mobile 'dirty air' monitoring unit recorded pollution levels
way above health guidelines in London today.

Evening Standard, 11 December, 1989

The Green Revolution successfully aborted, Jerry was looking
forward to a new golden age where the middle-class terror of
change (now officially called Amis' Syndrome) no longer dominated the city of his birth, where Technology might at last take its
true place as the first of the Graces. Here, at the centre, where
glorious new architecture was adding to the city's revivifying variety, he exposed himself to the entire Barbican before he fell
giggling amongst the cardboard boxes he had made his castle and
his monument.

'Mr Cornelius, pull yourself together.'

It was the voice of the Jolly Englishman himself. The air took
on a distinctive smell.

'Mr Cornelius! It won't do, you know.' This second voice from
the sky had learned to lose its frightened Midlands upwardly
mobile whine in a tone very much resembling authority – at least
the authority of a powerful schoolmistress whose flock was used
to terrified obedience.

'Bonk!' said Mrs Cornelius from her cave of egg-crates. 'Oo-er,
it's the vicar!' And she grunted.

'Mr Cornelius! We need your expertise!'

But Jerry was already moving, his scrawny legs carrying him
through débris and over sleeping bodies until he was able to mingle
with the firstnighters attending the première of *Adolf & Eva* which,
in its pretence at bad taste, was already getting rave reviews from
critics who liked to think they had courage. From the ramparts he
heard Una's disgusted shout. 'You cowardly little bastard.'

In the dark sky, the chopper pulsed. It sounded hungry.

3

Fortress Killing

A 23-year-old painter and decorator was yesterday convicted of the manslaughter of his middle-aged neighbours, who died trapped in their blazing home because they had turned it into a fortress to protect themselves from burglars.

The Independent, 10 Nov, 1989

Dodging and weaving, Jerry reached the outer walls of 'Blitzworld', created from the newly airstruck Docklands and returned to the days of her glory when she had blazed under the Nazi air fleet but never died.

'Blitzworld' was his current favourite of all the alternatives now available, isolating and containing his nostalgia without ever letting it contaminate reality. 'Parliamentworld', 'Newsworld', 'Marketworld', 'Cockneyworld' and 'Mayfairworld' all had their attractions, as had 'Blackworld', but of all London's boroughs (now retitled entertainment zones) 'Blitzworld' offered him the most.

Showing his pass, he entered the fire-blackened gates and escaped with relief into the Spirit of the War. From a freshly smoking crater came the sounds of happy camaraderie as punters shared their flasks of tea and thin sandwiches, breaking into a Vera Lynn medley at the drone of the air-raid siren. Setting his ARP helmet at a jaunty angle, Jerry looked about for something to loot.

'Coming in,' chorused the celebrants, 'on a wing and a prayer.'

This sentimental, co-operative, egalitarian future had been one he had been reluctant to see go, but it had already been stolen by Home Counties yuppies before it could get started. 'Say wot yer like, Jer,' his mum had said, 'them buggers reelly know 'ow ter turn yer emotional investments inter cash.'

He was still a little resentful that his own scheme, for 'Nukeworld', had been rejected on grounds of cost.

4

Green Guru summoned to No. 10 for Secret Talks

The Prime Minister has held a secret Downing Street meeting with Mr Jonathan Porritt, director of the environmental group Friends of the Earth, as part of the Government's growing embrace of green policies.

Sunday Telegraph, 10 December, 1989

Major Nye was looking at the afternoon broadcast from 'Parliamentworld'. 'My God, old boy, what frightful bounders these chaps all are!' His faint, grey moustache twitched once.

'Well...' Jerry expressed a tolerance beyond words. 'You know...'

The old soldier pulled himself to his feet. 'It's an odd place, London, these days. As if it hasn't settled down properly yet.'

Gloomily, Una Persson was cleaning her new M16 in the corner of the Blenheim Crescent basement. She paused, unable to miss the opportunity of a moral. 'London's become a mere monument to her own greed.'

'It's just a transition,' said Jerry lamely and turned towards the light... 'Oh, look, it's starting to rain.'

The Romanian Question

Dreams To Remember

All that day the train travelled at high speed westwards, through
Roumania. It did not stop, but slackened speed slightly as it
passed through the larger towns en route. Only the higher officials of the Roumanian main railway line knew of the passage
of the special, heavily-screened train, its destination or its pas-
sengers. Towards midnight, the Yugoslav frontier lay only a few
miles ahead. As the lights of Timisoara, capital city of Banat,
the rich wheat province of Western Roumania, began to glow
through the darkness, the driver sounded the engine whistle to
warn the station of his approach. The train slowed down to
pass through. Just as it left the station platform and was again
gathering speed, sharp flashes and the staccato cracks of rifle
fire burst from the thick undergrowth of the steep embank-
ments by the side of the railway track. Bullets spattered sharply
against the steel framework of the carriages and crackled
against the reinforced glass of the windows. The driver quickly
accelerated and the train shot forward at full speed towards
Yugoslavia – and safety. The would-be assassins, it was discovered later, were members of the Iron Guard, the Fascist
terrorists of Roumania who, at the behest of Adolf Hitler, had
brought about the downfall of King Carol, brought his realm
to ruin and degraded it to the level of a province of Nazi
Germany.

– A.L. Easterman,
King Carol, Hitler and Lupescu, 1942

Mourning the excessive fantasies of an unhappy celibacy, Jerry
Cornelius split with some feeling from the Carpathian convent
where, for the past few years, he had been holing up. Life looked
to him as if it might just be worth living again. Eastern Europe

was perking with a vengeance. Though it had to be said, some people were already waving goodbye to their first flush of Ruritanian innocence.

'My view of the matter, Mr C., is that we should've nuked the bastards where it hurts.' In middle age Shakey Mo Collier was growing to resemble the more disturbed aspects of Enoch Powell. His pedantry had a tendency to increase as his enthusiasm faded and Mo, Jerry thought, was nothing without his enthusiasms. He blew Mo a kiss for old times' sake and climbed into his coat-of-many-colours, his leather check. It still had the smell of a hundred ancient battles, most of them lost. 'Down these mean malls a man must shop.' He checked his credit the way he had once checked his heat. These were proving easy times for him. But he missed the resistance. Who had given him all this unearned power whilst he slept?

It was then that he realised he had dozed out a class war in which the class he had opposed, his adoptive own, had won back everything it had seemed to lose and now had no further ambition but to maintain its privileges with greater vigilance than last time. He was the unwilling beneficiary of this victory. He became confused, too sick to spend. He felt his old foxy instincts stirring. He grew wary. He grew shifty. He stepped back.

I'm Still Leaving You

What Jessica Douglas-Home observed as she touted the polling booths with her interpreter and driver was that only members of the Salvation Front were represented at the polling stations. Opposition members had everywhere been prevented from turning up. Opposition workers reported posters torn down and offices ransacked, even by the police. Opposition newspapers were mislaid or destroyed and despite a decree that campaigning must stop two days before the election, there was the last-minute distribution of a free newspaper publishing photographs of all the official candidates. 'Every one from the Ceausescu era,' says Jessica sadly. 'Simply a game of musical chairs.'

Sunday Telegraph, 27 May, 1990

The time machine was a sphere of milky fluid attached to the front lamp-holder of a Raleigh Royal Albert Police Bicycle of the old, sturdy type, before all the corruption had been made public. Jerry hated the look and feel of the thing, but he needed to take a quick refresher in 1956, to see if some of the associations made sense. At the moment, as he wiped the Bucharest dust from his handlebars and checked his watches, he was downright terrified.

Was it just the threat of liberty which alarmed him, or was the world actually on the brink of unimaginable horror as, in his bones, he feared? He shuddered. Whatever they might say, he had never relished the worst. Especially when the best seemed so much more within his grasp.

Yet this was the dangerous time. It always was. 'As power-holders lay down their arms, those who have known little power are quick to seek advantages.' Prinz Lobkowitz bent to pump up the front tyre, his wispy grey hair falling over eyes in which humour sought to disguise the concern he felt. 'And there is nothing to say they won't abuse that power as thoroughly as their predecessors down the centuries. It's the same in the Middle East. Most of these people have never experienced anything like the familiar democracy of the West. They have no faith in it. They have been supplied with myths which prove how degenerate and immoral it was. These are deeply conservative people. They worship their ignorance since that was all of their religion that was left to them. They defend their ignorance as others might defend a principle.'

'Sometimes you don't sound a lot different from the party hacks.' Jerry gave the front wheel an experimental bounce. 'That's a lot better. Thanks.'

Prinz Lobkowitz fitted the pump back on the frame. 'They are all shades, I suppose.'

Jerry got the bike into the proper rhythm and was gone before he could say goodbye. The pearly grey mist opened before him. It was good to be on the move again. He only hoped no-one had changed the old megaflow routes.

This would not be the best moment to be lost in Time, though God knew, it looked as if the whole of England was now in that situation. He had never imagined a future as miserable as this. He had thought the Sex Pistols had meant something more than a trend in T-shirts. They had all been bought over by lifestyle magazines.

He gazed wonderingly back at this unbearable future and found himself suddenly in a coffee bar in Soho talking to someone called Max, who waxed his moustache and wore a pointed beard, about Jesse Fuller and Woody Guthrie. These were the years of private obsession, of small groups of enthusiasts never acknowledged by the common media, not even *Melody Maker* which was full of Duke Ellington and referred to Elvis only on the cartoon page. 'This was before your enthusiasm became the common currency of the sixties,' said a Shade, 'and you thought you had achieved a better world. Then you sold it back to them for shares in Biba, Mary Quant and Ann Summers, just as they merged with the City.'

'Humbug!' Jerry desperately attempted to disengage from a morality he thought he'd discarded years before. 'I don't want any of this. Where's my mother?' She would understand. He had missed total immersion. When he was this aware of actuality, he tended to retreat in every complex way he knew. Time experienced at such relentlessly close quarters gave him the heebie-jeebies. He shivered. 1956 had been bad enough without this as well.

It was time to split again.

I Ain't Drunk

In the case of Roumania and King Carol, Goebbels had a superb opportunity to demonstrate his perverted talents. Ten years' experience as Hitler's supreme disseminator of calumny and hatred had made him master of every trick and twist of this iniquitous profession. Since he had made the science of Jew-baiting with the poison pen his speciality, he found no difficulty in applying his evil genius to the peculiar conditions prevailing in Roumania where, for many decades, the 'problem' of the Jews had been raised to a front rank political issue.

King Carol, Hitler and Lupescu

But the sixties and seventies made him cry. He couldn't stand the sense of loss. How had they all been persuaded to hand their keys back to their jailers?

Was freedom really so frightening?

Evidently a lot of Romanians thought so.

Born in Georgia

President Ion Iliescu pledged yesterday to keep Romania on the road to democracy and to end what he called the country's moral decay.

Reuter/Majorca Daily Bulletin, 21 June, 1990

'Don't tell me!' Jerry smiled at the air stewardess as she laid her towel at the edge of the pool. He leaned his arms beside it and tried to drag his pale body higher from the water of Tooting Bec Baths. 'You're psychic too!' Her answering sneer would have sunk the *Bismarck*. 'I knew it!' Jerry was in a fairly insensitive mood that afternoon. 'I like your taste in boob-tubes,' got him reported to the lifeguard, and 'Come fly with me' thrown out of the pool area.

As he slouched off across Tooting Common, whistling to his horrible dog, he wondered if his grandma was home from work and maybe good for half-a-crown, or at least a bag of toffees (she did half-time at Rowntree's). He jumped further backward until he was comfortably unaware of his free movement through Time and was able to turn his attention from the stewardess, still baffled by his sixties slang, to the toy-soldier shop back near St Leonard's Church in Streatham Hill, a few minutes' walk up the main road and down towards the Common. He wanted to make sure his naval gun-team was still there. He'd given the man 9d a week for it and he was only another 1/6d away; but he couldn't be sure of anything any more. Was he creator or the created? This unlikely thought made him pop into the quiet of the church and glare with some respect at the stained-glass prophets whom he now completely confused with God. For him, God had become a plurality of saints and angels. He'd had Rudolf Steiner to thank for that. Jerry – or someone like him – grinned into the dusty shadows of the Anglican sacristy. There was nothing left to steal.

Jerry tipped his hat to the new generation and turned back to his toys.

Two more weeks and he could land a team on Forbidden Island. His sailors almost within his grasp and the summer sun melting the sweet tar of Streatham, he sauntered down towards Norbury and Jennings' second-hand bookshop where he planned to trade his wholesome volume of *The Captain* for a novel called *Monsieur Zenith* by Anthony Skene, his current literary favourite and inventor of Zenith the Albino, the smoothest crook that ever smoked an opium cigarette. It was Jerry's ambition to smoke an opium cigarette as soon as possible. His elders by a year had already ventured Up Town to Soho and found it good.

Meanwhile, let some other Jerry carry West London for a while. He was settling down in the South. Here only Teddy Boys lay in wait for you with razors. Anything was better than Blenheim Crescent's mephitic presence...

But thought is resurrection. He found himself struggling to force his mother back into non-existence. Mrs Cornelius was unperturbed. She, of all people, was bound to survive. There wasn't a holocaust made that could get her. 'Why don' cher come 'ome, Jer?'

He gave up. With pouting reluctance he wheeled his big, heavy bike up the hill and down towards Elgin crescent. He was back in Notting Dale, immediately post-Colin Wilson. His bid for some other, less melancholy, past had failed again. Somewhere, he heard his Shade saying, I was happy once.

These weren't the kind of losses he had expected.

Midnight Drive

As usual in the Nazi propaganda of subversion, Goebbels did not scruple about consistency in his scurrilities with regard to Madame Lupescu, the king's companion of twenty years. Some of his 'stories' represented her as the instrument of 'capitalist profit-mongers, concessionaires and exploiters', others contained plausible tales to show she was the agent of 'international Bolshevism'. Contradiction of this kind never worried the Minister of Propaganda and Enlightenment. Hitler had laid down, in *Mein Kampf*, his fundamental principle of good political tactics and propaganda – the bigger the lie, the more easy its acceptance, the more effective its result.

King Carol, Hitler and Lupescu

'Eat yer tea, Jer. I'll be back in abart an 'ar.' Mrs Cornelius settled her hat and contemplated benevolently the slices of bread and Marmite, the Mars bar she had laid out for her son. 'There's some Tizer in ther cupboard.'

With the air of a mother who had more than fulfilled her duty she left for the Blenheim Arms.

Jerry took pleasure in his food. It was one of his favourite meals. The area door opened and he saw Old Sammy put his hesitant head into the room. 'Wotcher, young 'un. Ma in?'

'Pub,' said Jerry. 'Can I come and watch your telly later, Sam?'

''Course you can, lad.' Old Sammy was grateful for anyone willing, for whatever reasons, to accept his affection.

I Beg Your Pardon

Speaking after his inauguration in Bucharest's Atheneum concert hall, Iliescu was unapologetic about his government's role in dealing with street protests last week, although he admitted there had been excesses.

Reuter/Majorca Daily Bulletin, 21 June, 1990

The manners of these people, with their casual discourtesies and easy racialism, soon made Jerry as uncomfortable with the fifties as he had been with the eighties. What had changed? He was getting fazed again, almost as bad as he had become by the early sixties. 'Arse that way, elbow that,' he told himself ritualistically as he made his cautious progress – some lemming to its cliff – back to his Royal Albert.

He was experiencing a certain amount of deterioration. As he pedalled, the mist grew warm and began to stink, reminding him of the wartime factories of Newcastle, of heavy locomotives panting in the steely evening light; the only colour the vivid flames of furnaces and mills. He had no idea where he was.

'Time travel had for too long been a matter of instinct, its secrets the province of romantic bohemians and crazed experimenters.' Bishop Beesley spoke from somewhere at the centre of his steam-driven orrery, from some unlearned future. 'It's high time we brought System and Intellect to the Question of Time.' He pronounced some reasonable imitation of what he guessed was the current mode. Or was it post-mode now?

Jerry was beginning to sense his bearings. Somewhere from the late eighties he heard a howl of terrible xenophobia as a thousand intellectuals turned their hatred on the Unavoidable Present and many thousands of Moslems expressed their anger with two hundred years of insult which they had previously pretended to themselves was only the province of the ignorant and ill-educated amongst their neighbours.

I'd Rather Go Blind

Next day it was announced that the government had decided to form a new 'Party of National Regeneration', a fusion of all political parties into one 'National Renaissance Front'. There was no specific abolition of the former political factions, but by clear and unmistakable inference, they ceased to exist. Henceforth, Roumania was to be a One Party State whose principal members were to be nominated and whose purpose was to be 'the Defence of the Fatherland'. The leader of the new Single Party was King Carol. Elections would be held, it was stated, but only candidates approved by the Single Party leaders and declaring allegiance to it, would be permitted to seek the votes of the electors...

King Carol, Hitler and Lupescu

'All we have to remember now, Mr Cornelius, is that many of our new sister countries believe quite profoundly in the virtues of tyranny. To them the words "freedom" and "autonomy" are, on other lips but theirs, the ultimate obscenities. And as for a United Germany, God knows what this will mean to my constituents!'

Miss Brunner nervously adjusted her twinset and glanced at her watch. 'I'm on such a tight schedule, these days.' Reminded of that, she breathed a sigh of relief. All she knew was control. It so reduced one's anxieties.

Jerry scratched his stomach with a borrowed loofah. His fatigues were far too tight for him and if she wanted the truth, he'd cheerfully give it to her.

'I'm too old to be a revolutionary,' he said. 'I'm just trying to hang on to the gains we made. And that's why we had to act, Miss Brunner.'

'You won't get far,' she said. The movement of her hand to her perfect auburn hair was a kind of spasm. 'You're having trouble breathing as it is.' Unconsciously she reached for her own pulse.

263

'And don't think I'm afraid of any hidden gin bottles or whatever it is you believe you have.'

'I believe I have the killing-harmony, the power-without-fear, white-eyes!' His fingers twitching towards his needle gun, Jerry uttered something like his old mindless grin. 'What you people never allow for is just how short a distance you can push some of us before we stop going with the flow.'

'You disgusting old hippy.'

'I never was an old hippy, darling.' And he plugged her with one neat shot to the cortex. 'I was only reborn in the nineties.' He gave his wizened hands a wipe and returned to the video he had been planning to watch before she interrupted him. It was *Cat Ballou*. He was desperately in need of a new rôle model, even if it had died in the meantime. Concentrating on the credits, he reached for his pipe and his rocky.

Cold snap

President Iliescu of Romania claimed yesterday that the police and parts of the army had been 'psychologically incapable' of putting down anti-government protests, which was why he was setting up a new riot-control force. An unrepentant Mr Ionescu accused Western governments of overlooking the difficulties provoked in the police and army by the traumatic experiences during the December revolution. He also disclosed that he was considering a formal request to Britain to train the controversial new force.

The Times, 25 June, 1990

It just might be Hampton Court, he thought, wheeling his bicycle out of the maze at night. The Tardis – or police box – put the date around 1965, the year of his immaculate conception, when an empty winter had been filled with the warmth of very young children and an overwhelming sense of responsibility, to self and to them. Jerry now wondered if that hadn't been just before the depression set in. The times were a-changing and interpretations varied; he was all at sea.

Defeated again, he returned to Blenheim Crescent. It had been an age since he had cycled that far in the snow.

"Ere 'e is!' His mum came to the door, her sleeves rolled up on her red forearms and a huge knife in her right hand. 'A regular bad effin' penny, ain' cher, Jer?'

"Appy Xmas, Jer, boy.' His brother Frank's weaselly expression shifted between pacific leer and burning hatred. It was his common response to Jerry's arrival. 'Caff's on 'er way, she said.'

Jerry shivered. He was not sure he was emotionally ready for his sister's manifestation. Yet it was too late to worry.

Obediently, he took his old place at the table.

'Now, Jer – isn't this better than freedom?' Frank grinned across the turkey as their mother poised the knife, her sweat dripping from elbow to half-burned carcass, to mingle with her coarse gravy.

At last Jerry remembered what he had always loved in his sister and no longer felt afraid of her.

Our Love Is Runnin' Out

The knife-sharp air bit painfully into my face when I stepped from the Orient Express at Bucharest in the early hours of New Year's Day, 1938. The gloomy station, silent save for the shufflings of the few sleepy porters and the tired hissings of the engine, gave emphasis to the frigidity, as it were, of my entry into the Roumanian Capital. It was not a heartening beginning of my mission to investigate the real meaning of King Carol's nomination of the fascist, anti-semitic government of Octavian Goga.

King Carol, Hitler and Lupescu

Lying on the artificial beach at Nova Palma Nova reading a Large-type edition of *The Prisoner of Zenda* and listening to Ivor Novello's *Glamorous Night* on his Aiwa, Jerry congratulated himself: an earlier generation would have been reading *The Prisoner of Zenda* on a Blackpool or a Brighton beach. What Romania really needed at the moment was a decent Colonel Zapt. But then everything kept changing. Maybe Ruritania was no longer a viable model? The thought filled him with sadness. He looked up, expecting to see the towers of Zenda fading before his eyes, but his horizon was filled with neon, with the magic names of a different age – Benny Hill, Peter Sellers and Max Bygraves; McDonald's and Wimpy.

This vision disturbed him. These days almost any vision disturbed him.

Some sixth sense warning him, he looked up. Una Persson was tramping across the canary-coloured sand. She wore a Laura Ashley sun-dress and blue Bata strap-ups. In her hands was a heavy Kalashnikov.

That was enough for Jerry. He retreated into the romance of an earlier age and would have stayed there were it not for the touch of cold steel on his sphincter.

'I need some help, Jerry,' she said. She had removed one earphone. It was hideous. Her voice mingled with a hundred machine noises, the video arcades, discos and pinball halls, the traffic of road, sea and air.

'What?' He desperately tried to hear her. It was too late to try to cross her. 'Eh?'

'Come along now.' She reached towards his other ear.

'Damn you, Rassendyll,' he said. 'Can't they find some other poor devil to be king?'

'You ain't the king, boy. You'd be lucky to be queen for a day. You missed your chances.' Shakey Mo's little rat face twitched with a kind of lascivious rage. Hanging about near the steps up to the promenade, he had for obscure reasons smeared blacking on his face. He, too, was sporting a rather unfashionable olive green leisure suit. Things had to be bad when Mo got this patronising.

'Where the hell you been, man? Life goes on, you know, even if you haven't noticed.'

'I ain't drunk, I'm just drinkin',' said Jerry.

'You could have fooled me.' He removed his wraparound shades with a flick of the wrist once considered sexy.

'Which isn't saying a lot, really.' After a second's hesitation Mrs Persson dumped her rifle and the book beside the hot-dog stand. She couldn't make up her mind about them. Nothing stayed obsolete for long, these days.

When a Guitar Plays the Blues

The National Salvation Front government, accused by critics of being closely linked to the Communist Party of late dictator Nicolae Ceausescu, appears to be trying to mend the damage to its international reputation caused by last week's events.

Reuter/Majorca Daily Bulletin, 24 June, 1990

'It's not much of a job and you don't get a whole lot of respect.' Jerry brushed rain off his sodden fedora. 'The pay's no good and the hours are lousy – yet there's something in you has to go on doing it, the way other guys get hooked on dope or, maybe, a woman. Someone has to walk down those streets respectable people don't like to know about, especially when they might have a relative living there. Someone has to take the insults and the bruises and occasionally, the bullet, so that those respectable folks can sleep peacefully in their beds. In some ways you're a messenger between two mutually selfish sections of society – the Glutted Rich and the Vicious Greedy. Well, maybe that's exaggerating just a tad...

'There's a lot of people in between, a lot of little people. A lot of bad women gone right and good men gone down, and whores who should have been virgin brides in Wyoming, and judges who a more enlightened age would recognise as calculating psychopaths – and

all the rest; every piece of human flotsam, and every kind of
virtue... Courage-in-adversity, rotten wealth, Church-pure poverty,
damned near insane self-sacrifice and the pettiest, meanest kind
of greed you ever heard about. You wouldn't believe it. You don't
have to. Only I have to believe it. It's my job.'

Don't Touch Me There

I had hoped to be able to secure interviews with the leading
figures in the political drama which had set the world wondering and had created consternation in Roumania. I was hopeful
of being able to discuss the situation with the King himself, with
Goga, and with the most significant figure in Roumania, Cor-
neliu Zelea Codreanu, leader of the Iron Guard, fascist, terrorist,
murderer and most rabidly violent of Jew-baiters. Arrange-
ments to see King Carol and Goga were made with comparative
ease; to meet Codreanu proved a much more difficult task.

King Carol, Hitler and Lupescu

Jerry wasn't even sure of immortality any more. The rules kept
changing on him and the chronic vibrations were making him ill.

'You're overstretched, lad.' With a flourish of his pale grey
moustache, Major Nye guided the helicopter away from Dublin
where he had discovered Jerry wandering on the frozen Liffey.
'You need a bit of time to yourself.'

'I didn't think it was allowed.'

Clearly Major Nye found this remark in doubtful taste.

'There's not a lot left, after all,' Jerry added lamely. 'What with
the Ukrainian going off like that.'

'You're just depressed because of your dream of anarchy. Well,
old son, it seems it isn't to be.'

'Are you sure there's been no news from Scotland?'

'Not the kind you've been hoping for. I doubt if there's a black
flag left flying or an anarchist keel still in the sky. Those days are

over, dear boy, even in your fantasies. They never had a chance. Too romantic, even for an experienced India hand like me!'

The references were getting blurred. Jerry understood now why the only bits of history that were interesting were the bits that were almost never recorded. The slow turning of an honest Bavarian burgher into a Waffen-SS fanatic, for instance. These mysteries remained, so it seemed, the province of unreliable liars and braggarts, falsifiers of their own identities, the novelists.

'One's qualifications stand for nothing these days,' said Major Nye, turning happily towards Wilton and poetry. 'But I'm sure there's some sort of niche you can find for yourself.'

Jerry felt the old spirit slipping away again. He was regretful. He had never been able to reach Bucharest in the heyday of his powers.

'Here we are, dear boy. Keep your chin up.'

With cheerful confidence Major Nye put them down.

Cold Lonely Nights

Mr Iliescu, the son of a railway worker and a one-time favourite of Ceausescu, was not specific about who would be recruited into the new force, designed to deal with political violence. Already many miners have volunteered. Some opposition politicians and student leaders have likened it apprehensively in advance to a modern version of the Nazi brownshirts. 'We shall have to see about that,' the president replied when asked about its composition.

The Times, 25 June, 1990

The miles of underground concrete, like some vast, unpopulated parking garage, were lit by busy gas-jets set at alarming intervals. Between them were shadows, the stink of blood, the horribly uncleansable miasma of terror. He had to be in the foundations of some evil, if monumentally unimaginative, fortress. He had almost certainly made it to Ceausesculand. Propping the bike against a malodorous pillar, he swung off his rucksack. Beneath his sandwiches and his thermos he discovered a psychic map of the city. It was not as out-of-date as he had feared and Jerry found it easy to follow into the nineties. He paused to do the last of his Columbian Silver. At moments like this, grit and integrity only came in powder form. In some ways, he thought, it was like sniffing the dust of some ancient and forgotten empire; the nearest he got to dreaming, these days.

Strike Like Lightning

> I took up residence in the Athenee Palace Hotel and later in the morning after my arrival, I took stock of this most notorious caravanserai in all Europe. It was exciting to realise that here I was in the meeting place of the Continental spies, political conspirators, adventurers, concession hunters, and financial manipulators. Here at the crossroads, as it were, dividing Europe from Asia, in the centre of the Balkan cockpit, were hatched most of the plots and devilments that, in days gone by, upset a government here, fomented a revolution there and, on occasion, planned an assassination.
>
> *King Carol, Hitler and Lupescu*

Miss Brunner was beside herself. 'We put a stop to all that,' she said. 'We made a land where the English middle classes could bray with confidence.'

'Oh, it's not such a bad old world.' Gratefully Sir Kingsley lifted another pink gin to the kind of triangular sphincter which was his mouth. In fact, things were looking up, all in all, he thought, at the Jolly Englishman. He stared bleakly at his white, puffy fist and longed for his old pals. Most of them had failed to make it into the decade. Come to think of it, he reflected with a mourning grin, so had he.

Miss Brunner thought his attitude defeatist. 'You might be enjoying the decline, Sir K., but some of us aren't going to stand for it.'

'Fair enough.' The embodiment of the nation's literary aspirations offered her a weary leer. 'Bend over, darling.'

She couldn't resist power, no matter how deliquescent it had become. She giggled and ordered him another double. 'You were honoured,' she reminded him admiringly, 'for services to your country.'

'For services to Time, actually.' He accepted the gin.

'I do love you intellectuals.'

'Bugger Jane Austen.'

'Fuck George Eliot.'

'Pat Norman Mailer on the bottom.' At this, he recovered himself.

'Naturally.' On trembling palm she offered him her pork scratchings. 'How's your little boy?'

Not everything, she consoled herself, had gone to pot.

'I heard they named a pub after me in Magalluf,' said the old penman proudly. Then, almost immediately, he grew gloomy again.

'My luck, it's full of blokes in pink underpants drinking Campari-soda.'

Fanning the Flames

Denying any dichotomy between his speech to the miners and
his subsequent more measured address at his inauguration, Mr
Iliescu said: 'What is fundamental is who started the violence
and who provoked the violence.'

The Times, 25 June, 1990

Jerry's moped was acting up. It had never been as reliable as the Royal Albert, even on normal roads, and was behaving like a grumbling old dog as it picked its way along Romania's ancient tracks.

The great chasms and towering rocks, the gigantic torrents, gloomy forests and barren shale all inspired in him an awe of Nature. After less than two hours of this experience he found himself talking loudly to himself in German.

From Goethe it was but a short step to the Jewish Problem, something he had hoped to avoid on this holiday.

'Blut ist blut,' he sang resignedly. 'Sturm me daddy, eighty to the car...' and with this he began a descent into the cloud-hidden depths of a mysterious valley. So much for the subtleties of the human spirit! For him there were more urgent demands on his attention. How on earth had the English managed to make themselves the narrowest and most reactionary people in Europe and still see themselves as generous and enlightened? It was a wonder to him, and a privilege, to observe this fantastic progress at first hand. Gibbon, for instance, had been forced to speculate and, from his position, had found the decline of Rome almost impossible to accept. Increasingly, this had led him into those mighty abstractions the Victorians created from the stuff of the Enlightenment and which, they convinced themselves, were solid as the British Empire.

'Das Volk ehrt den Künstler, Johnny.'

Marrakech was looking better all the time. Jerry was glad he had lost none of his old instincts. In fact he seemed quicker on his toes than he had been in his glory days. He, better than anyone, knew when to head for the border.

You and I

On a certain day, the Jewish community was informed that the Yellow Badge had been introduced in all of Roumania. A sample was sent in with the strict injunction that in a few days the Yellow Badge must be ready and all Jews, men, women and children, were instructed to wear them. In Bukovina, this was immediately introduced ... This measure had a devastating effect on the mood of Bucharest ... People wearing the Yellow Badge were barred from street cars ... could not go to any offices or approach any authorities. This decree drew a pall over and had a depressing effect upon the city.

King Carol, Hitler and Lupescu

'Peru is getting altogether more interesting, now that a bloody writer's been beaten by a Jap.' Lifting a gentle hand from his Mars Supapac Bishop Beesley slipped a mini bar into his mouth. Outside, through the hotel window, dreamed the dusty streets of some South American capital. 'But it needs a better man than me to open up the interior properly. I haven't the stomach for it.' He descended with a sigh, inch by painful inch, into the largest armchair. 'Besides, a man in my position has to cultivate a certain detachment.' He looked thoughtfully towards the street where a tall old Englishman paused to peer up. 'Can that be Major Nye?'

The hushed tones of the serious professional Christian invaded his mouth and Jerry was startled by this apparent procession until he remembered that the bishop was expecting another visitor.

'Can we drop you anywhere tomorrow, bishop?' he asked carefully.

Beesley turned eyes upon him that were full of a ghastly benevolence. 'Perhaps, dear boy. You're very kind.' As if in sudden anxiety he glanced again at the window but the Englishman had strolled on. Jerry knew Beesley was never happy in Catholic countries, especially Latin America. He had been heading for some other Rio, some magical retreat, when the plane had been diverted here. He stroked his jowls and looked thoughtfully down at his sweat-stained tennis whites.

Jerry turned to leave.

'Do you know?' said Bishop Beesley with some resentment. 'The chap downstairs mistook me for a German this morning.'

'Don't worry, bishop.' The old assassin picked a crumb of

chocolate from the handle of the black mitre-case. Noticing how worn and shiny it had become reminded him how long the bishop had been on the run. 'Nobody else will.' He closed the door softly, as if upon a corpse.

Downstairs the electricity was off again and, as if waiting for the ride to begin, flies had settled thickly on the blades of the motionless ceiling fan. Others crawled across the darkened screen of a dormant TV still watched by the janitor, as if he perceived some drama denied to all but himself. Jerry glanced into the brilliant street, the glaring stucco, the graffiti and the Coca-Cola signs. Maybe it was time to go back to the wild side of life.

The Californian surf was beginning to sound good again and from somewhere overhead he was sure he could hear the comfortable presence of a rescue chopper.

There had to be somewhere else to go than a colonised Ladbroke Grove, the Cotswolds or a decolonised North Africa.

He had settled on Liberia even before the helicopter descended into a little square, blowing dust through the beaded curtains of the run-down shops and cantinas, sending dogs scattering reluctantly into the deeper shadows of the alleyways.

Professor Hira, his round brown face glowing with sweat and self-satisfaction, reached down a hand. 'Welcome aboard, old chap. Oh, by the way –' the Brahmin paused as Major Nye gunned the engine to keep her steady – 'Liberia's out now, too. Any ideas?'

Jerry gave in. Angkor Wat. Anuradhapura, Luxor and New York… all his favourite ruins had been taken over by someone. They'd even sold his roof garden to Richard Branson. To pay his debts, they said. He hadn't realised he owed anything.

He gave a hazy thought to Sid Vicious as he was lifted dramatically over the rooftops and spires into a pearly reality he had never hoped to find again.

'You missed the second coming,' said Major Nye. 'Didn't he, professor?'

'I think so. Or possibly just God's second childhood.' Hira giggled. He had a liking for mild blasphemies.

Devil Child

The reluctance of the army to rush to the aid of the government in the recent rioting has been interpreted differently by many Western intelligence experts, who claimed that many officers and soldiers were reluctant to oppose rioters who alleged that the government was run by neo-communists. As part of the power struggle the interior minister General Mihai Chitac, was dismissed after the rioting and control of the police switched from the interior to the defence ministry.

The Times, 25 June, 1990

Old Sammy came out of the kitchen into the alley. He was red with sweat. His stained white hat and apron fumed with the greasy heat of the chopshop whose flaring, agitated jets were the constant of his busy Friday night trade. He deep-fried pies and chops to order. Those boiling vats, in which all kinds of questions floated, reminded Jerry what eternal damnation must be like. No wonder those poor bastards were terrified. No wonder they clung to their ramshackle faiths – their habits which they could no more discard than the Jews in 1933 or the English in 1979. They were locked into self-made prisons, justifying all that was most cowardly and most cautious and most unjust in human society. He'd rather have Unitarianism which at least believed in handing out soup and a sandwich from time to time. Faith, he had to admit, was a bit of a baffling one. It couldn't be good for people.

Nothing fitted.

He'd ride with the tide for a while. After all, the cards were still settling. What had he been getting so angry about?

The sandwiches weren't, anyway, that bad. He'd recommend the Tuna Melt.

'I had a feeling I was getting in touch with the occult.' On his apron Sammy wiped fingers swollen and impure as his sausages. 'But I suppose that's typical at my time of life, isn't it?'

Jerry shook his head. He glanced carefully up the alley. 'Any port in a storm, eh, Sam? When in doubt consult your stars. What can you lose?'

'What *can* you lose, old son?' Sammy nodded with melancholy introspection, perhaps revealing all the many things he had already lost.

Above their heads was the blindness of the East End night in those precious years between the Blitz and the Thames Developments.

'There must be easier ways than this of making a living.' Sammy drained off another wave of sweat with his heavy arm and dashed the liquid to the concrete of the step. 'So long, Jerry. So long, squire. So long.' He went back to his chops and his pies. He had only recently introduced the pies to compete with a modern formica café across the street, and was not sure if they were worth it. They were bloody hard to fry.

Jerry, munching his free pasty, pushed his bike with one hand round the corner into the blazing white light of Whitechapel High Street, a salutary vision, where the wide roads were already gone through Leman Street and half the ruins of his youth. Leman Street had become little more than a slip-road and Wapping Old Stairs was blocked with corrugated iron on which posters for Tommy Steele and Bill Haley were already fading. The grey iron was bent and torn in places and through the gaps Jerry could watch the rain approaching across the moody waters of his Thames, where pieces of timber and old Tizer bottles jogged and drifted above depths which promised every horror. Even the agitated lapping of the water had a sinister, neurotic quality, and Jerry, never a keen East Ender, was glad when he got to the Tower and the waiting motor boat.

'We thought we'd lost you,' said Mitzi Beesley, decisively securing her Mae West.

'How was your mum?' Shakey Mo asked over his shoulder as he started the engine.

'She wasn't working tonight.' Jerry studied the water, swirling like a Mr Softee, and wondered just how many of these memories were actually his.

Frozen Alive

The lawyers and doctors, almost without exception, remained in Cernauti when the Russians took it over; a number of Buko-vina Jews, who had been living in Bucharest, left for Cernauti when the Russians came, stating that they preferred to live under Russian domination and subsist on dry bread than to live under Roumanian rule and be considered below contempt.

King Carol, Hitler and Lupescu

'Loathsome, uncouth, loutish.' Bishop Beesley waved an eloquent Yorkie. 'Or am I being unjust, do you think, to that scum of the earth? I like you, my dear sir, I really do. You're a wag, sir, if you don't mind me saying so.'

Nobody paid him any attention. The going was proving unexpectedly hard and it was all Shakey Mo could do to keep the armoured car on course. 'I still say it's no part of the Lake District.'

Major Nye wanted to offer them his definition of a gentleman. Eventually, to take their minds off their discomfort, they gave in, though Mo Collier's snorts and mutterings remained in the background.

'A gentleman,' Major Nye announced, 'should be courteous to all and considerate of all, respectful of all, no matter what their station or their sex. He should be thoroughly read in the literature of the day as well as that of the past, and should be conversant on matters of Science, Nature and the Arts, having some practical reading in moral philosophy and some practical understanding of all these things; he should also have a good knowledge of cookery, fencing, fancy sewing, water colouring, medicine and, of course, riding. He should always be able, with coolness and self-knowledge, to defend his actions, both morally and socially. He should have some accountancy and comparative religion, some household management, some training in the care of the sick and injured as well as the elderly. He must know the arts of self-defence, perhaps both Kara-te and Tai Chi, and certain aspects of infant responsibility. His education should emphasise courses in algebra, geography, history and politics, but should otherwise share the common curriculum.'

'You're a determinist then, Major Nye?' Professor Hira was the only one who had been listening.

'Not in the strictest of senses, old boy, no. In fact I think politics, like religion, are a man's own damned affair, pardon my French. But live and let live, eh?'

'Have you ever run across such a paragon as you describe, major?' Professor Hira adjusted his earpiece. The radio had, for days, been delivering Radio One, set to some antiseptic cycle of current singles repeated one after the other every hour. Professor Hira thought it a miraculous little system and was irritated by any suggestion that it was already hopelessly out of date. Modern technology could randomise anything these days.

'Not in this century, no, old boy.'

'Sometimes,' said Mo, 'you don't even need to do any kind of programme. It's the very latest in pseudo-technology. Wow!' His fingers played over endless invisible keys. He was programming an air-computer. His days were truly filled. 'Cerebral, man. Punch that code!' He could still function on simple levels and was useful for his old, instinctive skills. 'Bam! Psychedelic! Post-modern! Wow! Chaos!'

Years Since Yesterday

Iliescu said Romania had emerged in a state of moral decay from the era of dictator Nicolae Ceausescu, who was toppled and executed last December.

Reuter/Majorca Daily Bulletin, 21 June, 1990

'Gas,' said Captain Maxwell, the English engineer, replacing his stein of Pilsner Urquhart carefully upon the laminated oak, 'is the Future.' He glared with a kind of proprietorial benevolence around the bierkeller. 'That's where the fortunes will be made.'

From outside, in Wenzslaslas Square, the Australian Morris Dancers gave their precise rendition of the Flory Dance. They were said by some to be the hit of the Festival. He looked at Jerry before uttering a hearty laugh. It was as if someone had farted through their face.

Jerry gagged.

Playing For Keeps

One evening in the early weeks of the 'New Order' in Roumania, a group of armed men, in the green uniform of the Iron Guard, burst into the country house at Sinaia, as the old man of seventy sat at his desk in the study. They fell upon the 'Patriarch of the Roumanian People' and dragged him out of the house to the dark road outside. As he lay on the ground, they cut off his famous flowing white beard, riddled him with bullets, cut his throat, stabbed the already lifeless body and threw it into a sodden ditch by the wayside. When the torn, beardless corpse of Nicolai Jorga was discovered the next morning, there was found, stuffed in his mouth, a copy of *Neamul Romanesc*, dated September 9, 1940, containing the signed 'leader' entitled: 'On the departure of King Carol'. Thus did Roumania, under Hitler's 'New Order' directed by the Nazi Gauleiter 'Red Dog' Antonescu, achieve the 'moral restoration' which this Roumanian general swore to his King, Mihail, to be the holy cause of the overthrow of Carol the Second.

King Carol, Hitler and Lupescu

'Either the human race is going to have to improve its memory, lose it altogether, or get a new one.' Catherine Cornelius gave her brother a dismissive kiss. 'You can't fight that kind of amnesia. You might as well give up.'

'Never say die, love.' Mrs Cornelius went by with a pie. 'I carn't bloody believe it's Christmas again!' This was her great day of power and she was celebrating.

'God help us, every one,' said Jerry.

He shared a despairing wink with his sister.

'I think I'm going to have to slip out for a bit.'

She hated to abandon him, but there wasn't much worth saving at the moment.

Wound Up Tight

Two West German tourists and two Israelis were injured yesterday when a bomb believed planted by Palestinian militants exploded at the Dead Sea resort of Ein Gedi, police said.

Reuter/Majorca Daily Bulletin, 24 June, 1990

Bishop Beesley turned his head away. For some days now he had taken to wearing a grotesque *commedia dell'arte* mask under his mitre. This, together with the cramped conditions of their bunker, tended to hamper his movements until now he was content merely to raise at regular intervals a Snickers to his maw. They were beginning to object to his smell which, though sweet, had a distinctly rotten tinge. His daughter Mitzi had refused point-blank to get into the bunker with him and even now sat, with every appearance of comfort, in a wicker chair they had found for her and placed on the roof. From time to time she lifted her old Remington and sighted reminiscently along its barrel. The smoke from the ruins of the Barbican was beautiful in the late sunshine. A gentle breeze moved the purple heads of the fireweed and Jerry felt at peace again. He stretched out beside her, his chin in his hands.

'It can't keep going round and round for ever, can it?' He blinked 'Where am I?' He looked to where the armoured car was still parked. 'Romantic.'

'Only just,' said Beesley, his voice slurred and muffled by chocolate, his mask and the concrete.

Jerry was experiencing such extraordinary déjà vu that he could no longer register his surroundings. He glared at the smoke which had become a sort of screen on which were projected a sickening procession of images, each one only subtly different from the last.

'It's Time, I suppose,' he said. 'It seems all the same. What's wrong?' He raised himself up in alarm.

For once Bishop Beesley had an observation ready.

'*Reductio ad absurdum,*' he said with a hint of a blessing.

He rose suddenly, Mars wrappers rustling and falling about him like autumn leaves.

'Are they here, yet?'

Gradually, all the occupants of the bunker began to climb out until everyone was standing on the roof staring incuriously at the bland horizon.

'There's no time,' said Jerry, 'like the present.'

He was surprised that the thought did not any longer depress him.

Chapter titles by Lonnie Mack, Tinsley Ellis, Clarence 'Gatemouth' Brown, The Paladins, Koko Taylor, Katie Webster, Kenny Neal, Albert Collins, Roy Buchanan, Little Charlie & the Nightcats, Delbert McClinton, the Kinsey Report, Lonnie Brooks, all available on Alligator Records.

The Spencer Inheritance

I

'Leave Me Alone'

> I mean, once or twice I've heard people say to me that you
> know Diana's out to destroy the monarchy ... Why would I
> want to destroy something that is my children's future?

– Diana, Princess of Wales,
Television interview, November 1995

'Oh, cool! This –' with all his old enthusiasm, Shakey Mo bit into his footlong – 'is what I *call* a hot-dog.' His bearded lips winked with mustard, ketchup and gelatinous cucumber. 'Things are looking up.'

Close enough, in the cramped confines of the Ford Flamefang Mk IV, to suffer the worst of Mo's fallout, Jerry Cornelius still felt a surge of affection for his little pard. Mo was back on form, an MK-55 on his hip and righteous mayhem in his eyes. He was all relish again. Mounting the ruins of the St John's Wood Wottaburger, their armoured half-track rounded a tank-trap, bounced over a speed bump and turned erratically into Abbey Road. 'Bugger.' Mo's dog had gone all over the place.

'It's chaos out there.'

Major Nye fixed a pale and amiable blue eye on the middle distance. Neat grey hairs ran like furrows across his tanned old scalp. His sinewy body had been so long in the sun it was half mummified. They were heading for Hampstead where they hoped to liaise with some allies and carry on up the M1 to liberate their holy relics in the name of their dead liege, who had died reluctantly at Lavender Hill. The old soldier's steering was light and flexible, but sometimes it threatened to overturn them. Glancing back across his shoulder he voiced all their thoughts.

'This is going to be a good war, what?'

'At least we got a chance to lay some mines this time.' Colonel Hira brushed a scarlet crumb from his chocolate fatigues and adjusted his yellow turban. Only Hira wore the official uniform of the UPS. The United Patriotic Squadrons (of The Blessed Diana) (Armoured Vehicles Division) were famous for their eccentric but influential style, their elaborate flags. 'Those Caroline bastards will think twice before taking their holidays in Dorset again.'

A saccharine tear graced Bishop Beesley's flurried cheek. Seemingly independent, like toon characters, his fingers grazed at random over his face. From time to time he drew the tips to his lips and tasted them. 'Surely this is no time for cynicism?' His wobbling mitre gave clerical emphasis to his plea. 'We are experiencing the influence of the world-will. We are helpless before a massive new mythology being created around us and of which we could almost be part. This is the race-mind expressing itself.' His massive jowls drooped with sincerity. 'Can't we share a little common sentiment?' He squeezed at his right eye to taste another tear. 'Our sweet patroness died for our right to plant those mines.'

'And so her effing siblings could spray us with AIDS virus in the name of preserving national unity.' This was Mo's chief grievance. He was afraid he would turn out positive and everyone would think he was an effing fudge-packer like Jerry and the rest of them half-tuned pianos. 'Don't go forgetting that.' He added, a little mysteriously: 'Private money blows us up. Public money patches us up. Only an idiot of a capitalist would want to change that status quo. This is an old-fashioned civil war. A class war.'

Major Nye disagreed. 'We're learning to live in a world without poles.'

'Anti-Semitic bastards.' Mo frowned down at his weapon. 'They deserved all they got.'

'Are we there yet?' The cramped cab was making Jerry claustrophobic. 'I think I'm going to be sick.'

2

'Our grief is so deep...'

> ... when people are dying they're much more open and more vulnerable, and much more real than other people. And I appreciate that.
>
> – As above

The convoy managed to get as far as Swiss Cottage before a half-dozen of the latest 10 × 10 extra-sampled Morris Wolverines came surfing over the rubble towards them.

The hulls of the pocket landcruisers shone like pewter. The style leaders in all sides of the conflict, their streamlining was pure 1940s futurist. Their fire-power, from the single pointed muzzle of a Niecke 450 LS, was the classiest ordnance available. Those laser-shells could go up your arse and take out a particular pile if they wanted to. It was just that kind of aggressive precision styling which people were looking for these days.

'But can it last, Mr C?' Shakey Mo was taking the opportunity to retouch some of their burned paint. The fresh cerise against the camouflage gave the car the look of a drunk in the last stages of cirrhosis. Mo ignored the approaching squadron until almost the final moment. Then, nonchalant, he swung into his gunnery perch, pulled the safety lid down behind him, settled himself into the orange innertube he used to ease his lower back, flipped a few toggles, swung his twin Lewises from side to side with the heel of his hand to check their readiness, pushed up the sights, tested the belts, and put his thumbs to the firing button. A precise and antique burst. The rubble between their Ford and the rank of savvy Morrises suddenly erupted and clouds billowed. A wall of débris rose for at least twenty feet and then began to settle in simple geometric patterns.

'Here's some we laid earlier, pards!'

Mo began to cackle and shriek.

Following this precedent, ash rained across Kelmscott and all the Morris memorials. Ancient Pre-Raphaelites were torn apart for scrap, their bones ground for colour, their blood feeding the sand. It became the fashion to dig up poets and painters and own a piece of them. No grave was safe. Everyone now knew that such gorgeous paint was wasted in the cement of heritage. Heritage parks.

'Cementaries?' Jerry did his best with his associations. Why was it wrong to resist their well-meaning intentions?

What secrets could they possibly learn? Nothing which would embarrass me, of course, for I am dead. But secrets of the fields and hedges, eh? Yes, I've found them. It's easy with my eyes. Or was. Secrets in old stones, weakened by the carving of their own runes and the casting of dissipate magic. Desolate churches standing on cold ground which once raced with energy. Why is there such a cooling of this deconsecrated earth? Has the ether been leeched of its goodness by swaggering corporate capital, easing and wheezing its fat bodies through the corridors of privilege, the ratholes of power. Help me, help me, help me. Are you incapable of ordinary human emotion?

Or has that been simulated, too? Or stimulated you by its very nearness. Yet somewhere I can still hear your despairing leitmotifs. Messages addressed to limbo. Your yearning for oblivion. You sang such lovely, unrepeatable songs. You sank such puritan hopes.

But you were never held to account.

Blameless,

    you were blemished

only

in the minds

of the impure

Of the impure, I said,

but not the unworthy.

For this is Babylon,

    where we live.

Babylon,

where we live.
This is Babylon, said
    mr big.
What, mr b?
Did you speak?
Only inside, these days,
    mrs c,
for I am dead and my
loyalties are to the dead
I no longer have desire
to commune with the living
    Only you
    mrs c.
    Only good
    old mrs
    c.

Murdering the opposition:
        It is a last
        resort.
        He came up
        that morning
        He said
        From Scunthorpe
        or was it Skegness.
        You know, don't
        you?
        The last resort.

Don't blame me:
        You're on
        your own
        in this one
        I said
        Nobody

calls on
me
for a report.

Oh, good lord.
   Sweet lord.
   Let me go.
There's work to be done, yet:
   You don't know
   the meaning
   of pain,
   she looked over my head
   she looked over my head
   the whole time she spoke
   Her eyes and voice were
   in the distance.
   You may never know it,
   she said.
   You could die
   and never know it.
   And that's my prayer.
Loud enough for you, Jerry?
   Loud enough?
   She asked.
   There's an aesthetic
   in loudness itself.
   Or so we think.
   Can you hear me, Jerry?
   Jerry?
An anaesthetic?
   he said.
Oh, this turning multiverse
   is in reverse
And whirling chaos sounds
   · familiar patterns

in the shifting
   round
Yet still,
   they take the essence from
   our common ground
   They take our public
   spirit
   from
   our common ground.
We become subject
   to chills and bronchial
   seizures
Now we are paying that price
   Given that prize
   Severed those ties
   Those hampering
     second thoughts
   Those night rides
     down to where
the conscience still pipes
a piccolo
still finds a little resonance
among the ailing reeds.
Some unrooted truth
   left to die
down there.
Can you hear it?
Loyal to the end.
Loyal to your well-being.
Wanting nothing else.
Can you hear it?
Still piping a
hopeful note
or two.
All for you.

291

*

'You must be
fucking
desperate,'
she said.

The SciFi Channel:
Our ministers are proud
   to announce the
restoration of the English
   car industry
Record sales of light
   armoured vehicles
have made this a boom year
   for our
auto-makers.
   Bonuses all round,
   says Toney Flair
our golden age PM.
   Let's give ourselves
   A pat
   on the back.

The domestic arms trade
   has stimulated the
   domestic car trade
   The economy
   has never been
   stronger.

We are killing
   two bards
   with one
   stone.

Look at America.
That's their
lifeblood,
right?
You
know
what
I
mean?

You
know what I mean?
I mean
what
have
I
done?
I mean
why?
I mean
you
know
why?
I mean
you know.
Came out of the West
Out of the grey West
Where the sea runs
And my blood is at ease.
And this is where I rest.

3

Was Diana Murdered?

International crime syndicates are cheating Princess Diana's memorial fund with pirate versions of Elton John's Candle in the Wind...

Illegal copies of the song, performed at the Princess's funeral, are undercut by up to £2.50 and have been found in Italy, Hong Kong, Singapore and Paraguay. Profits will fund the drugs and arms trade.

Daily Bulletin,
Majorca, 26 September, 1997

'Gun carriages.' Major Nye lowered puzzled glasses. 'Dozens of them. Piled across Fitzjohn's Avenue. Where on earth are they getting them?'

Behind their battered Ford the smoking aluminium of the Morrises fused and seethed, buckling into complex parodies of Paolozzi sculptures. Abandoning his Lewises, Mo had used a musical strategy aimed at their attackers' over-refined navigational circuits. A few Gene Vincent singles in the right registers and the enemy had auto-destructed.

'It used to be glamorous, dying in a crash. But the nineties did with auto-death what Oasis did with The Beatles. They took an idiom to its dullest place. This wasn't suicide. It wasn't even assassination. It was ritual murder. How can they confuse the three? It was the triumph of the lowest common denominator. The public aren't fools. Don't you think we all sensed it?'

Finchley's trees had gone for fuel. Its leafy authority removed, The Avenue had the air of an exposed anthill. Ankle-deep in sawdust, people clustered around the stumps, holding branches and leaves as if through osmosis they might somehow restore their cover. They had no spiritual leadership. As Jerry & Co. rumbled past, waving, playing snatches of patriotic music and distributing leprous bars of recovered Toblerone, they lifted their rustling limbs in dazed salute.

'These places are nothing without their foliage.' Mo lit his last Sherman's.

The deadly oils released their aromatic smoke into the cab. Everyone but Jerry took an appreciative sniff. Jerry was still having trouble with his convulsions.

He had developed a range of allergies with symptoms so unusual they had not yet hit the catalogues. This made him a valuable target for drug company goons, always on the lookout for the clinically exceptional. New diseases needed new cures. But he was not prepared to sell his new diseases just to anyone. There were ethical considerations. This was, after all, the cusp of a millennium. There were matters of public interest to consider. The golden age of corporate piracy was gone. We were all developing appropriate pieties.

Mournfully Bishop Beesley saw that he was on his last Mars Megapak. Yet compulsively he continued to eat. Rhythmically, the chocolate disappeared into his mouth, leaving only the faintest trails. They slipped like blood down his troubled jowls.

'Seen anything from the old baroness at all?'

Mo scarcely heard him. He was buried in some distant song.

'You made

'the Age

'of the

'Predatory Lad.

'It paid you

'well.

'What price victory now, Mr C?'

'Eh?'

Jerry was still preoccupied with his physical feelings.

He lifted his legs and howled.

4

Das War Diana

I'm not a political animal but I think the biggest disease this world suffers from in this day and age is the disease of people feeling unloved.

– As above

Hampstead Heath was a chaos of churned mud and tortured metal given exotic beauty by the movement of evening sunlight through lazy grey smoke. In the silence a few bustling ravens cawed. Hunched on blasted trees they seemed profoundly uneasy. Perhaps the character of the feast upset their sense of the natural order. They were old, conservative birds who still saw some kind of virtue in harmony.

The house the team occupied had a wonderful view all the way across the main battlefield. Its back wall had received two precise hits from an LB7. The body of the soldier who had been hiding behind the wall was now under the rubble. Only his feet remained exposed. Mo had already removed the boots and was polishing them appreciatively, with the previous owner's Cherry Blossom. He held them up to the shifty light. 'Look at the quality of that leather. The bastards.'

He was upset. He had been convinced that the boots would fit him.

'You turn people into fiction you get shocked when they die real deaths.' Little Trixie Brunner, never less than smart, had agreed to meet them here with the remains of her squadron.

'Bastards!' Clinging vaguely, her mother drooled viciously at her side. Lady Brunner was having some trouble staying alive.

Trixie lifted disapproving lips. 'Mum!'

The infusions weren't working any more. Uncomfortably wired, Lady B. muttered and buzzed to herself, every so often fixing her bleak eyes upon some imagined threat. Maybe Death himself.

Jerry was trembling as usual. His mouth opened and closed rapidly. Lady Brunner smiled suddenly to herself as if recalling her old power. 'Eh?' She began to cackle.

Trixie let out a sigh of irritated piety. 'Mother!'

Until a month ago Trixie had been Toney Flair's Chief Consort and tipped for the Premiership when her leader and paramour took the Big Step, which he had promised to do if he had not brought the nations of Britain to peace by the end of the year. He would join his predecessors in US exile. It was the kind of example the British people now habitually demanded.

Trixie, growing disapproving of Toney's policies, had uttered some significant leaks before siding with the Dianistas whom she had condemned as upstart pretenders a week earlier. But at heart, she told them, she was still a Flairite. She was hoping her actions would bring Toney or his deputy Danny to their senses. Until the Rift of Peckham they had supported the Dianist cause. She would still be a keen Dianista if those twin fools the Earls of Spencer and of Marks, claiming Welsh heritage, hadn't allied themselves with the Black Stuarts and thus brought anarchy to Scotland. Rather than listen to all these heresies, her mother had stood in a corner putting pieces of Kleenex into her ears. One of her last acts in power was to make them both Knights of St Michael.

A shadow darkened the garden.

Jerry was compelled to go outside and look up. Limping over low was the old *Princess of Essex*, her gold, black and fumed-oak finish showing the scars of recent combat.

Mo joined him. He gazed approvingly at the ship. 'She always had style, didn't she?' he said reverently.

Jerry blinked uncertainly. 'Style?'

'Class.' Mo nodded slowly, confirming his own wise judgement.

'Class.' Jerry's attention was wandering again. He had found a faded ¡Hola! and began to leaf through it. '*Which?*' For the last couple of centuries Britain had seen her monarchs identify their fortunes first with the aristocracy, then with the upper middle class, then with the middle class and ultimately with the petite bourgeoisie, depending who had the most power. No doubt they would soon appear on the screen adopting the costumes and language of *EastEnders*. They were so adaptable they'd be virtually invisible by the middle of the century. 'Style? Where?'

'*Essex*.' Mo pointed up.

As if in response, the *Princess* shimmied girlishly in the air.

5

Dodi's Psychiatrist Tells All

> Those of us who met Diana can vouch for it, and the rest of us know it's true: She brought magic into all our lives and we loved her for it. She'll always be what she wanted to be – the Queen of our Hearts.
>
> *Diana, Queen of Our Hearts*,
> *News of the World* Special Souvenir Photo Album,
> September 1997

'It was then,' Major Nye told Trixie Brunner, 'that I realised a lifetime ambition and bought myself a good quality telescope with the object of fulfilling those two fundamental human needs – to spy on my neighbours and to look at the stars. But Simla seems a long time ago. I often wonder why they resented us so. After all, they didn't have a nation until we made them one. It was either us or some native Bismarck. Much better we should get the blame.'

'I believe they used to call that paternalism.' Trixie could not help liking this sweet old soldier.

'Quite right.' Major Nye squared his jaw approvingly.

His nasty locks bouncing, Mo swung round on the swivel gun-seat. 'Can I ask you a personal question?'

Trixie adopted that open and agreeable expression which had

become so fashionable just before the outbreak of armed hostilities. 'Of course,' she said brightly.

'How much time do you spend actually making up?'

'Not that long.' She smiled as if she took a joke against her. 'It gets easier with practice.'

'But about how long?'

'Why do you ask?'

'It would take me hours.'

'Hardly half an hour.' She softened.

'What about retouches?'

'I really don't know. Say another half-hour or so.'

'What about clothes? I mean, you're always very nicely turned out.'

'You mean getting dressed?'

'And deciding what to wear and everything. Say you change two or three times a day.'

'Well, it's not that long. You get used to it.'

'An hour? Two hours?'

'Some days I hardly get out of my shirt and jeans.'

'How long is a break in St Tropez?'

'What do you mean? For me? A couple of weeks at a stretch, at best.'

'And how much time a day do you spend working for others?'

Trixie frowned. 'What do you mean "others"?'

'Well, you know, lepers and all that.'

'That's hardly work,' said Trixie. 'But it does involve turning up and posing.'

Major Nye patted her gentle shoulder. 'The public is very generous in its approval of the rich,' he said.

'It's the poor they can't stand,' said Mo. 'What I want to know is how many big-eyed children will starve to death just because Kim the Stump got all the photo opportunities? Why isn't there more fucking anger? There's only so much charity to go round!'

'And nothing like enough justice.' Major Nye turned his chair towards the car's tiny microwave. 'Anyone fancy a cup of tea?'

He peered through one of the observation slits. A gentle mist was rolling over the picturesque ruins of Highgate. Marx's monument had sustained some ironic shelling. You could see all the way across the cemetery to Tufnell Park and beyond it to Camden, Somers Town, Soho and the Thames. It was a quiet morning. The gunfire was distant, lazy.

'Do you think it's safe to lower our armour?'

6

Now You Belong To Heaven

Then, amazingly, the masses who had prayed and sung the hymns, wept deeply as the service floated over London, began to applaud ... Once the hearse had passed, each and every one of us went home alone.

– Leslie Thomas,
News of the World, 7 September, 1997

Something in Jerry was reviving. He flipped through the latest auto catalogues. He felt a twitch where his genitals might be.

Rover Revenges, Jaguar Snarlers, Austin Attackers, Morris Wolverines, Hillman Hunters and Riley Reliants all sported the latest tasty fashions in fire-power. Their rounded carapaces and tapering guns gave them the appearance of mobile phones crossed with surgical instruments. They were loaded with features. They were being exported everywhere. It made you proud to be British again. This was, after all, what we did best.

But the politics of fashion was once again giving way to the politics of precedent. Jerry felt his stomach turn over. Was there any easy way of getting out of the past?

7

Diana's Smile Lit Up Wembley

The world is mourning Princess Diana – but nowhere are the tears falling more relentlessly than in Bosnia ... She met limbless victims of the landmines ... but she did much more than add another victim to her global crusade ... She made a despairing people smile again.

News of the World, 7 September, 1997

'Thirty years and all these fuckers will be footnotes!' Mo stood knee-deep in rubble running his fingers over the keyboard of a Compaq he had found. The screen had beeped and razzled but had eventually given him the Net. Taking a swig from his Gemini, he lit himself a reefer and flipped his way through the *Sunday Times*. 'Do they only exist on Sundays?'

'For Sundays.' Jerry was frowning down at a drop of machine oil which had fallen onto his cuff and was being absorbed into the linen. 'Do they exist for Sundays or do they appear any other days?' He was still having a little trouble with existence.

'We shouldn't have left him alone in the prozac vault.' Trixie Brunner brushed white powder from her perfect pants. 'You only need one a day.'

'I was looking for extra balance,' Jerry explained. He smiled sweetly through his wrinkling flesh. 'This isn't right, is it?'

Major Nye shook his head and pointed. Across the heaped bricks and slabs of broken concrete came a group of irregulars. They wore bandannas and fatigues clearly influenced by *Apocalypse Now*. This made them dangerous enemies and flaky friends. Virtual Nam had taken them over. Jerry sized them up. Those people always went for the flashiest ordnance. He had never seen so many customised Burberrys and pre-bloodstained Berber flak jackets.

They had stopped and in the accents of Staines and Haywards Heath were calling a familiar challenge.

'For or Against!'

They were Dianistas. But not necessarily of the same division.

Mo cupped his hands and shouted.

'For!'

Major Nye looked around vaguely, as if for a ball.

With lowered weapons, the group began to advance.

Major Nye thought he recognised one of their number.

'Mrs Persson?'

Carefully he checked his watches.

8

Princes Teach Charles To Love Again

> Princess Diana was named yesterday as the most inspirational
> figure for Britain's gay community. The Pink Paper, a gay news-
> paper, said a poll of its readers placed Diana way ahead of
> people such as 19th century playwright Oscar Wilde who was
> jailed for being homosexual or tennis star Martina Navratilova.
>
> *Daily Bulletin*, 26 September, 1997

'You never get a free ride, Mr C. Sooner or later the bill turns up.
As with our own blessed madonna, for instance. All that unearned
approval! Phew! Makes you think, eh?'

'I was his valet, you know.' 'Flash' Gordon's lips formed soft,
unhappy words. He was an interpreter attached to the Sloane
Square squadron. His raincoat was secure to the neck and pad-
locked. They had found him in some provincial prison. 'Up there.
He was a gent through and through but not exactly an intellectual. She was twice as bright as he and she wasn't any Andrea
Dworkin, either. I "wore the bonnet" as we say in Tannochbrae.
Some days you could go mad with boredom. Being a flunky is a
lot more taxing than people think. At least, it was for me.'

'Weren't you afraid they'd find out about your past?' Mo noted several old acquaintances amongst the newcomers, not all of them yuppies.

'Well, I was a victim too, you know.' Flash understood best how to comfort himself.

Una Persson, stylish as ever in her military coat and dark, divided pants, straddled the fire, warming her hands. Her pale oval face, framed by a brunette pageboy, brooded into the middle distance. 'Don't buy any of that cheap American shit,' she told Major Nye. 'Their tanks fall apart as soon as their own crappy guns start firing. Get a French one, if you can. Here's a picture –' she reached into her jacket – 'from *Interavia*. All the specifications are there. Oh, and nothing Chinese.'

'What's wrong with Chinese?' asked Jerry. He lay beside the fire staring curiously at her boot.

'Don't start that,' she said firmly.

But she answered him, addressing Mo. 'It's totally naff, these days. Jerry never could keep in step.'

'No free lunches,' said Jerry proudly, as if remembering a lesson.

'No free lunches.' Una Persson unslung her MK-50 and gave the firing mechanism her intense attention. 'Only what you can steal.'

9

Sign Your Name in Our Book of Condolence

As Mr Blair's voice echoes into silence, Elton John gives his biggest ever performance. He opens with the words – 'Goodbye England's Rose' – of his rewritten version of one of Diana's favourite songs, 'Candle in the Wind'. Billions around the world sing with him and remember the 'loveliness we've lost'. In Hyde Park, many watching on giant videos weep uncontrollably.

News of the World, 7 September, 1997

'It's not the speed that kills you, it's what's in the speed, right?' Sagely Shakey Mo contemplated his adulterated stash. 'You want to do something about that nose, Mr C.'

Jerry dabbed at his face with the wet Kleenex Trixie had given him. For a few moments he had bled spontaneously from all orifices.

'Better now?' Bishop B. looked up from the month-old *Mirror* he had found. It was his first chance to read one of his own columns, 'God the Pal'. He was getting along famously with the newcomers. They understood all about Christian Relativism, Consumer Faith and Fast Track Salvation. They had read his *Choice in Faith* and other pamphlets. They were considering tempting him to transfer and become their padre. Trixie was even now involved in negotiations with her opposite number. They used the *can* as their unit of currency.

Not having the stomach to finish them off, the Dianistas had brought a few of their better-looking prisoners with them. The allies now stood shoulder to shoulder, staring down at the foxhole they had filled with the cringing youngsters.

Mo felt about inside his coat and came out with a small, clear glass medicine bottle whose top had been carefully sealed with wax.

'See that?' He brandished the vial at the baffled prisoners. 'See that?'

'You know what that is? Do you? You fucking wouldn't know, would you? That, my dirty little republican friends, is one of *her* tears.' With his other hand he unslung his weapon.

As they heard his safeties click off, the half-starved boys and girls began to move anxiously in the trench, as if they might escape the inevitable.

'She fucking wept for you, you fuckers.' Mo's eyes shone with reciprocal salt. 'You fucking don't deserve this. But *she* understood compassion, even if you don't.'

The big multifire MKO made deep, throaty noises as it sent explosive shells neatly into each tender body. They arced, twitched, were still. Nobody had had to spend much energy on it. It was a ritual everyone had come to understand.

Mo slung the smoking gun onto his back again.

'You want to search them?' He winked at Trixie. 'I haven't touched the pockets.'

His visionary eyes looked away into the distance. Killing always heightened his sense of time.

Bishop Beesley murmured over the corpses while Trixie slipped into the trench and collected what she wanted. 'It was a culture of self-deception,' he said.

Trixie pulled herself up through the clay. 'Isn't that the definition of a culture?'

Apologising for the effect of the cold weather, Bishop Beesley urinated discretely into the pit.

Jerry turned away. He was asking himself a novel question. Was everything going too far?

10

Reflexivity

Last Sunday a light went out that illuminated the world. Nothing would turn it back on. The death of Princess Di, the fairytale princess, the human royal, left us all totally stunned.

I am not a Johnny-come-lately to sing the praises of our magical princess. Unlike many others who now describe her in such glowing terms but certainly did not during her life, I have again and again expressed my love for Diana.

When I got some readers' letters knocking her I was saddened. I wonder how they and all the grey men who put her down feel now? The people have spoken.

– Michael Winner,
News of the World, 7 September, 1997

'Islands within islands, that's the British for you.' The Hon. Trixie had long since given up on her race. It was her one regret that she had not been born a Continental. Her mother still shuddered if the word was mentioned.

Their convoy had broken through to the M1. Although heavily pitted and badly repaired, the motorway was still navigable. It left them more exposed, but it had been a while since any kind of aircraft had been over. Several friendly and unfriendly air forces were abroad, on hire to continental corporations. It was the only way to raise enough money to pay for the quality of artillery they demanded.

'We have had to learn,' PM Flair had announced over the radio, 'that we only have so many options. Economics is, after all, the root of most warfare. We can have guns and butter, but we can't have aircraft carriers *and* the latest laser-scopes. It makes sense, really. Only you, the warriors in this great cause, can decide what you need most. And if you tell us what you need, *we will listen.* I guarantee that. Unfortunately, I am not responsible for the failings of my predecessors, who set up the supply systems and who were as unrighteous as I am righteous. But we'll soon have the engine overhauled and back on the road, as it were, before Christmas. I have long preached the gospel of personal responsibility. So you may rest assured that I will keep this promise or take the Big Step in the attempt. Thank you. God bless.'

There were seven weeks left to go. By now the people's PM would probably be praying for a miracle. Ladbroke's and the Stock Exchange were setting all kinds of unhelpful odds.

Jerry himself had not ruled out Divine Intervention. Surely something was in control?

'It's not that long since you were collateral yourself, Mr C.' Mo attempted to revive his friend's self-respect. 'Remember when your corpse was the hottest commodity on the market?'

'Long ago.' The old assassin contemplated his own silver age. 'Far away. Obsolete icons. Failed providers. Lost servers. Scarcely an elegy, Miss Scarlett. Hardly worth blacking up for. Government by lowest common denominator. A true market government. Poets have been mourning this century ever since it began. Anyway, how would I remember? I was dead.'

'As good as.' Una Persson settled a slim, perfect reefer into her holder and fished her Meredith from her top pocket. Her elegant brown bob swung to the rhythm of the half-track's rolling motion and Jerry had a flash, a memory of passion. But it hurt him too much to hang on to it. He let it go. Bile rose into his mouth and he leaned again over the purple Liberty's bag. Something was breaking up inside him, mirroring the social fractures in the nation. He was nothing without his guidelines. This disintegration had been going on for many years and was now accelerating as everyone had predicted. Was he the only one who had planned for this? Had all the others lost their nerve in the end? He stared around him, trying to smile.

'Either stop that,' said Una, 'or pass me your bag.'

'Here we go!'

Ignoring the twisted and buckled signs which sought to misdirect them, they turned towards Long Buckby and their ideal. At some time in the past couple of years some vast caravan of traffic had come this way, flattening the borders and turning the sliproad into a crude highway, reminding Jerry of the deep reindeer paths he had once followed in Lapland, when he had still thought he could find his father.

He had found only an abandoned meteorological post, with some photographs of his mother when she had been in the chorus. Her confident eyes, meeting Jerry's across half a century, had made him weep.

A relatively unblemished sign ahead read:

WELCOME TO THE SHERWOOD EXPERIENCE
Sheriff of Nottingham Security Posts Next 3 Miles.
No admittance without Merry Man guide.
ROBIN HOOD'S FOREST
and FEUDAL FEUDING VR
(one price family ticket value)

'I told you we were near Nottingham.' Mo sniffed. 'There's nothing like that smell anywhere else in the world. God, it makes you hungry!'

'Takes you back a bit, eh?' said Major Nye. 'Now this, of course, is where an off-road vehicle proves herself.' The delicate veins on his hands quivered and tensed as he found his gears.

'Isn't it still relatively unspoiled?' Trixie tried to take the bib from her mother who clung to it, glaring and mumbling. Lady Brunner's lunchtime pap was caked all over her face and chest. 'The heartland of England. Where our most potent legends were nurtured.'

'That's crap, dear,' said Una. 'The only thing nurtured around here is two thousand years of ignorance and prejudice.'

'So she's right.' Colonel Hira rubbed softly at his buttocks. 'The heartland of England.'

'Fucking Tories,' said Mo.

'Right on!' Colonel Hira's chubby fist jabbed the overhead air.

'Haven't you forgotten how fucking concerned, caring and multicultural the conservatives really were, colonel?' The Hon. Trixie was furious. 'One more crack like that and you'll be whistling "Mammy".'

'I thought you were with the other lot.' Major Nye was puzzled.

Trixie made an edgy gesture. She hated argument. It was so hard to tell who really had the power these days.

'That doesn't mean I can't see all sides.'

Laughing, Jerry coughed something up.

As best they could, the others shifted away from him.

It was getting crowded in the steel-plated cab. The heat was unseasonal. What was going wrong with the weather?

'Greenhouse!' Jerry was reading his phlegm. 'We have to get back to Kew. Kew.'

'Kew?' Mo cheered up. He had always tried to avoid the Midlands.

'Queue?' Trixie shook a vehement head. 'Queue? Never again.'

'Kew,' said Jerry. 'Kew. Kew.'

'You should get that looked at.' From the shadows under the instrument panel Bishop Beesley surfaced. 'You could infect us all.'

Everyone was staring at him. They had believed him gone off with the renegades.

He adjusted his mitre. He shrugged his cassock straight and took a firm grip on his crook. 'There were small, unsettled differences,' he explained. 'In the end I could not in conscience take another appointment. My place is with you.'

'But you've wolfed the supplies,' said Mo.

'There was hardly anything left.' The bishop was all reassurance. 'Hardly a bite. Not a sniff. I wish I could tell you otherwise. A little jam would have been welcome, but no. These are harsh conditions and the Church must find the resources to meet them. I suggest that we pick up our holy charge and proceed directly to Coventry where negotiations are already in progress. They're well-known to have enormous stockpiles.' His mouth foamed with anticipatory juices. 'Rowntree's. Cadbury's. Terry's. Everything. Warehouses worthy of Joseph!'

'Coventry's the soft option.' Mo found the butt of his Monteverdi. Contemptuously he stuck it into his mouth. 'You want chocs, bishop, we should go to York. It's the obvious place. They always make the highest bids on this stuff.'

'Stuff?' Bishop Beesley was outraged. 'Is that any way to speak of such holy remains? The Church's motives, Mr Collier, if not yours, are of the highest. Coventry is much closer. Moreover the bishop there is well-disposed towards us. Did you hear what the Bishop of York had to say? Idolatry, he says! Step into the twenty-first century, divine colleague, I say. But when all the dust settles, security is our chief concern. As I am sure it's yours. We should never forget that ours is above all a profoundly spiritual quest.'

'Oh, for God's sake! Oh, Christ!'

Accidentally, Trixie had put her hand into Jerry's jerking crutch. Jerry's lips gave an odd spasm. 'Come again?'

II

Prince Harry to Meet the Spice Girls

Earlier, just outside London, the hearse had to stop before it joined the motorway so police could take away blooms from the windscreen. The flowers made a poignant mound on the hard shoulder. Once inside the Althorp estate Diana was laid to rest quietly and privately on an island set in a lake. Her day was over.

News of the World, 7 September, 1997

There were now some forty armoured cars, in various states of repair, and about a hundred mixed troops on rickshaws, mopeds, bicycles, motorbikes, invalid carriages and milk floats. Fifteen horsemen wore the tattered uniforms of the Household Cavalry. They were spread out for almost thirty miles, with Jerry & Co. in the lead, creeping along the B4036 to relieve the besieged manor of Althorp. The radio message had described a good-sized army of combined Reformed Monarchists, Conservative Republicans, Stuarts, Tudors, Carolines, Guillomites, New Harovians and Original Royalists, all united in their apostasy, their perverse willingness to diss the Madonna Herself. Camping around the walls like old queens.

'You hard girls. It's a conspiracy, isn't it?' Shakey Mo passed Trixie's dusted reefer back to her. 'I call you the Cuntry. You are the country, aren't you? You're running it, really. The old girl network. Your mum's their rôle model. Our madonna's their goddess. A monstrous constituency. A vast regiment!'

'Keep mum.' Jerry giggled into his bag. 'Keep it dark. Under your hat. Close to your face.'

Baroness Brunner began to cackle again. It was high-pitched. Some kind of alarm. Her hideous old eyes glared vacantly into his. 'It's all in the cards, lad. All in the tea-leaves. Cards and tea-leaves made up my entire cabinet for a while. That way I could control the future.'

'Wonky.' Jerry twitched again. 'It's going all wonky.'

'I warned the wonkers.' The old baroness sighed. Her work was over. She had no more energy. 'Where am I? Can I say wonkers? I told them it would go wonky. You can't say I was wrong.' Independent of her words, her teeth began to clack slowly and rhythmically. She drew a scented silk cushion to her face. In vivid threads, the cushion bore the standing image of the Blessed Diana, with a magnificent halo radiating from around her blonde curls, her arms stretched as if to hug the world in love, flanked by choirs of celebratory angels. There was some sort of Latin inscription, evidently embroidered by an illiterate hand.

Jerry watched her breaking up. She was in worse shape than he was. She had spent far too much energy trying to get her predictions to come true. It made a shadow of you in no time. It had been the death of Mussolini and Hitler. That's what made most presidents and prime ministers old before their time. Memory was the first thing to go. Which was embarrassing when you couldn't remember which secrets to keep.

Jerry sighed. There wasn't a lot of doubt. Things were starting to wind down again.

He shivered and drew up the collar of his mossy black car coat.

12

Two Billion Broken Hearts

We think Diana was killed through drunken driving ... We think. I think. But we do not know. I do not know. Every newspaper and news organisation, with the exception of the more excitable elements of the Arab media, has decided it was an easily explained crash. Lurid theories about her death abound on the Internet but that is the domain of students in anoraks – desperate like the fundamentalist Muslims, to pin something on the Satans of the Western security services and their imperialist masters. Yet people who read serious newspapers and watch serious television programmes still have their doubts. Perhaps in this uncertain world they need to find a perpetrator, they cannot accept that the most popular woman of her time was wiped out with her playboy lover in an ordinary car crash after a night at the Ritz.

– Chris Blackhurst,
Observer, 19 October, 1997

'Are you sure it's not a lookalike or a wannabe?' Sucking a pur-loined lolly, Trixie stared critically up at the slowly circling corpse. 'And he could be pretending to be dead.'

The swollen head, the eyes popping, the ears flaring, stared back at her as if in outrage at her scepticism. Oddly, the silver paper crown his executioners had placed on his head gave the Old Contender a touch of dignity.

'We're going to have to burn him.' Major Nye came up with his clipboard. He was counting corpses. 'Before his followers get hold of him. He's worth an army in that state.' He paused to cast a con-templative and sympathetic eye over his former monarch. 'Poor old boy. Poor old boy.'

The rest of the besiegers were either dead, dying or sharing a common gibbet. By and large the century hadn't started well for the monarchists. It looked like the Dianistas were soon going to be in full control of the accounts.

'Good riddance, the foul, two-timing bastard.' Mo had sat down comfortably in the grass with his back against the tree. He was cleaning his piece with a Q-tip. 'First he betrays his wife, then his mother, then his lover. He makes Richard the Third seem like Saint Joan.'

'He struck me as quite a decent, well-meaning sort of chap.' Major Nye glanced mildly at his board.

'I don't think we want to hear any more of that sort of talk, do we, major?' Trixie had the moral high ground well sorted.

'He gave her a lovely funeral,' said Bishop Beesley. 'That huge wreath on the hearse with "MARM" picked out in her favour-ite flowers. It made the Krays seem cheap. A proper people's send-off.'

'The man was a monster.' Trixie firmly held her spin. 'The Prince of Evil. The Demon King. That's all you need to remember.'

'But what of the Web?' Una came walking through with a scalp-pole she had liberated from the Shire Protection Associ-ation. 'Can you control that, too?'

'Like a spider.' Trixie's words were set in saliva. She tasted her own bile as if it were wine.

In a moment they would achieve the culmination of all she had ever dreamed.

'They're getting a raft ready to go to the island,' said Una. 'I knew you'd want to be there at the moment they dug her up.'

Trixie quivered. 'You realise this will give us power over the whole fucking world, don't you?'

'It goes round and round.' Una put her scalps into Jerry's willing right hand. 'Hold on to those for a bit. And come with me.'

They stumbled over the ruins of the manor, over the remains of tents and makeshift defences. Crows were coming down in waves. Parts of the battlefield were thick with heaving black feathers. It had been impossible in the end to save either the attackers or the defenders. But the island, by general consent, had not been badly shelled.

They arrived at the lakeside. A raft of logs and oil-cans was ready for them.

'Good lord.' Bishop Beesley gestured with a distasteful Crunchie. 'That water's filthy. Thank heavens we don't have to swim across. There's all kinds of horrors down there. What do people do? Sacrifice animals?'

'It's our duty to take her out of all this.' Mo picked up a long pole and frowned.

'Clearly the family no longer has the resources.' Stepping onto the swaying boards, Trixie Brunner assumed that familiar air of pious concern. 'So we must shoulder the burden now. Until we can get her into safe hands.'

'You're still sending her to Coventry.'

'That's all changed.' Bishop Beesley chuckled at his own misunderstanding. 'I thought it was the Godiva headquarters. She almost went to Brussels. But we've had a lovely offer from Liverpool.'

'Which we're not going to take.' Trixie's sniff seemed to make him shrink. 'Ten times her boxed weight in generic liquorice allsorts? That's pathetic! You're thinking too parochially, bishop. Don't you realise we have a world market here?'

'She's right.' Una began to pole them out over the water.

'America. Russia. China. Wherever there's money. And the Saudis would buy her for other reasons. It's a seller's market.'

'Russell Stover. Hershey's.' Convinced, the bishop had begun to make a list. 'Pierrot Gormand. My Honeys Tastes a Lot of Lickeys.' Thoughtfully he popped the last of his Uncle Ben's Mint Balls into his mouth. 'Sara Lee. Knott's Berry Farm. Smucker's. America. Land of Sugar. Land of Honey. Land of Sweetness. Land of Money.' His sigh was vast and anticipated contentment.

'Syrup?'

13

We'll Win World Cup For Diana

The Royal Family often seem to behave in ways which could actually be called unpatriotic, and their denial of Diana, the world's sweetheart, was the biggest betrayal of all. But then, what can you expect from a bunch of Greeks and Germans...

Her brave, bright, brash life will forever cast a giant shadow over the sickly bunch of bullies who call themselves our ruling house. We'll always remember her, coming home for the last time to us, free at last – the People's Princess, not the Windsors'.

... We'll never forget her. And neither will they.

– Julie Burchill,
News of the World, 7 September, 1997

'We might have guessed the yellow press would be here first.' Trixie had the air of one who was glad she had anticipated the right make-up for an unexpected situation.

She glared furiously down into the empty grave.

'Who are you calling yellow?' Frank Cornelius brushed dark earth from his cords. 'Anyway, I wasn't here first, obviously.' His features had a blighted look, as if he had suffered severely from greenfly.

'But you know who was, don't you?' Una Persson poked impatiently at him with her long-barrelled Navy Colt. She had chosen it because the brass and cherrywood went best with her coat but it was a bugger to load. 'That earth's still fresh. And the coffin looks recently opened.'

Bishop Beesley was shattered. He sat on the edge of the empty grave licking the wrapping of his last Rollo.

'This is sacrilege.' Mo paced about and gestured. 'I mean it's inconceivable.'

As usual at times like these, Jerry had risen to the occasion. 'I think we're going to have to torture you for a bit,' he told his brother. 'To get the information we need.'

'That won't be necessary, Jer.' Frank's smile was unsure.

'Yes it will,' said Jerry.

'It was all legit.' Frank spoke rapidly. 'The upkeep of the site was tremendously draining, as you can imagine. After the old earl went down outside South Africa House at the battle of Trafalgar Square, there was a bit of a hiatus. The surviving family has responsibilities to its living members, after all. They brought a copter down while you were shelling the house. She'll be in Switzerland in an hour or two. Procter and Gamble have acquired the cloning rights. This is democracy in action. Think of it – soon, anyone who can afford one gets one! Charities will snap them up. Live! Oh, Jerry, this is what we've dreamed of! Of course, she doesn't actually belong to the people any more. She's a corporate property. It's Princess Diana™ from now on. A dually controlled subsidiary, People's Princess (Kiev) PLC, own all the copyrights and stuff. But there'll be more than enough of her to go round. Charity gets a percentage of those rights, too. PP are a company with compassion. Their chairman's a notorious wet.'

'I wish you'd tell us all this after we've tortured you,' said Jerry.

Frank sank to his knees.

'Sorry,' he said.

'*You're* fucking sorry.' Mo unhitched his big shooter, unsnapping the safeties, going to Narrow Ribbon Fire and pulling the trigger in one fluid, chattering movement which cut Frank's head from its body. It bounced into the grave and rested in the desecrated mud looking up at them with mildly disappointed eyes. A groan came out of the torso as it slumped onto the stone. Blood soaked the granite.

'Loose cannon.' Mo seemed to be apologising.

Jerry was getting pissed off. He rounded on Trixie. 'I told you this was strictly cash. I should have got it from you up front. And now this little bastard's robbed me of my one consolation.'

But Trixie had been thinking.

'Wait here. Come with me, Mo.'

She began to tramp through the mud towards their raft. She boarded it and Mo poled his way to the shore.

While Una Persson did something with the grave, Jerry squatted and watched the Hon. Trixie.

She and Mo walked up the shore to where they had parked their Ford Flamefang.

Una came to stand beside Jerry and she too studied Trixie and Mo, watched as they dragged old Baroness B. from the cab. Trixie's mother made peculiar stabbing motions at the air, but otherwise did not resist. Her teeth were half out of her mouth and her wig was askew but the worst was the noise which came from her mouth, that grating whine which people would do anything to stop. In her heyday, men and women of honour had agreed to appalling compromises just so that they might not hear her utter that sound again.

Even after Trixie had stuffed her mother's moth-eaten wig into the rattling mouth, the old girl kept it up all the way back to the island.

Jerry was beginning to realise that his recovery was temporary. He reached for his purple bag and looked on while Trixie and the rest bundled the noisy old woman into the coffin and tacked the lid back on. There were some unpleasant scratching noises for a bit and then they knew peace at last.

'It's a pity we didn't keep one of those gun carriages.' Mo was polishing the top.

'They won't know the difference in Coventry.' Trixie pushed

Jerry towards their car. 'Check the raft. Have a root around. We'll need all the bungee cords we can get for this one. Once we get to the car, she'll have to go on the roof.'

'I'm not sure of the wisdom of deceiving the Church.' Bishop Beesley fingered himself in unusual places. 'Where does devotion end and sacrilege begin?'

'Don't be ridiculous.' Trixie started to haul the coffin back through the mud towards the waiting raft. At the waterside Jerry and Una took it over from her.

She paused, catching her breath. 'Nobody can go further than the great British public. Besides, Mum's an authentic relic in her own right. Surely she's well worth a lorryfull of Smarties? It'll be the muscle we need to get us out of trouble. And if she's still alive when they open the box, they've got an authentic miracle. Who loses? A deal's a deal, vicar. Any port in a storm. Isn't modern life all about responding appropriately to swiftly changing situations? And isn't the Church all about modern life?'

'Besides –' Mo gestured in the direction of the real world – 'we haven't got much choice. We're going to have to buy petrol.'

'Well,' said the bishop, 'we'd better not tell the men.'

'We'll divvy up after Coventry, say.'

This began a fresh round of intense bargaining.

'There is another alternative…' Nobody was listening to Mo. He shrugged and stepped down towards the raft.

'But I understood I would receive part of my share in confectionery.' Bishop Beesley was close to panic.

At a signal from Una, Jerry helped Mo aboard, then loosed the mooring rope. He and Mo began to pole rhythmically through the detritus towards the bank.

It was some minutes before Trixie and the bishop noticed what was happening and by then Mo and Una were loading the coffin onto the roof while Jerry got the Ford's engine going.

'Now Church and State will have time to establish a deeper and more meaningful relationship.' Una opened her *Diana of the Crossways* and began comparing it to her charts. 'Someone has to preside over the last rites of that unsatisfactory century.'

After his brief flurry of energy, Jerry was winding down again. 'It suited me.'

Major Nye's face appeared at the window slit. He was puffing a little. 'Hope you don't mean to leave me behind, old boy.'

'Can't afford to, major.' Una's spirits were lifting. 'We need you to drive. Climb aboard.'

As Major Nye's legs swung in, Jerry shifted to let the old man get into the seat. The others settled where they could. The cab had not been cleaned and the smell of vomit was atrocious. From overhead on the roof there came a faint, rhythmic thumping which was drowned as Major Nye put the car into gear and Mo took his place in the gunnery saddle.

Their followers limping behind, they set off towards Coventry, singing patriotic songs and celebrating the anticipated resolution.

'All in all –' Jerry sank back onto his sacks and rolled himself a punishing reefer – 'it's been a tasty episode. But it won't go down too well in the provinces. I'm beginning to believe this has been a poor career move. Market forces abhor the unique.'

What would I know? I say. What would I know? I am dead and a friend of the dead.

We get no respect these days.

The Camus Referendum

(In Memoriam: Douglas Oliver)

Wahab

Farther Down The Line

All of a sudden, then, I found myself brought up short with some though not a great deal of time available to survey a life whose eccentricities I had accepted like so many facts of nature. Once again I recognised that Conrad had been there before me ... I was born in Jerusalem and had spent most of my formative years there and, after 1948, when my entire family became refugees, in Egypt.

– Edward Said,
London Review of Books, 7 May, 1998

Jerry took the July train out of Casablanca, heading East. There was a cold wind blowing. It threatened to pursue them to Cairo.

'It's like you've been telling them for years.' He was leafing through *Al Misr*, thinking it could do with a few pictures. 'They're academics and politicians mostly, debating whether or not flight is possible or if it is whether they should allow it, and everywhere above them the sky is full of ships.' He frowned. 'Is that a quote? If we're living on the edge of the abyss, Miss B., I think we should make the best we can of it. Love conquers all. A bit of vision and we'll all be more comfortable.'

'I have had visions since I was a child.' With prissy, habitual movements Miss Brunner arranged her *hadura*. She was calling herself General Hazmin but her old, green fundamentalist eyes still winked above her yashmak. Her accompanist, Jerry's current lover, snored lightly in the corner chair while the grey, flat roofs of Casablanca began to flash past faster and faster. 'Originally of the Prophet, but later of ordinary people from history, or people I did not recognise, at least. I always felt very close to God.'

'Me, too.' Jerry settled himself into his deep chair as the train torqued up to sound minus ten. 'With me, of course, it was Jesus. Then the Middle Ages, mostly. Then the nineteenth century. Now we're somewhere between the end of one millennium and the beginning of another. The blank page between the Old Testament and the New. I had no idea what it was all about. These days I just see things in shop windows. They always turn out to be something ordinary when I examine them. Maybe it was the dope in the sixties? They sell you any old muck now.' He patted his heavy suitcase.

'This is the age of the lowest common denominator. I blame America.'

'Don't we all?' She stared vacantly at the blurred landscape. 'A ram without a brain, a ewe without a heart.'

He blushed. 'Impossible!'

She looked into the whispering corridor. 'Flight is so unfashionable, these days.'

Dos

American Tune

His life was dedicated to the United Kingdom, and he always spoke for all the people of this fair land. Enoch warned us about Europe, about excessive immigration, and he reminded us of our heritage and history. If only we had all listened...

– Stuart Millson,
This England, Summer 1998

'A mature democracy is surely a democracy which orders its affairs by public debate and reasoned agreement. An immature democracy is one where affairs are settled by conflict, by adversarial court cases, authoritarian laws resisted by civil liberties groups. Didn't America lead the way in this appalling devolution? Why would any democracy want to repeat that mistake?' Prinz Lobkowitz looked at his dusty drawers and coughed as if embarrassed.

'Immature or corrupted, the body counts are the same. They were almost up to the 100,000 target last year. It's a big market, major. A lot of citizens. A lot of good gun sales. All I need is for you to give me the slip.' Jerry took dust from his eyes with a fingertip, glaring at the disturbing fan above. 'And if you could spare a little something for the journey...'

'Of course.' Lobkowitz found his documents. 'Ugh!'

'That was probably me.' Shakey Mo Collier spoke from the shadows where he had been posing with his new ordnance. Lazily he flipped and zipped. 'You had Marmite or something in there. I thought it was resin or ope but I couldn't get the lid off without using my knife. Sorry. You'd know if I was *trying* to make a mess.'

'Thanks.' With insane deliberation Lobkowitz began to whistle 'Dixie'.

Drei

Valentine

> I dreamed I was in England
> And heard the cuckoo call,
> And watched an English summer
> From spring to latest fall,
> And understood it all.
>
> – Enoch Powell,
> *Collected Poems*

'The land of cotton.' Major Nye took Una her gin sling. She was hypnotised by the waters of the Nile white against the steel-grey rocks. 'The river runs a merrier course nearer to her source than her destination. What?' He sat down in the other chair as she turned, uncrossing her legs. She wore Bluefish, longing for authenticity in pastel luxury. And elegant beyond understanding, he thought. She was unassailably beautiful these days. They sat at their old table on the terrace of the elegantly guarded Cataract

Hilton. Fundamentalists had made tourism a luxury again. It was wonderful. Indeed the fundamentalists were very popular in America now because they had successfully prepared for Western business and attendant human rights legislation by reducing their national economies to zero and attracting the benign authority of the democratic corporations.

Una and the major were surveying neighbouring Elephant Island for an EthicCorp™ which had already done miracles in Egypt. And everyone admitted *DisneyTime*™ had turned Alexandria into the thrusting modern metropolis it was today. They had even removed the original city to the Sinai between *Coca-Cola*™ University and *Sinbad's Arabian Fantasy*™, in a successful effort to improve trade, tourism and education in the region. Who could complain? In *LibraryWorld*™ the scrolls could almost be real.

'Of course.' Una concentrated on a pleat. She shook her skirt again. 'We are making a rod for our own backs, major. Or, at least, putting all this tranquillity in jeopardy.'

'It's share and share alike nowadays, Mrs P.,' Major Nye tipped his cap towards the river. 'We all have to take a little less. Like the War, what?'

'What war?'

'Last one. Big one. What?' He frowned. 'Are you joking, Mrs P? Or are you in trouble?'

She reassured him. 'Just a joke, major. In poor taste.'

'I know exactly what you mean.' He offered her a bowl of cherroids. 'These are dreadful.'

Arba

Heartland

'If two quarrel, the Briton rejoices,' has long been a proverb. In the course of centuries but few had seriously endeavoured to catch the measure of Mephistopheles, and none had succeeded. The wilder the turmoil in Europe, the more might

England rejoice, for countries that had got their heads battered were afterwards easily the most docile.

Hindenburg's March on London,
Germany, 1913, Eng. tr., 1916

'Okay, Mr C., So you never caught *The Desert Rats*. Then rely on me like an old-fashioned officer and I will get us through, okay? There isn't a World War Two movie I haven't seen at least twice and I've always been very fond of a wasteland.' Mo's voice was muffled by his respirator, a black and belligerent snout. 'Here we go!'

The half-track's caterpillars whistled impotently over the sand. Another shell made a neat, noisy crater only a few yards away. They wiped at their goggles with dirty gloves.

'Libyan.' Sniffing, Shakey Mo paused in his busy handling of the gears and gunning of the engine. 'You can always tell.'

'But we're so far from the border.' Bishop Beesley's camouflaged mitre oozed from the conning tower. 'And a long way from the Basra Road.'

'Never very far, bishop.' Shakey Mo did something angry to the machinery and it lurched upwards, back onto the blitzed concrete of the road. 'Not these days. Not ever.'

Pyat

Across the Borderline

Then in the year 1870 something quite unheard of happened. About that time there all at once appeared in Europe in the foreground a youth in the fullness of his strength – young Germany! He was a sprig of the good, stupid old-German Michael, who had fared especially badly owing to his horizon bounded by the church tower, and his secluded mode of living. Michael had to sit very far behind in the European State class, and during the last five hundred years he was always several decades behind the others. Young Michael, however, the fair-haired, blue-eyed fellow, was of a different mould! To the schoolmistress on the other side of the Channel he looked a very slippery fish!

Hindenburg's March on London

'They've been chopping up children, mostly, as far as I can tell.' General Hazmin had removed her yashmak and now wore a massive gasmask, designed to resist the most fashionable mixtures. It gave her the appearance of a Hindu goddess. She moved ponderously through the village. Every so often, when Jerry slowed down, she gave the rope a tug. He had begun to enjoy the sensation. His giggling grew louder as she dragged him, for a moment, through the gobs of bloody flesh. 'Oh, Christ!' He shook. 'So cold. Oh, fuck.' General Hazmin was discovering the frustrations of trying to punish a creature which had either experienced everything or was grateful to experience anything. 'You are no longer human, Captain Cornelius.'

He shrugged. 'I never was. Was I?'

'We are all born human.'

'Somewhere back on the clone line, sure. It's the type, though, that's important, isn't it? Cro-Magnon, I mean, or Neanderthal. We should never have got mixed up. It's not their faults.' He had a mood swing. He had begun to weep over the remains of a little girl whose throat had been slit and whose mother's hands had been cut off before she, too, had been killed. 'Their brains can't make the connections most of us make. They look human. But they're not quite. Thirty per cent of the population, at least? Genetics are so important these days, aren't they?'

Una Persson had taken the rope from General Hazmin's gloved hands. She swung her lovely hair as she looked back at him. 'So which are you, Jerry, love?'

'Bingo bango bongo, I should never have left the Congo.' Jerry sometimes wished he hadn't abused his *Homo superior* status so frequently and so self-indulgently. 'I used to be the world's first all-purpose human being. I was really happy in the jungle. Just like Derry and Toms. A new model of the multiverse. But it all turned back to shit. Africa should have negotiated new borders for herself. That's where the trouble began. I should know. I started it.'

'Yes, right. You and bloody Sisyphus.' Una exchanged some enjoyable glances with General Hazmin. 'What shall we do with him this time?'

Six

She's Not For You

Successive generations of our politicians have failed, or in some cases actively betrayed, their country's interests. Now only the ordinary people can hope to reverse the tide of bureaucracy and centralised control which is already engulfing every participating nation in Europe. Are there enough people who care or dare to do something about it? Or is *Land of Hope and Glory* finally to be replaced by *Deutchshland Uber Alles*?

Letter to *This England*, Summer 1998

'I'd like to stop off in Algiers as soon as possible.' Una had slung Jerry over her best pack camel. He rubbed his face on the animal's hide. He moaned with tiny pleasures. 'I had a wire from my agent. We're doing a revival of *The Desert Song* in Marrakech next month. I promised them I'd get you to sing.'

'Blue heaven and you,' croaked Jerry as he bounced. 'One alone. We are the Red Shadow's men. One for all and all for one. Or is all one, anyway? One or the Other? Never more than two? I can't believe in a simple duality. The evidence is all against it. Once a clone... Clone away, young multiverse. Clone away. Oops. Oh! Oh! Yes! Watch it, Stalin. The cells are out of control.'

'Damn!' By accident she had struck him full across the buttocks with her camel whip. She took some rags and a bowl from the saddlebags and tried to save the fizzing, strangely coloured sperm running down the animal's flanks.

This amused him even more.

Sebt

What Was It You Wanted?

SIR: I have recently returned from a business trip to the Arabian gulf and was immediately struck by the presence there of a British export which is rarely found anywhere else in the world. Why is it that when we travel several thousand miles to somewhere as alien to us as Bahrain or Dubai we can still buy a pint of good English bitter, yet those closer to us (geographically and politically) never stock anything but lager and pilsener? One could tread the pavements of French towns for hours and never find even a smell of anything like traditional English Ale.

Letter to *This England*

'Imperialism breeds nationalism and nationalism needs guns. America supplies both, just like ICI and Dupont make bullets and bandages. It's the trick the rubber trade learned early on. Condoms or rubber knickers. There's always a market.'

Una signed the form and handed over the remains. From his tank Jerry opened and closed his mouth. Tubes ran from all his other orifices. 'What?'

'You'll be fine,' she said.

The whole tribe surrounded him now. They seemed proud of their bargain. Discreetly, they pointed out the peculiarities of his anatomy. He was enjoying an unfamiliar respect.

'It is beautiful,' said one of the young women. Like the other Berbers, she wore no veil. Her aquiline features were striking. Her green eyes were exceptional. 'Some kind of cuttlefish?'

Una shook her head.

'Not nearly so interesting. Or intelligent. It's the light. See?'

Ocho

Getting Over You

I had allowed the disparity between my acquired identity and
the culture into which I was born, and from which I had been
removed, to become too great. In other words, there was an
existential as well as a felt political need to bring one self into
harmony with the other ... By the mid-seventies I was in the
rich but unenviable position of speaking for two diametrically
opposed constituencies, one Western, the other Arab.

– Edward Said,
Between Worlds

'You were monumental in Memphis.' Shakey Mo was trying to
cheer his exhausted chum. 'What a tom, Jerry. What a comeback!'

'Too many.' Jerry smiled sweetly into his restored reflection.
'Too much.'

Mo wasn't really listening. With a thumbnail, he scraped at a
bit of hardened blood on his barrel. 'It was a shame about Grace-
land. Could have been a crack. But nobody's got any money, these
days. It had to go to a private buyer. Nothing like the smell of an
old Vienna.'

'Land of Song.' Jerry slipped a comb through his locks. 'Land
of Smiles. Where there's a drug there's a way. Millions will pay
through the nose to visit that historic toilet.'

Mo put his gun down and carefully got out his maps. 'Now all
we have to do is find a drum.'

'Boom, boom,' said Jerry.

'I meant a gaff.' Mo folded the filthy linen. 'Sometimes I wonder about you.'

Enia

The Most Unoriginal Sin

Your paper talks about the balkanization of American society and the imminent train wreck we're facing. Any suggestions on what readers can do to help turn this around?

I urge your readers to become very aggressive in fighting for the enforcement of the nation's civil rights laws ... The civil rights laws passed in the 1960s are, for the most part, not enforced or are weakly enforced. A white man like me can pretty well discriminate against Americans of color every day of the week – in housing, employment, public accommodations, schools – with no fear of being punished under the civil rights laws. For example, it's estimated there are 4 to 8 million cases of racial discrimination in housing each year, and yet very few whites are ever punished, even mildly, for this massive discrimination...

– Joe Feagin,
Southern Poverty Law Center Report, June 1998

We don't have to worry about the Europeans. All the British and the French are waiting for is American leadership.

– Bob Dole to Congress, 1995

The American general had all the flaky wariness of his kind. He wasn't used to being in this position. Nobody spoke his language. He made complicated, aggressive movements with his cigar to show he was on top of things. His inexperienced lips trembled with frustration. His boy's eyes shifted uncontrollably, sensing the necessity of self-reliance but having no appropriate training, only the rhetoric. The Chlue were as mystified by him as the Sioux by Custer. But, like the Sioux, they had no problems with the idea of genocide. They had some sense of what his rituals meant and were wary of them. Perhaps they recognised the traditional American warm-up to a necessary action. When sentimental speeches failed, there was only the rocket.

The black tents were pitched all along the shallow valley. Sweat and animal dung, cooking fires, tajini, couscous. A noise of goats and ululating women. Horses. Metal. A subtle, pervading odour of cordite, a faint, blue haze of rifle-smoke. In the distance were the banners of the Rif and the Braber. All the Berber clans were assembling. Only Cornelius could have brought them here. He was one of themselves. Their cause was his. They asked little more than freedom to roam.

The general settled his plump bottom onto the director's chair which he had brought with him. Everyone else sat on carpets.

'Tell these bastards that they're Berber-Americans now. They can vote. We've given them several choices.'

In Arabic, which all the Berber tribes could understand, Jerry said:

'You have no choice. If you do not sell him your villages, he will have you all killed by fundamentalists.'

This made sense. Sheikh Tarak, their spokesman, gave it some thought.

'Tell them about human rights.' The general was impatient. 'War crimes.'

'He will then kill the fundamentalists. So all but him and his corporation will perish.'

'You will not perish, dear friend.' Tarak's old eyes remained amused. 'We'll sell him the villages. After all, it's only fifty years or so since our noble grandfathers wiped out the bastards who used to own them.'

'They'll sell.' Jerry turned to the general. 'But they want a royalty.'

'Royalty. Fucking royalty? Don't they know we've abolished all that in America.' He began to roll up his plans. 'This is going to be an eco-complex, not a fucking casino.'

'They say there's no royalty on egos.' Jerry responded to Tarak's enquiring eye.

'Good!' The handsome old sheikh understood perfectly. 'Let them build their hotels. Then we will come back upon a great *harka*. And lay waste to everything. Thus it begins again.'

'He's prepared to negotiate a lease,' Jerry told the general.

Tisa

Don't Give Up

Our passion for a city is often a secret one. Ancient, walled cities like Paris or Prague, or even Florence, are introspective, closed, their horizons limited. But Algiers, in common with a few other ports, is as open to the sky as an eager mouth, an unprotected wound. Algiers gives you an enthusiasm for the commonplace: how blue sea ends every street, the peculiar density of the light, the beauty of the people. And, inevitably, amidst all this unprotected generosity, you scent a seductive, secret ambience. You can be homesick in Paris for breathing space and the whisper of wings. In Algiers, at least, you can sample any desire and be certain of your pleasures, your self, and so know at last what everything you own is worth.

– Albert Camus,
Algerian Summer

In Marrakech Jerry sat back at his café table and watched the German tourists boarding the evacuation buses taking them to their planes and trains. The Djemaa el-Fna, the great Square of the Dead, had lost none of its verve. In fact, since the departure of the Germans a rather gay, lively quality had returned to the city. The storytellers were already drawing large crowds as they described the Rif's decision to drive the infidels from their territory. 'There is a tendency to play to the lowest common denominator, even here.' Prinz Lobkowitz leaned to freshen Una Persson's cup. 'Sugar?'

Mo Collier was bored brainless. He had set his vibragun on its lowest notch and was giving his back a massage. 'You got to admit, Prinz L., that they do a nice coffee. The krauts. I've never found this Turkish stuff much cop, even when you call it Greek stuff. Or Moroccan stuff. But your German, now, given half a chance, knows his Columbia from his Java and can brew a bean with the best. If only the rest of Fritz's food was edible, they could have become a nation of restaurateurs and we'd all like them now. They always meant well. But they should've brushed up on the old cuisine and not tried for the macho image. It doesn't suit them. It makes them even more ridiculous than most. They should have gone on laughing at the Prussians. Talk about the lowest CD of all, eh?'

'Bismarck was a great leveller,' Prinz Lobkowitz agreed. 'And so was Hitler, for that matter. An odd record, really, for so benign a race. They just want to bring the best they have to everyone else.'

The tourists were squeezing themselves through the double-wide doors as hard as they could. There were no street boys on hand to push them in. Their proffered francs and marks lay on the ground where they had been thrown back from the crowd. The Rif had made examples of surrounding villas owned by German infidels. The Marekshis were in a jolly mood. The Germans had no power now. Their marks were a bad memory. Some of the Berbers had brought food and video-cameras and were filming the sweating Teutons, in their damp, grubby whites, as they silently embarked.

Una eyed the swollen bottoms with some interest. 'Do you think they're growing into Americans?' she asked. 'Or are Americans descended from them?'

'Hard to tell. What an aggressive gene, eh? The Germans used to think of themselves as undeveloped Englishmen. They had that in common with the Americans. Now, of course, they need no models. They are all kingsize. They have their wealth instead.'

'Some day.' Mo was in a visionary mood. 'People will hunt them. Not much sport, though.'

'German?' Major Nye parted his lips in a silent laugh. His pale blue eyes were almost lively. 'I thought they were all Scotch. You know – MacDonalds, Campbells, Murdochs. Those chaps own everything. The most aggressive people on earth. Devolution was the best idea the English ever had. Now, with nobody else to blame, the Scotch and the Irish can go back to fighting each other. We can just hope they won't start marching on London again. They drink too much. And then they decide to claim our throne. Those sectarian battles never cease. They're a tradition.' The old soldier savoured the delicate mint. 'Because a few purse-mouthed Yankee scrooges refused to pay for the army that had protected their backsides, borrowed a couple of old English political principles, such as no taxation without representation, to offer a moral reason for welshing on their bills, their descendants now continue to give high-sounding reasons for not coughing up their fair share and see the "Celts" (actually mostly Danes) as fellow sufferers under the British heel. How long did this suffering last? The peculiar thing is that it's the most aggressive Americans – low Protestants, Scottish Rites Lodge, Orange Lodge – who swallowed the myth. The very people who would have been fighting the Catholics just as their Scotch-Irish cousins do now. Have you noticed, by the by, that all the soldiers in the regiments which massacred the Indians had Irish names? Their Indians, I mean. Not Kipling Indians. Though come to think of it...'

As the muezzin began his electronic call from the Booksellers' Mosque, Una Persson bowed her head over her black cup. 'That's progress for you.'

'And Heinz,' said Mo. 'And Sara Lee.'

'What?' Jerry was distracted. He murmured the responses.

'General foods.' Mo seemed to offer this as an explanation.

They allowed him a moment's time for himself.

'Nestlé's,' he added.

'Mo?' said Jerry.

'I thought we were doing one of those guessing games. The seven most powerful food corps. Like the names of the seven dwarfs. What's that?' Mo's ear ticked.

'Six,' said Jerry. 'Unless Private Murdoch doesn't count.'

'It's like adding a Greedy. Seems there should be one but there isn't. Okay, no junk media. How about Pepsi?'

'Drinks mostly. And burger chains.'

'That's food, too, though. Same with Coke.'

'We should stick to – you know – general foods. Basics.'

'Are we counting services?'

'No.'

'Then you cut out McDonald's.'

'Okay. Three.'

'Right,' said Mo, narrowing his eyes. 'Let's think of the rest.'

The last prayer called, the square was filling with its evening population. A wash of deep scarlet and glittering gold raced out of the shadows of the surrounding market stalls – the acrobats had arrived. The fire-eaters and snake-charmers and conjurors called their audiences to them. Fortune-tellers were busy with their cards and bones. A squeal of flutes. A mumbling of drums. Dark shapes moved boldly around the perimeter and the Pakistani fakir, originally an engineer kicked out of Saudi, lowered himself onto hot coals.

There was a smell of roasting mutton, of chestnuts, of jasmine and warm wax.

Una sighed at the texture of it. Her relaxed fingers traced eccentric geometries over the china. She folded down the collar of her black car coat and unbuttoned. Her chest foamed, white flecked with red. It was her linen, no longer constrained. She hadn't had time to change. She had come straight from the theatre with Jerry. She reached to caress his cooling hand. She had no fear that she was setting a precedent. If it didn't exist now, it wouldn't exist.

She stroked his rapidly growing nails. Entropy and the absurd. You had to love it.

Jerry raised his head. He smiled. He purred. A jaguar. 'My brain's changed.'

Major Nye beamed upon the crowd. He had not looked so

dapper since the last time he was here, with Churchill, in '44. The prayer having ended, he returned his cap to his head.

'What a blessing religion can be.'

(Thanks to Willie Nelson and *Across the Borderline*)

Cheering for the Rockets

I

Noon

There is this same anti-Semitism in America. I hear the swirl and mutter of it around me in restaurants, at clubs, on the beach, in Washington, in New York, and here at home. No basis exists for the statements that accompany it. 'The Jews,' people say, 'own the radio, the movies, the theaters, the publishing companies, the newspapers, the clothing business, and the banks. They are just one big family, banded together against the rest of humanity, and they are getting control of the media of articulation so that they can control us. They have depraved every art form. They are doing it simply to break down our moral character and make us easy to enslave. Either we will have to destroy them, or they will ruin us.'

– Philip Wylie,
Generation of Vipers, New York, 1942

Let a Jew into your home and for a month you will have bad luck.

Moroccan proverb

Let an American into your home and soon he will own your family.

Lebanese proverb

We call them 'sand niggers'.

Coca-Cola senior executive in private conversation

A nation without shame is an immoral nation.

– Lobkowitz,
Beyond the Dream, Prague, 1937

'They appear to have broken another treaty.' Jerry Cornelius frowned and removed something like a web from his smart black coat. Slipping his Thinkman™ into his breast pocket he fingered his heat. His nostrils burned. There was a wired, cokey sort of feel to the atmosphere. Probably only gas.

'Pardon?' Trixie Brunner, dressed to kill with a tasteful UN armband, was casting about in the dust for something familiar. 'So fill me in on this one. Who started it?'

'They did, naturally.' The UN representative was anxious to get the interview over. They had staked him into the ash by way of encouragement and the desert sun was now shining full on his face. His tunic flashes said he was General Thorvald Fors. The Pentagon had changed his name to something Scandinavian as soon as he got the UN appointment. It sounded more trust-worthy. He had already explained to them how he was really Vince Paolozzi, an Italian from Brooklyn and cursed with a mother who preferred his cousin to him. His familiar family remi-niscences, his litanies of favourite foods, the status of his family's ethnicity, his connections with the ultra-famous, his mafiosities, the whole pizza opera, had finally got on their nerves and for a while they had given him a shot of novocaine in the vocal cords. But now they were exhausting the miscellaneous Sudanese phar-maceuticals they'd grabbed at random on their way through Omdurman. The labels were pretty much of a mystery. Jerry's Arabic didn't run to over-the-counter drugs.

'I see you decided to settle out of court.' Jerry stared at the gen-eral, trying to recognise him. There was a memory. A yearning. Gone. 'Are you on our side?'

'What we say in public isn't always what we mean in private?' The general's display of caps seemed to be an appeal.

'A legalistic rather than a lawful country, wouldn't you say? That's the problem with constitutional law. Never has its feet on the ground.'

Lobkowitz came to look down at the general. He was behaving so uncharacteristically that for a second Jerry was convinced the old diplomat would piss on Fors. The handsome soldier bureaucrat now resembled a kind of horizontal messiah.

The Prinz fingered his fly. 'Nowadays, America's a white recently pubescent baptist festooned with an arsenal of sophisticated personal weaponry. Armed and ignorant. Don't cross him. Especially if you're a girl. Captain Cornelius, we're dealing with Geronimo here, not Ben Franklin. Geronimo understood genocide as political policy. He knew what was happening to him. Somehow inevitably that savage land triumphed over whatever was civilised in its inhabitants. They are its children at last.' Prinz Lobkowitz turned in the rubble to look out at the desert, where the Egyptian Sahara had been. His stocky fatigue-clad body was set in an attitude of hopeless challenge. His long grey hair rose and fell in the wind. His full mouth was rigid with despair. He was still mourning for his sons and his wife, left in Boston. For the dream of a lifetime. For peace. 'Our mistake.'

Jerry sniffed again at the populated air. 'Is that cordite?' He touched his lips with his tongue. 'Or chewing gum?' He had pulled on a vast white gelabea, like a nightshirt, and a white cap. His skin had lost some of its flake. He wondered if he shouldn't have brought more power. He'd only come along for the débris.

'All that informal violence. Out of control. Reality always made Yanks jumpy.' Shakey Mo licked his M18's mechanisms, feeling for tiny faults. 'They're good at avoiding it, of forgetting it. If it can't be romanticised or sentimentalised it's denied. Fighting virtual wars with real guns. That's why they export so much escapism. It's their main cash crop. That's why they've disneyfied the world. And why they're so welcome. Who wants to buy reality? Fantasy junkies get very aggressive when their junk is threatened. You all know that sententious American whine.' He tasted again. He was hoping to identify the grade of his oil. He had become totally obsessed with maintenance.

'If I were Toney Blurr I would stick a big missile right up Boston's silly Irish bottom. Where the republican terrorists' paymasters live. Remind them who we are. Bang, bang. And it would make the Protestants feel so much better. People in the region would understand. They admire that kind of decisive action. CNN-ready, as we say. Such a precise, well-calculated single, efficient strike would cut off the terrorists' bases and supplies and lose them credibility with their host nation. Bang. Bang. Bang.'

Everyone ignored the baroness. Behind her yashmak her mad old eyes glared with the zealotry of a recent convert. Since her last encounter with Ronald Reagan she had become strangely introspective, constantly trying to rub the thick unpleasant stains from the sleeve of her business suit. Not that she had been herself since three o'clock or whenever it was. There was a lot to be said for the millennial crash. It had questioned the relevance and usefulness of linear time.

'Universal Alzheimer's,' said Jerry. 'Where?'

'Eh?' Lady B.'s wizened fingers roamed frantically over her ice-blue perm. 'Would you say it was getting on for four?'

'Water...' General Fors moved pointlessly in his bonds, the stakes shifting in the ash, but holding. His uniform was in need of repair. His cheeky red, white and blue UN flashes were offensive to eyes grown used to an overcast world. Even his blood seemed vulgar. His skin was too glossy. They hadn't been able to get his helmet off easily so Mo had spray-painted it matt black. General Fors was also mainly black. His face gleamed and cracked where the paint had already set. 'Momma...'

'You're coming up with an unrealistic want list, pard.' Jerry was the only one to feel sorry for him. 'Anything more local and we'll happily oblige.'

'Home...'

'You are home. You just don't recognise it.' Mo's guffaw was embarrassing. 'Home of the grave. Land of the fee. You discount everything you have that's valuable. You sell it for less than the traders paid for Manhattan. Now all that's left are guns and herds of overweight buffalo wallowing across a sub-continent of syrup. They don't hear the distant firing any more. Or see the clouds of flies.'

'Fries?' said General Fors.

Prinz Lobkowitz had now relieved himself. His hopeless eyes regarded the general. 'You had a vital, successful trading nation reasonably aware of its cultural shortcomings. Which everyone liked. We liked your film stars. We liked your music. Your sentimental cartoon world. And then you had to take the next step and become an imperial power. Burden of empire. Malign by definition. Hated by all. Including yourselves. You're not a country any more, you're an extended episode of *The X-Files*.'

'Missiles!' The general tried a challenge. His head rolled with the fear of it.

'All used up now, general. Remember? HQ filled them with poisoned sugar and wacoed them into your own system. The bitterness within. Double krauted. Flies? You think this is bad. You should see California.' Babbling crazy, Mo appeared to take some personal pride in the decline.

'You told him this *was* California.' Any hint of metaphor made Trixie uneasy and simile got her profoundly aggressive. 'Is that fair?' She cleared her throat. She patted her chest.

'Lies...' said General Fors. His big brown eyes appealed blankly to heaven. The sun had long since disabled them.

'I call it retrospeculation.' A goat bleated. Professor Hira came waving out of the nearest black tent. With their vehicles, the Berber camp was the only shelter in a thousand miles. The plucky little Brahmin had an arrangement with the sheikh. He was still wearing his winter djellabah. He had his uniform cap on at a jaunty angle. Behind him, above the dark folds of heavy felt, the tribe's cycling satellite dish forever interpreted the clouds. 'Anyway. What does geography mean now?'

'Lies...'

'Too right. You dissed the whole fucking world, man. Then you ojayed it. But not for ever. You were neither brave, free nor respectful. Once we couldn't use your engines what could you offer us except death?' Shakey Mo stepped in the general's lap, crossing to the useless desert-cruiser and climbing slowly up the camouflage webbing to his usual perch on the forward gun tower. 'Not that I approved of everyone leaving the UN.'

'We are the UN,' explained General Fors. 'At least let me keep my Ferraris.'

'Your mistake was to get up the Mahdi's nose, mate. A poor grasp of religion, you people. And what's worse, you have bad memories.' Pulling down the general's shades, Mo set himself on snooze. Gently, his equipment fizzed and muttered, almost a lullaby. He swung slowly in his rigging. From his phones came the soothing pounding of Kingsize Taylor and the Dominoes.

To be fair, General Fors had got up all their noses. Leaving old Lady Brunner wandering about in the dried-up oasis, the rest of them moved into the desert leviathan's shade. They felt uneasy if they wandered too far from the huge land-ship. Her Kirbyesque aesthetics were both comforting and stunning. But her function left something to be desired. The *General Gordon* had been breaking down ever since they'd fled Khartoum. The vehicle had been the best they could find. At a mile to the gallon it wasn't expensive to run. The world was full of free gas. From somewhere inside the ship their engineer, Colonel Pyat, could be heard banging and cursing at the groaning hydraulics and whispering cooling systems. Sometimes it was hard to tell the various sounds apart. The machine had its own language.

Jerry wondered at the sudden sensation in his groin. Was he pregnant?

He paused and looked up at the pulsing sky. At least they'd had the sense not to fly.

2

Non

Last winter, in the first precious weeks of war, our Senate used three of them to argue the moral turpitude of one member. That is as sad a sight as this democracy has seen this century.

– Philip Wylie,
Generation of Vipers

We kept reporting to our officers that there were large numbers of Germans all around us, together with heavy transport and artillery, but the brass told us we were imagining things. There couldn't be Germans there. Intelligence hadn't reported any.

Survivor, the Battle of the Bulge

For some weeks after their arrival in Bosnia the Americans spent millions of dollars in a highly-publicised bridge-building exercise. The whole time they were building it local people kept telling them there was an easy fording place about half a mile downriver. Intelligence had not reported it.

Survivor, Bosnia

You have to tell the White House and the Pentagon what they want to hear or they won't listen to you. That's how we got blamed for the Bay of Pigs after we'd warned against it.

Ex-CIA officer

WE DON'T DIAL 911

Commercial Texan home signboard
painted on silhouette of a sixgun

'Everything's perfectly simple.' General Fors had rid himself of his various stigmata and had repainted his helmet a pleasing apple-green. His attempts at Arabic lettering were a little primitive, but showed willing, even if his crescent looked like a sickle. 'It's just you people who complicate everything. We were so comfortable.'

They had made him security officer and put him near the revolving door. The hotel was deserted. Through the distant easterly windows guttered a wasteland of wrecked cars and abandoned flyovers, a browned world.

'Too many you know darkies.' Jillian Burnes, the famous transsexual novelist, was the only resident now. She was reluctant to leave. She had been here for six months, she said, and made a little nest for herself. She had come on a British Council trip and lost touch for a while. Her massive feet up on the Ark of the Covenant, she was peeling an orange. 'This operation was aimed at thinning them out a bit.'

'So far it seems to have firmed them up a bit.' Jerry was helping the general buckle his various harnesses together. He dusted off his uniformed back. 'All this red plush is a natural sand trap.'

In the elegant lobby, its mirrors almost wholly intact, they had piled their booty in rough categories – domestic, religious, entertainment, military, electronic, arts – and were resting at the bar enjoying its uninvaded largesse. Even the sky was quiet now. The customers had all fled on the last plane. And the last plane had gone down in the rush. They could have been in New York or Washington. Had there still been a New York or Washington.

Giving the general a final brush, Jerry wondered why so much of Jerusalem was left.

The other British Council refugee was dwarfish Felix Martin, son of the famous farting novelist, Rex. A popular tennis columnist in his own right and virtual war face for the breakfast hit *Washington Toast*, Felix dabbed delicately at his dockers and looked tragically up at Trixie.

'Baby?' said Trix.

'Have you been over here before? Is that blood, do you think?

3

None

> But, until man is willing to pay the cost of peace he will pay the
> price of war, and, since they must be precisely equal, I ask you
> to consider for how many more ages you think man will be
> striking balances with battles? ... But recollect that, to have
> peace, congresses will be compelled to appropriate for others
> as generously as they do now for our armies, and the taxpayers
> will have to pay as willingly, and as many heroes will have to

dedicate their lives to the maintenance of tranquility as are now risking them to restore it.

– Philip Wylie,
Generation of Vipers

Man is still so far from considering himself as the author of war that he would hardly tolerate a vast paid, public propaganda designed to point out the infinite measure of his private dastardliness and he would still rather fight it out in blood than limit the profitable and vain activities of peace in order to study his personal conscience.

– Philip Wylie, ibid.

Once you get it [your market economy] in place, you'll take off like a rocket.

– Bill Clinton
to the Russian Duma, 1 September, 1998

'They must have felt wonderful, bringing the benefits of German culture to a world united under their benign flag.' The three had strolled out to what was probably the Reichstag or possibly a cinema. The set, so spectacular in its day, had received one of the first strikes specifically aimed at Disney. Jerry picked up a fluffy Dumbo.

'These aren't Germans.' Trixie tucked everything back in. 'These are Americans.' She remassaged her hair.

'Did I say Americans? They loved the Nazis, too. I remember when I worked for Hearst in '38. Or was it CBS? Good old Putzi. A Harvard man, you know. Or Ford? Or Goebbels? Or '49? Uncle Walt admired the artwork and slogans, but he thought he could make the system function better over here. And they were, indeed, far more successful. Still, the patterns don't change.'

'You have to take the jobs where you find them.' Trixie, in sharp black and white, pouted her little mouth. In her day she had firmly enjoyed the ears, tongues and privates of cardinals and presidents. She was a prettier, modern and more aggressive version of her old mum, who had been bought by a passing trader.

'It's what the fourth estate is all about.

'It's what the public says.

'It's what we say.

'I mean, this is what we say, right?' Felix was having some trouble getting his sentence going. He didn't like the look of Mo's elaborate ordnance. 'Are those real guns?' His melancholy nose twitched nervously above prominent teeth, a glowering dormouse. Tough cotton shirt, serviceable chinos, jumper, jacket, all bearing the St Michael brand. Marks guaranteed middle-class security. Land's End. Eddie Bauer. Oxfam gave him the shudders. He was strict about it. His life was nothing if not exclusive.

He withdrew into his clothing as if into a shelter. It was all he had left of his base.

'Oh bum. Oh piss. Oh shit.

'Oh bum. Oh piss. Oh shit.

'Oh bum.'

'Hallelulla,' said Jerry. He was beginning to feel his old self. 'Or is that Hallelujah?'

'Bum again?' Trixie scented at the wind. 'Was that Felix. Or you?'

'Childish bee. Where's the effin' loo, lovey?' Jillian Burnes hefted her magnificent gypsy skirts and stepped lushly into the shaft of light coming through the roof. 'Must be the Clapham Astoria.' For years she had survived successfully on such delusions. 'I used to be the manager here.' She swung her borrowed mane. She fluttered her massive lashes. She smacked her surgical scarlet lips. 'This is what comes of moving South of the River. What actually happened to the money?'

'Computers et it.' Mo was admiring. He had found some more glue. 'The Original Insect et it. Millennium insect. Ultimate bug. Munch munch. Bug et everything. Chomp. Chomp. Chomp. Et the time. Et the dosh. Et the info. Et the control. Et the entire lousy dream. The house of floss. It all went so quickly. Gobbled up our world and all its civilisation and what do we have to show for it?'

'Some very picturesque ruins,' she pointed out. 'Heritage sites. Buy now while they're cheap. Especially here at the centre of our common civilisation! Imagine the possibilities. Yes. Yummy.'

'Yum, yum, yum,' said Jerry.

'Yummy. That's so right,' said Trixie.

'Fuck all,' said Mo. 'I mean fuck off.'

'How?' Jillian swung like a ship at anchor. Then she remembered who she was. She sighed, as if making steam, and continued her stately progress across the floor. Mo traipsed in her wake.

'Lies,' said the general.

Jerry whacked at the old soldier's head with a sympathetic slapstick. 'Those aren't lice. They're locusts.'

4

No

> To maintain our low degree of vigilance we had to adopt the airy notion either that nobody was preparing for war or else (since almost everybody was) that the coming war could not touch us. We necessarily chose the latter self-deception.
>
> – Philip Wylie,
> *Generation of Vipers*

> … The news out of Jonesboro, Ark., last week was a monstrous anomaly: a boundary had been crossed that should not have been. It was a violation terrible enough to warrant waking the President of the US at midnight on his visit to Africa, robbing him of sleep till daylight.
>
> *Time*, 6 April, 1998

> It is our goal to teach every school child in Texas to read.
>
> George W. Bush election commercial

'Faid-bin-Antar' touched his cup to the samovar and his servant turned the silver tap. Amber tea fell into the bowl. Listening with delight to the sounds it made, the old sheikh seemed to read meaning into it. His delicate, aquiline face was full of controlled emotion. Behind the Ray-Bans his eyes held a thousand agonies.

Brushing rapidly at his heavy sleeve, he stared through the tall ornamental window to his virtual garden where Felix Martin's head, its bushy brows shading uncertain eyes, continued to present his show. His body had been buried for twelve days. His ratings were enormous. The virtual fountain continued to pump. The antique electronics flickered and warped, mellow eccentricities. Sepia light washed over Jerry's body, giving it strange angles, unusual beauty. Jerry was flattered. He was surprised the generator had lasted this long.

'We who work so hard for peace are insulted by every act of aggression. When that aggression is committed by individuals, whatever cause they claim, we are outraged. But when that aggression is committed in the name of a lawful people, then we have cause to tremble and fear the apocalypse.'

The sheikh sighed and looked carefully into Jerry's painted features. He turned his head, contemplating the dust.

'For fifty years I have struggled to bring understanding and equity to North and South. I have brought fanatics to the discussion table and turned them into diplomats. I have overseen peace agreements. I have written thousands of letters, articles, books. I have dissuaded many men from turning to the gun. And all that has been destroyed in a few outrageous moments. Making diplomats into fanatics. To satisfy some pervert's personal frustration with the United States and to make an impotent president and his over-privileged, under-informed constituency feel good for an already forgotten second. The very law they claim to represent is the law they flout at every opportunity.' Sheikh Faid was still waiting for news of his daughters.

Jerry took a handful of pungent seeds and held them to his nose before putting them in his mouth. 'They're trying.'

But the sheikh was throwing a hand towards his glowing, empty screens. His voice rose to a familiar pitch.

'As if any action the Americans ever attempted didn't fail! They never listen to their own people. Those officials are all swagger and false claims. True bureaucrats. When will it dawn on them that they have lost all these phoney wars. When will they be gracious enough to admit failure? How can they believe that the methods which created disaster at home will somehow work abroad? They spread their social diseases with careless aggression. It's a measure of their removal from reality. There was a time, sadly, when the US people understood what a farce their representatives made of things. They used their power to improve the world.' He beamed, reminiscent. For a heartbeat his eyes lost their pain.

'I used to enjoy those Whitehall farces when I was a student. Do they still run them? Brian Rix's trousers fell as regularly as the sun set. Simpler satisfactions, I suppose.'

'Failure,' Jerry said. 'They don't know the meaning of the word. Imperialism's no more rational than racism. That's why they fly so well together.'

'Well, of course, you know all about imperialism. You'll enjoy this.' With both hands the sheikh passed Jerry the intricate cup. 'The English love Assam, eh? Now, what about these Americans?'

Jerry shrugged.

He reached beyond the carpet to run his gloved hand through the ash. It was fine as talc. You could powder a baby with it. 'We're defined by our appetites and how we control them. They've made greed a virtue. What on earth possesses them?' He tasted and returned the glittering cup.

Folding his slender old fingers around the bowl's delicate ornament, Sheikh Faid savoured his tea. He considered it. He scented at it.

Jerry wondered about watching a video.

After a while, Sheikh Faid began to giggle softly to himself. Behind him the endless grey desert rose and fell like an ocean. The wind cut it into complex arabesques, a constantly changing geometry. Sometimes it revealed the bones of the old mosque and the tourist centre, but covered them again rapidly, as if disturbed by memories of a more comfortable past.

Soon Sheikh Faid was heaving with laughter. 'There is no mystery to how those Teutons survive or why we fear them. It is a natural imperative. They migrate. They proliferate. Like any successful disease. It's taken them so little time. First they conquered Scandinavia, then Northern Europe and then the world. And they wonder why we fear them. That language! It reminds me of Zulu. It buzzes with aggressive intelligence. It cannot fail to conquer. What a weapon! Blood will out, it seems. Ah, me. It costs so much blood. The conquest of space.'

As if remembering a question, he reached to touch Jerry's yielding knee. Signalling for more tea, he pointed to the blooming horizon.

'It is their manifest destiny.'

Philip Wylie (1902–1971) wrote Gladiator *(1930), the direct inspiration for the Superman comic strip. The co-author of* When Worlds Collide *and* After Worlds Collide *(1933 and 1934), he wrote a number of imaginative and visionary stories including* The Disappearance *(1951). His non-fiction, such as* Generation of Vipers, *is relevant today. His essay on 'Science Fiction and Sanity in an Age of Crisis' was published in 1953. His work was in the Wellsian rather than in the US pulp tradition and remains very lively. He scripted* The Island of Lost Souls *(Dr Moreau) (1932) and* The Invisible Man *(1933). Other books included* Finnley Wren, Corpses at Indian Stones *and* Night Unto Night. *Much of his work was a continuing polemic concerned with his own nation, for which he invented the term 'momism' to explain how sentimentality and oversimplification would be the ruin of American democracy.*

The Visible Men

Or, Down the multiversal rabbit hole

'That a cat's cradle?' Miss Brunner peered down at a naked Jerry Cornelius tangling his hands in a mess of guitar strings. A red Rickenbacker twelve lay beside him.

'It's twine theory,' he said. Frank was absorbed in his own calculations covering the large slate propped on his mum's kitchen table. 'He got a bit confused. Too many Es. Too much reverb.' He followed her gaze. 'G? Somewhere in the seventh dimension.'

'He's a simple soul at heart. Easily led...' Major Nye stroked his pale moustache. He'd come in with Miss Brunner hoping to take Mrs Cornelius out. 'Is she here at all?'

'Pictures with Colonel Pyat.' Frank spoke spitefully. 'IT at the Electric. I'll tell her you called.' His horrible feet in a bowl of soapy water, he frowned over his equations. What had been in that third syringe?

'Pip,' said Jerry. 'Pip. Pip.' The strings coiled into a neat pile and vanished. He beamed.

Frank wondered why Jerry could charm and he couldn't?

Jerry strolled into the basement room sniffing. At the window, Jerry stopped to test the bars. In the kitchen Jerry cursed as he felt about in the toaster. From the front door upstairs Jerry called through the letterbox. They were all naked, save for black car coats. Jerry stood up pulling on his underpants. 'Sorry I'm not decent.'

Miss Brunner turned away with a strangled word. 'What...?'

'Interdimensional travel.' Jerry knotted his wide tie, copping Frank's calculations. 'Though not very sophisticated.' He reached to rub out a figure.

Pettishly, Frank slapped him. 'Just the air cooling. Entropy factor. Anyway, your sizes are all slightly different.'

'All?' Jerry frowned at the versions of himself. 'If I had a black hole they'd follow me into it. As it is...'

Frank scowled. 'You and your bloody multiverse. Energy's bound to thin out if you're that profligate.'

'Crap.' Jerry holstered his vibragun. 'Effectively energy's limitless. It's Mandelbrot, Frank. Each set's invisibly smaller. Or invisibly bigger. Depending where you start. You don't go through the multiverse – you go up and down scales of almost infinite but tiny variability. Only the mass varies enormously, making them invisible. That's why we're all essentially the same.' With scarcely any echo, identical voices came from each identical mouth: 'Only after travelling through billions of sets do you start spotting major differences. The quasi-infinite, Frank. Think how many billions of multiversal planes of the Universe there are! Vast as it is, with my box you can step from one end to the other in about ten minutes. Go all the way round. Your mass compresses or expands accordingly. Once I realised Space is a dimension of Time, the rest was easy!'

'Pervert! You and your proliferating clones.'

'Clones?' Miss Brunner licked her lips. 'Are they edible?' She adjusted her powder-blue two-piece.

'They're not clones, they're versions. When you dash about the multiverse, this sort of thing happens. I prefer to shrink. But denser, you rip holes; drag things in. Nobody sees the universe next door because it's too big or too small. Fractional, of course, in multiversal terms. Problem is, bits of one universe get sucked into another. They're all so close. Déjà vu…?'

'Carry on like this, young man –' Major Nye straightened his cap – 'and you'll cause the end of matter. You'll have your chaos, all right!' Feelings hurt, he made for the basement door.

'That's ridiculous.' Miss Brunner repaired her face. 'Why aren't your clones…'

'Duplicates.'

'Why aren't they too big or too small to see?'

'That's the whole trick.' Jerry preened. Now in sync, his rippling duplicates followed his every move. 'Getting us all to the same scale. Expansion and compression. Your atoms only change mass, maintaining identity. See, we're either too huge to perceive the next universe or we're so massively tiny we merely pass through it without noticing it. Either way you can't see 'em. Until I use this little gadget.'

With a disapproving pout, she clicked across the parquet.

'You change your mass relative to theirs, or vice versa, and they become visible. At first you feel a bit queasy, but you get used to it.' Picking up the small black box from the table, he showed her the display, the triggers. 'Have a go. It's easy. Everything's digitalised.'

'Certainly not. I have enough trouble controlling my own world.'

'But this gives you millions of alternatives. Immortality of sorts. Admittedly, the nearest billion or so are boringly alike. But most people, like you, love repetition...'

'Rot! Utter dissipation! Double Deutsch, I call it!' Grumpily, Major Nye closed the door. Through the bars they saw him climb the area steps, pushing aside three more Jerrys staring at one another in some confusion.

Upstairs the front door opened.

'Oh, blimey!' Dismayed, Jerry peered around for a hiding place. 'Mum's back early.'

'You'll have some explaining to do.' Frank smirked.

But Jerry was already fiddling with his box and wires. As Mrs Cornelius waddled into the room, exuding a delicious smell of greasy fish, Jerry shrank into a corner, his duplicates following. Everyone stared after him.

'Fairyland again!' Miss Brunner was contemptuous.

'The major said Jerry 'ad a message. Where's 'e gorn?' Mrs Cornelius lifted huge blue suspicious eyes. A plump hand carried chips from her newspaper to her mouth.

'Climbing the bloody beanstalk, as usual.' Defeated, Frank faded.

Mrs C. roared.

Walking the Hog

I

The new Pera could never be to Jerry's taste. He had been born in ruins and run-down glory and it was always a comfort to visit your childhood. Now there was a powerful movement to abolish the past in all its complexity and replace it with a simplified child's version easily manipulated by populist politics. When you walked into the Pera Palas these days the old gilt and plush was gone, replaced by the smell of frying bacon.

'Not much of an improvement, I'd say,' grumbled Major Nye staring at his plate of international porridge. With a sigh he reached for the salt, changed his mind and took up the sugar shaker instead. 'Oh, my lord! I do apologise.' He had knocked over condiments which even now dripped on the bright patent leather of Dr Didi Dee's fashionable Louboutins. The eight-inch heels took a foxtrot step backward. Didi worked hard to keep her image. She was a model, as she pointed out frequently on television, to all the Afro-American girls out there with dreams; she was the new Oprah. Once again Jerry wondered if the demagogue came first and gathered the crowd or the crowd created its own creatures out of whole clay. He skirted the drooling bottles and made the usual gentlemanly courtesies in which Didi so delighted. Slowly withdrawing her hand she shook back the hair of her new Ravemaven wig and sat down with him at a table less brightly lit than the others. Once the lounge abounded with discreet, dark corners, the murmur of a million plots. Or was he morphing his memory into an urban myth?

You had to avoid such processes at all costs or there was no point in being immortal. Someone had to retain the past's complexity. That, surely, was what everybody prayed for and why prayer took on a far more spiritual perspective in secular nations like France and England?

'You still favour the longer style of haircut, I see.' Didi's glowing black eyes looked critically into her Martini. 'No, I mean it. It suits you. You wouldn't be Jerry Cornelius otherwise, always trapped a minute or two in the future, a minute or so in the past. Time-thief. Culture vampire. Identity provider. I'm not complaining, sweetheart. We all go to university, these days. Your instinctive style never gets old.'

'Happy to oblige.' Jerry looked around the early-morning restaurant. His work here was done. He took pleasure in Didi's coded small-talk washing over him. Her father had been a high-ranking KGB colonel and she had grown up reading Paustovski and the other survivors of the Stalin days. Some of them had to be understood on so many levels they were almost infinitely divinable. Language had become another of her first lines of defence. She carried more armour than *The Alaskan Queen*. And, because he had no desire to penetrate those defences, they were friends.

Major Nye was still apologising. Jerry noticed that his old friend's cuffs were beginning to fray and that his jacket was a little too big. The suit had been made in the day when quite uncon-sciously the major had carried more muscle. Jermyn Street once seethed with chaps from the colonies buying their discreet weaves and pinstripes. These days even the Foreign Office ordered its suits from Hong Kong and Mumbai. The UK had too few pat-terns to choose from.

2

Jerry jumped ship in Bangkok. He was tired of working with crews of Burmese slaves and their cruel Thai masters. Three pub-lic torturings and two killings were in his view a wasteful way of catching fish. The slave trade lacked all its old ethics. His father would never have permitted such treatment.

At the Wonshott Hotel he arranged to meet Prince Wu Ling, last of the Ming pretenders. He owned property in Shanghai and Macao and had many investments on the Pacific Rim. He wanted

Jerry to get him six new Bristols which his drivers could ferry to Paris.

'That's at least two years' production!'

'I didn't say when I wanted them, Mr Cornelius.' The prince examined the bottom of his teacup. 'I'm a patient man, as you surely know. That's the secret of my success. The business community has been waiting since 1940 for this moment. Another decade and we shall no longer need to pretend. We shall have private armies larger than the nation's. Democracy gives the population the illusion of control. Teams to support. The communists and other authoritarian governments are learning this. Not many of us will survive the century, Mr C.'

Jerry parted the curtains and stared down at the distant street. 'This probably isn't the best place to look for jeans.'

'Oh, you have a year or two left.'

Jerry wondered if he had any children to remember.

3

Jerry got off the train in Or-du-bain. The green and white peaks neatly surrounded him on three sides. On the fourth side blue water rose slowly to join the pink and gold dawn. He had made a long journey, through a dozen time zones and twelve distinct versions of recent history, had been thrown off the train in Geneva and had hardly got back on again. He really was getting too old for this. And as for faking another poet, he thought he would rather throw up.

'I blame the drugs.' With an expert smile the old aristocrat removed his hat, extending his hand. 'On time as usual, old boy.'

'That's not what everyone says.' Jerry looked with distaste at the parked Smart car. 'Is that for all of us?'

'Both.' Prinz Lobkowitz grew impatient with his friend's reluctance to march to the new tunes.

'All?' Jerry was still having difficulties with his identities. 'But you told me that these wind farms are destabilising the weather?'

'That's what the figures suggest. We have the technologies in place now. There's precious little chance of us replicating earlier mistakes. All we need to do is slow down a little. Wu Ling thinks it's the secret. I gather you disagree.'

'It's not that.' Jerry lifted an apologetic shoulder. 'I don't care. I'm used to speed. You know how that one goes.'

'Speed? It's a drug, surely?'

Jerry sniffed. 'That's true of everything. Do you know the exact time?'

'Today?'

'Take your pick.'

'Well, this is Switzerland, after all. I've never heard so much ticking.'

'Persevere. It's in here somewhere.'

Prinz Lobkowitz pursed his lips.

Jerry could tell that he would get away with nothing of any value if he stayed too long in this environment. From somewhere came the familiar strains of 'Jerusalem'. What was the point of looking for old clues? The new ones were just as useful. 'But what do we need all this energy for?'

The old aristocrat shrugged. 'I don't know. Take your pick. Music? Hospitals?' With some embarrassment he replaced his dove-grey homburg on his glittering hair and led the way towards the car where his liveried servants were carefully harnessing the horses.

4

M. Pardon made an awkward, embarrassed gesture towards his hastily knotted tie. 'You're looking for an Oriental solution to an Occidental problem, aren't you? It isn't all about domes and towers. I suppose I'll never get used to your terrible shortcuts. They'd kill me, I know.' His little pink cheeks were spotted red, as if he'd been bitten.

They were meeting in their usual rendezvous where the Canal

St Martin's glassy green water plunged underground beneath a bust of the actor Lemaître who looked a little desperately across the Rue Faubourg-du-Temple towards the statue of La Grisette. *Les Enfants du Paradis*! Both pieces of sculpture had grown a little greyer since he had last seen them.

Jerry waved his bandaged hand. 'I got this in Tanzania.'

'A bite?'

'Where do you suggest?'

The Frenchman waved his manicured hand towards Le Phare over on the corner near the Franc Prix's displays of cut flowers. Jerry could smell them from here. All those colours! At the restaurant waiters were setting the outside tables for lunch. 'The quiche is always good.'

Arm in arm the two men crossed the street. Jerry breathed in the sudden waft of warm tar. This heat-wave was likely to last for the rest of the year.

'Tanzania, eh?' M. Pardon chose a table. 'A special kind of monarch. Johannus Carolignas, maybe?'

'Always.' Jerry leered as only one of his age and background could. 'Firbank's for the memory.'

'Shouldn't that be mammary?'

M. Pardon sat down carefully with his back to the square. 'Oh, lord. Time's sliding back to the Stone Age. Isn't it?' He sighed as he took in the lunch menu. 'What's to be done? What's to be done?'

Jerry checked the blackboard menu. 'Is that the only way out?'

'Of course. Unless you want to get back to the Aegean. All that ancient limestone. Those early artists! Primitives?'

'Apart from the toilets? Yes?' Jerry had lost interest in the arts. Graffiti still engaged him sometimes. He fingered his fly.

M. Pardon was ahead of him. 'My hand has only to move a little to the right and you will never find your fantasy world again, my old *mon vieux*...'

Jerry did what he could to hide his disappointment. He turned his head, listening. Somewhere in the distance, possibly La Villette, pocket battleships fought gun to gun. It was impossible, these days, to enjoy a quiet evening at home.

Lunch quickly over, M. Pardon pulled on a lilac glove, placed a lilac homburg on his head and, signalling for Jerry to rise, guided him up Rue Faubourg-du-Temple to Avenue Parmentier and the entrance of the Goncourt Métro. 'There's much to be said, Monsieur Cornelius, for living *La Vie Imaginaire*. And anyone can do it without too much of an effort, in one way or another. But, let's face it, the alternative hasn't done anyone much good. Who's living in a fantasy world? Obama or Danny the D-and-D freak? Believe me, you'd be wise to stay in Narnia.'

Jerry spat dramatically into the gutter.

'What's up?' asked M. Pardon.

'Nothing,' said Jerry. 'Just a frog in my throat.'

'Is it over yet?' Pardon seemed in an unusually obstructive mood. He pointed up into the west. Above them, more or less following Avenue Parmentier, the sky was full of drones. 'You take from the State, you take from the People. The theft of the People's wealth has become routine.'

'Who are we fighting now?'

'WalMart.' Pardon's eyes had a sort of glee. 'Now, I was going to suggest you visit my friend Cantonlac. He practises Chinese medicine, these days.'

'Really?' Jerry remembered the first time he had come across Cantonlac eating a big cane roach in mistake for a date and then insisting it tasted like fried chicken. 'Call me old-fashioned but I think I'll wait to see my GP in London.'

M. Pardon began to descend the steps into the Métro. Jerry refused to follow him. He cast about for transport. He really did need to get to Bengazi.

'Oh, take my boat if you must. It's in Deauville. The usual mooring.' He looked up through the railings, his eyes full of tears. 'Ownership of the world is now almost wholly in the hands of the great Brand Families. It suits us to remain discreet. Just as the dictatorships made one last-ditch stand to form a true republic before collapsing.'

Frowning, Jerry framed a question but Pardon had vanished.

Jerry, turning back towards République, thought of the Grand

Khan of China, who ruled an empire of many millions. He wondered if it were still relatively easy to get to the Far Indies where he had hoped to join the entourage of the fabled King of the Christian East, Prester John. They had once marched together against the so-called Six Pagan Lords of the Congo, being narrowly defeated at Kananga.

But those were the easy years, he thought, before the spread of sophisticated fire-power when a man with a sword looked good on a camel.

Jerry sighed and turned up the collar of his black car coat. Where were the legends of yesteryear? Jill Bell had once taken fifty men with her into the Tanzanian wilderness and created an empire. Who would try that now without back-up from China, India, Russia or at least some high-profile sportswear brand?

5

Sitting on a toilet just outside Karachi, Jerry read a yellowing newspaper. On the other side of the door he could hear the TV conversation clearly. Chiefly for his benefit his host had clicked on CNN.

'It was a bloody few hours, the People's Revolt,' declared ex-President Hershey-Heinz, stepping down from the throne he'd occupied for less than three years. After handing his fortune over to the People he had flown from Havana to Kingston, where Keith Richards had offered to go bond for him. The ex-president's family had bankrolled the Stones' last tour, Old Men Know Best, perhaps their most successful. Jerry remembered meeting Hershey-Heinz backstage. The Fix were opening for the Stones. They had all grown up together. Jerry, of course, still looked about thirty and had died eight times to his certain knowledge. *You'd think with all that experience I'd be a better musician.* He still had trouble tuning his Rickenbacker 12.

Everywhere in the region coups established fresh governments, most of them popular, and began the clean-up as they called it.

Jerry wasn't at all sure he was enjoying Utopia. He could see that this was going to be a decade of upheaval and only a rough settling of the political landscape. Elected representation came and went so quickly, these days. Didi had estimated that there was a new fair and legal election held in the world about once every two and a half minutes.

Wiping his bottom on the news, Jerry contemplated a quick trip into 1965 to see his mum. Mrs Cornelius had a way of helping him get reorientated. He turned up the volume on his headphones. Dead Giveaway were singing their latest hit, 'The Infant Disposal Song', from their album *Life in Our New Cemetery*.

He had already heard the thunder and now as he stepped out of the shed it began to rain heavily. Was this how it would be from now on?

6

The Fix were back together. Jerry had managed a couple of rehearsals in New Delhi. The songs were mostly his but he found them hard to remember. He had been away from Louisiana too long.

> Jackhammer Jack never runs with the pack.
> Jackhammer Jack don't cut you no slack.
> Jackhammer Jack got a fine new shack –
> By the muddy Mississippi where the alligators at.

He had raised the stand so he had to strain to reach the mike. It gave the impression that he was trying harder than he actually was.

Outside in the mud the audience was slowly coming together, singing along with the band. There was nothing like performing for a bunch of people who knew and enjoyed your stuff.

He was briefly nostalgic for the old days when they had gone out as Pegleg Pierre and his Cajun Rhythm Kids. Katrina had scotched that. Now everyone but him had to sit down to play. He thought back to those innocent times. He had been in love with a sculptress called Winnie Two. One day she had presented him with something she had been working on in secret. 'There you are,' she had said. 'I've made you a rose.'

He still had it somewhere.

He took a sweet breath of the dusty old air. It had not rained anywhere in this state or Mississippi or Texas for almost two years. For a while, before the band re-formed, he had run illegal Evian to Baton Rouge in regular Exxon trucks. The stuff always smelled faintly of gasoline. The city was still in the process of suing Hannibal, Missouri, for damning the river upstream.

Jerry was enjoying being on stage again but even so he would be glad to be back in 1970 in a world where he had been able to count his identities.

7

'Only by accepting the miraculous can we begin to rescue ourselves. Mutuality is the natural condition of humankind. It was our willingness to help one another out which got us through the Stone Age. Our misplaced pragmatism, our misdirected reliance on materialism as a moral and economic system, determines our desperate times. We could have created a decent, trusting world if we had invested the same effort we put into trying to destroy one another. Religion? Maybe. But not as we know it...' Professor Hira, the chubby Brahmin, paused his V and started his lecture again. He had to be word-perfect by Sunday. He reached to press the record button of his Sony ICD PX139 and looked up as Jerry entered his office.

'Oh, good lord, Jerry. You do pick some bad times. I'm up to my eyebrows in work!'

'Glad to hear it, prof.' Jerry was brash, just back from his base and looking a bit pale. 'Hope they're paying well.'

Hira's expression showed he still found Jerry irredeemably vulgar. 'I heard Didi and you had fallen out. Some lie she thought you'd told.'

'Lies? Oh, yes, They've multiplied. Like flies.' He smiled. 'They keep the sun off the meat.'

Hira wasn't amused. 'Never have so many human souls lied themselves to perdition.' He wiped his mouth. 'The lie is necessary currency in our contemporary world. Everyone is good at it. Some are very, very good. We judge a person's character by their ability to fib. Some consider themselves artists and embellish their stories. Some work to make them true. I'm watching them as best I can but it's the ones who attempt to turn lies into truth you really have to watch, you know.'

'I thought everyone did that.'

Hira preferred to take Jerry seriously. 'Reality only rarely survives their abuse. And they, poor creatures, are assigned to that unholy pit, where great wealth can be found, where every lie is rewarded, where every reality is in fragments, where gloom, despair and disappointment are felt for eternity. But you already know my math. Radiant time and so on.'

To Jerry, Hira sounded a bit confused. 'Have you been dabbling in religion again, prof?'

Hira was wounded by this. 'Religion is my life. Do you know how long I prayed before I agreed to be part of this new energy investigation? Solar power? Tidal power? Wind power? All require considerable contemplation. Fire, water, air...' He shrugged and then resumed his position. His body language wanted Jerry to leave.

'No earth?' Callously, Jerry lit a long Sherman's and flipped a dead match into his old friend's waste bin.

'Earth is what we're trying to save.' Hira got a big white handkerchief from his pocket and blew his nose. From somewhere outside the sound was repeated by a bull elephant sensing the presence of a female. With a shudder, Hira replaced the linen in the pocket of his white, baggy trousers. 'You can't remain cynical about this, Jerry. The human race could be looking at annihilation!'

'Serves it bloody well right,' said Jerry. 'It's the animals I feel sorry for. Don't you? They didn't really have much to do with creating the situation. Still, when you got to go you got to go, eh? Or am I wrong?'

'You're impossible, Jerry.' Hira struck what he hoped was an impatient pose.

'No, prof.' Jerry turned to leave. 'Just a bit unlikely.'

8

Didi Dee rocked on her heels, hardly noticing Jerry as he slipped back into her bedroom and kissed her lightly on her bare shoulder. She was trying to get the wrinkles out of her slip. 'I should have done my ironing today.'

Jerry showed her what he had found.

She stared unintelligently at the figures and diagrams, reading the fading words. 'Radiant Time? What the fuck is that?' She gave them back to him, rubbing her arm.

Jerry rolled them tightly and snapped the bands back. He wondered how Didi could punch his buttons in that way. Turning up the collar of his black car coat he opened the door and walked downstairs. He was beginning to regret becoming his father's executor. It wasn't as if the house was worth much. The fake Le Corbusier walls were beginning to lean outwards and the top floor threatened to fall in. He left by the front door.

A few moments later he had revved the engine of the old Duesenberg and thoughtfully put it in gear. The rhythm of the engine echoed the beat of her heels as she descended the spiral staircase. 'I'm coming with you.'

Jerry sniffed nostalgically. Speed was speed. Didi knew how best to haunt him.

He waited while she settled herself in the passenger seat. With a sigh, he took off the handbrake and turned on the music.

'What's the time?' he said. 'My watch has stopped.'

Epilogue

The Dodgem Decision

It was not their accomplishments that Jerry disliked so much as their attitudes. It had been such a mark of English literature, certainly since Chesterton. It was traceable in all the donnish 'novels' and detective stories, the fantasies of people like Tolkien, Williams and Lewis, the work of self-styled 'poets' like Conquest, the music of Vaughan Williams and Eric Coates, reaching its final depths in the ill-constructed, soft-minded concoctions of John Braine, Kingsley Amis and the rest.

An attitude of spirit.

Just as the harmonium corrupted Indian classical music, so had the operettas of Gilbert and Sullivan subtly corroded the quality of English thinking. Attitudes that aimed at reinforcing opinions rather than analysing them, at preserving conventions rather than expanding them.

Pints of beer in the good old English pub. Jolly jokes in the senior common room. The most that a novel can hope to be is an amusing pastiche or a work of sociology. Even a light comic narrative became a 'protest', a piece of melodramatic wish-fulfilment became 'an indictment of society', and a bit of conventional stream of consciousness became 'experimental'.

2

Driving the Phantom VI along the front at Brighton, Jerry looked out to sea. It was inescapable, he thought. It was large. It could not be comfortably dealt with. It was a fact. An old woman staggered out into the road in front of his car. He hardly noticed the bump.

3

He reflected on the desperate search for a label, on the way in which the word Surrealism had been resurrected to stand for anything that was not a 'realistic' narrative. Most of the stuff the publishers presented under this label bore as much similarity to surrealistic texts as Ardizzone bore to Ernst. But then what was 'the new fiction' but a label? He glanced at the copy of *New Worlds* on the seat beside him. The slogan for that month read: 'What do you need?'

4

He had reached Hove with its bland white blocks facing not towards the sea but onto neat green squares where old women, all wool and chocolates, trailed their decrepit domestic pets and a faint smell of rotting underlinen. This, of course, was where the shopkeepers came to die, to complain that the sea didn't have enough sugar in it, to be bullied by beer-reddened newsagents and overcharged by decaying waitresses. On the whole they took it passively, as if their past lives could be redeemed by the punishments and indignities inflicted by this suburb by the sea. And yet at the same time they appeared to seek reassurance that their lives had not been useless, selfish, narrow and full of spite. Perhaps this was why they clung onto existence (hoping that if they could live another year or two they would receive some sign), obsessively comforting their ruined bodies. To cater to this unvocalised hope there were the Health Food Shops and the *Daily Express*. But the *Daily Express* saw itself in a humbler light, directing the pilgrims on to the revelations of Alan Whicker and David Attenborough.

5

Music critics who had praised the virtues of The Beatles had given authority to the opinions of the tone-deaf who now praised anything from the Electric String Band to The Doors. A similar process, where the virtues of Kipling and Chesterton were praised, had made it possible for all those critics whose bad taste encompassed anything from Ian Fleming to Kingsley Amis to praise the books and get away with it. Such critics recognised similar attitudes in the writers they admired and so assumed them to have the talent and craftsmanship of their predecessors.

It's the rambling English drunkard who made the rambling English narrative, thought Jerry, completing the U-turn and driving back towards the West Pier. And it was left to Leavis to confuse intellectual rigour with moral rigour, to mistake, in the final analysis, fiction for sociology. What's it about, then? Symbolism was a stale joke. There was no substitute for imagination. He passed the ambulance where they were carefully carrying an old lady on a stretcher. Things had come to a pretty pass when the work of Firbank was ignored in favour of his imitator Waugh whose prose, diffuse in comparison with that of his master, was thought to represent the best of English style.

If only Connolly had heeded his own warnings; if only he had convinced contemporaries like Karl Miller and Kenneth Tynan. The muse had become a fat old lady in a bathing machine, a stern Presbyterian Scottish aunt. The schools produced nothing but anachronisms. Their revolutions were not intellectual but vaguely political and therefore boring. There was nothing more old-fashioned than the speeches of the last members of the Old Guard, the student revolutionaries. The 20th Century Confusion.

6

Feeling that he was familiar enough with the attitudes of the Brighton authorities, he parked the Rolls-Royce on a double yellow line and got out. He crossed to the promenade and looked down on the beach.

A column of constables, headed by a local magistrate with the honest stupid face of an unsuccessful salesman, carefully searched the litter baskets for offensive reading matter. Each was armed with a stick of rock shaped like a walking stick, and with these they picked among the soiled copies of the *Daily Mail* and the *Sunday Telegraph*, the chip bags, the old sandwiches and the lolly wrappers. Jerry lowered his sack to the ground and opened it, throwing out copies of *The Crying Game*, *I Want It Now*, and *Musrum*. The constables were too immersed in their search to notice the fluttering things that hit the beach like dying crows.

7

The sun set and Jerry stayed on the dodgems as he had for the past four hours. He was badly bruised on his right knee and had grazed his hand, but the dodgems on the East Pier were among the best in the country and he wanted to make the most of them. For an hour he had been pursued by a middle-aged man in an orange car. He recognised his old friend from Burma, Captain Maxwell. He had lost weight. Jerry turned his dodgem and rammed the orange car head-on. Jarred, Captain Maxwell scowled, but did not look at Jerry. He had little sense of humour, Jerry remembered.

8

Driving slowly along the front under the lights, Jerry wondered why there should be a need for a new fiction. Were there really new ideas circulating? New subject matter? Probably. But even if there were not, it was always better to try to extend the range of fiction. Stylistic revolution always preceded the contextual revolution and that was in progress already. Though few admitted it, the revolution was as good as accomplished. This place, he thought, heading into a side street, it's like some Margate of the mind.

Most of the books published in England were already dead before birth. It was disgusting, really. One would have expected a certain amount of development in the field of preventive medicine. Captain Mackenzie had suggested a contraceptive on the fountain pen as a suitable remedy. That way they could scribble all day and do no harm to anyone.

Perhaps someone had suggested it first to Mackenzie?

Dead languages were taught in the universities; the languages were formal, often very beautiful, and certainly quite complex. Learning them imposed a certain necessary discipline, perhaps. But the language was no longer relevant to the present day. One might just as well attempt to produce a narrative in classical Greek in the manner of Homer. Not a bad exercise, of course, like a lot of pastiches, but hardly vital.

All the experiments in style of the first half of the century had been attempts to freshen the approach to the old concerns. Many writers of the period had abandoned them, eventually, because they had discovered that the old techniques were better suited to the old concerns. But now elements of those styles were being used as they had never been used before. He turned the car towards Lewes.

9

As he checked the fuses, Jerry glanced up, afraid that the moonlight had caught his silver swastika cufflinks. He had chosen them with special care. It was best to know all the implications of an action.

He backed away from the building, making his way to his parked car. As soon as he was in the Phantom VI he touched a stud on the dashboard.

Behind him there was a roar as the books went up. He stuck an arm out of the window and waved at the crowd; then he drove back to Brighton.

10

Pleased with his naïveté, Jerry wondered what else he could do before he left. He was so tired of debate. The facts remained. It was boring to be so explicit. It pleased nobody. He fingered the gold Star of David at his throat. How evolved everything was. It was time to be moving on.

11

Old men in Harris Tweed sports jackets with leather patches on the elbows wandered along the asphalt talking about jazz and science fiction, about politics and even religion.

They considered their tastes and opinions to be radical, vital. It was such a shame.

Jerry Cornelius leaned against the one remaining wall of the library. Why did the establishment of any generation always consider themselves progressive? By the time they achieved power their battles were old, whether they had been won, lost or forgotten. If the policemen were getting younger, the BBC producers were getting older.

12

The gestures of fear. The words of self-comfort. The talk of crafts-manship by those not skilled enough to construct a simple traditional narrative. The provincial philistinism that, as an act of pseudo-rebellion, was so much easier to cultivate than an informed attitude. At least, thought Jerry, Chesterton could construct a decent enough essay. He thought of *Writing in England Today* with its sad substitutes for the essay – of *The James Bond Dossier* of which the most damning thing that could be said was that it was not wil-fully bad (the only joke was Amis's reference to it as 'belles-lettres'), his particular contribution to that body of work which included a Latin translation of *Winnie-the-Pooh*. Cardigans, cardigans, cardi-gans. With their woollies and their brandy, the academics were no better or worse than the poor old ratbags dying in Hove and Wor-thing and Bognor Regis. Who were they fighting? Why were they running away? The bawling of opinions (Amis's review of *Lolita* was as wearying as Nabokov's opinions of everything) had become the substitute for reasoned argument. It was accepted everywhere in England as a good enough substitute.

13

London drew closer and Jerry began to relax. He switched on the radio. The persistent confusion of art with politics was madden-ing. English critics chiefly argued with the moral attitudes they believed they discovered in works of fiction and seemed unable to discuss the qualities of the fiction. They approved of books whose moral attitude, as they saw it, they shared, disapproved of those with which they couldn't agree. Faced with books that refused to be interpreted, they dismissed them. Later academics would do worse. They would provide 'keys'.

14

In his house overlooking Holland Park, Jerry watched the autumn light as it faded. If a new fiction existed, its concerns were with new ways in which a narrative could be constructed and presented, as well as with thorough familiarity with subject matter still regarded with suspicion by the older members of the establishment and by its younger members as something startling and shiny with which to pep up the old forms. Only the most recent generation of writers – chiefly American and English – were able to deal with it in a completely relaxed way, taking it for granted as they took the H-Bomb for granted, for they had grown up with it. Computers and spaceships, among other things, had been the subject matter of their childhood reading. Some contemporary fiction was now actually dealing with contemporary situations, images, events, ideas, attitudes, characters. And a little of that dealt with the subject matter in a manner that suited it. If people found the form unfamiliar, impossible to appreciate, it was perhaps because they thought the same about the stuff that the form was attempting to deal with. Most publishers, magazines, journals, were incapable of knowing what the modern public wished to read, and they blamed their falling sales on everything but their own judgement.

15

The documentary fiction of the fifties, that still appeared in establishment magazines like *Evergreen* and so on, had been, quite evidently, the precursor of the new fiction. The documentary stuff had dealt with the subject matter but at best it was semi-fiction, dramatised reportage, excellent journalism. It had been left to a new generation to take it and apply imagination, to create a synthesis, a true form of fiction. Perhaps it would take still another generation to produce the masterpiece. But the use of the word 'generation' was too loose, Jerry thought as he opened the window to smell the smoky autumn, for a good many years separated Via, Geddes, Ballard, Matthews and the rest, and their differences of approach, of course, were quite as marked as their similarities.

16

Jerry switched on his new light machine and tuned it to the stereo, sat down at his IBM 2000 and began to compose a book. He had planned it for 4,000 words, but now it seemed it would emerge at 4,250. He hoped that the extra length would not bore the reader. He selected a 10/11pt imitation Times for the main text and would probably not bother to justify the right-hand margin. He would run off 2,000 copies at first and see how it went. If it went well he might transfer it to disc. He would have to ask his distributor.

It was strange, he thought, how even a few months ago a writer could not control every stage of his work's production, that it would involve editors, publishers, agents, contracts, compositors, printers, binders, and the rest. He could remember how he had once been prepared to operate in that system. It was hard to believe how it had been possible. Now his only concern was with the efficiency of his distributor.

Hey, how does this thing work!?

17

Historical analogies were always suspicious, Jerry thought; yet it did seem that the reportage disguised as fiction and the fiction disguised as reportage preceded the emergence of a true fiction form. But the whole subject was beginning to tire him. There were stories to write. One only produced essays when one was not actually doing the work. That was why interviews with novelists and film-makers were always misleading. Usually they only had time to give the interviews, or write the articles, between their creative patches. So they usually appeared jaundiced, tired, cynical. 'It's all a con.' Their work remained and it meant a great deal more than any amount of analysis by the person himself or his critics. The work was the fact. It needed no rationale. To have a positive attitude was to have at best a limited one. Live and let live, thought Jerry. But there was a time when the bastards wouldn't give me a chance.

18

He watched the television before he went to bed. Its red gun was misfiring and this gave the pictures of Vietnam, Biafra, Czechoslovakia, the spaceflight and the latest heart transplant, a distinct green cast, as if everything took place under the shade of gigantic tropical trees. He switched off.

You had to think fast, read fast, write fast these days, but never hastily. It was the only way.

Maybe it was time to leave the hothouse.

(Ladbroke Grove, 1968)

Acknowledgements

'The Peking Junction' first appeared in *The New S.F.*, edited by
Langdon Jones, Hutchinson, 1969.

'The Delhi Division' first appeared in NEW WORLDS No. 185,
edited by Michael Moorcock & James Sallis, December 1968.

'The Tank Trapeze' first appeared in NEW WORLDS No. 186,
January 1969.

'The Nature of the Catastrophe' first appeared in NEW WORLDS
No. 197, edited by Charles Platt, January 1970.

'The Swastika Set-Up' first appeared in CORRIDOR No. 4, edited
by Michael Butterworth, Winter 1972.

'The Sunset Perspective' first appeared in *The Disappearing
Future*, edited by George Hay, Panther, 1970.

'Sea Wolves' first appeared in *Science Against Man*, edited by
Anthony Cheetham, Avon, 1970.

'Voortrekker' first appeared in FRENDZ Nos 3–5, June/July 1971.

'Dead Singers' first appeared (as 'All the Dead Singers') in INK,
5 October, 1971, and (as 'Dead Singers') in *The Lives and Times
of Jerry Cornelius*, Allison & Busby, 1976.

'The Longford Cup' first appeared (cut) in PENTHOUSE Vol. 8
No. 7, October 1973, and (uncut) in *The Lives and Times of Jerry
Cornelius*.

'The Entropy Circuit' first appeared in *An Index of Possibilities*,
edited by The Catalogue, Clanose/Wildwood/Arrow, 1974.

'The Entropy Tango (fragment)' first appeared in *The New Nature
of the Catastrophe*, edited by Jones & Moorcock, Millennium
Books, 1993.

'The Murderer's Song' first appeared (in German) in *Tor zu
den Sternen*, edited by Peter Wilfert, Goldmann, 1981, and

(in English) in *Tales from the Forbidden Planet*, edited by Roz
Kaveney, Titan, 1987.

'The Gangrene Collection' first appeared in CITY LIMITS, 18–25
January, 1990.

'The Romanian Question' first appeared in BACK BRAIN
RECLUSE, edited by Chris Reed, Spring 1991.

'The Spencer Inheritance' first appeared in THE EDGE No. 7,
edited by Graham Evans, May/June 1998.

'The Camus Referendum' first appeared in GARE DU NORD Vol. 2
No. 1, edited by Douglas Oliver & Alice Notley, 1998.

'Cheering for the Rockets' first appeared in INTERZONE No. 137,
edited by David Pringle, November 1998.

'Visible Men' first appeared in NATURE No. 7,091, May 2006.

'Walking the Hog' first appeared in *Kizuna: Fiction for Japan*,
edited & published by Brent Millis, 2011.

'Epilogue: The Dodgem Decision' first appeared (as 'The
Dodgem Arrangement') in SPECULATION No. 23, edited by
Peter Weston, July/August 1969, appeared (as 'The Dodgem
Division') in *My Experiences in the Third World War*, Savoy, 1980,
and (as 'Epilogue: The Dodgem Decision') in *The Lives and
Times of Jerry Cornelius*, Harrap/Grafton, 1987.

Artwork:

Frontispiece & end-piece, by Harry Douthwaite, from the covers
of *The Final Programme*, Avon, 1968.

Dedication page artwork, by Mal Dean, first appeared in *The
Final Programme*, Allison & Busby, 1969.

Epigraph page artwork (adapted for 'The Peking Junction', 'The
Longford Cup', 'The Entropy Circuit', 'The Romanian
Question' and 'The Visible Men' title pages), by Douthwaite,
first appeared in 'Further Information', NEW WORLDS No. 157,
edited by Michael Moorcock, December 1965.

'The Delhi Division', interior artwork, by Dean, first appeared in
NEW WORLDS No. 184, edited by Moorcock & James Sallis,
November 1968.

'The Tank Trapeze', interior artwork, by Dean, first appeared in
  NEW WORLDS No. 186, January 1969.

'The Nature of the Catastrophe', interior artwork, by Dean,
  adapted from the front cover of NEW WORLDS No. 191, edited
  by Langdon Jones, June 1969, also adapted for the front cover
  of *The Nature of the Catastrophe*, edited by Moorcock & Jones,
  Hutchinson, 1971.

'The Swastika Set-Up', interior artwork, by David Britton, first
  appeared in CORRIDOR No. 4, edited by Michael Butterworth,
  Winter 1972.

'The Murderer's Song', interior artwork, by Dean, first appeared
  (in 'The Firmament Theorem' by Brian W. Aldiss) in NEW
  WORLDS No. 191, and (in 'The Murderer's Song') in *The New
  Nature of the Catastrophe*, edited by Jones & Moorcock,
  Millennium Books, 1993.

'The Camus Referendum', interior artwork, by Britton, first
  appeared (in 'Niki Hoeky' by Charles Partington) in NEW
  WORLDS No. 215, edited by Britton, Spring 1979, and (in 'The
  Camus Referendum') in the TIME CENTRE TIMES Vol. 4 No. 4,
  edited by John & Maureen Davey, D.J. Rowe & Ian Covell,
  May 2000.

MICHAEL MOORCOCK (1939–) is one of the most important figures in British SF and Fantasy literature. The author of many literary novels and stories in practically every genre, he has won and been shortlisted for numerous awards including the Hugo, Nebula, World Fantasy, Whitbread and Guardian Fiction Prize. He is also a musician who performed in the seventies with his own band, the Deep Fix; and, as a member of the space-rock band, Hawkwind, won a platinum disc. His tenure as editor of NEW WORLDS magazine in the sixties and seventies is seen as the high watermark of SF editorship in the UK, and was crucial in the development of the SF New Wave. Michael Moorcock's literary creations include Hawkmoon, Corum, Von Bek, Jerry Cornelius and, of course, his most famous character, Elric. He has been compared to, among others, Balzac, Dumas, Dickens, James Joyce, Ian Fleming, J.R.R. Tolkien and Robert E. Howard. Although born in London, he now splits his time between homes in Texas and Paris.

For a more detailed biography, please see Michael Moorcock's entry in *The Encyclopedia of Science Fiction* at: http://www.sf-encyclopedia.com/

For further information about Michael Moorcock and his work, please visit www.multiverse.org, or send S.A.E. to The Nomads Of The Time Streams, Mo Dhachaidh, Loch Awe, Dalmally, Argyll, PA33 1AQ, Scotland, or P.O. Box 385716, Waikoloa, HI 96738, USA.